SONG OF THE TIDES

Song of the Tides

A Novel

Tom Joseph

The University of Alabama Press   Tuscaloosa

The University of Alabama Press
Tuscaloosa, Alabama 35487-0380
All rights reserved
Manufactured in the United States of America

Designer: Michele Myatt Quinn
Typeface: Minion

∞

The paper on which this book is printed meets the minimum
requirements of American National Standard for Information
Sciences-Permanence of Paper for Printed Library Materials,
ANSI Z39.48-1984.

Library of Congress Cataloging-in-Publication Data

Joseph, Thomas A., 1950–
    Song of the tides : a novel / Thomas A. Joseph.
        p.   cm.
    "Fire Ant books."
    Includes bibliographical references and index.
    ISBN 978-0-8173-5484-8 (pbk. : alk. paper) 1. Calusa Indians—Fiction. 2. Indians of North
America—First contact with Europeans—Fiction. 3. Spaniards—Florida—History—16th century—
Fiction. 4. Indians of North America—Florida—Fiction. 5. Florida—Ethnic relations—History—
16th century—Fiction. 6. Florida—History—To 1565. I. Title.
    PS3610.O677S66 2008
    813′.6—dc22

                                                                                            2007044234

For Nana

AUTHOR'S NOTE

Though *Song of the Tides* is a work of fiction, every attempt has been made to follow accurately the written accounts from the era made by European visitors. Unfortunately, while archeologists have compiled a wealth of material knowledge of Calusa culture and history, theirs was not a written language; nor do oral records survive. We do know that the Calusa returned to their capital city, now called Mound Key in Estero Bay, and thrived for a time into the seventeenth century. Tragically, European diseases and the slave trade from the north took their toll. The Calusa tribe was largely extinct by the mid-1700s, though some Calusa refugees are known to have been transported to Cuba on Spanish vessels and might possibly have living descendants today.

Of the mostly Spanish letters and memoranda that survive, three are primary and make for fascinating reading. Gonzalo Solís de Merás's *Memorial* recounts his brother-in-law Pedro Menéndez's journeys in La Florida, including his historic meeting with Carlos and marriage to the cacique's sister. I read two versions: John E. Worth, translations prepared for 2004 Summer Stipend, National Endowment for the Humanities, "First-Contact Narratives from Florida's Lower Gulf Coast: An Annotated Translation Project," and Jeannette Thurber Connor (translator),

Pedro Menéndez de Avilés, Adelantado, Governor and Captain-General of Florida; Memorial by Gonzalo Solís de Merás (Florida State Historical Society, 1923). The 1575 Memoir of Hernando d'Escalante Fontaneda on the Country and Ancient Indian Tribes of Florida—he did finally make it to Spain—is both captivating and agonizingly incomplete. I used a few short passages verbatim in Escalante's otherwise fictitious journal entries, as well as his list of Calusa towns for place-names and as inspiration for characters' names, since Fontaneda's is the only known documentation of Calusa language. Dr. Worth also translated Fontaneda's memoir for the same project; others include David O. True's version of Buckingham Smith's translation (Glade House, 1944); translations are also available on the Internet. The letter from Father Juan Rogel to Father Jerónimo Ruiz del Portillo, April 25, 1568, found on pp. 230–278 of John H. Hann's Missions to the Calusa (University Press of Florida, 1991), is the best document we have on Calusa spirituality, though of course it is filtered through the Jesuit's point of view.

Many thanks to ethnohistorian John Worth, assistant professor of historical archaeology, Department of Anthropology, University of West Florida, for sharing both published and unpublished sources including his own translations, for his fine-toothed review of the manuscript, and for his confidence in the book as a work not only of history but of fiction as well.

Thanks, too, to William H. Marquardt, curator in archaeology at the Florida Museum of Natural History and director of the University of Florida Institute of Archaeology and Paleoenvironmental Studies, whose knowledge of and insight into all things Calusa, as evidenced in his archeological research, his many writings, and the fabulous Calusa exhibit at the Florida Museum of Natural History in Gainesville, is unsurpassed. Merald Clark's brilliant and meticulously authentic illustrations have helped me to visualize the Calusa culture, environment, and the people themselves. His drawing of the character he knew as Cacica, who became my novel's Aesha, graces the book's cover.

This novel could not have been written, or re- or re-rewritten, without the help of many. Kathy Olberts helped me get started, and my sister Shauna Deb encouraged me throughout. The critiquing, editing, and unflagging support of Annamarie Beckel, Michele Bergstrom, David Brainard and Joey Wojtusik kept me from trainwrecking. Without Phil Paterson, Northern Writers would never have been born. David Peterman translated and shored up my Spanish and is as true a friend as a writer can have. And many thanks to all who read and commented on early drafts of the manuscript.

To my daughters, Nikki, Jessica and Hillary, the girls, even if you're girls no longer, and my wife, Jeanne, who first brought me to Southwest Florida on our honeymoon in 1973, you're always here with and for me—how can I thank you enough? And to Nana, Anntiva, Mom, who introduced me to the living world of the Calusa, you were and are my inspiration.

For those who have caught the Calusa itch, I can't recommend highly enough a visit to the Randell Research Center in Pineland, Florida (www.flmnh.ufl.edu/rrc/) at the historic site of Tanpa. Also, in addition to the sources listed above, the following make excellent reading: Darcie A. McMahon and William H Marquardt's *The Calusa and Their Legacy* (University Press of Florida, 2004); John H. Hann's *Indians of Central and South Florida, 1513–1763* (University Press of Florida, 2003); Albert Manucy's *Menéndez* (Copyright 1983 by the St. Augustine Historical Society, Pineapple Press, Inc., 1992); Robin C. Brown's *Florida's First People* (Pineapple Press, Inc., 1994); and Frank Hamilton Cushing, Phyllis E. Kolianos, and Brent Richards Weisman's *The Lost Florida Manuscript of Frank Hamilton Cushing* (Florida Museum of Natural History, 2005).

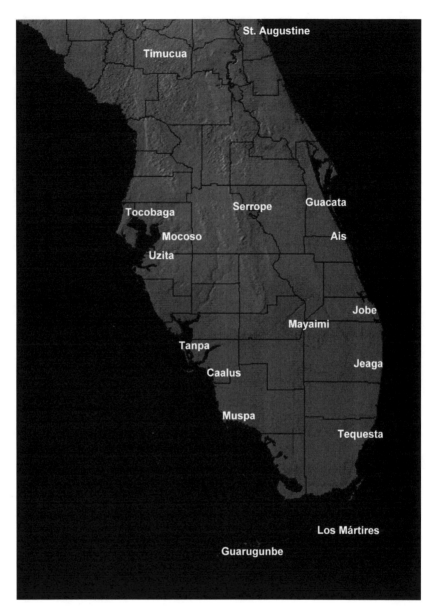

Figure 1. Sixteenth-century Florida.

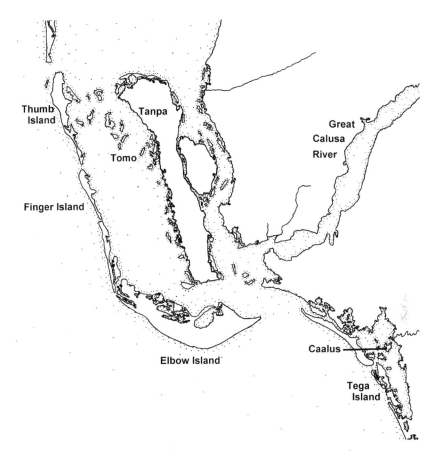

Figure 2. Calusa environs.

SONG OF THE TIDES

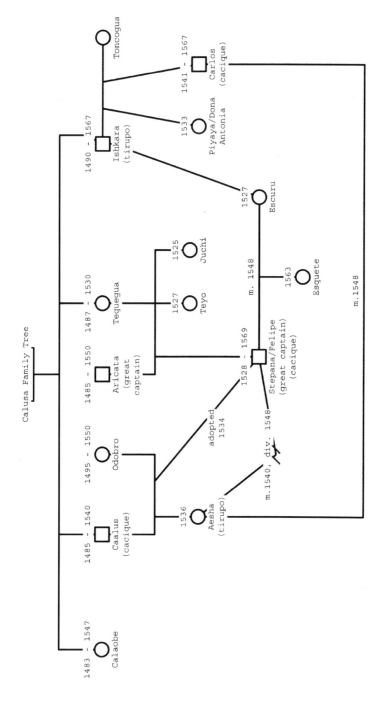

Figure 3. This family tree uses actual names, dates, and relationships to the extent they are known or can be interpolated. The remaining entries are invented by the author and are not inconsistent with historical accounts.

ᔌ One ᔌ

I was born too late. I should have been cacica.

To many, the idea of a female leader was preposterous. But my father, Caalus, was the great unifier of the people of Escampaba, the people who now bear his name. It was his duty to pass to his offspring the royal insignia. Caalus produced no sons, though, only me. To wear the beaded leggings, to place the pearl amulet around my forehead, to carry the ruler's staff, those were my birthrights. I was born too late. By that time, he'd given them to Stepana.

Stepana. My cousin. Once my husband. Ever my adversary. Child of my father's sister and the warrior Aricata, born eight years before me. For all that time, despite Ishkara's potions and the parade of wives the vassal tribes sent Father, he remained childless. Before the council, Aricata was as sharp of speech as he was of spear. "Cacique, how many women have you lain with? All barren? Ha. Already there is whispering, not only in Caalus but throughout Escampaba that their paramount leader possesses the manhood of a jellyfish. The only way to quiet the tongues is to name a successor."

The great captain had the people's ear. He had slain the stranger named Ponce, the leader of the Spanish invaders who had dared to land on Escampaba's shores. Aricata's arrow delivered Ponce to the land beyond and sent his wind ships fleeing. It didn't matter that Father knew the strangers would return. Aricata was the people's hero. His influence was pervasive, his ambition limitless. The longer Caalus held off naming an heir, the louder the whispers became.

It was Ishkara who presented the solution after retreating to the sanctuary of the inner temple to listen to the gods, and my same dear uncle who, as tirupo, the people's spiritual leader, presided over the ceremony at which Caalus adopted Stepana as his son. Though Father recoiled at the very sight of the youth whose head was as swelled as his belly, he understood Ishkara's good sense. In so doing, Stepana came out from under Aricata's control and into Father's. It would seem.

For all the moons my mother carried me in her womb, I am told all of Escampaba held its breath. When I was born female, though, tongues wagged more than ever. Men claimed all the high positions, from tirupo and great captain down to the councilors and clan heads. But on the rare occasion that only a female child was born, she alone would carry the blood of the cacique. She could rule. It had happened in the provinces.

As Father called the people to assembly, they wondered: would Caalus be so daring as to attempt to entitle a female? Would he sever the bond that made Stepana his son and successor? He was, after all, the most powerful leader the people had ever known.

Powerful, but not foolhardy. To rouse the wrath of Aricata was to weaken all of Escampaba. Nor would Father break a sacred promise, even one he lamented. He announced to the people: his daughter would not rule. Instead, when she came of age, she would marry Stepana.

To pledge me to Stepana was another decision as abhorrent as it was necessary. I had not even the consolation of an unhurried childhood. It was not Father's wish that I marry at the age of four suns, yet that was his order. I was born too late and wed too soon. And that is but the beginning of my story.

No. My story begins much earlier. For who am I but a strand of palm fiber braided into the belt of my ancestors? My story is the story of my people. It begins, truly, in the time of quiet, when the people knew themselves not as the Calusa, the followers of Caalus, but only as the people. Even then, they had a name for their watery homeland. There, in the maze of island-dotted, shallow-water bays protected from the open sea, tidal waters washed in and out, mixing with fresh water from the rivers of the mainland's interior. It was not an ancient world; in fact, the oldest stories spoke of a time when the land and sea met much closer to the setting sun, and the ground was dry, the climate arid. Now, though, the sea had risen, creating a vast underwater flat covered with sea grasses and teeming with life. In the shallows the walking trees took hold, forming a web of interlocking roots, nursery and sanctuary for small fish, shrimp, and crabs, which in turn fed the profusion of birds, fish, and animals that the gods had sent to populate this bountiful place.

The people's name for their home was Escampaba, the Bay of Plenty.

In the time of quiet, there was enough for everyone. Fish swam thick in the waters, and conchs, clams, and whelk were so plentiful that the people's cities rose on heaps of discarded shells that formed tall mounds topped with homes and temples. Everything the people needed came from the sea and the thin strips of land upon which they lived. The fishermen made cord from the fiber of the sabal palm and wove it into nets, which they floated with pegs from the cypress tree and weighted with heavy shells, and the fish swam into their nets. Women wove baskets from vines and creepers and roots and stems and filled the baskets with oysters for roasting and steaming. Men fashioned cups and bowls from whelk shells, carved as things of beauty as well as of utility. They harnessed fire to hollow out the pine tree for canoes, sturdy crafts that could glide through the shallows or stand up to the waves of the open sea. With whelk shell chisels and cutting blades made from the teeth of sharks, they shaped and sculpted wood into masks for use in their ceremonies.

The gods were pleased with the people. It was a time of abundance.

In the quiet time, the people, my people, lived in harmony with the cycles of sun and moon. They gave thanks to the gods, to Sipi, who ruled over the heavens, land, and sea, to Nao, who presided over human affairs, and to Aurr as well, who aided in time of battle. For even in the quiet time, the people had conflicts. Long had their canoes explored their watery world, paddling up the coast to the north, where they found the followers of Tocobaga, and to the south, past the vast swamp at the foot of the mainland, along the great long appendage of the Gator Tail Islands, and farther yet to the rising sun lands of Tequesta. The time of quiet was threatened then by the voices of others who spoke words the people did not understand.

No, this story is not mine alone. It is that of Tanpa, whose followers built a majestic, high-mounded city traversed with waterways and a deep canal clear across his wide island to gain safe access to the great river that poured from the interior. These feats, grand in vision and exhaustive of labor, opened the trade route to the tribes on the immense Lake Mayaimi. Tanpa was wary, but as he bartered the people's dried fish for the others' roots and whelk hammers for their pots of clay, they learned to live together in a truce constructed of mutual fear and respect.

It is the story, too, of Muspa, he of the city at the edge of the vast snaking labyrinth of channels and walking tree islets to the south. Muspa was a tirupo who moved freely about the world of spirits, summoning health with the sea turtle or disease with the spider, fruitfulness with the dolphin or demise with the white pelican. His people excelled in woodcarving, fashioning smooth masks and graceful figures, polishing them to a fine sheen and preserving them with fat or decorating them with pigment made from charcoal, ground shells, or berries. It was these masks that the people used in their ceremonies, these figures that they prayed before. Muspa's people earned renown throughout Escampaba as masters in the twin realms of the spirits and artistic beauty.

And of so many more. Of the smaller villages of Yagua, Estantapaca,

Queyhcha, Sinapa, Tomo, Metamapo, and of the tiny out-island settlements, whose inhabitants shun both the congestion and protection of the cities, and who come together only during the festivals.

And can it be said that mine is not the story of our enemies, too? Of Tocobaga, whose fishermen follow the migrating schools of fish into Calusa waters and whose warriors sneak in at night to steal nets and canoes. And, of course, of the Spaniards, those strangers from afar who returned, just as Father predicted, on their fearsome and fabulous floating villages.

Here, from the refuge of the sacred inner temple where the gods spoke to Caalus and to Ishkara, let all those whose waves have washed over our shores speak while I listen, listen to the counsel of the very waves themselves, pushed to the shore, then sucked back to sea in their endless rhythmic breathing that sustains all of life. For it is nothing but life that I seek, life for my people. Let me hear all the voices until, at last, they speak as one. Only then will I act.

I am Aesha, the bird that dances between the waves. Tonight, my vision will be completed. Tonight, my story may end.

⤚ Two ⤘

Caalus stood before the temple, the shadow of his compact, muscled body projecting oddly long and angular onto the latticed walls. He dared not go inside for fear of disturbing Ishkara. For eight days now, his brother had secluded himself in the sanctuary of the inner temple. Only a journey of great import would have kept him there so long. Caalus turned toward the gold-tinted light of late afternoon, gazing past the central canal and its harbored entrance, past the low walking tree islands dotting the placid bay, past even the far-off lookout station on Tega Island. Osprey Eyes, the people called him, and Caalus felt complimented with the comparison to the startling yellow-brown orbs, fierce and keen, of the fish hawk. He strained to see farther yet, out to sea. That was where the strangers would come from. Soon. Then Tanpa, Muspa, and the others would believe. They'd see the wisdom of his counsel. If by then it wasn't too late.

He didn't blame the other leaders for doubting. Like the wispy clouds that precede a storm, only rumors had blown in first of a race of hairy-faced strangers who traveled in colossal canoes that could carry an entire settlement yet required no paddlers, only the winds to fill their cloths. The men who steered them, said the chattergulls, were puny, pale-skinned, and laughably ugly, with hair all over their faces and bodies. Yet these strangers from afar could control the winds. They were clever beyond imagination. They came from a land beyond the sun, sent by the gods themselves. Perhaps, some suggested, they *were* gods.

The stories spread like fire on the grasses, taking on a sinister edge. The strangers carried astonishing weapons whose darts struck like lightning, exploded like thunder, and killed anything in their path. They wielded glinting knives as long as a man's leg, slicing off the noses and ears of those who refused to do their bidding. It was impossible even to run from them, for the strangers would unleash a wolf-like demon that could outrun a deer and devour you whole in crocodile-like jaws. Soon accounts were told around every campfire in Escampaba of the strangers' hideous tortures, until it was quite impossible to separate truth from tale.

The same stories could be heard at the chiefs' council fire. Caalus, the young headman of the small island in the central region, was a newcomer to the informal assemblies that took place during festival time, having only recently become a chief after the passing of his father to the land beyond. He listened closely to the counsel of Tanpa and Muspa, leaders of the people's great cities to the north and south. Here were men who'd come from a long line of powerful chiefs of the same name, who enjoyed the admiration of all. Yet when finally it came Caalus's turn to speak, he did not defer. In a voice that was respectful yet firm, he said, "We must band together under a strong single authority, a central council with leaders from throughout the islands. Only then will we be able to coordinate the defense of all." Above the grumbling, he added, "Please, I implore you. Our fishing grounds are becoming ever more congested. How are disputes to be settled? And we should be expanding the trade networks collectively, not haphazardly." But the others, fiercely independent, balked. One way or another, the people had always coped with their enemies and settled their internal differences. They feared the power of a central leader more than they coveted the benefits.

Then a traveler came to Caalus, an Arawak from the islands to the south and east, far beyond the farthest corner of Escampaba. He claimed to have lived amongst the strangers and that he spoke some of their words. Spaniards, he called them. They were monsters whose cruelty knew no bounds. Descending upon the Arawak in search of wealth, especially the shiny ore called gold, the invaders enslaved the natives by the thousands, demanding payment in gold and toil. The Spaniards' cacique was a man named Juan Ponce De León, whom the strangers called Adelantado, "supreme leader." His fearsome companion, Bezerillo, was not a demon but may as well have been—at a point of its master's finger, the giant dog would rip you to shreds.

The traveler called himself Guacanoa. Facing the standard punishment for failure to deliver the required tribute of gold—the cutting off of his hand—he'd fled by canoe into the night, not daring to make landfall for days on end until, nearly expired from thirst, he came to Caalus.

Caalus gave Guacanoa water, food, and a good bed. After the man had rested, Caalus learned that the strangers numbered, as far as Guacanoa could say, only in the hundreds. With their superior weapons, they lost but few of their men in battle and so had been able to subdue vastly greater numbers of Arawaks, who, being a peaceful people, had few weapons of their own.

Instead of despairing from Guacanoa's tale, Caalus took solace. The strangers were not gods but men. The most human of purposes motivated them: greed. They ate, slept, shat, and bled. Their numbers were not overwhelming. Perhaps they were capable of cruelty, but what men weren't? Caalus brought Guacanoa to Tanpa and Muspa along with a new idea. The waters of Escampaba possessed treasures that far outshone the strangers' yellow rocks. "We'll trade with them as we have with the interior tribes. We'll make them allies." And finally, his ultimate argument: "If we devise no such strategy, perhaps Tocobaga will."

Though the mention of Tocobaga, the people's hated enemy to the north, raised some eyebrows, still many resisted. Who would sit on this council? Where would it be located? What if they disagreed with a decision? They moved at the pace of the manatee, acted like the lumbering sea animal, too, burying their heads in the sea grasses, then rising to snort out a blast of hot air before descending below the surface again.

So Caalus waited, waited while the dread mounted like dead fish on the shore after a strangling tide. Waited while his brother, the tirupo, searched the spirit world for clues to mastering this new menace. From atop the island's highest point, Caalus watched the sun dash the sky with its fiery light as it descended toward its nightly meeting with the sea. Soon another night of quiet would fall upon Escampaba. How many more would there be?

The wind ships were coming. Ishkara felt them as he could feel a storm still far out at sea, with his bones and joints. Like a wall that rose to the sky, they blotted the sun, casting a shadow that darkened the bay, the island, the temple. They must be very close, too close to see what pushed them forward. "Heh-emm." With a loud slurping sound, Ishkara swigged casine from the cup of the right-handed lightning whelk. Until his vision cleared, the black drink would be his only nourishment.

Ishkara sat cross-legged on his straw mat. Here in the temple within the temple, in the room that none but chief or tirupo could enter, where resided the tribe's most sacred masks and images, he could confer with the gods. They were right before him: Sipi on the ancient white deerskin; Nao, the graceful half-feline, half-human figurine; Aurr, the carved ivory-billed woodpecker with its blood-red head. Why did they not speak? Did the coming of the strangers, like that of the swirling, killing blue-sky storms, signal the gods' anger? Or was it possible that these strange men were sent by unknown gods residing in a place beyond Ishkara's imagination, beyond even the reach of Sipi? For hours and days, Ishkara had prayed for guidance, yet all he heard was silence, all he saw was darkness. The gods had abandoned him.

Or had they? In the empty void before him, Ishkara noticed the dim light of a small flame flickering weakly in the distance. Intrigued, he moved toward it ever so slowly, fearful that his slightest motion would extinguish it. But as he drew near, it floated away, just beyond his reach.

Again he approached, and again the flame drifted away. And a third time. Finally, summoning all his patience and skill, Ishkara crawled at a conch's pace, moving imperceptibly, reaching not with his hands now but with his mind, his will. Farther he stretched, almost touching the flame, though still he could feel no heat. Where had the flame come from? What did it signify? What did it have to do with the strangers and their wind ships? He could see the flame but not the source of the fire. Closer. He must come closer yet, must find the source.

As Ishkara inched forward a final hair's width, the flame suddenly exploded. Dazzling bursts of light danced before him, shooting sparks of yellow, blue, and green, leaving him dazed and blinded even as he tried to shield his eyes with his hands. Only gradually did he realize what had happened: sunlight was showering into the sanctuary. Then he heard his brother's voice: "The wind ships. They've arrived."

Word had come from an out-island fisherman breathless as a flopping flounder. An enormous canoe had beached on a shoreline near his fishing grounds. He'd been throwing his net in the sea grass when he heard noises, as if a group of woodcarvers were scraping and pounding. Paddling around a corner, he came upon the massive vessel pulled up on land and lying on its side, with several men cleaning and scraping barnacles off its bottom. When pressed further—what did the men look like? How many were there?—the fisherman threw up his arms. He could give no more information. He had turned and fled.

"What have you seen?" Caalus asked Ishkara. "What is your counsel?"

Ishkara rubbed his stinging eyes. He felt so much older than his twenty-three suns. Though Caalus was five suns his elder, it was Ishkara who bore the tirupo's burden of communing with the spirit world. Not even the chief could countermand a decree of the gods . . . if there was one. "Shadow. I see only darkness."

"But brother, in all that time, eight days it was, you've seen nothing?"

Ishkara would not speak of the small flame. It had eluded him, as if the vision belonged not to him but to someone else. "This new menace," he said instead, "it's different. Always before we knew who and what we were fighting. I cannot guide you. I've seen nothing. I've failed."

"Or is it the gods who've failed us?"

Ishkara winced at Caalus's words. "The gods have tested us many times. Please, brother, do not doubt. The answers will come."

"I have no time for waiting. Answers or no, the wind ships are here."

Blinking still, Ishkara hung his head low.

Caalus put a hand on Ishkara's bony shoulder. "Forgive my harshness. No one knows the difficulty of your journey better than I. I have no choice, though. I am chief. I must act."

"If I can't guide you, I must still urge caution."

"But the ship appears to be disabled. We may be able to take it quickly."

"It could just as easily be a trick, a decoy. Perhaps a larger force lies hidden, waiting to attack. Was it not your hope to approach them peacefully?"

Caalus unclenched a fisted hand, then balled it again. "It's difficult to overcome the warrior's instinct."

"I fear that our weapons will fail us," Ishkara said. "We must use our wits. I tell you, there's great danger here. Brother, please. Caution."

Caalus looked kindly upon his brother, who was taller by a head but thin as a slipper shell and pale as one, too. Ishkara's long hair fell uncharacteristically loose from his neglected topknot. The eight days had taken a toll. "You must rest and eat," Caalus said. "I'll contact Tanpa and Muspa. We surely must act in concert. In the meantime, I'm sending a scouting party. Is this truly a wind ship? Why is it pulled up on land?

Are there others? And how many men are there? There should be answers to these questions at least."

More waiting. It was two days before the scouts returned. They reported sighting the great canoe from afar. It had already launched and was moving under the power of cloths mounted on tall posts, three square ones and a triangular one, their bellies filled by the breezes and puffed taut. The wind ship moved to sea at Open Mouth Pass, steered south, and anchored just offshore of the base of Elbow Island. The scouts left two of their number to keep watch.

Out to sea? Caalus could delay no longer. Leaving Ishkara to await word from Tanpa and Muspa, Caalus led a party of twenty canoes on the half-day paddle to Elbow Island, bringing Guacanoa along as interpreter. There, perhaps three arrows' distance from the shore, floated the most magnificent vessel that Caalus had ever laid eyes on.

The stories hadn't exaggerated by much. The wind ship was massive, twice longer and wider even than the royal barge, Caalus's two-log catamaran. Four tall poles, thick as mature pines, extended high in the air, steadied by a maze of ropes. Lashed to the posts were cross-poles that held the wind cloths, rolled up now by means of more ropes. Wood boards, stacked and glued tight to each other, ran its entire length, curving to a pointed bow. But perhaps most impressive was the vessel's depth. The wind ship had a wood platform—a floor, really—extending its length and breadth. Below, there must be an abundance of room for cargo. Imagine, a dry room for storing trade goods.

Caalus blinked and refocused. So entranced had he been with the wind ship that he'd ignored the strangers themselves. Perhaps twenty men stood on the vessel's platform. They were too far away to distinguish their features or what weapons they might carry. Caalus wondered how many more were hiding in the depths.

The young chief and his party beached on Elbow Island, where a crowd was gathered. A man, one of the scouts, inched forward. "If you please, there has already been an incident with the strangers. This morning, before you arrived."

It took great effort for Caalus to tug his eyes from the wind ship.

"We watched them through the night," said the scout. "This morning, they began to pull their anchor. We feared they would leave. So we paddled to them—some of the fishermen who'd gathered here helped us—and tried to put their anchors back down. That was when," the scout's eyes grew so wide his very soul could escape them, "the strangers attacked."

"Attacked?"

"They launched a canoe. No, not a canoe. It resembled a small wind ship with paddles instead of cloths. Backward paddles. Each man pulled on two. They chased our canoes all the way to the beach. We fled, but they jumped out and ran after. They wrecked two of our canoes and grabbed four women and took them back to the wind ship."

"There was no fighting? No bloodshed?"

The scout shook his head. "We dared not attack for fear they would kill the women."

Caalus's eyes flicked over the crowd. Out of the fifty or so, there might be a dozen able men to join his forty warriors. The numbers were insufficient, even if there were no more Spaniards than those he'd already seen. He had to stall for time and reinforcements.

He gestured to Guacanoa. "Will you undertake a mission for me?"

"I will. It's to you I owe my life."

"Go speak with the strangers. Tell them to remain anchored. In a few days, I'll bring them gifts. In return, they'll release the four. Tell them I have the shiny ore. Gold."

"But you have only the small pieces I've given you. They're guanin, of very poor quality."

"They don't know what I have and don't have."

When Guacanoa returned but a short time later, his teeth chattered with fear. "The Adelantado himself is on board."

"What did he say?"

"I . . . when I saw him, I feared getting too close. I shouted to him from a distance. He responded, but I could not make out what he said. I know but little of his tongue. I heard a growl, too. I think it was his beast. I beg you, do not take them lightly."

Caalus comforted the Arawak. "I won't attack him, not now. My plan is to trade for the women. But warriors will back me up."

Reinforcements trickled in slowly from nearby islands, though none yet from Muspa and Tanpa, who had long distances to travel. Caalus pleaded for patience. But as he feared, the warriors, mostly young men, itched for action. There was no central command, no coordination. The next day, twenty canoes attacked the Spaniards, trying to cut their anchors. The Spaniards sent a back-paddling canoe full of fighting men. Their weapons spit fire and exploded, the noise booming over the open water. Five warriors fell. Four others were captured after they fell from their canoes.

That night the Adelantado sent two of the prisoners back. Although they couldn't relay the Spanish leader's words, Caalus understood the meaning. The Spaniards preferred not to fight. The next morning Caalus gathered the pieces of guanin and, flanked by the eighty-odd warriors now present, approached the ship. Up close, it was even larger, towering over his log canoes as if they were child's toys. Pale-skinned, grim-faced men stared down. So did the glinting eyes of their fire spitters.

"*Venimos en paz.* We come in peace," shouted Guacanoa from the bow of Caalus's canoe. "We wish to bring you gifts, and gold."

An older man with a long nose and pointy, fur-covered chin looked down at them. He said something in a tongue that Caalus could not understand.

"He says that we may come forward. The others must move back," Guacanoa translated.

But before Caalus could give the order, a canoe sprinted for the ship's bow, paddled by Aricata, one of Caalus's own young warriors who was as short of diplomacy as he was of patience. He lunged for the anchor rope, his bone knife drawn.

The strangers were ready. Their weapons flashed and barked. Aricata fell back in his canoe, clutching his shoulder. Already, Caalus saw the other warriors hoisting their bows and atlatls. There was no stopping now. Caalus fitted a spear into his atlatl and hurled. With force that could as easily split a sapling or a head, it struck its target square over the heart. And glanced off. The man was wearing protective covering as hard as turtle shell. He pointed his weapon at Caalus. The chief flung himself to the floor of his canoe, heard the thunder. Something rushed past him, whistling like a plummeting hawk. As he took up his paddle, he saw three more warriors fall. "Retreat," he shouted.

From a distance, the strangers' weapons could do no damage, but neither could the warriors' spears. They tried arrows, but the Spanish arrows, shot from a bow held curiously crosswise, flew farther. Through the day, the warriors made periodic runs at the Spaniards, but few of the Spaniards fell, and many of Caalus's men floated face down. By nightfall, the blue ocean was turning red. Only a handful of able warriors were left to gather the dead and wounded and to paddle, shamefaced, back to the city.

Caalus left behind three scouts. Several days later, they returned. The strangers had moved about the bay for a few days, sending a landing party here and there to explore, carefully avoiding any settlements. Then, sailing southward, they disappeared.

The defeat at Elbow Island was a bitter one, Caalus's alone to bear. It didn't matter that he hadn't ordered the attack. He was a headman. Women had disappeared; warriors had died. Caalus prepared to lose any influence he'd begun to enjoy amongst the chiefs of Escampaba. He'd be fortunate to retain his position in his own home city.

Ishkara prepared the dead, dispensing their lesser souls, those of the shadow and the reflection, to the animal world, there to inhabit those marvelous beings; and he carried their remains, and of course their eyes, in whose pupils resided the third, eternal soul, to the Island of Bones. As he led the people through the customary nine-day grieving period, word began to trickle back from the settlements. To Caalus's astonishment, he was hailed as a hero throughout the islands. Neither Muspa nor any village to the south reported seeing the wind ships. They'd vanished. Caalus had driven them off.

He posted sentries on every out-island and sent patrols far out to sea. Though rumors still abounded, and stories of occasional sightings from the tribes to the east continued, none could be verified. Caalus's own patrols saw nothing but endless ocean.

If the people were pleased at the strangers' disappearance, Caalus was full of regrets. Hadn't the Adelantado, in releasing two of the captives, sent a message? If only Caalus could have met the strangers' chief face-to-face, he might have come to know the man. A great opportunity had been lost. Caalus lamented, too, the loss of Guacanoa, who had fallen to a Spanish arrow, for with him died the possibility of learning the strangers' tongue.

Most of all, though, he regretted his failure to capture the wind ship. Such a marvelous vessel. He summoned the people's finest canoe builders, drew for them the picture still so vivid in his mind's eye. The builders shook their heads. "We burn our canoes from logs. The construction you describe is altogether different. Each log has been individually sawn square and glued to the next. What are we to use? Our saws are made from sharks' teeth and mackerel jaws. They'd wear out on a single log. And that is only the beginning. How are the logs joined one to the other? How are they bent and held to shape? How is the great weight of the wood platform and wind cloth posts supported?"

"Build a small model."

They did. It broke apart. The glue, made from pinesap and deer's hooves, would not hold.

Ishkara warned his brother. "You waste far too much time trying to duplicate these wind-powered monstrosities. The people complain that you're obsessed and envious. Forget the wind ships. They are the work of demons."

"Not demons. They may cast their shadow over you, but I've seen them up close. They're the work of men—powerful and dangerous—but in the end, still men."

"No, brother, there is more than that. I returned to the battle site. There are spirits about, spirits that show no respect for our gods. Besides, you have greater concerns. You must turn your attentions to governing."

So Caalus sat with Muspa and Tanpa and said to them, "When the wind ships return—and they will—they must know that they face a single, unified adversary. We must be ready to fight as one. Only then will they respect and fear us. This we have already recognized. Now we must create the means by which to put it into practice." The two leaders concurred. And so they agreed to divide Escampaba into three provinces. While each would retain much autonomy in local affairs, Caalus's city would be recognized as both the central trade hub and the seat of authority in the affairs of battle. And Caalus would become cacique, the paramount chief of all Escampaba.

To solidify his new position, Caalus issued two proclamations. First, every village must pay tribute in the form of food, skins, or other valuables. Second, Caalus alone would be permitted, indeed required, to lie with multiple wives, though his successor would be, as tradition dictated, born of a union with his sister. Some villages came quickly into line. Yagua, Estantapaca, and Queyhcha pledged their loyalty with precious blood relations, sending sisters and daughters to Caalus. The cacique rewarded their families with seats at his nine-member council table. Others, Sinapa, Tomo and Metamapo among them, were reluctant. Caalus tolerated the tacit rebellion. Soon enough they would have to make a decision to join him or suffer the consequences at the hands of the Spaniards.

Meanwhile, he set his greatly expanded labor force to work. His small city-island had been modeled after Tanpa, with two principal mounds, one for the temple and one for his own living quarters, bisected by a canal dug into the island. Now Caalus ordered his own mound expanded, not in height lest it eclipse that of the temple, but in breadth, so that it could hold a proper palace and council hall. The central canal was widened and a large, circular water court dug at its terminus in the island's center. A broad plaza was built at the foot of the water court with ramps spiraling up both mounds in the manner of shells. Caalus ordered, too, a high seawall constructed all around the island and extended at the central canal's entrance to create a sheltered harbor. Now the island was far better protected from both weather and invaders.

On the barrier islands stretching the length of his territories, islands of great natural beauty but lightly inhabited because of their exposure to those same enemies, Caalus placed a series of lookouts who could quickly relay messages to each other by means of signal fires. The Spaniards would not slip in unnoticed again.

For season upon season, Caalus occupied his people with the preparations. Though the Spaniards did not show themselves, shocking reminders of their cruelty washed onto the shores of Escampaba in the form of bedraggled, sad-eyed refugees from the islands to the south, especially from the one called Cuba. All came with tales of horror. Some spoke a bit of the Spaniards' tongue. Caalus allowed them to settle on a nearby island, hoping their skills would prove useful when the time came.

Eight cycles of the sun had passed when the Spaniards returned. The lookouts spotted two wind ships, even larger than those in memory, enter at Elbow Island. Following at a discreet distance, they watched the vessels anchor just off the mouth of the great river of the interior. To their astonishment, from the strangers' ships walked a herd of giant deer. The strangers climbed upon their backs and rode them into the woods. With the help of these animals, as well as of sharp-bladed saws and chopping tools, the Spaniards, who numbered about two hundred, cleared a large area of trees in a mere two days' time and began to erect log lodges for the men and pens for their other strange animals large and small.

Strangers building a settlement in the heart of Escampaba. This time Caalus did not even consider talk. He launched a surprise attack with five hundred warriors. And though he lost more than a hundred and fifty men, the Spaniards were routed, for Caalus's warriors had learned to aim their arrows and spears at the strangers' unprotected faces and legs. The pointy-chinned Adelantado Juan Ponce himself fell wounded with an arrow in his thigh.

Afterwards, the young warrior Aricata paraded blood-dripping, pale-skinned heads through the city of Caalus, pausing frequently to rub the gore into the scarred muscle of his misshapen left shoulder. "Do not expect their leader's return," he told the adoring throngs. "The arrow he fell to was my own. It was tipped in poison." To reward Aricata's bravery, Caalus betrothed to him his youngest sister, Tequegua, then named Aricata great captain, war chief in charge of all warriors.

But the cacique refrained from rejoicing. Once again, the ships had escaped. They were like the wind that blew them. They could not be contained.

☙ Three ❧

The people now shared a common name, Calusa, the followers of Caalus. Caalus's storehouses overflowed with treasures both fundamental and fanciful: deer hides, antlers, and bones; barracuda, mackerel, and shark jaws; egret, heron, eagle, and osprey feathers; tortoise and sea turtle shells; cypress knees and gumbo-limbo knots. Ishkara took possession of the roots, seeds, and plants, establishing an orchard of the fruit-bearing coco plum, hog plum, and mastic trees and rooting the vines of wild grapes from throughout the region: muscadine, frost, summer, and pigeon grapes. An exotic bush sent from the Gator Tail Islands, whose seed coverings produced lather when rubbed between the hands, promised the potential of replacing sand as a scrubbing agent, and the hard brown seeds of this same soapberry plant made excellent buttons. Near the temple he grew gourds and bird peppers, the former for use in the casine ceremony, the latter because he loved their fiery flavor. Papaya, too, the sweet exotic fruit grown by Tanpa. But Ishkara especially prized his row of hackberries, whose sweet red seeds he chewed incessantly.

But nothing was as important to Ishkara as the healing plants: saltwort, nickerbean, wild sage, sea purslane, trailing wedelia, white stopper. With these the tirupo made poultices for wounds, salves for the stings of rays and catfish, and teas to aid itching, relieve burning urination, stop bleeding or running bowels, and a hundred other purposes. Under Ishkara's guidance, the island of Caalus became the medicine pouch of Escampaba.

Caalus's palace grew, too, as he added rooms for the growing multitude of more than thirty wives. More than any other, this custom reinforced alliances and ensured the loyalty of villages too remote to control directly. For the most part, the distant chiefs sent their daughters willingly, for the practice elevated their status too, since the offspring of such marriages would be nobility by virtue of Caalus's blood.

There was only one problem. The marriages produced no children.

Ishkara gave Caalus a tea of the rock tree leaf for strength, fed him a broth of boiled tadpoles for virility. The tirupo donned the mask of the dolphin, known to couple fruitfully with many partners and shook a snakeskin rattle above Caalus's head, a ceremony that should have driven out the spirits spoiling his brother's seed. But the spirits were strong. They'd arrived, Ishkara was certain, on the sails of the wind ships. Although the ships had been driven away not once but twice, their evil lingered.

And other wind ships returned. Not to Calusa waters, but to those of Tocobaga, Uzita, and Mocoso, only a few days' paddle to the north. New Spanish leaders named Narváez and Cabeza de Vaca came to replace the fallen Adelantado Juan Ponce and reportedly rode their giant deer inland. Neither Caalus nor Ishkara took much solace either from the knowledge that the old Adelantado had indeed died from Aricata's arrow or from the new Spaniards' terrorizing of Calusa enemies. They were too close.

More suns passed, that great being making his slow journey north toward the anchor star and back south again, wet season followed by dry, endless unrelenting heat followed by the short uneven cold or mild days. Ishkara sired two daughters, Escuru and Piyaya, while Aricata fathered two daughters of his own, Juchi and Teyo. But while the palace halls rang with the sounds of girlish games and songs, there remained no male offspring in the royal family. And no germination at all of Caalus's seed, though his nights were even more demanding than his days.

When Tequegua bore Aricata a son, everything changed.

Ishkara named the boy at an unusually early age: Stepana, Cheeks Full of Milk. He refused weaning, screaming day and night for the breast even at three suns, then punishing Tequegua by biting the nipple that fed him. As soon as the boy had a name, Aricata began to speak openly of the need for a successor to Caalus. The great captain was as insistent as he was crude, proudly strutting about the city without breechclout, parading his own productive loins as he proclaimed the inadequacies of Caalus's: "Perhaps the cacique should enlist my services not only in the arena of war, but also in that of love." As time went on and Caalus remained childless, Aricata's demands grew ever louder. "Name an heir, Cacique. You're a young man no longer. If you die without one, you'll plunge the people back into chaos."

Long had Caalus regretted the day he offered the hand of his sister to the man as thorny as prickly pear. Aricata was always itching to lead raiding parties, not only against real enemies like Tocobaga but against friendlies like the Ais, Guacata, and Tequesta that failed to pay tribute goods, even if they were only a moon overdue. The only diplomacy Aricata practiced was to be found at the end of a saber club.

Caalus well knew whom the great captain had in mind. Unfortunately, Aricata had spoken the truth. Ishkara's potions were of no use. Caalus was doomed to remain childless.

Seeking the counsel of the gods, Ishkara ducked under the arched entrance of the inner temple. The masks of each clan and village, some realistically rendered, others fantastic combinations of man and animal, filled the woven mat walls, their shell bead eyes glaring down on his shoulders with a tangible weight. Ishkara turned to the altar at the center of the sanctuary, bowing to the Creator Sipi, portrayed on the hide of the white deer as the likeness of a barracuda pierced by harpoon. "Ancient One," he implored, "we have repelled the strangers, and yet their spirits linger to make mischief on us still. Did you send them? Are you angry with us? Tell me, what must we do?"

But Sipi, sometimes tempestuous, sometimes benevolent, always temperamental, refused to answer. Ishkara turned next to address Nao, the panther-man who kneeled and bowed in contemplation. "So often you've shown us the safe course through the shoals of human defiance. Tell me how to advise my brother." But neither would Nao respond.

Instead, it was the tall figure of the war-god Aurr, carved from a hard knot of fine buttonwood and painted black, red, and white in the exact likeness of the greatest of the woodpeckers, which beckoned to Ishkara. The polished eye seemed to take on the malevolent grin of Aricata. The ivory bill was ready to peck.

Ishkara relayed the vision to Caalus. They knew what they had to do.

The ceremony was usually reserved for the rare and tragic instance where both parents have perished. Always, relatives or neighbors would take the child in. Sometimes, though, the bond would be so strong, the love so absolute, that the new parents would adopt the child as their own. Forever after, no distinction would lie between adopted and natural child.

With his lancet of fish bone, Ishkara scratched the hands of both cacique and child and placed their palms together. The blood mixed and combined. Stepana was now the child of Caalus and, as first-born male, entitled to the royal insignia. Caalus placed around his new son's forehead the large pearl amulet attached to the beaded fillet. The cacique leaned down to fasten the identically beaded leggings. When Stepana came of age, Caalus would pass to him, too, his ruler's staff made of the rock wood.

The Calusa had a successor.

Afterwards, the boy licked his hand and smiled. Caalus shivered.

Wasn't that gesture, that delight in the taste of blood, so reminiscent of Aricata? Stepana might now be Caalus's child, but it didn't stop him from exhibiting his former father's brutishness. He was broad of frame and used his size to advantage, delighting in besting other children in spear throwing or push-and-shove, then, in a cruel child's imitation of the adult world, forcing them to pay tribute to him of the fish they netted or the clams they collected at low tide. He had a special craving for oysters, which, even at six suns, he could eat by the dozen. The boy's fat face had a perpetual sneer, even when addressing his elders. Even his new father.

Caalus detested the new son who'd come to live in his palace. At least now, though, Aricata was neutralized, forced to express gratitude in public even while in private he fumed over his loss of leverage. Caalus finally felt free to turn his attentions elsewhere. He traveled to some of the villages that had remained holdouts, still acting on their own, fishing and gathering where they would, delaying or refusing tribute altogether.

One such settlement was that of Tomo. It was small but ancient, with modest ridge-shaped mounds and a long history of strong leaders as headstrong as they were intelligent. The current chief was no exception. Tomo wasn't threatening, he was simply aloof. He promised nothing. Nevertheless, he feted the cacique with a grand feast and entertained him with a performance by his daughter Odobro. She sang of the sea, her voice rising and falling, now whipped to a tempest, now becalmed. While her eyes, dark as the black drink, stared past Caalus, seeing only the storm of which she sang, her long fingers swayed and swung, weaving her story as a deer bone shuttle constructs a net.

Caalus hadn't the heart to come down on Tomo. The next morning, he bid the errant chief goodbye. Stepping onto the royal barge, he was stunned. There, already aboard, stood Odobro.

"Your father sent you?"

She shook her head.

"Then why have you come?"

"To sing for you." Tall and yet slender with youth, she displayed none of a youth's hesitation.

"You'd leave your father and home simply because it's your duty to sing for me?"

"No," Odobro answered. "Were it my duty, I'd come. But I'd never sing. I sing because it's my desire."

At first, from Odobro's lips came only slow, mournful ballads full of longing for the sights, sounds, and smells of home. As time went on, though, she began to open up, to sing of all around her. She sang of the fiddler crab, and her music crawled upon the walking-tree roots. She sang of the woodpecker, and her notes darted forward to peck the tree. She sang of the puffer fish, her cheeks inflated with air, and the song billowed and fluttered. She laughed then, and so did Caalus.

Soon, she sang of the life that grew inside her. The spell was broken. Odobro carried Caalus's child.

Speculation littered the shores like shells after a storm. Caalus's contempt for Stepana was well known. Yet the cacique had shared blood with the child. The bond could not be broken. Or could it? This was Caalus. Who could object?

The chattergulls feasted. Aricata could object, that's who. It was no secret that he still doted on the boy. Surely, if Stepana were disinherited, Aricata would revolt. What of the warriors under his command, yet who had pledged loyalty to Caalus? Would they go with Aricata or turn on him? And what of the rest of the populace? The Calusa would be torn apart.

The child was a female. That settled it.

Or did it? Men might govern Calusa society, but blood was blood. Rare though it happened, a sole female child could become chief. It had happened in the provinces. The gurgling baby carried the true blood of her father. And his eyes. As Odobro bore the babe around the city, all took notice of the yellow-brown orbs that looked, even in infancy, focused, penetrating, old.

For nearly three moons, Caalus said nothing. He disappeared with Ishkara for days on end, clearly struggling. Finally, Caalus called his councilors and people to the council hall. The royal insignia would stay with Stepana. When his new daughter came of age, though, the two would wed.

Caalus's blood would continue into the next generation.

◦⌐ Four ⌐◦

Mother woke her at dawn. As always, she sang:

> *Little pearl, awake, arise.*
> *This day promises a bright surprise.*
> *First-born, who wishes so to be large.*
> *Today will float on the royal barge.*

Instantly, First-born sprang from her sleeping bench. "Where are we going?"

"If I told you, it would not be a surprise."

As if a ride on the royal barge were not wonder enough, First-born arrived to find both Father and Ishkara already seated on the high platform spanning the two pine canoes. What luck having Father here. For the longest time he'd not come to play with her or to stroke her hair as she fell asleep, even though she was certain he was not away to the provinces, for she had heard his voice in the palace. Though Mother would not speak of it, First-born feared that Father was ill.

Today was surely First-born's lucky day. She had her mother and father to herself, and her uncle, too, for once free of the dark confines of the temple. She scampered up and wriggled between the two men. Ishkara reached over to pinch the flesh on the underside of her arm. "Ah, child, I see your mother spoils you." He pinched harder.

First-born looked at him hard and did not cry out, for she knew he was testing her. Without mask and body paint, he was not so scary, this tall, stringy man with the single egret feather atop his neatly coiled top-knot. She reached over and pinched him back, and Ishkara smiled at her with dark-stained teeth. First-born glanced quickly over at Father. Though he too smiled, black, puffy pockets drooped below his eyes. She stretched to touch two red scabs on Father's neck. They looked painful.

Father scooped her in his arms and somersaulted her in the air. "Don't look so serious, child." First-born yelped with delight. She stood between the two men as the heavy craft launched into the central canal. Soon the twelve strong servant-paddlers had the twin canoes slicing through the harbor entrance and into the bay, skimming over the light chop of the blue-green water. Mother sang a song of the ocean.

Mama's gonna sing you a song of the tides
Who lift the mighty ocean and take it for a ride
Squeezing through the passes, then on the flats they glide
Mama's gonna sing you a song of the tides.

Push on toward the shoreline, set the waves at play
Cover up the oyster bars and grasses in the bay
Dip the knees of the walking trees into a bath of salt
Flood on up the river until it's time to halt.

Mama's gonna sing you a song of the tides
Who with their friends the wind and moon forever will be tied
Tireless, they lift their load and carry it with pride
Mama's gonna sing you a song of the tides.

Draw back from the beaches, leave their line of shell
Expose the barren mud flats—both their treasures and their smell.
Slide back through the passes, out to sea, and then
Moving moving moving, they're moving once again.

Moving moving moving, resting, moving once again.
Moving moving moving, resting, moving once again.

"You're taking me to the sea."

"Sometimes I fear you're far too clever for a child of only four suns. Yes, to the sea."

First-born's eyes skipped. The open sea was too dangerous for children. If Father and Mother were taking her there, she must be growing up.

Mother kept singing that song about the tides all through the ride, a lively song that the paddlers kept rhythm to. The barge glided through the water, paralleling the chain of islands that separated it from the sea. Each time they reached an opening between islands, First-born bounced to her feet. "Now we'll turn out to sea." But they kept paddling on. It was mid-afternoon and First-born was fighting to keep her eyes open when they entered the shallows and made landfall.

First-born couldn't contain her disappointment. "You said we were going to the sea."

"Be patient, child," Father said. "It's very close. Listen."

He was right. She could hear the ocean's voice. She took Mother's hand and dragged her toward the noise, zigzagging through the scrubby brush and vines. "Are there no people on this island, Mother?"

"None. That's why I love this place. Now, watch your feet. There are sand burrs there."

But First-born would have gladly endured a thousand stick-tights to reach that sound an instant earlier. She raced to the top of the small sand ridge, then stepped down upon a glimmering white beach. The sand was warm. Fine and soft, too. First-born sat down and took two big handfuls. So powdery and clean. The air, too. On the breeze were the scents of only salt and water, not of the tidal mud that clung to the air at home. First-born saw the waves hitting the shore, first here, then there, and she heard the rhythm. They were making Mother's song.

She leapt to her feet and ran to the ocean, the sand squeaking under her bare feet. The instant she reached the water, a wave rolled in and bowled her over. She lay wet and spluttering in the sand, not knowing what to make of the situation. Mother came to the water's edge and scooped her up. She was laughing. So First-born laughed, too.

Mother set her back down, and First-born watched the waves crash in, then draw back, in, then back. Some smallish shore birds with reddish-brown wings and a big black spot over a pure white breast were there, birds she'd never seen before. Following the waves down on short orange legs, they pecked the sand, then scampered back just as the next wave approached. What fun! First-born approached the water, more carefully this time, and chased a retreating wave down the slope of the beach. As the next rolled up, she squealed and scurried away. Then down. Then back up. The ocean was playing a game with her. First-born ran down and slapped the water with her foot, then dashed back up before the waves could touch her back.

The smell of sea, the crash of waves, the squish of wet sand, and all those birds playing the wave game. It was a long time before First-born looked up to see Mother, Father, and Uncle sitting on the beach, watching her. Mother sang out to her:

Child who flits between the waves
Quite as clever as you are brave.
Scream and shout, run and play
For you, there's none other than today.

"Look at this." She ran to show Mother and Father the olive shell she'd spied. Not like the old, faded ones she occasionally found in the bay. This one was bright, lustrous, as alive as the tides. She put it in Father's hand. "It's the most beautiful thing in the world. It's for you."

Father pulled her to him. "The next most beautiful thing, after you."

It was exactly as Ishkara feared. As the four watched the sun fall toward the open ocean, he stole a glance behind, his seer's eyes perceiving what the others could not. Three shadows extended up the beach, long and healthy, darkening the sand with firm if exaggerated outlines. The fourth was faint, gossamer, like a spider's web that cannot be touched without breaking. It belonged to Caalus.

A half-moon earlier, when Caalus had taken ill, Ishkara had detected immediately that his brother's shadow-soul had departed. It was the easiest of the three souls to lose, for it could slip away in the dark of any moonless night, leaving its host listless and lethargic. Ishkara had gone to the woods and found it, then reinserted it with agave pins through the nape of the cacique's neck—you could still see the scabs. Instructing Caalus to stay indoors, Ishkara surrounded the palace grounds with fire to discourage the shadow-soul from attempting another escape. So as to deter his reflection soul from fleeing, he ordered Caalus not to gaze into a calm pool of water. And he checked and rechecked his brother's eyes. If the third and most important soul, which resided in the pupil of the eye, clouded over, it was a sure sign of turning toward the land beyond, for that soul was eternal and guided you there, even as the others left the body to enter one of the lesser animals.

Today was the first time Caalus had ventured out. Ishkara had tried to dissuade him. "Brother, you may be cacique, but when it comes to affairs of the souls, you must listen to me."

"Today Odobro takes my child for the first time to the sea. I'll not miss that."

"You're too weak. If your shadow-soul takes flight again . . ." Ishkara let the words hang.

"Some ailments even you can't repair. Besides, if the people do not see me leave my bed, I am as good as departed anyways."

"At least, then, I will accompany you."

"Father, where does the sun go at night?"

"It sleeps in the ocean."

"What does its bed look like?"

"No one knows. It is far away, in a place no canoe has ever reached."

"You could go there, Father. You're cacique. You can go anywhere."

Perhaps, Caalus thought, his shadow-soul already had. He prayed for the courage to follow it. The land beyond was the last great mystery.

"Look, Father, it's so big. And it's melting." First-born stood transfixed as the sun went through its nightly ritual, one she'd seen many times, but never with a view unencumbered by the outer islands. As the sun burned from yellow to orange to fire red, it fell ever faster, melting and spreading into the sea. As the last tip disappeared, the girl let out a gasp, jumping into her father's arms.

"What, child? What did you see?"

"The last spark of the sun. It was green. It was there just for an instant, and then it was gone."

"She's a receptive one," said Ishkara. Then, to First-born, "You're fortunate indeed to have observed the sun's green shadow. Some go a lifetime without witnessing it, for to see it, the air must be clear, the seas calm, and your spirit full and strong."

"This is the most wonderful place I've ever been. I want to stay here forever."

Odobro laughed. "Would you settle for one night?"

Now, the girl smelled roasting fish. The servants had built a fire on the beach and were cooking a large stingray they'd speared in the shallows.

First-born ate serving after serving, making Mother toss her head back and giggle. With a fourth plateful in her lap, First-born fell fast asleep.

Caalus inched closer to the fire. "She must marry. Now, while I still breathe."

Odobro's smile vanished. Her arms encircled her husband's waist. "No. You're not leaving us. Ishkara will restore you. He must."

Ishkara shook his head sadly. "My powers are not unlimited, and neither are Caalus's. If we don't perform the marriage, Aricata might well cancel it and wed Stepana to Juchi or Teyo. They're his blood."

Odobro drew away from Caalus. "You'd fight that, though. We'd fight that together."

"And plunge all of Escampaba into chaos," said Caalus. "Wouldn't Tocobaga love that? And"—he pointed to sea—"wouldn't that be just the foul air that the wind ships would return on? We must remain unified. At all costs."

Odobro's arms went up involuntarily, as if cradling her baby. "She's barely weaned."

Ishkara poked the fire, setting sparks dancing skyward. "It is highly unusual. Yet, it would be accepted. I'm sure of it."

"You'd have my child sharing a bed with that fat lout?"

Caalus stroked Odobro's long hair. "It will be a marriage in name only. She'll continue to live with you."

Odobro pushed him away. "You speak as if you're already gone. Go, then. Leave me alone."

Caalus walked down the beach. Tiny bits of green light shaken from the setting sun winked at him from the sea. Ghost crabs scuttled sideways on the tide line, illuminated by a bright half-moon. Wouldn't First-born love that game, cornering and catching the skittering creatures? Perhaps he should wake her. No. He was too weary. And though Odobro's pain grieved him, the discussion was not finished. He returned to the fire.

"Ishkara, you must declare yourself regent until Stepana is of age."

"That won't be easy. Aricata is the people's hero. He'll push hard."

"You must resist. Aricata must never hold power."

"Stepana will be even worse, though."

"No." A smile touched Caalus's sallow face. "By the time Stepana is old enough to reign, First-born will be nearly grown. She's the child of Odobro. We'll see who will rule whom."

"If the child is to wed," Ishkara said, "she will have to have a name."

"You mustn't rush it," exclaimed Odobro. "A name is a serious matter."

"Serious, yes, but have you not observed her today, running on tiny legs, flitting amongst the waves like the shorebird aesha? I see many waves in front of her, waves she must face or avoid, conquer or escape. This child will be forever dancing between them. Aesha. That will be her name."

A royal wedding should have been a grand festive gathering, filled with dancing, singing, and tears of joy. Instead, the guests shed only tears of grief. Caalus had to be carried to the council hall and seated on his raised bench, his condition obvious to all. After Ishkara performed the ritual, Odobro snatched her child from Stepana's grasp and fled to her chambers. Heaping plates of oysters converted his grumbles to grunts. Otherwise, an eerie silence prevailed.

A scant moon later, Caalus could not see his image in the bathing pool. In three days' time, his lifeless body was borne to the temple, accompanied by six servants who would attend to him in the land beyond. Ishkara thanked the servants profusely, then slew them swiftly, mercifully, cutting their throats and bleeding them quickly.

All of Escampaba mourned. The men ran in long, looping circles around their islands all the day long, following each other in heaving silence. Mothers fed their children only once a day, and the adults fasted altogether. Several of the clans, to demonstrate both their grief and affection for the departed cacique, sacrificed children to join him in his next life. Ishkara vanished into the temple for the proscribed four days, there to capture the cacique's third, undying soul and contain it with the mortal remains. Ishkara boiled the flesh from the bones and poured the broth into the sea. Afterwards, he placed the bones in a buttonwood box carved with the image of the osprey into which were inset two lustrous pearl eyes.

As for the actual eyes of Caalus, those receptacles of his eternal soul, Ishkara preserved them in a wooden bowl coated in cedar oil and filled with a brine of seawater and herbs. He fitted the lid, sealed it with glue from the strangler fig, set it in the container. "Rest in darkness, my brother," he whispered. "But guide me to the way of light."

At last the tirupo appeared, wearing the mask of the black vulture. "It has been done. Caalus's remains have been preserved and shall rest in the temple forever. And the cacique, who loves the people still, has spoken to me and implored me to take custody of the ruler's staff until Stepana has come to an age at which he is able to rule."

Not even Aricata could dispute the pronouncement, at least in public. In private, Ishkara tried to soothe his anger, adding, "Only for a period of two suns. Be patient."

"I am not a patient man."

The role of regent was as uncomfortable as it was unfamiliar. Although all eyes were often upon him as tirupo, from behind the mask Ishkara had always been able to observe others freely. Now, with an all too public face, he found himself constrained to mask his emotions instead of letting his masks emote. He knew what he had to do, didn't object when three villages sent him wives; in fact, he'd encouraged them in most persuasive terms to do so. Although he never allowed visitors to bow palms up before him—an act reserved for a cacique alone—he sat upon the ruler's bench exactly as Caalus had, his brother's staff in hand. Ishkara moved his sleeping quarters to the palace. Increasingly, by day he was to be found at the council hall. The tirupo and regent raced constantly between palace and temple mound, between responsibilities and sanctuary.

Before long, there was born to him a son. When he brought the infant to the temple and placed him in front of Caalus's shrine, the deceased cacique spoke again. With the birth of a blood son to Ishkara, there were now two legitimate heirs. The regent must delay handing over authority until a sign came indicating who was the better choice.

A red-faced Aricata stormed into the temple, his bone knife drawn in one hand, war club waving in the other. But Ishkara, wearing the mask of the she-wolf, let out a spine-chilling scream that halted Aricata in his tracks. "Stop. Hear me out."

"Be quick about it," Aricata hissed through clenched teeth. "I told you, I am not a patient man. My club awaits your head."

"Do you really think the people will support you?"

"The people fear me."

"And still love Caalus. Do they not now call themselves Calusa in his honor?"

"Aesha is wed to Stepana. He is the rightful heir."

"Perhaps. But Caalus speaks through me. Do not forget, my powers are strong. Aricata, my brother and friend, you do the people splendid service as their great captain. You are a hero. Remain so."

Grudgingly, Aricata lowered the club. "Calusa." He spat on the ground. "Someday that name will be a long-forgotten memory."

Instead of a defeat, Aricata interpreted his skirmish with Ishkara as endorsement of his military tactics. The regent stood silent as Aricata expanded his authority, enlarged his forces, improved his weapons. His warriors roamed farther afield, demanding ever greater tribute in return for the protection of the Calusa state. Indeed, Ishkara realized the necessity of military might. His eye was ever on the horizon. A force of nine wind ships and six hundred men had landed in the territory of Uzita, a mere two days' paddle from the northernmost reaches of Calusa territory. For now, they avoided Escampaba. Ishkara had Aricata to thank for that.

After a time, though, the grumbling of those subject to Aricata's strong-arm diplomacy grew louder. Aricata clamped down harder yet. Ishkara understood all too well the great captain's plan. Soon his power would be too great for even Ishkara to suppress.

At twelve suns, the spirit of woman was swelling in Aesha's girlish body. Her legs had lengthened until she stood shoulder-to-shoulder with her mother, and from her tanned chest, small protuberances bulged. She still dashed about with the exuberance of a child, but when occasionally she slowed to a walk, her long black hair swished across the small of her back with the pledge of womanhood. Her lips wore the pout of adolescence. Her eyes, though, revealed no hint of ambiguity, danced no line between childhood and maturity. Her mother might gaze past you. Aesha stared through you as does the fish hawk through water. Exactly like her father.

Ishkara's son, now seven suns, acted much older. He seemed to have understood from infancy the weight of his position, and he greeted each day with a gravity that deflated the buoyancy of youth. Surrounded by older cousins and sisters, the tight-lipped boy seldom spoke, but his silence was anything but a sign of stupidity. His brooding brown eyes took in everything.

Ishkara chose his name carefully: Carlos. To the ear, the sound was scarcely distinguishable from that of Ishkara's beloved brother, yet the name was more powerful still. Carlos was said to be the supreme ruler of the Spaniards, a man-god to whom all the strangers bowed. A name could hold great power. The boy would need every advantage.

Ishkara gave Carlos one advantage more. Caalus had spoken to the tirupo once again. Carlos was to be given the royal insignia. The marriage of Aesha and Stepana was to be annulled, and Aesha would instead wed Carlos. To this arrangement, Odobro gave her willing consent. She even suggested the further step of Ishkara's adoption of Aesha as his daughter. That way, any offspring of the marriage would be the rightful heir.

This time, Aricata merely snorted. "You name him after the fur-faced cowards who hide from us? You declare the scrawny infant cacique? Do what you will. It is I who keep the people safe, I who command the warriors. Stepana will not be cacique. He'll be more powerful yet. He'll succeed me as great captain."

"Agreed."

"I have one condition more. Stepana shall have another bride, one of my choosing."

"Yes, of course. And who will that be?"

"Escuru. Your eldest daughter."

⤙ Five ⤚

In the moon of turtle laying, when the air hung soggy over the tepid bay, Carlos wed Aesha and Stepana wed Escuru in a single ceremony. The idea had been Ishkara's. Why not? There was already widespread whispering that Stepana's marriage to Escuru would give him status equal to the young heir's. Ishkara would let the evening unfold, let the people observe for themselves who was the more noble.

The two brides, cousins in fact, could have been twins. Identically tall and slender, their black hair was gathered with polished tortoise shell hairpins, their faces painted in thin patterns of red, blue, and indigo, ears adorned with buttonwood pegs inset with oyster pearls. Their demeanors, though, could not have been more dissimilar. As they approached Ishkara on the raised platform in the center of the plaza, Aesha, the girl-woman, walked with poise, looking about her with a steady, penetrating gaze. Escuru studied the ground as if she balanced on a precipice. Who would have guessed that Escuru was the elder by five suns?

When Stepana and Carlos entered the plaza, Ishkara actually heard a few snickers bubble up from the crowd. The young child barely reached the navel of his older cousin, and he had to take two steps for each of Stepana's. The large carved gorget hanging from Carlos's neck seemed to make his shoulders droop, and his etched leather breechclout hung nearly to the ground, threatening to slide off his little-boy buttocks. In contrast, Stepana marched in erect as his throwing spear. An enormous array of necklaces and bracelets dangled from his thick neck, biceps, and calves. Beneath the ornaments, Stepana's bare chest and back were painted in bold, thick red and black strokes. Warrior strokes.

Carlos and Stepana stood before Ishkara. With a grand flourish, Stepana removed the pearl amulet he'd worn for the past six suns and placed it around Carlos's forehead. The boy's head wobbled as he struggled to keep it upright. When Stepana put the beaded leggings around Carlos's calves, they promptly fell off. Chortling laughter erupted throughout the crowd. Ishkara had to stamp Caalus's ruler's staff on the ground for order.

The couples faced each other, thumbs on each other's navels, drawing their partners into their innermost sanctuaries. Stepana, his hands circling Escuru's waist so that his fingertips touched at her back, spoke his marriage promises in a deep, clear voice, concluding, "I pledge these vows not only to you, my beloved, but to my new third father and to my people, to whom I dedicate my service and my life."

As for Carlos, he squeaked.

As Ishkara invoked the name of Sipi, the couples stood in tubs of seawater and drank cups of rainwater, sprinkling the last drops on each other as well as kicking and splashing with their feet. Then the crowd cheered, the conch horns blew, the girls' choruses sang, and the mismatched couples stepped down from the marriage platform, Carlos tripping over his new leggings and nearly sprawling to the ground before Aesha caught and righted him. Cold sweat welled up on the back of Ishkara's neck. He'd miscalculated, and badly.

The gifts of food were presented next, platters of boiled and roasted fish, raw oysters, clams and scallops, sabal palm hearts, persimmon cakes, and countless fruits and berries. As was custom, the two couples would eat their fill before the other guests were served. Escuru and

Aesha ate sparingly, and while Carlos made a show of taking a man's portion, he struggled to clean his plate and finally left his spoon in his thick, starchy coontie pudding. Not so Stepana. Over and again he returned to the tables to gorge on roasts of venison, raccoon, and bear. He snatched the choicest morsels of rare delicacies: the flipper of the sea wolf, the nose of the manatee, the tender flesh of the unborn blacktip shark. Clams and oysters disappeared down his gullet unchewed. He popped the tiny, scorching bird peppers that had been Ishkara's gift without the hint of a grimace. In between, he swigged gulps of casine, the black drink, then went to the shadows to purge. The spectacle impressed a certain element. A crowd of boys and young men surrounded Stepana, urging him on, tossing boiled shrimp in the air, which Stepana caught in his mouth and dispatched with a crunch.

Ishkara should have felt satisfaction. Instead, all he could think was, mate to my daughter? Father one day to my grandchildren? Ishkara, he who was immune to the purgative effects of casine, fled to his fruit grove and emptied his stomach. The stench of fruits rotting at his feet matched the taste in his mouth. He forced himself to return to the celebration, though he could not bring himself to join it. Standing in the shadows behind the bayberry torches, struggling to breathe the sodden air, he saw Carlos, only seven suns, attend to his new wife, following her every movement with alert if unsmiling eyes.

Stepana, on the other hand, was bent double over a banquet table, rubbing greasy hands over his distended belly. Ishkara scanned the crowd, praying he would not find Escuru. But there she was, as he knew she'd be, standing in the background, watching her new husband grab every shapely thigh and buttock that passed within reach. Several of the elders shook their heads. Ishkara stepped from the shadows. He strained to smile a ruler's smile, a father's smile, and approached his daughter.

She fled, slipping into the hazy, liquid veil of the night.

Ishkara didn't try to pursue her. Instead, he turned toward the hide drummers, who were beating out a spirited rhythm for a group of energetic dancers, amongst them Piyaya. Plodding and heavy of foot, his second daughter nevertheless kept to the center of the circle. That was Piyaya, as steady as Escuru was tremulous. Aesha was there too, thankfully oblivious to both Stepana's pawing and Escuru's shame. Good. Why should she too suffer? As she stepped and glided to the cadence of the drums, the bead and shell bracelets on her wrists and ankles rustled, the belt of double panther's paw shells, which Carlos had collected himself, clacked and rattled rhythmically.

When the drummers paused, Aesha worked her way to Ishkara's side. "Escuru left. I saw."

"It's not your concern."

"Ah, but it is. I wanted to run after, but that would only have called more attention to her. So I danced."

"As well you should. It's your wedding. It should bring you only happiness."

Aesha sighed. "I have wed now twice before my first bleeding. To feel nothing but happiness is far too much to ask."

Well into the night, when some of the elders were beginning to leave, Aricata approached Stepana and leveled an elbow at his son's ear. Groaning, Stepana rose and staggered toward Ishkara. "With your permission, I have a gift for your new daughter." Then, lurching to Aesha, he opened his hand and produced a circular disk the size of a large sand dollar. Its outer ring sparkled like the moon on the sea, and in the center a polished button shone like the setting sun. Silver and gold.

"Beauty for a beauty," he announced in a loud voice. Then, under his breath, "Don't let this ceremony deceive you. You're still mine and always will be. I eagerly await the coming of your womanhood. By the looks of you, it won't be long."

Aesha turned away, but Stepana grabbed her by the arm. "You think to humiliate me by refusing it? Ha! You disgrace only yourself."

Aesha stood impassive as Stepana pawed her hair, fondled her neck, and pressed the hulking circle of metal between her breasts, directly over her heart. The disk that outshone the sun felt as cold as the sea in the numbing moon.

Heat. Barely past dawn and already the oppressive heat and humidity had driven Ishkara from his mat. Not that he'd slept. He'd been steeped in a rancid brew of despair and rancor all night. He called for Stepana.

Stepana rubbed his eyes and picked a crust from the corner of his mouth. "My third father, you wake me early from my wedding bed. The marriage, I'm pleased to report, has been consummated." He reached under his loincloth and scratched himself deliberately. "May I now return to my duties?"

"Fool. I didn't send for you to inquire of your sexual prowess. The thought of you lying with my daughter is a more powerful emetic than an entire gourd of casine."

Stepana raised two fingers to his nostrils and sniffed. He began to say something, then reconsidered. "Now that you are my father," he said instead, "tell me. How is it you are able to hold the black drink down?"

Ishkara's stomach churned, but he willed on his face an impassive glare. "It's I who'll ask the questions. The gold and silver medallion. Where did you get it? No double-speak now. I address you not as father but as keeper of the ruler's staff."

The smirk vanished from Stepana's mouth. "My third father, you may choose not to believe me, but the staff is something I respect. My vows last night were sincere. The disk came from the north, on the small island of Toempe's clan. He traded for it."

"Did he say where it came from?"

"I remember his exact words: 'From the mines of Onagatano, on the mountain where stands white frozen water.'"

"And how did you obtain it?"

The sneer reappeared. "I am the great captain of Escampaba."

"Future great captain. And only then by declaration of the cacique or his regent. Never forget that, Cheeks Full of Milk. This Toempe, does he have more?"

"No. I made sure of that." A full grin now.

"I'm sure you did." Ishkara shook his head and breathed deeply. "You act as if this is all a child's game. Need you be reminded? The shiny rocks are not to be toyed with. In pursuit of them, the Spaniards enslave, they wage war, they kill. The disk you recovered is not some mere bauble. Its magical powers may hold the secret to controlling these invaders."

"It will protect Aesha, then."

Ishkara prayed that was true, though deep in his bones he doubted it. Now, the crucial question. He jabbed a bony finger into Stepana's still-greasy belly. "Do you have more?"

"No. I swear it."

Ishkara locked eyes with Stepana. For a long minute, neither flinched. Finally, not shifting his gaze, Stepana said, "I speak the truth. Know this about me, third father. Though I respect your position, I back down from no man. Now, how may I serve you?"

Ishkara forced his voice to sound as even as Stepana's. "Find me more. Bring me gold. Nothing is more valuable."

"With pleasure, third father. With pleasure."

Ishkara didn't have long to wait for gold and more.

It was a searing, sticky day in the moon of the killing winds. There had in fact been a bad gale several days earlier, not a blue-sky storm but nearly as bad. Preceded by three days of long, building swells, the storm hit with a fury, coming from the sea, yet blowing from the mainland. Caalus, with its conch seawall and embankments, had withstood the storm with minor damage. Now, in the irony of the season, the wind had vanished, inviting armies of biting sand flies and chiggers to assault every corner of the city. Not even the palace mound could capture a breeze.

Those who weren't languishing in the shade shelters near smudge pots sought what little refuge they could find in the too-warm waters.

The stillness of the afternoon was broken by the whoop of voices in the distance. A party of canoes, Calusa canoes, approached from the sea. They were heavily laden, crowded to the brink of capsizing. As they entered the harbor and proceeded down the central canal, a throng of citizens followed. Descending from the palace to the plaza by the water court, Ishkara was not surprised to see Stepana at the lead. What followed behind, though, took the tirupo's breath away: pale-skinned captives.

Stepana jumped triumphantly from his canoe. "I've brought you presents from our vassals the Tequesta. The mighty wind ship of these . . . *my* prisoners dashed upon the rocks. I give them to you, third father, and the cargo, too."

A cheer spread through the crowd as Stepana's company unloaded boxes of goods and herded the prisoners at spear point onto the terrace. Ishkara inspected the party of strangers. There were forty or more, men and women both. Bruised and bedraggled, they cowered together, fear draining the color from their already pasty faces. This was no war party.

"Blood. We will have their blood," someone called from the mob.

"Our fathers died at their hands."

"We will have revenge."

"My people," Ishkara shouted over the crowd. "Be silent. Let us thank the gods for delivering the strangers to us."

"Let us thank Stepana."

At that moment, Stepana clapped his hands and two men carried over a heavy chest. Stepana opened it, reached in and pulled out a rectangular block a bit larger than his hand. He raised it above his head so it caught the light of the sun. "Gold, third father." He reached into the chest again. "And silver."

The mob cheered even louder. "Gold. Silver. Blood. Give thanks to Stepana!"

Ishkara had to beat the ruler's staff on the ground repeatedly to quiet the people. Nearly choking on the words, he announced, "Yes, our thanks to Stepana. You've done well. Now, take these captives to the temple."

Stepana began to do as he was told, but the crowd refused to let him through. Yelling again for blood, they began to close in on the prisoners.

Stepana approached Ishkara and shrugged his shoulders. "The people want more."

Ishkara surveyed the unruly gathering. Stepana was right. Straining to make himself heard, he shouted, "Patience, my people. We must do this properly. I will call you to the temple tonight. There will be sacrifices."

The sentry outside the palace storeroom had dared not bar either the young ruler-to-be or his mate from the tightly guarded room. While Ishkara prepared for the ritual, Carlos and Aesha stood before the heap of goods salvaged from the prisoners' ship. Methodically, the boy inspected each new object, picking it up, feeling its texture, sniffing it. He held in his hand now a short wooden handle whose end had been pounded into a heavy piece of wedge-shaped metal. A weapon? No, more likely a tool. Carlos felt the sharp blade, made a chopping motion. How inferior Calusa whelk-shell hatchets were in comparison.

"Look at this." Aesha picked up another device, a thin, cup-shaped piece of metal with a handle that made the cup hang upside down. Inside it was suspended a small ball. When Aesha swung the cup back and forth, the ball hit the sides, making a beautiful tinkling noise. How astoundingly clever. Aesha cheered. Even the taciturn boy smiled.

"And this." Aesha traded the music cup for a smaller tool that looked like two knives joined together. As she pressed the halves together, the twin metal blades made a ringing click, more percussive than the cup, yet still most pleasing to the ear. "It's another music maker." She opened and shut them, rhythmically swishing and clicking the blades.

Carlos took them from her and ran his fingers along the edges. Then, inserting thumb and middle fingers into the holes at the base of the blades, he brought them to Aesha's ear and cut off a lock of her hair.

Aesha gasped, stared at the even-cut strands. Naturally, the people had hair-cutting blades. But not like this two-knife contrivance. "More," she said. "Cut off more. Cut it to here." She touched her shoulder.

"But only those who are shamed have their hair cut off."

"No. This is different. These are wonderful. Cut."

As the cutters sang their merry tune, long, straight strands of black fell on the floor like piles of grass. Swish-click. Aesha patted her shortened locks and giggled. Then, "oh." She gasped again.

Carlos held before her the most wondrous instrument of all. It was so . . . simple, nothing but a piece of hard, flat metal. Yet it was polished so smooth that it showed her reflection-soul. Aesha studied her hair, her face. Never had she seen her features in such detail: the tiny cracks in her skin, the fine hairs of her eyebrows and lashes. Even her nose had hairs. She looked at her own eyes. Intense yellow-brown irises stared back at her.

She turned the reflection-maker toward Carlos. "Is it still there?"

"What?"

"My face."

"No. My face is in it."

"Then where did mine go?"

Carlos shook the reflection-maker up and down. "It must be as in a pool of water. Your reflection-soul enters, and returns whenever you appear."

"Then it must contain the souls of the prisoners."

The two stared at the polished rectangle. Then Carlos said, "No. The Spaniards have no souls."

"How can you say that?" She tinkled the music cup again. "Their cleverness is as great as the gods."

Before Carlos could answer, a conch horn sounded. The sacrifices were about to begin. The people who had fashioned these treasures were about to lose their heads.

The wolf mask's exaggeratedly long ears were held on with wooden pegs. As Ishkara danced about the temple, howling, the crowd that had jammed the temple's large outer chamber howled with him. At the center stood two pale, naked Spaniards, their hands and feet securely tied. The first was an older male whom Ishkara judged to be the shipwreck's leader, for the tirupo had observed him comforting the others. The second was younger, certainly less than twenty suns, though it was difficult to tell with these smallish, hairy beings. To the side, huddled together, were the rest of the captives. Though Ishkara feared what the crowd might do, he wanted to observe their reactions. That was why he'd chosen both the leader and the young one.

"By the order of Sipi, and with the consent of our great cacique Caalus, I offer these lives to Aurr. I call upon our great captain to carry out the sacrifice."

With that, Aricata stepped forward and shoved the older Spaniard to the ground, two warriors holding him chest-down. Instead of dispatching the man himself, though, Aricata called forward Stepana and handed him his saber club. To the roaring approval of the crowd, Stepana held the stout instrument in front of him and turned slowly so all could admire the twelve gleaming sharks' teeth set in a straight groove and lashed tight with rawhide. Raising the club high above his head, Stepana brought it down with the full force of his weight. There was a crunching noise as the man's neck snapped, and a ripping sound as the sharks' teeth cut into his flesh. Blood spurted onto the temple floor. Four times more Stepana struck, finishing each blow with a back-and-forth sawing motion. Then he grabbed the man's hair and pulled the head from the body.

The people roared their approval. The prisoners gasped. Blood dripped. Carlos stared. The head stared back. At the back of the royal platform, where she'd been ducking low to avoid the attention her shortened hair was sure to cause, Aesha squeezed her eyes shut.

Ishkara beckoned, and Stepana brought him the head. His hands cupped, Ishkara reached forward and, with a quick twist, pulled out the eyes. Holding them at arm's length and facing his people, Ishkara intoned, "May Aurr devour the souls of our enemy, that he may know them and advise us well." He placed the eyes in a whelk bowl and set it in front of the woodpecker image. Stepana impaled the head onto his spear, later to be placed in front of the palace, then turned to the second, younger captive. When Stepana dispatched the boy, Ishkara kept his focus on the prisoners. Some retched, others covered their eyes or wept. Not so different from ourselves, Ishkara thought. Not gods. Humans.

Ishkara treated the remaining captives as he would any defeated enemy, offering them as gifts to nobles and lesser chiefs. To heal the wounds of families who had lost fathers and brothers in the battles long ago with the strangers, he ordered frequent sacrifices.

In a rare moment of verbosity, Carlos asked his father, "Why do you keep always a head on display? The palace is never free of the Spaniards' stench."

"It will show the people that these strangers are not to be feared. They bleed, they die, they stink like mere humans. They do not even make useful slaves. For all their skill in working metal, they are actually quite dim-witted and will not do what I tell them. Perhaps they leave the able at home and send only the stupid."

What a pity. Even by the use of signs, he could communicate but little with the strangers. Ishkara called for the Cubans who still lived in Calusa waters, but more than thirty suns had passed since their arrival, and their ability to speak the Spaniards' tongue had extinguished with disuse. In an effort to penetrate the mystery of the strangers, the tirupo, acting as a conduit for Aurr, consumed the eyes of the sacrificed himself. They were as rubbery as the sap of the gumbo-limbo tree, impossible to chew. Once again the fundamental nature of the Spaniards eluded Ishkara. They guarded their essence tightly; it was as hard to pierce as their reflection-makers. Or were they simply as soulless as they were flavorless?

That was why he spared the boy. The captives had shown some cleverness, hiding the child in their midst, though of course eventually he'd been discovered. From his size, Ishkara first guessed the child to be near Carlos's age. Good. The younger he was, the better the chance of training him. On closer inspection, though, the Spaniard's face showed the thinning of adolescence, and he had hair beginning to grow beneath his armpits. When the tirupo peered inside the boy's long blue breechclout, he shrunk away as if scalded by Ishkara's touch.

Ishkara took the young Spaniard to the palace storeroom. "How old are you, child?"

No answer. The boy stared at the ground.

"Tell me what you know of these goods. What are their names and uses?"

Not even a hint of a response.

"Do you want to die like the others? No, I don't suppose a threat will help. Very well, I've decided to keep you here at the palace. You will serve me personally."

It was even fruitless to try to communicate with this one by means of signs, for the youth would not even look at him. The boy may as well have been a conch. How he could be made useful, Ishkara had no idea . . . until Aesha and Carlos wandered into the storeroom. Both immediately sat down next to him, reaching out, touching his skin and garments. The actions only caused the Spaniard to turtle farther into his shell.

"This boy," Ishkara said. "You're curious about him?"

The two nodded.

"He won't talk to me, even in his own tongue."

Gently but firmly, Aesha lifted the boy's chin up, cupped it in both of her hands, studying his face. "Don't be afraid," she said, stroking his cheeks. "We have no clubs, no spears." Then, to Ishkara. "Can't you see the fear? You must give him time to get accustomed to us."

"Of course I see the fear. But I haven't the leisure of time."

"Let us work with him." Aesha could hardly contain her excitement. "Please. Spare this one. We'll get him to talk. I promise."

Ishkara stroked his chin pensively.

"He must be someone important," Aesha argued. "Why was he the youngest on board? He's a smart one. I can see that, too."

"As are you, my Little Bird. Very well, he's yours to command. For now. Deal with him as you wish."

Aesha clapped her hands. "Come, Carlos. Let's get started. We'll feed and bathe him, then dress him properly."

"He's neither infant nor child's toy," Ishkara cautioned. "Do you remember the baby raccoons you discovered a few moons ago, that you thought were so cute, their eyes barely opened, their ears so short and tails so slender?"

"I know, I know," said Aesha, rubbing a still-scabbed forearm. "And their teeth so sharp." Then, her jaw jutting now, she added, "But afterwards I made them my friends, didn't I? We'll do the same with him. You'll see."

The two took the Spaniard to the bathing house and tried to strip off his breechclout, but the boy fought so hard they decided to leave him in there alone. "Use this." Aesha tossed him a pod of soapberry. "And scrub hard." She demonstrated.

He seemed to understand. When he came out, his skin was pinkish and his hair, snipped, no doubt, by the cutting tool, less greasy. He still insisted on wearing the filthy breechclout, though, made not of woven palm or deer hide but of a blue cloth that encircled each of his legs.

Aesha stooped to one knee, bent her head low to look into the boy's downcast eyes. "I am Aesha," she said, pointing to herself. Then, stabbing a finger, "and this is Carlos." At the name, a spark of recognition lit, though it quickly turned to confusion.

Aesha had a servant bring the boy a bowl of fish chowder, and he gulped it down. "Another?" she asked, but he made no response. She took the bowl away but left the clamshell spoon, which he seemed enamored of, turning it over in his hands as if it were something extraordinary.

"No matter what Father says, this boy acts like an infant," Carlos said. "These are the mighty Spanish who fill the people's souls with fear?"

"He's been taken from his family. He's frightened beyond words." Aesha petted him as she'd tried with the baby raccoons. "See? He doesn't bite." Then she tapped her forehead. "I know what we should do. Come. Follow me."

She led the Spaniard to the storeroom, where she retrieved the reflection maker and put it in front of him. For the first time, the boy raised his eyes, looking at himself. He removed a smudge of dirt from his nose, ran his fingers through his hair.

"What's this called?" Aesha said, placing her hand on the polished surface.

A noise came out of his mouth.

"Did you hear that?" Aesha asked Carlos. Then, to the Spaniard. "Say it again."

"Mirror."

"Mira." She tried to wrap her tongue around the unfamiliar sounds. "In our language," she spoke deliberately to the boy, "we do not have a word for this miraculous device. The closest I can come is, 'standing pool.'" She laughed. She thought a hint of a smile crossed the boy's face. Then it vanished, and he seemed to vanish too, into the depths of a black and solitary pool.

Within a few days, she'd ascertained the boy's name: Escalante. His age was thirteen suns, identical to Aesha's. She was making progress. As more days went by, though, she learned little more. When she tried to give him some comfort by returning him to the storeroom, he merely sat in a corner, his arms wrapped around his chest. Aesha knew that he was able to communicate. He simply didn't want to. His appetite, too, had diminished. Aesha feared the boy wanted only to die. She wasn't sure why, but she actually liked him, though he was a defeated enemy. Like the raccoons without the mother, he was so alone.

Perhaps the best thing was to get him out amongst the people, amongst the song and laughter of everyday life. Naturally, everywhere she led him, a crowd followed. The boy was unwavering—he refused to acknowledge anyone, drawing inside himself even more tightly. Yet it was from one of the curious that a breakthrough came. They were at the waterfront. As usual, Escalante sat immobile, oblivious of the boy-men who were teaching some of the children canoeing skills in the shallows. One of the older of the boy-men—Iqi, she thought, was his name—steered his canoe so the bow brushed against the Spanish boy. When the startled Escalante looked up, Iqi motioned for him to get in. The boy looked back at Aesha—at least that was something. She quickly waved her assent.

Escalante picked up a paddle and immediately began digging the blade into the water. A grinning Aesha shouted, "Ah, so that's what he wants. Take him for a ride."

The boy had either paddled a canoe before or had been secretly observing, for his strokes were clean and sure. The canoe shot away from the island.

"He's escaping," someone shouted.

"He can paddle all he wants, but he won't get far," Aesha laughed, for Iqi was steering the canoe in circles.

For several minutes the Spanish boy flailed furiously, sweat dripping down his back. Finally, he set the paddle down and buried his face in his hands, his breath labored with great heaving sobs.

Iqi waved to Aesha to get her attention, then pointed away from Caalus. Aesha quickly nodded agreement. Give the boy some time to collect himself.

Iqi maneuvered the canoe out of sight, into the network of islands in the bay, paddling steadily, silently through the shallow channels. At length, pointing to the shore, in a soft voice he asked the mute Spaniard, "You see these? They're the walking trees, the mothers of our lands and nurses to the crabs and fishes. We call them this because they wade into the sea to make new territories. Do not their roots look like feet?"

Stopping in the lee of the wind, Iqi wrinkled his nose at the fetid smell of mud exposed by the falling tide. A few canoe lengths away, a green heron caught his eye. Iqi tapped Escalante on the back with his paddle and, when the boy turned around, pointed to the heron. Its yellowish legs took a few wary steps down the small branch on which it stood, and the bird flicked its tail twice, then became still again. Almost imperceptibly, ever so slowly, it stretched its short neck forward, black-in-yellow eye fierce and focused. Then, in an astonishingly sudden motion, it stabbed at the shallow water. Its beak came up, a small minnow speared on the end.

Escalante looked back at Iqi and mouthed a few words that Iqi did not understand. No mind. The Spanish boy was smiling.

Iqi led the boy around several cays, identifying the small and great egret, the white ibis and its brown little brother, and the various herons, saying their names slowly, miming their distinguishing characteristics, imitating their squawks. The Spaniard was looking at him now. Iqi brought a floating clump of weed into the canoe and turned it over to expose dozens of tiny shrimp and crabs, a couple of baby puffers, and a thin, wriggling pipefish. Spying a shell moving along the bottom, Iqi scooped it from the shallows and tossed it to Escalante. Iqi curved his hand into the shape of a claw.

It didn't escape Aesha's attention that, when the two returned, Escalante clutched the hermit crab in his hand. It was a good sign. The boy was holding on.

13 August 1549

When they killed first Captain Fernández and then my dear brother, I wanted only to die. I know it is only a matter of time before I will join him and the others. One by one, the savages have murdered them in the most hideous and unspeakable manner, while the populace cheers as if watching some kind of sporting match.

And yet, for now they've spared me. They seem to have some kind of plan for me, though I know not what it is. They have placed me in the palace of their priest king, if that is what he can be called, the very butcher who tore the eyes from my poor brother's severed head. There, I have writ it, though it calls up the images that haunt my every moment and invade my restless dreams. Ne'er shall I forget the tortures. Some day I will have my revenge. I live only for that.

I am in the care of a girl and a younger boy, son and daughter of the priest king. They feed me and speak to me in their primitive grunts. I do not want to eat, and yet with the smell of food, my mouth waters and my hands reach out despite my will. I do not want to understand them, I want only to be left alone, and yet in spite of that, I am beginning to learn. The boy is named Carlos and the girl Aesha. She is thirteen years old, for she made that many marks in the dirt and pointed to herself. I refuse to look at her, as I refuse all contact with this murderous race, and yet my eyes, as my hands and ears, disobey me. She, as the others, wears nothing to hide her shame. They go naked, except only some breechclouts woven of palm, with which the men cover themselves. The women do the like with a certain grass that grows on trees, a grass that looks like wool, although it is different from it.

The very same age as me, and yet she sings to me and fusses over me as if I am a child. It is she and her race that are children. They worship as miracles even the simplest of life's conveniences: a mirror or a scissors. I hate them for their ignorance. They look at me as one might look at a dwarf or harelip. I hate them all.

Let them come for me. I am ready to die. I shall never reach Salamanca. The ship is in pieces, all of us captured. If only I could steal a weapon, I would at least take one with me: the priest king, or the one who brought the club down on García. He smiled. He enjoyed it. Lord, grant me the strength. I can be a boy no longer.

My trunk is gone as are the gold bars my brother and I carried to Salamanca. I am left with nothing but my memories, my will, and these water-stained pages I found in the room where they put the wreckage from our ship. I shall not give them up. This is my solemn pledge.

"Ur-nan-do-day-es-ca-lon-tay-font-a-nay-da." Aesha had to slow her tongue to a lightning whelk's crawl to pronounce for Ishkara the boy's full name. He had left a place called Car-ta-hay-nya, a half-moon's sail to the south, bound for the Spanish homeland, though Aesha had no inkling where that might be. The boy came from a noble family, for he had indicated, if Aesha understood correctly, that the gold and silver bars discovered amongst the wreckage belonged to him. Why had they entrusted him with such wealth? Why were neither his mother nor father aboard the wind ship? "I freely admit," she told Ishkara, "I still have questions."

"That is a very safe statement. When have you ever been without questions?"

"The other objects we have recovered—hatchet, scissors, bell—are all quite ordinary," Aesha explained to Ishkara. "Imagine. Ordinary."

"You are speaking his tongue? You've done well."

"I know a few words. But more every day."

"And the boy—he is learning to speak with us?"

Aesha shook her head. "He . . . can't."

"Or won't. If he is no use to me . . ." Ishkara let the rest of the sentence drop.

"You must give him time. He is much troubled. Often, I hear him cry out in his sleep."

"Perhaps I need to persuade him a bit."

"No. He fears you greatly. When you are near, he begins to shake. Please, I beg you to have patience. He trusts me. Let me take him away for a while. I will teach him not only our tongue but our ways."

"And where would you go?"

Aesha's eyes danced. "To the Thumb. To the island of my naming."

A hint of bemusement sneaked over Ishkara's face. "Ever the clever one. You always find a way to do exactly what you want. So be it. I'll tell the servants to prepare provisions for you and Carlos."

"No. I mean no disrespect, Father and Uncle. But Carlos is too young to be of help." She paused. "And no servants."

"You'll not go alone. It's far too dangerous."

"Of course not. But the boy must not be intimidated. I have a plan."

"Why does that not surprise me?"

"I wish to place Escalante under the tutelage of Iqi. There is already a bond between them."

"Yes, I know him. He came to Caalus only recently. His father died in a storm, I believe. His mother re-wed, brought him here. I've seen him with the children. He's a good one—strong and yet gentle. He'll make a fine teacher. Very well. But I won't give this strategy of yours forever. Already the people complain that you treat the captive like nobility. With Stepana whispering in their ears, they call for more blood. Always more blood."

"No. You mustn't."

"I'll give you until the festival of the flaming stars, Falko."

"But that's less than three moons away."

"Aesha, my Little Bird. You were like a child to me even before you wed my son. I wish I could spare you the troubles of the adult world. Go to your island. Work with the Spaniard. I wish with all my souls that you succeed. But when you bring this Es-ca-lan-tay back, he will speak. Either to me in this world, or to Aurr in the next."

∾ Six ∾

Aesha leapt off the loaded canoe when it was still in waist-deep water, nearly capsizing the dugout and dumping both Iqi and Escalante in the bay. She splashed to shore, the touch of the island bringing shiver bumps to her flesh. It was even more beautiful than she remembered, though its attraction was hard to pinpoint. The vegetation was scattered and scrubby, full of sabal palms, saffron plums, and sapling live oaks. Small dunes formed around clumps of grasses that caught blowing sand; disk vine gridded the open areas between them. From the crest of the island, little more than her own height, she could easily see, at least from the narrow base of the Thumb on the southern half of the island, to both bayside mud flats and seaside beach.

Perhaps that was what attracted Aesha: the openness. No seawall buttressed the shorelines, no shell middens dominated its landscape. No drying racks, no sun shelters. No palace. No temple.

And no footsteps dimpled the powdery white sand that sparkled like polished pen shell. Aesha sat and scooped handfuls of it over her legs and feet until she was buried from the waist down. She basked in the warmth, closed her eyes to take in the island's blend of fish and flowers, salt and sand. She loved every tantalizing scent. This was a place where she belonged.

Moving, moving, moving, resting. The waves sang her mother's song. She gave herself up to sound and smell and womblike warmth. Yes, resting.

"Moving once again." It was a different voice, a not so melodious one. She looked up, expecting to see Iqi before her. But no, he was still unloading the canoe with Escalante.

"Close them again. You'll see me."

She did. "Father!" He stood over her, young, healthy, unadorned by a cacique's accessories.

"Yes, my First-born. You're not alone in being captivated by this place."

"Father. You're here. But your bones lie in the temple. How can that be?"

"Still asking questions, I see." He smiled at her. "The wisest of men—and women—are those who never stop." Then his yellow-brown eyes went serious. "But for those in our position, of whom so much is expected, answers are demanded. From now on, young as you are, you'll need to have answers, too."

"I do," she reassured him. "I will, but first . . ."

"I'm afraid there can be no 'but first' for you," he said, sadness thick in his voice. "Responsibility lies heavy on you. Be strong, First-born. Do as your own voice bids you."

"I will. Father, have you seen the boy, the Spaniard? I brought him here. I was right to do this, was I not? Father?"

But he was gone.

She kept her eyes closed, trying to cling to his image, his voice, even as she became mindful of the surf again. *Moving, moving, moving, resting. Moving once again.* Reluctantly, Aesha wriggled from her sand hole. There was so much to teach the Spaniard, and now she was more convinced than ever that so much depended on it, on her. Ishkara would spare the boy only if he could be made useful. Useful. She would make him that and more. Surely his destiny was to be far larger. Someday his people would return. Whether they would wage bloody war or come in friendship might all depend on what Escalante told them. She saw her mission clearly. He must become a person of the islands, of the walking trees, of the beaches. He must learn not only the tongue but also the stories, the songs of sun and wind and tides. Then, when the time came, he would speak as a Calusa. He would sing the praises of Escampaba.

She brushed the sand from her skin, saw Iqi strolling toward the shore, the boy following. Already, Escalante's skin was darkening. Once his hair grew long—as hers would have time to while she was here, thankfully—Iqi would teach him to wind it into a proper topknot. The sun and salt would soon take care of the ripped and ragged Spanish garments he insisted on wrapping about his thin torso. His nose was too long, his face too narrow, but Aesha was confident. He could be made to look Calusa.

Would he ever act so, though? While life sometimes flickered in the boy's dark eyes, too often he still cast them to the ground. Ah, the ground. Why not start there? "Come." She took him by the hand. "Observe the gifts of the sea." She led him along the beach, following the undulating lines of shells and debris that marked the tide line. Stooping as she walked, Aesha showed Escalante cockles and canoe shells, cones and bubbles, augurs and tusks. She picked up a long, looping spiral of what looked like seaweed. "Look closely. This is the egg casing of the lightning whelk. You see the tiny shells inside? They grow"—she moved a few steps up the beach to hoist a heavy shell with yellow bands and brown stripes running up its spiral—"to be these. For us, this is as valuable as your gold, for it is upon the back of this shell that our cities are built."

Escalante proved a keen observer. Each time he found an unfamiliar specimen, he showed it to Aesha. "That," she pointed to her earlobe, "is a baby's ear. Very delicate. You always find them at the top of the tide line because they're so light. This heavy brown one is a fighting conch. Their whorls can be spiked or knobless, their lips brown, orange, or even purple. And that one's the flat half of the scallop shell. It looks like the palm frond you wave before your face on a hot day. So we call it a fan. *Shutun.* Say it."

The boy nodded, but he would not speak the Calusa word.

Iqi engaged Escalante in more practical pursuits. They chopped down several sapling pines, buried them vertically in a circle, and bent them inward until they could be lashed together with strips of bark. Over the domed framework, they braided mats of reeds, tightly woven at the roof to repel the rain, more loosely lower down so the walls would let in the breeze.

Under Iqi's patient tutelage, within a moon's time Escalante could set a gill net in the sea grass for specks and catfish, throw a cast net at schools of cruising mullet, stalk the flats with a spear for stingrays. One day Iqi showed him how to pound bark and twigs from the fish fuddle tree into a powder. They placed it into a weighted basket and set in the water. Moments later, they were scooping stunned fish from the surface with dip nets.

During moonlit nights, as Iqi pointed out the night birds, the curlews, nighthawks, and bitterns, the Spanish boy learned to twist palm fiber to make cord to repair the nets. As his fingers struggled to make the correct knot, he shoved the net away in frustration. Iqi was a patient teacher, though, and before long the boy's fingers grew nearly as nimble as his tutor's.

Still, though, he didn't speak. Aesha knew that he understood, for when Iqi instructed him, he would nod his head and obey. Neither did Escalante speak much in his own tongue, save for an odd nightly habit of touching his forehead, chest, and shoulders, then folding his hands in front of him and speaking softly. Sometimes, then, tears would come.

Iqi spoke little more than the Spaniard. He avoided being alone with Aesha, taking his meals after the other two were finished, coming to his sleeping mat late and rising early. One hot night, too full of worry to sleep, Aesha came outside to cool off and found Iqi standing still as a heron at the water's edge. A bright three-quarters moon lit his bare back and outstretched arm. She approached silently, hardly breathing, though, strangely, her heart was beating hard. Her nostrils took in the musk of Iqi's man-smell. At sixteen suns, he was nearly full-grown, broad-shouldered, muscled, smelling of fish and work. She felt something stir inside her, deep, beyond the edge of understanding.

Iqi turned to her then, nodded, and began to walk away.

"No!" Her voice was shrill, not what she intended. "Stay. What are you doing?"

He showed her his fishhook tied to a roll of twine. On the hook was a partially crunched sand flea.

She turned the hook over in her hand. It was made of bone and wood, the sharpened stick and strong, curved sliver of bone joined by tightly woven cord. Its small size meant that the fashioning must have been all the more difficult. "You made this yourself?"

He nodded.

"Who taught you?"

"My father."

"I have heard he's in the land beyond. What happened?"

Iqi's eyes flicked out to sea. "A storm."

"Please. Explain."

"A blue-sky storm blew over Sinapa, where we lived. The waters rose. Father went to check the grave mounds to make sure the fathers and mothers wouldn't drown. He never returned. We found him beneath a fallen mastic tree. It was gigantic, the oldest on the island. Its time had come. And his."

"He must have been a very great man for Sipi to have chosen him to accompany such an old being."

"For me, the greatest of all." His eyes darted to her. "I mean no offense."

"I take none."

Iqi waded a step into the water, bent and scooped his hands along the ledge just past the shoreline's edge. Holding his hands up to the moonlight, he sifted through the sand and shell until he found a plump sand flea. It played dead in his hands, then nearly squirmed away before he could grab and impale it on the fishhook.

"May I?" she asked.

He handed her the cylindrical wooden line reel that held the twine. Twirling an arm's length of line in a tight vertical circle, Aesha tossed the hook into the trough of deep water just beyond the shore. Moon-splattered light danced in the gentle surf, fluttering on the crests, tickling the shadows. "It's dazzling," she said.

He nodded.

"They're the tears of Sipi," she said. "The stories tell us that is where all life came from."

Iqi watched her line.

"You know the stories, do you not?"

He nodded again.

"And it's to the sea that the souls of the departed return. So the stories say, too." She knew she was baiting him just as he'd baited the fishhook, but she couldn't help it. She had to hear his voice again.

"No, the stories say otherwise."

That voice. That smell. The stirring again. "And what do they say?"

He glanced at her, eyes narrowed, brows furrowed. He stayed silent.

"Yes, of course I know what the stories say," she told him. Then, touching his forearm (oh, to touch him, too), "But I will let you know a secret. The teachings say that when I die, my shadow and reflection souls will enter lesser animals, but my third soul, my eye-soul, will stay with me, with my bones forever. The secret is this: I don't believe the teachings, not fully, anyway. Do you know why?"

She didn't expect an answer, and it didn't come. "Because," she picked up, "as soon as I came to this island, I saw my father. He"—a tug on her line stopped her. She pulled on it. Too late. She brought in an empty hook. "Caalus doesn't live only in the box in the temple," she continued. "He visits here as well. He spoke to me."

Iqi dug another sand flea, rebaited the hook, his warm hand circling hers. "Sometimes my father spoke to me as well," he said. "But once I came to Caalus, only in my dreams."

"Mine told me to be strong, to do what I must."

"What is it you must do?" he asked.

"That's a question for a lifetime," she said. "But a lifetime is made up of moments, and in this one, what I must do is catch a fish." She broke away from him, flung the baited fishhook into the gentle surf. This time, she concentrated fiercely on the line in her hand. When the fish pulled, she snapped her wrist back sharply. The fish was on. Gently, she brought the line in hand over hand, paying it out when the fish struggled, then pulling it back in until at length she dragged a fat pompano onto the beach. Iqi captured and unhooked it, then held it aloft so the moonlight gleamed on its silver flank. "I understand why your father visits you here," he said. "I could ask no more than to stay on this island always."

He gutted the fish with long, sure strokes of his bone knife, then washed it and wrapped it in seaweed to keep it cool. He handed her the package.

Aesha smiled and patted the sand. "Come sit with me. Tell me the story of Sipi's first days."

His eyebrows creased again. His lips shut tight.

"I want only to hear your voice," she said. "It's as strong as your hands. Why do you so seldom use it?"

"It is as thick, too. I am but a ground dweller."

She reached to take his hand and pull him toward her. "Then you should be comfortable here. Sit. Please."

Iqi settled beside her, facing the sea. "If it's your command, I'll recite the story."

"Not a command," she said. "But it is a desire."

"I will tell it then as my father told me, for I know no other way." He drew in a deep breath. "It was to just such a spot as this that Sipi first came when the land and sea were new. He sat as we sit here and sifted his hands through the sand. In just one handful, there were too many grains to count. Scooping some water from the sea, he tried to count the drops; but in that single cupful there were too many drops to reckon."

Aesha watched those strong hands talk. They made the tight shape of a cup, then parted ever so slightly to let the water slide through. Then he reached outward, one hand higher than the other, grabbing the air and pulling it down and back. "He set out in his canoe to explore," Iqi said, "riding the tides through the bay, watching the walking-tree mothers at work creating the lands. A thousand shades of green dazzled his eyes. 'Such a place I've found. Is it not wondrous?' Sipi proclaimed. But no one answered. And though this world was a miracle to behold, Sipi began to feel lonely."

Iqi turned his head to look up the sand beach, his neck muscles taut but his face relaxed, peaceful. "Looking behind, he saw that his shadow followed, and Sipi was much comforted. But then clouds came over the sun, and his shadow disappeared. He approached a pool of water and saw his reflection and was gladdened again. But then the wind came up, and his reflection vanished. Feeling more alone than ever, Sipi returned to the beach, once again to sit at the water's edge."

Thick of tongue? Her father could not have told the story more expressively. Nor even Ishkara.

Iqi was quite oblivious of her now. "For the remainder of the day Sipi sat until finally the sun began to fall toward the sea. The clouds parted, and his shadow reappeared, longer than ever. Sipi smiled, for the shadow cheered him. The wind calmed; his reflection spread out across the sea, and again Sipi smiled. He watched the sun turn orange, then red, and plunge below the surface, spreading a pool of flames upon the still waters. At the moment the sun vanished, there flashed a ray of green, its hue as brilliant as if the thousand greens of the trees and plants and grasses had been concentrated in a single beam. It lasted but an instant and was gone so fast that Sipi wondered if he had only imagined it. He turned toward his shadow to ask, but the shadow had vanished. He searched for his reflection, but it, too, had disappeared. Such splendor, and yet now Sipi felt more lonely than ever."

Iqi tilted his head skyward, the words bubbling out. "The moon appeared then, greeting the sea with its silvery light. So moved was Sipi that tears sprang from his eyes, mixing with the moonlight sister, falling into the womb of the sea. Sipi fell sound asleep. As he slept, all the fishes of the sea were born. Later in that long night, some crawled onto land and became the animals. Others flew into the air and became the birds. Another walked upright and became our first ancestor. And when Sipi awoke, he was never alone again."

Iqi turned finally to Aesha. She lay on the sand, eyes closed, lids fluttering. Gently, Iqi picked her up, cradling her, and carried her to the shelter. She put her arms around his neck, sighed in her sleep, her lips pursed into a slight smile.

9 October 1549

They try to fashion me as they do their primitive tools, scraping and whittling away at me. My clothes have rotted from my body, and I had no other choice than to construct a breechclout in the Indian way. There is little to it, two strands of palm that circle my waist and one that extends between my legs, ending in a kind of broom that is tied in the rear with a certain grass. Surely it won't last long. Yet, it seems to stay fastened even when I swim. The rash between my thighs has, thankfully, subsided.

I know their aim though I don't know why. They aim to make me Indian. I do not shy from learning their skills, for when I escape I must know how to survive in this alien world. I have learned to tip a wood spear with the poison spine of a catfish or the tail of a stingray. From the leg bone of a deer, I made a certain kind of fish catching de-

vice, not a hook exactly, but a needle-like gorge that the fish swallows and then gets lodged in its throat. From that same deer I fashioned a knife that is rudimentary but sharp enough to draw blood readily. And they let me keep it. Someday I will turn it upon them.

But first I must learn more. These Indians make all manner of tools from the shells that wash up on the beach: pounders, gouges, hatchets, scrapers, and cutting blades of an astonishing variety. Some shells they use whole, others they chip away all but the strong center column. When a handle is needed, they find a piece of wood and use strips of deer hide or woven cord to attach them. Then they use these tools to work with bone, wood, or other shells. I carved my own wood bowl and dip into the pot of fish stew with a shell ladle. There is little to eat other than the fish or creatures of the sea, but of those there are plenty. When I escape, I shall not want for food.

The days fly by quickly. I am ever busy. Only at night do I have time to think, to plot, to grieve. Sometimes such exhaustion overtakes me that I fall asleep while praying. The next thing I know, the one called Iqi is shaking me awake and the girl called Aesha is talking to me in her grunting chatter. I understand most all of what she says now. It is a much-abbreviated language these Indians speak, a word or two standing for an entire thought. This, of course, is not surprising. They are a primitive people of lowly intelligence. The one thing I shall never do is speak their guttural words.

She watches me even as I write this. Ha. She knows nothing of what I have written. From the confusion in her face, I understand that her people possess no written language at all. Inferiors. After I escape, I shall return and conquer. It will be laughably easy.

The sea was hungry. It chomped at the beach, chewing and digesting huge mouthfuls of sand before spitting them back out again, building an offshore sandbar. The ocean's bite marks could be seen on the waist-high ledge that now ran along portions of the beach. It was no day to be out on the water, but that was exactly where Iqi had sent the young Spaniard. Aesha understood. To become a man, a boy had to be challenged. So she'd tried to control her nerves as Escalante launched the sea canoe through the high breakers, then disappeared into the rolling swells.

He executed the difficult put-in flawlessly. He was learning quickly. But there was so little time. Less than a moon until Falko.

Escalante's head popped into view as the canoe rose on a high swell. Steering square with the breaking waves, the Spaniard surfed his way to shore, then scrambled out and pulled the canoe up the beach ledge. He was wet, panting and grinning as he made his way up to the ridge where Aesha and Iqi sat.

Seeing him in the canoe had given her an idea. "You paddle well," Aesha said. "I want you to take part in a competition, a race. You know what this is?"

Escalante gave the slight nod that said he understood.

"Soon we must return to Caalus for the festival of the burning stars. Boy-men bring their canoes from every corner of Escampaba to race each other around the island. It's one of the highlights of the festival."

"He'll never win," said Iqi. "For though he is skilled, he's too small. Look at him."

Aesha surveyed the boy. "He's as tough as dried otter meat. And even tougher on the inside. Besides, winning is not the goal. He needs only to stay in the pack. Let him be invisible. It will show him to be one of us."

"But you forget that each contestant must build his own canoe."

"Then you'd better get busy."

By the next day, the wind had subsided. The three went to a nearby island where a grove of tall pines grew and selected a thick, straight specimen. Felling and limbing it with conch axes, then lashing it to the canoe and floating it back was the work of an entire day. The following morning, under Iqi's guidance, Escalante placed coals on the log's surface and began to burn away the inside, using wet mud from the bay to control the extent of the burn. Ignoring the acrid smoke from the smoldering green wood, the boy scraped away the charred area, then began the process anew. Little by little over the next long days, the canoe took shape until it was hollowed to a uniform thickness from bow to stern and both ends were beveled upward. Finally, using sharkskin shagreen, Escalante rubbed the wood to a smooth finish. He then carved a button-wood paddle with widely flared blade. "It's much wider than normal," Iqi explained. "More blade will give you more powerful strokes."

When Escalante launched the canoe and it tracked straight and true through the water, he came back beaming. Aesha returned the smile, but her stomach clutched with fear. She was more convinced than ever of the significance of keeping this boy alive. Yet his stubborn refusal to speak put him in great jeopardy. He seemed otherwise to be thriving now. Why was he so obstinate?

Trust. Somehow she hadn't fully gained it. What more could she do?

With Iqi's help, Escalante pulled the canoe high up on the beach. Iqi ran his hands along its length, nodding approvingly.

She would give him something, that's what. Something important. Something he could hold secretly, establishing the trust between them. She ran to the shelter, then returned to stand beside the Spaniard.

"I want you to have this," she said, and handed him the gold and silver disk Stepana had given her. She hated it, had hidden it out of sight in a corner of the hut.

Escalante wouldn't reach for it, though.

"Please. Take it. Just don't show it to Stepana. Don't show it to anyone. It belonged to your people. It should be yours. Do you understand?"

He nodded, took it now.

One last try. "Why do you not speak in my tongue? Ishkara is not unkindly, but he demands it. Otherwise, you'll meet the fate of the others. Please."

The clenched jaw spoke only too loudly.

Aesha turned to the sea. A flock of gulls and terns hovered low over the water, diving on a school of baitfish moving along the sandbar. Over and over again the birds swooped, plummeted, and plunged. Aesha focused on a single small white tern. It flapped and flopped in the midst of the shrieking maelstrom, bobbing and diving until finally it surfaced, a finger-long fish held triumphantly in its beak.

Then a large gray-white gull darted by to wrest the meal away.

The Falko moon fell at the beginning of the dry season, when the temperatures were still warm but the sogginess had usually left the air, when huge migrations of fish flooded the passes, when the oysters became plump and firm and the sand flies and mosquitoes retreated. In fact, the moon was poorly named since the festival was always held on the no-moon night, its very purpose being to celebrate the sacrificial burning of the heavenly stars. Naturally, these sacrifices could and did happen at any time, Falko moon or not. However, on certain nights in this season the sky would flare with bursts of flame followed by arrow-like trails of smoke as one star after another caught fire, then fell from the heavens. Then, the people would know that, just as captives were offered up to Aurr, so the stars of heaven were being sacrificed to Sipi.

Serious as were the underpinnings of the festival, the people had long joked that Falko was a fine excuse for a celebration. Whether stars burned on that night was not important because, most assuredly, romances did. When at evening's end all fires were extinguished so that the heavens could be viewed, it was a signal for coupling to begin. Wedded or not, any woman of regular bleeding and any man with seed were permitted to lie together on the night of Falko.

Falko was the favored festival of nearly every Calusa.

And this was to be Aesha's first. She awoke early and crept from her room, taking care not to wake Carlos on his mat beside her. He'd been brooding ever since her return, in a huff at having been left behind. Neither would he be invited to tonight's festivities; not even the cacique-to-be could violate the rules. She did not want to let his ill humor ruin her special day.

Slipping into the thatch-walled bathhouse, she scrubbed her skin hard with soapberry to clean off the lingering grit of out-island living, then rinsed with ladles of fresh water. Falko Day was a chance to show off your bravery, skill, and talents. And your beauty. She braided a single osprey tail feather into her hair—that to remember her father by—and painted a simple circular design on her left shoulder. She would wear no other ornaments today, only her charms.

Feeling invigorated, she decided to show herself off to Mother. As she scurried toward Mother's quarters at a far end of the palace, though, he was there, Carlos, looking ever grave. Aesha sighed. Her tag-along husband. She had no choice but to tolerate him, for the moment anyway. "Come," she said. "Let's walk amongst your subjects. And do try to smile. It's Falko."

Carlos's frown deepened.

Descending from the palace mound to the plaza, Aesha's nostrils flared. Already the air was steamy, not from the weather but rather from enormous pots of all-in-one stew. Mmm. The harmonious blend of dozens of ingredients from sea and land danced their way through her nose straight to her growling belly. Fifty cooking fires, maybe more, lined the central canal that was already crowded with early-arriving canoes. She wished she could sample every pot. She would make certain to stop at Escuru's fire. Last Falko, Escuru's all-in-one stew had held more than a hundred varieties of fish and mollusks, roots and herbs, animal and bird flesh. Again this sun Stepana had spread the word. Anyone bringing an exotic morsel would be wise to stop at Escuru's fire first.

Aesha and Carlos wandered through the display of wares spread out on the plaza. A tightly woven basket of peeled grapevine caught her eye. Deep red marlberries had been added to some of the vines during boiling, allowing the weaver to introduce a brightly colored pattern into the design. Another basket of sabal palm roots had been fashioned in the shape of a sea turtle, the checkered motif remarkably resembling the animal's shell. A third, made from saw palmetto stems, stood nearly as tall as she. She peered inside, and two children squealed with delight.

Ah, to be a child with no cares again. She'd even be willing to endure the humiliation of returning alone to her bed upon the dousing of the fires. Or would she? She sighed. The answer didn't matter. There was no turning back.

Beyond the baskets, a large crowd had gathered to admire a wood panel upon which was carved and painted the image of a kingfisher. Aesha knew instantly the carving must have come from Muspa. Though its proportions were perfectly rendered, the carving was fanciful, too, its blue, white, and black checkered pattern at once inaccurate and somehow perfectly capturing the bird's essence. Painted pearls fell from its mouth. How clever. The kingfisher was ever chattering. Behind it stood a double-bladed paddle, asserting the bird's claim of authority over the sea. Aesha's thoughts drifted to Escalante. May he distinguish himself today. At least, may he not suffer the shame—or worse—of an overturned canoe.

As they strolled toward Escuru's fire, Carlos took Aesha's elbow. "I made something for you while you were away. I give it to you now to remember me through this day . . . and night." He handed her a large sunrise clamshell. On the inside was painted a picture of Carlos himself, wearing an elaborate headdress and plaited wrist and leg bands. His hands reached into the air in a dancer's pose. "Dance with whoever you want tonight," he said, "but I'll be there with you. Remember who I am. The next cacique."

"And only seven suns. A mere child, no matter how old you try to act."

"Nearly eight. Don't forget I was born during the Falko moon."

"And don't forget it was *my* father who was the last cacique. Don't forget who *I* am." Aesha shoved the shell back at him. "You've been whining ever since I returned from the Thumb. It doesn't become you.

Don't think I'll do your bidding solely because of who you are. Ever."
Her eyes burned a hole in the air between them.

His burned back.

The conch horn sounded. The canoe race was ready to begin.

As Stepana paddled to the start line, he waved to the throng of onlookers lining the water court, chuckling inside. Sometimes his ideas impressed even himself. It had not taken him long, once he got wind that the Spaniard was entering the race, to commandeer a canoe. It was simply a matter of explaining the consequences of noncompliance to Iqi. Yes, that was his extra stroke of genius. The runt's mentor would not be in the water to look out for him. Stepana had to hand it to Iqi—the commoner's canoe paddled effortlessly. Stepana could not have built a better one himself. Correction. He had, as required, built this craft with his own hands. Would anyone dare dispute that?

The canoes lined bow-to-stern and packed tight side-by-side at the water court somehow made way for Stepana to wedge Iqi's craft into position at the front of the pack. He looked over both shoulders. Where was the runt? Nowhere to be seen. Maybe he had lost his nerve.

Ishkara kept his remarks short. "You race for the glory of Sipi, the honor of Escampaba and the joy of Falko. Now go."

The spectators cheered, urging on their favorites as the canoes pressed forward. Stepana dug his paddle into the water in an all-out sprint, racing to keep near the front of the pack, knowing full well that he'd be unable to keep up the pace for long. But then again, he didn't need to.

The more than one hundred fifty canoes splashed out of the central canal. Though his breath came in heaving gulps, Stepana managed to keep up with the leaders as they exited the harbor. "Aiyee," he cried at the top of his lungs. "Aiyeee!" Just as he hoped. The canoes beside him paused momentarily, confused at his use of the war cry. "I am your leader," Stepana shouted. "The rest of you will follow . . . or die."

Thanks be to Aurr, the canoes next to him slowed. As those farther back caught up, Stepana heard the word being passed. He eased up, put a forearm to his sweaty brow, and labored to catch his breath. At a relaxed pace now, he circumnavigated the island. No one dared to overtake him.

As once again they approached the harbor and cheering spectators, Stepana picked up the pace. This canoe of Iqi's truly was a beauty, though with Stepana's weight it did ride a bit low in the water. A dozen other canoes kept just behind him, vying, no doubt, for second place. Good. It looked like a race.

Then, out of the corner of his eye, Stepana saw a canoe on the far side of the pack edge even with his. The paddler was small of stature but smooth of stroke as he forged ahead. Bare back glistening and topknot braided, the boy could have been any young Calusa. Except for the exaggerated nose of his profile. The Spanish runt. And in that instant, too, Stepana knew that he'd seen that identical beak-like profile elsewhere— beneath his ritual saw.

As they turned into the central canal, Stepana redoubled his efforts, and his canoe lurched forward with every stroke. But the waters that yield reluctantly to the wind gladly carry the froth. The boy's canoe skipped ahead, crossing the finish line first.

Stepana jumped from his canoe and splashed through the water toward the Spaniard. Escalante met him with raging eyes. Stooping to make sure he could be heard over the crowd, Stepana yelled, "Let me be the first to congratulate you. Enjoy your victory. Soon, you will die."

The boy replied in short, clearly enunciated Calusa words. "You killed my brother. I will have your head. It is the Calusa way."

In the anthill dance, the participants line up one behind the other, each holding the waist of the dancer in front, forming a line that winds through the crowd until eventually head and rear come together to form a circle rotating around the fires. On the stomping three-beat signal of the hide drums, all the ants scatter, running into the crowd, coaxing new dancers to the circle. As Aesha hopped and shuffled around the fire, she tried to keep an eye on Escalante, though it was difficult with the swarms of congratulators surrounding him. When the signal came, she ran to the Spaniard and pulled him forcefully toward the re-forming line of dancers.

And he spoke to her. "I won. That's what you wanted."

"And it's what *you* wanted. You've chosen to speak and to live. It's a joyous day for both of us." She turned away from him, wiggled her buttocks into him. "Let's dance." As they took their place in the circle, she wasn't sure what was hotter: the fire before her or the heat of his hands squeezing her hips. On the next signal, as others scattered the two clung together . . . until another set of hands ripped Escalante's forcefully away.

"You dance most seductively. Later you'll continue the performance in my bed."

How could the fat brute have sneaked up on her? She should have detected Stepana by smell alone. "I'm already wed."

"To a boy with a penis the size of a turtle's tail. Besides, tonight is Falko. Oh, I forget. You're a young one." He licked his lips. "This is your first."

Aesha whirled and skipped out of range, throwing her fiercest look back at Stepana. But her heart beat uncontrollably. The man who always got what he wanted had endured one humiliation today; he wouldn't tolerate a second. He stepped toward her.

Then a third set of hands were upon her, steering her to the circle as the drumming started again. Iqi's. "You're shaking," he whispered.

"Stay with me. Don't let go. Please."

He held her, danced with her until the drums stopped for good and the voice of Ishkara boomed out. "Extinguish the fires that we may see the burning stars." The people cheered and ran to fill their empty pots with seawater. A huge cloud of steam enveloped the plaza.

"Take me away from here," Aesha whispered. "Away from Caalus. I need to smell the sea, to see the stars."

"Stepana took my canoe."

"We'll take it back."

"But ..."

"Don't worry about that blowfish. He puffs up to enormous proportions, but a simple prick with the pin, and he shrinks back to size."

Iqi didn't pretend to understand. This young girl-woman who shook like a palm frond one moment planted herself like a mighty mastic the next. His was not to understand. He obeyed.

As they left the plaza, Aesha spied Escalante. So tightly was he hugged by three girls that she feared the boy might suffocate. His eyes met hers for a moment, then darted to Iqi. Then he pulled the girls even closer, sinking his face into a ring of soft flesh.

They found the canoe in the shallows by the water court. As Iqi paddled from the harbor, Aesha rested her back against his knees. "Away," she said. "Take me to our island."

"It's too far. I could paddle all night. We still won't reach it."

"To the sea, then."

Through Tega Pass and up the shoreline he stroked, until the lookout platform disappeared in the moonless night. Aesha rose and dove from the canoe. The warm water felt wonderful and she submerged repeatedly, washing away smoke, sweat, fear, and anger. The sea made her feel pure again. And such a night it was, a thousand stars winking suggestions, urging her on. Her bare bottom waggling at Iqi as she dove, she surfaced first on this side of the canoe, then on that, spitting water at him. Finally, she extended her arm so he could help her back in. But when he did, she pulled with all her might. He didn't resist. He splashed in beside her.

Pressing her body to his back, she hung on as he swam her toward shore. Then, in waist-deep water, she spun him so he faced her and squeezed him in a way that left no doubt what she wanted.

He wriggled from his breechclout, embraced her, supported her as she wrapped her legs around his waist. She winced in pain at first, her nails digging into him; but soon she relaxed. And then moved with him. And then with urgency.

Aesha thrust herself on him over and over, throwing her head back, seeing in the whirling sky the fiery bursts and smoking trails of burning stars. Like knots of wood in a bonfire, they ruptured in explosions of red and orange, darting off in random directions. One alone, then three at once, then two aimed directly for each other. Then, her vision blurred, as Iqi, too, exploded.

∽ Seven ∽

Ishkara wasn't sure why he felt so fatigued. True, he was entering his six-tieth sun, not ancient but certainly exceeding the norm now. Aricata, Odobro, and others of his age had set forth on their journeys to the land beyond. An increasingly persuasive voice told him the time was nearing to join them.

But not yet. Despite his constant worry, the skies over Escampaba were fair. As clouds so often skirted the islands only to build up and re-lease their loads on the mainland, so too the Spaniards continued to steer clear of the Calusa. Of course, that simply led to more concern—were Calusa enemies conspiring with the strangers? For that matter, what of the people's allies? A link between the Spaniards and even distant tribes could prove disastrous. But no—the stories that drifted in spoke only of shipwrecks or bloodshed. The latest was typical. A Spanish holy man who walked ashore near Tocobaga had been promptly clubbed to death.

There could be no better news.

And now he had the boy as interpreter. He wasn't surprised that Aesha had succeeded; she was endowed with a superior talent for persuasion from both her father and mother. Escalante now spoke and lived as one of the people. Ishkara permitted him to move about freely. Already the boy's presence was reaping political dividends: who else could boast a personal Spanish servant?

There was more yet to be thankful for. Even the cruelest of men could lose their taste for blood in old age, and Aricata in his elder suns had developed a tempering voice. When the great captain's remains were placed on the Island of Bones, that canal-surrounded mound reserved for the nobles, Ishkara recognized his passing with fasting, running, and song, hoping that the respectful conduct might help to moderate Stepana's excesses. And indeed, the young great captain seemed to be using surprisingly good sense in setting the boundaries of his mischief. He had a murderous reputation, yes, but Ishkara couldn't deny that Stepana's atlatl waving was keeping the neighboring tribes, even Tocobaga, quiet. Perhaps Ishkara had underestimated Stepana's shrewdness. He was nothing short of amazing, even if much of his energy was spent in self-promotion. The man had a nose for Spanish gold, a tongue that could put the masses in a trance, and a brilliant sense of timing. His forays to the far corners of Calusa influence never failed to extract Spanish treasure; his triumphant returns always attracted huge crowds.

Perhaps Ishkara had underestimated the great captain's loyalty as well. The regent had persuaded one of Stepana's young warriors to keep a close eye on the valuables. He reported that Stepana was turning over everything, withholding nothing. Ishkara's stockpiles overflowed. He ordered a large buttonwood chest built and kept under constant guard. At Aesha's suggestion, he installed as the primary sentry her friend Iqi, whose loyalty, even in such a sensitive capacity, was beyond question.

How did the magic hold sway over the Spanish? Ishkara waved his hoop of scallop shells before the open chest, shook his crab claw rattle, fingered his string of divining pearls. But none of the talismans could pierce the strangers' spells. The glittery metals bombarded him with dazzling light, making it impossible to focus. To understand a thing, one had to see it clearly. Perhaps that was how the gold and silver worked their sorcery, by blinding him, blocking contact with his innermost soul.

Ishkara had no choice but to shut his eyes tight and peer inward. He rolled the oddly shaped pearls one by one between his thumb and fingers, letting his breathing calm and his mind settle until time stood aside and he could see around its edges. That was when the vision came. The great stores of gold and silver rose from the chest, suspended in the air. They began to move then, to feign and rush at him as would a cornered animal. Gold bars whizzed by his head at ever increasing speed. Ishkara resisted desperately the urge to cringe and duck, forced himself to sit frozen, head erect. Faster and faster the metals circled, until they had formed themselves into a whirling windstorm, a blur of motion with Ishkara in the middle. Still, he didn't budge. He compelled his mind and body to remain in vigilant composure, his eyes to see only the calm blue center inside the spiraling storm.

The gold and silver returned to the chest. Ishkara sprang up and slammed shut the door.

Why did the metals mock him? Could it be that the Spanish understood their evil and were only too happy to unload them upon the Calusa? Ishkara slumped to the ground. The more of the precious metals he amassed, the more they seemed to drain his strength.

Or perhaps his weariness had a simpler explanation. Until Carlos came of age, Ishkara was obliged to perform the duties of both cacique and tirupo. For the latter, Ishkara was suited in both temperament and training. More than anything, he wished to return to the cultivating of his gardens and the preparation of salves and remedies, tasks for which increasingly he relied on Aesha. Tending to matters of state left little time for the concerns of the souls. He feared that his absence from the temple and neglect of the gods would result in catastrophe. Many suns had passed since the last devastating blue-sky storm. Perhaps the vision of the whirling gold was just such a warning.

One thing, at least, was apparent. He must prepare Carlos.

There was so much to teach the boy, and though he was still of such tender age, Ishkara couldn't delay it any longer. He called before him Piyaya, she of the thick frame, solid, dependable, and loyal. "Second daughter, I must thrust upon you a grave responsibility, one that I dare not entrust to Escuru, though she is the elder. I must retreat to the inner temple with Carlos. We are not to be disturbed. You will be my eyes and ears while I am gone. Keep them open wide."

They climbed the miniature mound and crossed the threshold into the sanctuary, the smell of the fresh thatch Ishkara had laid tickling their nostrils. Ishkara placed his hands upon Carlos's shoulders. "Here, my son, and here alone, I will speak of the secrets of the heavens and earth, or so much as has been revealed to me. This is sacred knowledge; we must both cleanse ourselves, I to impart it, you to receive. During our time here we will fast and drink only of the black drink. We will not leave until we receive a sign. To do so would be a signal that the gods do not approve."

Carlos blinked, his eyes adjusting to the subdued and somber light. Slowly, he took in the room, the mask-filled walls, the central altar displaying the sacred images of the gods, the ornate box containing Caalus's remains. Turning toward his father, he said, "Approve of me, you mean."

Those eyes. Eyes that hadn't yet seen ten suns, yet looked so much older. "My son," Ishkara said, "you look so serious. I don't mean to frighten you. We dwellers of the Bay of Plenty have been blessed with gifts of strength, cleverness, and bravery. To survive, indeed to prosper, we need merely to live by these gifts and to give thanks to the gods. This is a lesson we learned long ago. Sit down now, and I will tell you a story."

He waited while Carlos folded his knobby legs beneath him and settled on the palm thatch mat. "Of all Sipi's domain," Ishkara began, "he loved most the fine sand beaches of the barrier islands. Long ago, in the very dawn of the time of quiet, the people lived upon those thin necklaces of land with their gentle, cooling breezes that blew away the biting bugs. Life was easy. Too easy. The people reaped riches from the sea and congratulated only themselves, quite overlooking the need to thank the gods.

"Sipi, they forgot, is both Creator and Destroyer. His fury was swift and certain. From up above he whirled his finger, and the breezes circled around each other faster and faster, until they built into a fearsome windstorm. The waves crashed onto the beaches and raced across the islands, carrying trees, homes, and bodies. The winds destroyed even the shelters on the highest ground. No one escaped Sipi's wrath."

"But Father—" Carlos began, then quickly fell silent.

"My son, here in the inner temple feel free to speak."

"How did the people know that Sipi made the storm and not Aurr, who is always making war?"

Ishkara smiled. "The Ancient One is the cleverest of all. Exactly so the people could not mistake where it came from, Sipi left a hole in the middle of the storm through which the people could look up at his domain, the sky and heavens. Thinking the tempest was over, they ventured from their hiding places. Then the winds shifted, coming from the opposite direction and hitting with even more ferocity. Many more lives were lost. The islands were left in shambles, and the people fled, terrified, into the bays of Escampaba to the domain of the walking tree.

"Still, though, Sipi's temper wasn't quelled. He unleashed pouring rains. For days upon days, the rains came down, raising the water in the ocean until the lands of the walking tree began to disappear. The people retreated to the last high places, where they huddled together with the animals, shaking with terror.

"Now, the most clever of the animals, Raccoon, asked the people, 'What have you done to so enrage the gods?' And the people said they did not know, for they were so paralyzed by fear they couldn't reason. So, Raccoon said, 'You must stand aside. I will see what can be done.'

"First, Raccoon appealed to Osprey, cacique of the birds. 'This rain is a message from the gods. Please, carry us to the mainland, that we may seek higher ground on which to lead better lives.' But Osprey declined. 'Why? The gods are not angry with the birds. If the land disappears here, we will simply fly elsewhere.' Then Raccoon appealed to Tarpon, cacique of the fishes. 'Let us ride upon your back to the mainland, that we may find shelter.' But Tarpon, too, declined. 'The gods are smiling on the fishes. We live already in a world full of water. We rejoice in the rain.'

"Raccoon, perched precariously on the last tip of dry land, plunged into the water. Down and down he dove, until he found the bottom. Surfacing with a clump of mud in his paw, he laid it upon the ground. The other animals followed his lead. Soon the land was restored.

"The people cascaded their thanks upon Raccoon, who replied, 'Do not confer your thanks on me, direct it to the gods.' And the people knew then how they had erred. Now we live humbly in the land of the walking tree and the mounds we have built upon it in imitation of Raccoon and the animals. Only the foolish—or the truly pious—live upon the beaches, for they are the sacred lands of Sipi."

Ishkara saw the look of confusion on Carlos's face. "What is it, my son?"

"How did the people speak to Raccoon?"

"In the time of quiet, the people could talk to the animals, and the animals to the people. The trees and grasses, the sun and moon, the rivers and the tides all spoke to the people, and the people listened and knew how to live their lives. These things speak to us still. We have only to listen."

Ishkara walked to the image of Sipi upon the altar at the center of the sanctuary. Etched into the hide of the white deer, circling the barracuda-like figure, were nine fanciful designs. "These"—he ran his finger over them—"are tongues of various beings, tongues that remind us of the importance of speech, of stories and of listening." He let out a tired sigh. "But the people have forgotten how to listen with their souls. They want their leaders to tell them what to do, how to live. And so we do. Not by choice, only by necessity.

"My son, my throat grows dry. Let us drink." Ishkara ducked from the inner temple. Moments later, he returned with a large deerskin pouch and a pan of hot coals from the fire that always burned in the temple entrance. Plucking the glowing embers with his thumb and forefinger, he placed them in the small fire pit, then covered them with wood shavings. A lively flame sprang up. Ishkara bade Carlos to feed the fire with larger twigs.

"Father, how do you touch the coals and not get burned?"

"A mystery, no? Actually, not so much of one." He showed his calloused hands to Carlos. "Many so-called mysteries would be better termed practice. Now let me show you how to brew the black drink." From his pouch he drew a bundle of stiff green leaves and put them into the well-blackened pot he'd laid over the fire. "The leaves come from the yaupon holly. First, we parch them." He let them wilt and dry until they nearly began to burn, then filled the pot with water. As it heated up, Ishkara pulled from his pouch a long-necked gourd with a small hole at the top and a larger one in its side. "I grow these gourds myself, as you know. You'll soon see the result."

When the water had come to a boil, Ishkara dipped the gourd into the pot so that the hole in the side was submerged. Soon, steam began to rise from the top hole, and with it, a breathy, whistling noise. "Hear the song of casine," Ishkara said.

The gourd moaned and wailed, howled and whistled. "It sings to our loved ones in the land beyond," Ishkara explained. He removed the pot from the fire and, with the gourd, transferred the contents to a deep wooden bowl. "Now, the leaves must steep. Smell. Not at all unpleasant, no?"

Carlos sniffed tentatively and wrinkled his nose.

Ishkara laughed. "You'll get used to it soon enough. Now watch the casine work its magic." Dark color began to swirl into the liquid.

Ishkara now placed the ceremonial cup before his son. "This right-handed whelk is one of the rarest of shells. As perfectly formed as the common left-handed shell, it reminds of the reflection soul, for whom all the world is identical yet opposite. I stumbled on this shell when I was a boy not much older than you. I've never found another. Would that I had the luxury of time to wander the shallows for more treasures." He dipped the whelk into the tea, now a uniform dark, rich brown and poured the contents onto the fire. "The first cupful is for the gods."

As the fire hissed and popped its thanks, Ishkara filled another cupful, then sipped from it with a loud "heh-emm." "The second cup is for the elder." He drank slowly and noisily, his head bent over the cup.

Hunched over like that, hair faded and thinning, skin sagging from muscles that were no longer there, an elder, yes. Carlos couldn't help but notice.

Ishkara finished, dipped once more and handed the cup to the boy. "And the third for the future cacique."

Carlos held the cup rigidly at arm's length. "But I'll spill my belly."

"Perhaps." Ishkara sat cross-legged and said no more.

Carlos brought the steaming cup closer and sniffed at the tea once, twice, then brought it to his lips, blew on it and sipped, imitating his father's "heh-emm." "It's good. Not bitter." He took another swallow.

"I'm pleased, my son, at your bravery. Now that is enough for the moment. The casine is a stimulant. It will always be available in the inner temple. By drinking small amounts at first, you'll build a tolerance. Later, you'll have an advantage over the others who drink it only at special ceremonies. Even Stepana. The people will take note."

"But Father—isn't that a deception?"

"I prefer to call it training. As I've already told you, the people will always seek a leader. Will you have it be you or someone else?"

"Heh-emm." Carlos sipped. This time the tea was slightly bitter. Ishkara took it from him. "A single sip is enough for now.

"Let us speak now of some of the great mysteries: of the sun and the moon and the tides. We recognize these heavenly fixtures not only as objects but as beings. And are they not? All living things exhibit habits. The sun awakens on the mainland and sleeps in the sea. The moon is the sun's younger sister; she stands for him at night, but dares not outshine him and so displays her full glory only one night in thirty. The tides serve both sun and moon. They run strongest when the moon is full, yet being a bit lazy, are always falling behind the sun's schedule."

"Ah," Carlos brightened. "That's why the tides come later each day."

"Excellent. You see the importance of observation? Many mysteries can be understood by observing and listening to the heavens and seas. They are part of us and we of them. By living in rhythm with their patterns, we prosper. They are mysteries no longer. But"—Ishkara took another swallow of the black drink—"there is one mystery that we have not completely unlocked. Death. Death is the last great unknown."

Carlos's perpetual frown deepened.

"To speak to you of death, let me first speak of the souls. The first two, those of the shadow and reflection, are shared amongst all creatures. When a man dies, those souls leave him. We recognize in the animals the spirits of our departed: the curiosity of the child in the playful antics of the otter, the daring of the warrior in the sudden attack of the bobcat, the dignity of the elder in the stately carriage of the great blue heron. But what then becomes of the souls of those animals when they die?" Ishkara raised his eyebrows and fell silent.

Carlos deliberated a long moment, then said, "The stories say . . ."

"Ah, yes, the stories say. What do they say?"

"That the soul passes to lesser and lesser beings until it disappears."

"You've learned well. But here is a secret: we do not know."

The frown etched farther yet into the young face.

"I know your trouble," Ishkara said. "The stories are truth. Every Calusa can recite them. They've been passed along from our fathers' fathers, and we in turn tell them to our children and grandchildren. They can be questioned only by a privileged few. Isn't it odd that the gods choose as special those who challenge the natural order of things? As cacique, you'll be one. You'll have to select a tirupo, recognize that person of special talent to hear the unheard when he shows himself. For only together can you hope to unravel the mystery of death."

"I've already found my tirupo," Carlos said. "It's you."

Ishkara's darkened forefinger traced absently along the puffy blue trails running up the back of his hand. "I'll be here for you as long as I can. But as the black drink reminds us, every living thing passes from this world to the next. I'm not a young man anymore."

"When you speak like that, it scares me, Father."

"And me. But to identify his fears and thereby deny them their power is every man's challenge. I'm no exception." Ishkara shifted in his cross-legged position, lifting the weight off each side of his buttocks, throwing his shoulders back, then settling back down. "But we were speaking of the souls, and we've not yet discussed the third, the one seen in the very center of the eye. It is this soul that makes a pelican a pelican, a dolphin a dolphin, that makes you and me human. In our carvings and our paintings, we celebrate this third soul, the soul of the individual, above all the others. Often we call it the greatest of the souls. Yet, we must be ever mindful: we recognize it as only one part in three. Humility. Don't let the lesson evade you. For if it does . . ."

"The blue-sky storm." Carlos's finger spun in a circle.

"That's right. Or some other catastrophe: famine, or the strangling tide, or drought. This season is far too dry. I fear it will get worse. As cacique, the people will look to you above all others. On your shoulders will be their thanks or their blame. Try as I might, I cannot protect you from that."

"I don't wish you to, Father. I know my responsibilities. I won't run from them. Please go on. You were speaking of the third soul."

"Yes, the third soul. We know, do we not, that this soul stays with a man even after he dies?"

This time Carlos cocked his head.

Ishkara laughed once more. "Ah, good. You begin to question. No, we do not know this. Here in the temple, the voices of Caalus and of the ancestors sometimes speak to me. But here lies yet another mystery. Sometimes, the voices are silent. Sometimes when I speak to Caalus, he doesn't answer; he is elsewhere. The same is true when we go to the Island of Bones. We hear the voices of our loved ones speaking to us. Sometimes. And so, we perform trials. Sometimes we keep the bones of a departed one intact and bury him in a certain position. Sometimes we lay out several individuals in a pattern like the rays of the sun. Sometimes we let the bones become clean in a charnel house, then break them up and bury the remains of many men and women together. Then we observe. Do the voices speak more strongly as individuals or together?

"Never, though, do we lose respect for our dead. We know that the souls of the departed hold power over us. They can be mischievous or worse. So, we break up and scatter with their bones their favorite possessions, their spoon or bowl or sleeping mat, that are so much a part of them that the implements have absorbed portions of their souls; and we hope that in so doing, we release the souls. So, too, we surround the Island of Bones by water so that the souls may remain undisturbed and will not venture out."

Wincing, Ishkara rose and stretched, shook first one leg, then the other. "And if I don't move these old bones around, they too may never venture out again. My son, I wish it weren't necessary to burden you at such a young age with the great imponderables. I promise to stay close to you in life even as I prepare for death. And after my leaving I will try to reach you from the other side. That will be my last and greatest challenge.

"But I have spoken long enough. Now, you must speak to me. Tell me what you've observed about the world."

Carlos sat in silence, twirling on his finger a lock of hair that had escaped his topknot. Finally, "The central canal, it points directly at Tega Pass."

"Yes, you observe keenly. And what of the islands—the barrier islands, Sipi's playground?"

Carlos gave a puzzled look.

"Sipi chose to align them to face the anchor star, who never moves. If you were a bird and could fly a direct line over that long chain of islands, you'd fly straight into the anchor star. The sun's path across the sky travels perpendicular to that line. Recognizing this order, we align our cities and water paths similarly."

"But Elbow Island is crooked. It doesn't line up."

"True. That makes it a most powerful place. It's no coincidence that it was at Elbow Island that we first encountered the Spaniards. The spirits are strong there. We see the gods' work not only in the perfect, but in the atypical, too. I must tell you another story. I promise a short one."

"May I try some more of the black drink?"

"Of course. Just sip it slowly." Ishkara dipped half a cup and handed it to his son. "Soon after Sipi had created all the world's inhabitants, his brothers Nao and Aurr came to inspect his handiwork. Nao, being of even disposition, praised his elder brother profusely. But Aurr was jealous. 'I will do better,' he said. 'I will create my own creature. It will hatch from an egg as a bird, yet will not fly. And despite having neither wing nor leg, it will travel on both land and water.' And so, Aurr created the coral snake and, for good measure, gave it a deadly bite.

"The prideful Sipi was not to be outdone. He conceived of not one but three beasts that swim as the fish but breathe as the animal: the dolphin, the manatee, and the whale. And are they not the most magnificent of the water creatures? My son, praise always the work of the gods in the animals and in the plants as well. By what power do some trees have the strength always to hold their leaves? We're not sure. But we revere them. We build our masks and our canoes and houses from the pines, cedar, and spruce trees. And of course we brew the black drink from the leaves of the holly evergreen. It stays in your belly?"

Carlos nodded. A yawn escaped his mouth.

"Even the black drink's effects don't last forever. You've listened well, my son. Stay with me awhile longer. I will explain why I brought you here now." And Ishkara told Carlos about his vision of the swirling bars of gold and silver. "I'm bewildered by the glittering metals of the strangers. These rare treasures hold much power. Yet it is a dangerous power indeed. I believe they may have been sent to destroy us. The metals and the strangers themselves may be a test of the gods. I have begun to prepare, but there is much more that will fall to you. That is why you, too, must prepare."

Ishkara walked to the wall of the inner temple, paced its perimeter, caressing each mask with his rough fingers. "Twenty-four clans have brought me their symbols. They may look imposing, alarming even. Do not fear them, rather draw strength from them." He removed and carefully donned the mask of the crane clan, the carved cypress base of the long-necked bird perched atop his skull, its head and beak projecting far above, its fanciful plumage trailing behind. "How clever was the craftsman." Using strings running through the hollow neck, Ishkara worked the crane's beak open and shut, made its tail feathers rise and fall as he flapped his arms and strutted about. "Yet, are not even the finest recreations of the birds, fishes, and animals but feeble imitations of the actual creatures created by the gods?" Ishkara moved to the altar now to inspect the images of the gods. "As these portrayals, sacred though they are, still are but mere representations of the gods themselves. I will leave you now. Come, touch the images yourself, speak to them that the gods may know you and answer back."

"But father, you said we mustn't leave the temple."

"I will take my mat behind the altar. Take your time. I'll be waiting for you."

Carlos cautiously approached the image of Sipi, put a tentative finger on the edge of the deerskin stretched over its wood frame. Cracked and dry. Very old—as old as the Creator himself? Carlos listened for the voice of the Old One as he ran his fingers the length of the skin. He thought of the stories his father had told him. Sipi was proud, proud and vengeful, temperamental, too. To be feared . . . and faced. "I am Carlos," he whispered. "I bow to you, but I don't turn away. Speak to me, please."

No voice. Carlos repeated the greeting with Nao. Again no answer. Turning to Aurr, then, he said, "Someday, I'll need your help. I'm sure to face many enemies. Speak to me now, that I may show you my courage."

Neither, though, did Aurr respond. So Carlos waited, determined to display the patience of an adult. He noticed that the dim light in the temple had changed, grown dimmer yet. It must be nighttime.

The waiting made him nervous. What if the gods refused to recognize him? Nevertheless, Carlos sat as still as an egret waiting in ambush, resolved to remain there forever if need be. Waited so long the light was changing again. Waited as his back ached and his bladder cried to be emptied.

Finally, it was his thoughts instead that emptied. Yet in the blankness, there was something there . . . a feeling. Faint but distinct, it pulled him to the carving of Nao, to the long, lithe human body kneeling in both repose and readiness, to the alert yet serene panther's face. Nao was ever watchful; nothing escaped his gaze. Nao presided over the interactions of men with both a strength and understanding no human could match. As Carlos touched the carving, he felt the strength of authority flow into him. Yes, it was Nao who would guide him. He was certain.

"Father," Carlos shouted. "It's Nao that speaks to me." A pause. "Father?"

A loud snort announced Ishkara's presence. He rose to embrace his son. "You've done well. Very well."

"I have," Carlos said, grinning now. "I'm one of the chosen. I'm sure of it."

"Let us give thanks," Ishkara said. "Remember, humility." He bowed low, praying silently to the gods.

Carlos joined him. He tried to pray, but he was just too excited. No words came.

"Try again," Ishkara said.

"You hear my thoughts."

"No, I hear your fidgeting."

"I'm sorry, Father."

"You'll learn. You simply must practice. The time has come now to leave the temple," Ishkara said.

"But we only barely arrived."

Ishkara put an arm under Carlos's armpit to lift him upright. "The effects of the casine are strong. Three nights have come and gone, my son. You'll return here often to drink, to pray, to consult. Now, though, it's time we return to the people. As Nao would surely remind us, there are practical concerns to address."

Practical concerns there were. As the dry season continued unabated, the level of the city's rainwater cisterns fell dangerously low. Ishkara allowed Carlos to accompany him to dawn council meetings, where they debated a proposed proclamation that every family be required to devote two days per moon carrying freshwater from far up the mainland's rivers, beyond the reach of the tides. To the astonishment of both Ishkara and the councilors, Carlos spoke up. "If you please, there may be a better method. The families carry water inefficiently in wooden bowls. We must build much larger containers made to the shape of our largest canoes. Let the canoes be paddled by revolving work parties, so that they stay ever busy. Laborers who have no time to fish or hunt will be fed from communal pots, to which all families will be required to contribute."

The system worked. Carlos, it was clear, had a gift for the practical. It was time for him to move about in the world.

⸙ Eight ⸙

They traveled with a sizeable staff of servants charged with paddling for them and protecting them, but Carlos preferred to take the lead in a solo canoe, and Escalante usually followed just behind. Upon reaching their destination, the exotic Spaniard would shock the audience by speaking in the Spanish tongue and then astound them by repeating the words in Calusa. Aesha, eighteen suns now, was not one to miss an adventure and always accompanied her husband. Flashing intense yellow-brown eyes immediately recognizable by all, she spoke eloquently of the need for unity and allegiance. But it was Carlos, the young ruler-to-be, grown tall and increasingly muscular in his thirteenth sun, who impressed the most, delivering his message of Calusa supremacy with an air of complete self-assurance. "I win them over with praise, not threats," he told Aesha. Indeed, he steadfastly refused Stepana's offers to escort them, though he did of course allow the great captain's bowmen to flank the royal entourage. "I make them proud of who they are." The three were rewarded with pledges of loyalty and tribute on a scale that Ishkara had never imagined. The temple's walls crowded with clan masks.

Far and wide they traversed the Bay of Plenty, a series of bays really, the settlements scattered amongst the sandbars, shoals, oyster reefs, and walking-tree cays. Carlos, in his systematic thoroughness, tried to visit every settlement, even the small colonies of a few dozen family members living in thatched huts atop their barely elevated, flat-topped shell platform. They stayed longer at the larger cities, stopping for two or three days to be feted and toured. Carlos was fascinated by each location's individuality, how it contoured to both the shape of the land and the makeup of the clan. At Estantapaca, where several families shared equal influence, eight canals led like rays of the sun from the central temple mound to round water courts in front of identically sized mounds. At Cutespa, a strict hierarchy prevailed, with the headman's mound highest and the remainder of gradually diminishing height, each farther from the center. The water courts at Metamapo were square instead of round, recognizing, as that chief explained, four influential families at the terminus of each. Carlos committed the geographies of both designs and personalities to memory.

While Carlos met with the headman, Aesha wandered the bush with the clan's healer, learning new plants and herbs and novel uses for familiar ones, mixing salves, brewing teas, helping to treat the infirm. As for Escalante, he watched them both, watched everything, then made scratchings on his thin rectangular pieces of bark.

"What are you drawing?" Aesha asked him one day.

"I'm not drawing."

"I've seen you do this often. Please, tell me. Show me."

Escalante reluctantly showed her the page.

Aesha examined it closely, turning it around in her hands. "This bark is cut from an unfamiliar tree. And the subject, I can't make out any creature. It seems to be a series of symbols."

"Symbols, yes. I'm"—he searched for a Calusa word—"I'm talking with paint" was as close as he could come. "In my tongue, it's called writing." He explained how every Spanish word could be represented by a precise combination of a mere handful of letters. "They're quite simple. I learned them as a child."

"Simple? No. This is amazing. Write something for me."

He picked up a sea grape leaf, dipped his small brush into his jar, and painted five figures on it. "There. This is for you. Actually, it is you."

She held the leaf as if it were the most precious treasure in the world. "The first and last of the symbols—they are the same?"

"Yes. It's your name. Aesha. At least, this is how I believe it should be rendered."

Mouth agape, she traced a finger lightly through the letters.

"Writing is how we remember history, how we learn the word of God."

"Teach me." She scrunched beside him, very close, her moss skirt brushing his bare thigh.

Escalante put the brush in her hand and guided it to make the awkward scratchings that pass for a novice's letters. She practiced copying her name on leaf after leaf, bending forward, concentrating hard, the tip of her tongue projecting from the corner of her mouth.

As always, he watched. Watched her practice until the pot of Indian paint was empty. Still she wrote like a child.

But she moved like a woman. She smelled like a woman.

Oddly, Carlos was not taken with the Spanish letters. "How will they aid me? No one will know what they mean."

"We'll teach them."

"The impression we make on the people is already overwhelming. When the Spaniard speaks, they listen as if to the gods. I'm concerned that the people come out only to view him, not me. I don't trust this 'writing.' It could be another Spanish trick."

As soon as they returned to Caalus, Aesha raced with the scratched markings to Ishkara. Surely, he would understand. "Think of it. By this means, you may speak to someone many days' paddle away, and then they may speak back to you."

Ishkara was unmoved. "We accomplish the same with our messengers."

"Who often give the message their personal twist. The Spaniard has told me that by means of these symbols the gods speak directly to every Spanish child. Even in the far-off city of Cartagena, Escalante heard them."

"What use then would be our stories, our campfires?" Ishkara picked a coal from the fire and held it to the sea grape leaf until it burst into flames. "You see, this writing of yours is not so permanent."

Aesha's eyes, too, flamed. "You can destroy the object, but I can create another. It's the knowledge that matters."

"Be careful, my Little Bird. Do not grow too charmed with the Spaniards' ways."

"I don't fear them. They hold no power over me. How are we to contend with the Spaniards unless we learn their habits?"

Ishkara shook his head. "You exhibit all the certainty of youth. I fear wisdom will come to you at a great price."

"My uncle and father, I intend no disrespect. But you grow old and pinched, and live in the past."

15 August 1554

Five years come and gone. I cling to my calendar scratched onto these crumbling sheets as I cling to my fading identity. My hair has grown long; it reaches my waist. My body is hard and brown and smells of the shark liver oil that repels the biting insects. From my voice, deepened now, come the utterances of a Calusa. Their words come unciphered into my head. I no longer have to think of their meanings.

Though I reach only to the shoulders of this race of giants, otherwise I too closely resemble these savages to be distinguished. Perhaps that is what protects me, for each year when they sacrifice a Christian in order to feed the idol that they worship, the one they say eats the eyes of humans, they look past me to another. I pray that I might myself be struck blind to spare me from witnessing their gruesome dance around the hideously disfigured head, and yet I cannot help but feel relief as well.

Even so, they recognize and exploit my differentness. They show me off like a prized possession to their brother Indians, who listen raptly to my words as if I am the messenger of the Lord Himself. Deep into the interior of La Florida have I traveled with these Calusa who hold sway over their far-flung kin. I dare boast that I have seen their lands as has no other civilized man. I even returned to where my ship was lost, a place the Indians call Tequesta, situated on the bank of a river which extends into the country the distance of fifteen leagues. This river issues from another lake of freshwater which is said by some Indians who have traversed it more than I to be an arm of the Lake of Mayaimi. On this lake, which lies in the midst of the country, are many towns of thirty or forty inhabitants each, and as many more places in which people are not so numerous. They have bread of roots, which is their common food the greater part of the time; and because of the lake, which rises in some seasons so high that the roots cannot be reached in consequence of the water, they are for some time without eating this bread. Fish is plenty and very good. There is another root like the truffle over here, which is as sweet. And there are other different roots of many kinds; but when there is hunting, either deer or birds, they prefer to eat meat or fowl. In the rivers of freshwater are infinite quantities of eels, very savory, and enormous trout. The eels are nearly the size of a man, thick as the thigh, and some of them are smaller. The Indians also eat alligators and snakes and animals like rats, which live in the lake, freshwater tortoises, and many more disgusting reptiles which, if I were to continue enumerating, I should never be through.

These Indians of Tequesta occupy a very rocky and a very marshy country. They have no product of mines or things that we have in our part of the world. The men go naked, and the women in a shawl made of a kind of palm-leaf, split and woven. They are subjects of

Carlos and his tribe, and pay them tribute of all the things I have be-
fore written, food and roots, the skins of deer, and other articles.

Before their painted chiefs I stand and speak. These words in my
native tongue keep me alive. And yet, will it not be the final mocking
irony when, someday, I forget how to speak them? Five years. So much
has faded. I am a savage and a sinner, lying with women, sometimes
two or three together, so unrestrained are their ways. And their ways
are now mine. Am I a Spaniard still? Will ever I be again?

All I have left are these words. I dare not give them away, even to
her. I let her copy the letters. Even that is too much. Naked and hea-
then, shameless and godless though she is, still I cannot stop myself
from drawing her near me. She cares for me; I need as a reminder
only to grasp the gold and silver medallion she gave me long ago. But
she is wife of the man who soon will be their king, whose influence
grows as does his body. I acquaint with her at my peril. He can de-
stroy me.

What more have I to live for anyway?

Day upon day, Iqi ascended the curving ramp up the palace mound to
take his position in front of Ishkara's chest of treasures. It wasn't a long
climb, a few moments' trek to the plateau that stood ten men's height
above the plaza; but each time he reached the summit, the second highest point in all of Escampaba, Iqi felt an odd light-headed sensation: *I*
wasn't meant to live at these dizzying heights.

Those around him, though, treated him as if he belonged. Together
with the nobles, a handful of artists and craftsmen, and a small number
of Stepana's lieutenants, Iqi was fed from the nets and snares of the
commoners, invited to dine on delicacies only the higher-ups could enjoy. But Iqi could barely stomach the meat of the sea wolf, could only ru-
minate that he'd rather witness that larger cousin of the otter playing
in the sea. And along with the flirtatious looks from unmarried women
came challenging glares from his equals: what had Iqi done to deserve to

dine from their nets with the privileged few, to receive the adulation of the women they sought?

Unwelcome by those he belonged with, awkward with those he was thrust upon, Iqi barely noticed the passing of the moons and suns. He lived numbly, saw everything, everyone from a distance. In the ever more thickly populated city, Iqi was utterly alone.

Except for Ishkara. He came often to sit before the Spanish riches, always with a handful of red hackberry seeds for Iqi to munch on. Iqi was quick to withdraw to a respectful distance, but often Ishkara beckoned him to stay, sometimes even inviting him back to wander amongst the royal gardens. There, Iqi would see Aesha tending to the plants, picking this and that for Ishkara's infusions. Iqi would linger there, watching the dance of her long fingers, the rhythmic swish of her hair as black as the boiling kettle into which she dropped the healing herbs. He dared not speak to her, nor she to him, for Ishkara did not leave them alone. Kindly though the great leader was to him, Iqi understood this was a line he could not cross.

Ishkara knew it was time for Carlos to govern.

Carlos selected the implements and attire of the cacique carefully, his travels throughout Escampaba having convinced him that his greatest challenge was to become and remain cacique of *all* the people. He wished to rule by acclamation, not fear. So for his headdress he chose not the feather of a single bird as had Caalus, but instead the distinctive plumes of the white egret, the black crow, the redheaded woodpecker, the small green heron, the brown pelican, the great blue heron, the roseate spoonbill. He replaced the pearl amulet of the cacique-to-be with a gold chaguala, a tablet made of the Spaniard's precious metal into which was etched Carlos's personal design, a complex pattern with two teardrops harkening to the tears of Sipi and a series of circles within circles resembling a third, all-seeing eye. On one arm, Carlos strapped the tail of the raccoon; around the other hung the teeth of a bear. To his knees were strapped the fringed leggings that only the cacique could wear, this new pair woven in the humble pattern of the fisherman's net. The staff of the cacique, too, was modest, less than an arm's length and terminating in a grooved knob. Instead of the traditional tassel hanging from the ruler's staff, Carlos displayed a braided lock of Aesha's hair, reminding the people of his connection to her father, the great unifier.

Around his neck and waist, the new cacique wore the gifts of many chiefs: bone beads, carved columella pendants, strings of pearls and ancient sharks' teeth. Though weighted down like a heavy cast net, Carlos moved without effort now, his frame grown large and sturdy, belying his youthful age of only fourteen suns. His face, painted heavy with the warrior colors of red and black and also with the statesman's white, had matured, too, drawn tighter, leaner, even as it bore his perpetual look of solemnity.

In a ceremony attended by more than two thousand, Ishkara knelt before his son, hands extended, palms up. Carlos, seated upon the cacique's bench, placed his hands over his father's, then on those of the nine councilors who followed, and finally on the more than a hundred visiting chiefs and headmen who knelt before him, presenting gifts from their home villages and cities. Last of all came Stepana, who bowed low even as he held his atlatl high in the air in a gesture that was somehow both subservient and swaggering. A great celebration followed, with much food and endless cups of casine that Carlos drank with gusto. It was not lost upon the people that the young cacique spilled his stomach not once.

The very next morning, Ishkara moved his sleeping mat from the palace to the temple.

Carlos governed with a maturity beyond his age. Presiding over the councilors, he listened intently from the ruler's bench, then spoke quietly but firmly, making pronouncements in his confident manner. When Tocobaga—testing, always testing—crossed to the Calusa side of Two

Rivers Bay, Carlos himself paddled (with Stepana this time) in a force of forty warrior canoes that turned the opposing cacique back without a fight.

Stepana collected still more gold and silver, which he presented, always in a very public performance, to the new cacique, who was now the keeper of the Spanish treasures.

And still the Spaniards stayed away.

Under Carlos, Escampaba prospered. He seemed to have a better way of doing everything. New, larger fish corrals were built with openings that were below the surface on high tide so that schools of mullet could be driven into them. Then, as the tide ebbed, the trapped fish could be harvested at leisure. Carlos, too, made plans for a new council hall attached to the palace. The great building would be the largest in all of Escampaba, able to accommodate inside a crowd as large as had attended Carlos's coronation.

A building to hold two thousand? The people gasped. Then they went to work.

Only Aesha seemed dissatisfied. On the rare occasions that Carlos visited her sleeping mat—for he now had a flock of new wives—she was distant, cautionary. "You are but sixteen suns now. Knowing your youth, your councilors take advantage of you."

"And what evidence of this do you see?"

She chose not to answer directly, rather continued. "And Stepana is more dangerous than ever."

"Dangerous, yes. To our enemies." Carlos put his hands on her shoulders. "You worry too much."

She laughed without mirth. "You were always the worrier."

"As cacique, I must be warrior, not worrier. Enough talk. That isn't why I've come to your mat."

Aesha received him, but for her there was no pleasure. Sweaty and troubled, she fell into a twitchy, tortured sleep. She was no longer on her mat but outside, somewhere intimately familiar and yet entirely unrecognizable. Smoke and flames were everywhere. Three high snaking tongues of fire appeared before her, probing, licking, rubbing up against each other, intertwining, then unraveling again in a dance both repulsive and erotic. What was burning? Her eyes teared. Too much smoke. She squeezed them shut and shrank back, turning her head from the searing heat. But even with eyes closed, the inferno burned bright, as if it were at once outside and inside of her. She tried to yell for help but her voice came out a feeble shriek; she lay paralyzed as the flames, distinctly snake-headed now, caressed and stabbed her prone, naked body with stinging pleasure-pain, moving up and between her legs, then winding round her belly, back, and breasts. Too late, she realized that the flames had become stout cords, digging into her skin as they bound her tight. She writhed and wriggled, frantically twisting to free herself. With desperate strength, she struggled loose and gulped a breath of smoke-free air. They were gone.

No. Surreptitiously, the flames had locked and braided themselves into the long black strands of her hair. They pulled at her now, tugged at her scalp until she was being lifted from the ground and whirled round and round. Smoke and flames were everywhere; she was being sucked in, drawn to the center of the raging firestorm.

Panting, drenched in sweat, she awoke. Carlos was gone.

She went to the temple to tell Ishkara of her vision. "Your powers are strong," he told her. "It is the future you see."

"But what does it mean? Why can I not see more clearly what is burning?"

Ishkara sighed. "We see only what the gods allow us to. Long have I known that a fateful future awaits you. I fear it won't be a peaceful one. The snake is Aurr's creation." He took her head in his hands, gently ran his fingers through her hair. "Our stories tell us that the hair is our source of potency. Long ago, you cut it off with the strangers' implement. But it has grown back longer and stronger. In your vision, you met the flames with your strength. That is a good sign. For you and for the people."

"For the people?"

"Don't forget that a lock of your hair adorns the ruler's staff. With your fate hangs that of all Escampaba."

ᔕ Nine ᔕ

Nine-times-nine cypress posts set in a wide circle served as the bones of the great building, each carved and painted in a story scene. A skin of woven palm walls was lashed tight to the posts, with open-air windows in every third span to help dissipate the heat of all the anticipated bodies. The scale was truly grand, the council hall's circumference a three-hundred-pace walk. Its crowning achievement, though, obvious to all who craned their necks from below, was its roof. Shaped like a gigantic inverted basket, the palm thatch dome, supported by a complex lattice of timbers designed by Carlos himself, reached skyward to an impossible height, taller and broader than the most towering fig or mastic tree. Viewed from a distance, the council hall exactly resembled the setting sun melting and spreading as it fell into the sea.

Inside, the building was divided into two sections. The first was a semicircular amphitheater featuring a raised platform in its interior for Carlos, his dignitaries, and his councilors, backed by a high wall decorated with animal carvings from throughout Escampaba. Behind that wall were the cacique's personal quarters, rooms for his sisters, wives, servants, and a rapidly expanding troupe of boisterous children.

It had taken four suns to complete the project, and Carlos's status had grown as lofty as its roof. Too high, claimed the ever vocal chattergulls. "He challenges the gods to blow his palace down." But the gods did not. They filled Calusa waters with astounding runs of fish so thick the water turned black, combined with good rains that filled the cisterns to overflowing and sweetened and swelled the fruits and berries. It was a time of abundance in the Bay of Plenty. At the age of twenty suns, Carlos's popularity was unprecedented. Everyone applauded the young cacique.

Everyone, it seemed, except his principal wife. Instead of tending to her husband's needs, Aesha passed her days at the temple with Ishkara. When Carlos complained, Aesha shot back, "He's your father. Haven't you noticed how thin of face he's become, how slumped of shoulder? Our population grows ever larger, and so do the people's needs. Ishkara can no longer keep up. Someone needs to gather his herbs, to mix his potions. I've brought you these for your swollen jaw." She handed him leaves from the toothache tree. "Chew them."

The leaves brought relief. Temporarily. But as below the aching tooth festers the decaying root, so between Carlos and Aesha the trouble lay deeper. Children. Or lack thereof. Carlos was not afflicted with the same malady as Caalus had been. That much was evident from the nursery noises emanating day and night from his wives' quarters. But he and Aesha remained infertile.

"Aren't there enough runny bowels soiling the floors of your grand achievement already?" she protested.

"It's from you that I desire an heir."

"Then why do you forbid Piyaya from marrying? Your poor sister deserves more than a bare mat and an empty womb."

"The people demand an heir from two royal parents. If you don't produce a child, she will. But only by you will my offspring carry the blood of Caalus. These others in the hallways I don't call children. They're annoying noisemakers, no more."

"You leave the door open for Stepana to employ the same tactics as did Aricata."

"Pfff." Carlos let the breath escape loudly across his lower lip. "The offspring are visible proof of my vigor, just as the marriages confirm my alliances. They're a political necessity."

"As was your marriage to me. It was, and is, nothing more."

"Why do you hate me so?"

"I don't hate you, but neither does that mean I bear for you automatic love. You were a child when we wed. You followed in my wake as ducklings chase their mother."

"I follow no longer. I'm cacique now."

"A title that rightfully was mine. I accept that outcome; it was the best for our people. But you'll never sway me with demands for obedience."

The two fell silent. A palmetto bug scampered across Carlos's legs, then hid at the edge of Aesha's sleeping mat. Carlos crushed the roach with his fist. "I am cacique," he repeated. "And you will be the mother of the next. That is what matters. For us and for the people you cherish so dearly."

Aesha went to see Ishkara, but he threw the problem back at her. "I have shown you the healing properties of plants and the songs that activate them, the use of my masks in summoning animal spirits, even the methods for luring back a wayward soul. You must discover your own fertility remedy." He rolled his shoulders back to straighten his spine. "That is, if you truly desire one."

Aesha's response came out in a stammer.

Ishkara waved a hand at her. "This is not for me to hear." His head began to droop forward again, and he stared at the temple floor. "I expend all my energy in battling the Spanish spirits. I cannot keep them away forever. They do mischief between you and Carlos, just as they did with my brother."

"No one sees that. They see only prosperity."

"And you? What do you see?"

"I still see flames. And the smoke only grows thicker."

"Yes," he agreed. "Thicker." And closed his eyes, looking to an inner space.

Aesha shook her head sadly. She couldn't bring herself to reveal the whole truth to Ishkara. There were faces in the flames now. Some were pale, covered with hair, unrecognizable, others all too familiar: Stepana and Escalante. But never Carlos. He was conspicuously and consistently absent. How could she explain that to Ishkara?

There was another presence in her nocturnal visions. He waited patiently as she struggled to find him through the smoke, to draw close and press against him so he could shield her from the flames. She saw him only in glimpses. But Iqi's smell and the feel of his good, strong hands were embedded in her memory from long ago.

She encountered him on the palace mound from time to time, where Carlos's gold and silver chest was fuller than ever. It was plain to see in Iqi's joyless manner that he was miserable as one of the chosen elite. His only source of pleasure came when he played with the children of the palace. He kept a nickerbean seed wrapped in a piece of shagreen. When the children approached, he'd rub the bean over and over on the rough surface, then toss it to them, inevitably eliciting a squeal of delight when they caught the hot object. They'd pass it between each other until it cooled off, then give it back to Iqi with the predictable demand, "Again." All too soon, though, the children would be shooed off by their mothers, and the light would dim from Iqi's face.

Though Iqi didn't speak of his melancholy to Aesha, it filled her with guilt for sending him to the palace mound to begin with, and then for leaving him so long to languish there. He didn't deserve the fate she'd thrust upon him.

In truth, she'd been selfish; she simply wanted him near, though she'd never dared more than exchange pleasantries, not even at subsequent Falkos. A wife of the cacique did not look elsewhere, much less the principal wife. And so, she lay on her mat at night, desire burning at her loins. Sleep, when it finally came, brought no relief, only more flames.

She didn't know who was the more despondent.

As always, in Aesha's dejection, her thoughts turned to her island. It was then the fair breeze of inspiration blew in. The Thumb. She'd send Iqi there; he'd be so much better off. And someday the opportunity would arise to visit him far from the prying eyes of idle wives with nothing better to do than to stir the pot of rumor and scandal.

Then and there, she made a decision. She'd take no fertility remedy. To the contrary, on her travels Aesha had consulted many healers about conception and childbirth. Cat's claw bark was easy to come by. You had to take large doses. But it worked; it prevented conception. Likewise, the bark of the hackberry tree, that very tree whose seeds Ishkara loved to chew, could regulate her cycle, induce her bleeding if need be. And if those didn't work, a tea of the trailing wedelia, usually used to help push out the afterbirth, could expel an unwanted baby. Up to now, she'd left it to the gods' will whether she'd bear Carlos's child. She'd ensure their decision didn't change.

"There's danger living on the outer islands," Aesha told Iqi. "You'll have only your wits as protection from storms or invaders."

"Then I'll have no protection at all," he replied, grinning.

"You don't have to go," she said.

"I remain here only at your direction and Carlos's."

"That's a mistake I can never forgive myself for. I won't let it continue. You may leave this island and go wherever you like."

"I told you once there's no place I'd rather be. In my memory, I've only grown fonder of it."

Now the difficult part. Aesha churned inside, but she tried to keep her expression steady as she spoke to Carlos. "If the Spaniards come, they'll likely arrive from the sea to the north. You could post no one more reliable than Iqi to watch for them."

"I already have two sentries in the area." Carlos furrowed his heavy eyebrows, deepening the crease across the bridge of his broad nose, a line that had become permanent even at twenty-three suns. "That's not why you send him there, though."

"He's wretched in Caalus."

"He's a conch eater. He serves at my impulse. Already he's been elevated far beyond anywhere his ground-dwelling imagination could have dreamt. And he protests his circumstance?"

"No. He would never complain."

"So you do so for him. I'm not unaware that he bedded you before I did, nor of the way you still look at him. You intend to visit him at the Thumb." It was a statement, not a question.

Very well. Carlos had opened the door. "To collect plants for Ishkara. To see, perhaps, the face of my father. To hear the songs there. And to see Iqi, yes."

The crease between Carlos's brows tightened. "Go, then. As my father would remind me, you'll somehow inevitably get what you want anyway. But if you carry his child, I will kill him. I'll kill them both."

She didn't answer. Cat's claw grew on the Thumb. Hackberry, too.

There was yet another complication in Aesha's affections: Escalante. She couldn't help herself: she was consumed with knowing everything about him and his people's ways. At times he gave her glimpses of the father and mother he left in Cartagena or of the place to which he was traveling, Salamanca, a place he called home even though he'd never seen it. It was, he said, a city of magnificent buildings built of stone and wood, of moving shelters on wheels drawn by powerful, obedient animals, of temples of worship lit with all the colors of the rainbow. More often, though, he shut her out. "Those places mean nothing to me now. They are as dead as my brother. You wanted to make me one of your own? Well, you've succeeded."

"No," she told him. "You have your language still, your writing. You must teach me so it stays alive."

But he would do no more than to apply the letters to her own words.

"Se-le-tega," he wrote, chuckling at the irony. It meant *come to the look-out, see if there be any people coming.* A phrase he longed to hear. And was convinced he never would.

To Aesha, it was as if it were a game to him, to draw her near, yet to keep her far. She saw that he was attracted to her, saw it in the swelling bulge below his loincloth when she sat close. But he made no advances toward her, didn't dare to. For this she was grateful, for though he fascinated her, she didn't care to bed him. Enigmatic and alien, yet maybe underneath he was not so different. Many women visited his sleeping mat, but he took no wife. To love one you cannot have was not so different at all.

Escalante was not the only Spaniard in Caalus now. Carlos, seeing the Spaniard's usefulness, had spared others, sacrificing only those that Ishkara required for the yearly rituals. The new arrivals included several women and a six-toed man by the name of Barbu who had been shipwrecked near Guarugunbe in the Gator Tail Islands. Many of the women soon carried the children of Calusa nobles; Barbu, the man of curious footprints, became a second interpreter.

Across the mainland a five days' journey from Caalus was a powerful chief named Oathchaqua of the tribe of Ais. Located on the coast where the sun awakens, the Ais were rich in Spanish treasure as well as prisoners. So distant was Oathchaqua's tribe that neither Caalus nor Ishkara had considered an alliance feasible. Carlos had other ideas. He sent Barbu, escorted by Stepana, to Oathchaqua with many presents. As had become Carlos's custom, they included a wood copy of the cacique's teardrop tablet. In return, Oathchaqua would know what was expected: the hand of his daughter. Barbu, flanked by a considerable warrior force, relayed Carlos's message through one of Oathchaqua's Spaniards. If the Ais chief cooperated, a silver amulet would in one sun's time replace the wood one, signifying his proven loyalty. The advantages of friendship with Carlos were numerous. So were the hazards of refusal.

Oathchaqua sent his daughter back with Barbu. En route, though, warriors from the tribe of Serrope ambushed the party as they lay on their sleeping mats and captured the daughter and her attendants. The impudent Serrope then spit salt spray into Carlos's eye by wedding the daughter himself and releasing Barbu to Oathchaqua instead of to the Calusa.

Carlos's grip was not as firm as he hoped.

The cacique was livid with Stepana. "You allowed my future wife to be snatched from under your snoring nose. The chattergulls are buzzing like mosquitoes after a rain. It is you that blundered, but I who will pay the price. If you don't reverse this catastrophe, Serrope will be emboldened, and we'll never see Oathchaqua's riches again, not to mention his daughter."

"Cacique, before sending me on this mission, you didn't consult me, you merely gave me an order. I could have told you then: the Ais are too distant, Serrope too well armed. You were overreaching. You can order me back, and I will go . . . to my probable death. Will you die beside me?"

"I'm not afraid to die."

Stepana drew himself erect and stared Carlos in the soul of the eye. "Nor am I. But I prefer to die to protect my people, not to compound an error in a too-distant realm."

Aesha was no more sympathetic. "Why must you attempt to spread your influence so wide?"

"Pfff. A large net gathers more fish."

"And too heavy a catch tears the net."

"I control fifty major cities and villages now; the small settlements between are too numerous to count. Our territories have expanded beyond anything your father or mine imagined. I give the chiefs and headmen my personal insignia; they shower me with tribute and wives."

"They shower you with trouble, as you've just seen."

"Stepana will manage the trouble."

Aesha was appalled. "As he managed Oathchaqua and his daughter? How can you know he didn't make a pact with both Serrope and the Ais? It's just the kind of incident Stepana would revel in. By embarrassing you, he gains esteem for himself . . . and adds a secret ally, too."

"Your imagination spreads wilder than creeping vines in the rainy season."

"And what of the Spaniards? And these others I've heard of from Escalante—another race of the white-skins? You should be drawing in, defending our home, not expanding."

"These new strangers and the Spanish want only to kill each other off. So Escalante has said."

"But you know of Ishkara's vision. There is much danger."

"My father grows old. He may have misinterpreted. The gold and silver have done us no harm. To the contrary, they fortify our alliances. Escampaba is stronger than ever. I've heeded my father's advice. I've prepared."

But Aesha still saw flames.

12 November 1564

The French are in La Florida. Oh bitter satire that it is the heretic Huguenots that have built a fort, gained a foothold in this hostile land. Will they give me my freedom from the Indians only to hand me the noose when I profess my true faith? Where is my King? Where are his soldiers?

Nine Spaniards we now number in Escampaba, if Spaniards you count us still. Thanks be to God for their arrival, for I had lost track of my calendar, lost the will to pen these pages, nearly relinquished my last shred of civility and crossed the line to a state of savagery from which I would never have returned. The year is now Fifteen Hundred and Sixty-four! I've been captive fifteen years, lived longer among the Indians than among my own people.

The Spaniards bring precious little news. Like me, they are cast-

aways come from Havana or farther south, having never seen Spain or gone too long to remember. Some of the women have succumbed already to heathenness, taking Indian mates, producing bastards only faintly recognizable as European. But I have at least received news of a new king. Carlos has yielded control of Spain and its overseas empire to his son, Felipe. My new king will surely recognize the importance of this unexplored, untamed land. Such a man of the world he is: son of the Holy Roman Emperor and of Queen Isabella of Portugal, married to Mary of England and now, I am told, to Elizabeth de Valois, daughter of the French King Henry. Could it be we've reconciled with the French? Woe to be so far removed, unaware of whom to count as friend or enemy.

Truly, these Indians of Carlos are nearly civilized in their capacity for conspiracy and maneuvering. The oddest and most indecipherable of all is Stepana. He who wielded the death club on my very brother, he who swore those many years ago to do the same upon me, now treats me as confidante. It is from Stepana, not the Spaniards, that I learned of the French fort. He serves Carlos, he told me, but is himself the rightful cacique. Someday, he said, he will have the office that is rightfully his.

I made no judgment on his remarks. I know not why he tells me these things, whether he woos my loyalty or spies on me. I dare not trust him, trust anyone. Even her. At day's end, whether I lie with one of them or retire to my quarters alone, I am equally solitary.

I may be damned to hell for voicing these faithless thoughts, but I cannot help it. In this godless land, am I also without You?

Oh, to be on her island again. Aesha drank it in like sweet water from an underground spring, drank in the long line of white sand, the cooling breeze, the tangy salt air. As the wind rustled the sea grapes and the waves rattled the shoreline's shell necklace, once again the island sang to her. She spent the entire first day sitting in a single pile of shells the tides had deposited, finding within an arm's length delicate baby's ears, tiny wentletraps, yellow, orange, and purple scallops, a pen shell that held the soul of a rainbow, a starfish that of its heavenly sister. She delighted in the antics of a reddish egret splashing, hopping, and stomping its feet as it hunted minnows on a shallow sandbar. The tide came in and went back out; she never moved until the sun, a giant red eye on the horizon, winked green and disappeared.

Then, finally, the crackle of Iqi's fire and the aroma of his quahog chowder drew her. She ate with relish, enjoying every chewy bite of clam, every tender morsel of boiled sable palm heart. Iqi waited until she put her bowl down, then kicked sand over the fire. "Come." He took her hand and led her across the beach, his eyes searching the sand under the dim light of a sliver moon until he came upon a wide track leading from the water's edge up the beach. "We're in luck," he whispered. "Follow me."

He dropped to hands and knees; she did the same, crawling up the track toward a dune of sea oats. Iqi gestured with his hand to stop, put a finger to his lips. Aesha heard a rustling sound in the dark beyond them. At length, it died down and was replaced by a rhythmic noise of moving sand. Finally, that too ended.

"We won't disturb her now," Iqi said aloud, and he led Aesha around the dune. "There. She's a big one." He wasn't exaggerating. The she-turtle was huge, two arms across. Iqi led her a mere body's length behind the turtle, which squatted over the hole she'd dug with her hind flippers. Plop. An egg fell in, and another. "Watch this now," Iqi said, pulling Aesha closer. "Don't worry. She's busy; nothing will interrupt her."

As Aesha leaned over the hole, a squirt of fluid came down on the new eggs. Plop, plop, squirt. Into the deep hole the eggs fell two at a time, then were squirted with oil. Over and again the sequence repeated itself, more than a hundred having dropped when finally the turtle began using her back flippers to cover the hole. Finishing, she smoothed the sand flat, then made her way down the sloping sand toward the beach.

"She . . . she's crying," Aesha said.

Iqi laughed. "They do look like tears, don't they? I suppose they are, though the purpose, I'm sure, is to flush the sand from her eyes. Now that she's finished laying, do you want to eat her? I might need help rolling her over."

"No." Aesha grabbed his arm. "Let her go that she may lay again."

The mammoth turtle crawled to the sea, where, with a final thrust of her flippers and wiggle of her tail, she disappeared. Aesha backed close to Iqi, wiggling, too. His arms wrapping her from behind, they stood a long time, inhaling each other's scents, listening to the softly lapping waves.

Aesha moved his hands to her moss skirt, pushed them down to slide it over her hips. She stepped out of it, dropped to the sand, and gave herself to Iqi then, pulled him to her on the warm beach under a blanket of stars that blinked the music of the heavens. She took him in, took him in as a woman is meant to, enveloping, nurturing, reveling with him in a sea of pure sensation, bringing their love to completion. And in so doing, became complete herself.

In her dream that night, once again Aesha ran with her namesake bird as it poked at sand fleas with its upturned, pointed beak, all the while dodging the lapping waves. In her sleep, she smiled.

For moments, she did know peace.

She awoke the next morning to the aroma of brewing tea. Iqi squatted next to the fire, feeding it with small twigs. She rose and strode to him, still naked, and pressed herself to him, giving him a close-up whiff of her woman's perfume. Then they were joined together again, clamped as tightly as the halves of a clamshell.

The tea was lukewarm and very strong by the time she tasted it.

"I can't stay," she told him.

"I know."

"Will you be lonely?"

"For you, yes."

"You could return to Caalus with me."

"Though I might return with you, I could never be with you there."

"Someday," she said. "I promise. Do you believe?" She studied him over her whelk cup, his plain, broad-nosed face, unpainted, sun-browned body, sinewy, muscled legs, and wide, flat feet that could support him forever in a motionless squat.

"Yes. Someday," he repeated. "But not there. Here."

"I don't know when that day will come," she said. "If you find someone else, I'll understand."

He looked up and down the deserted beach and smiled.

"It could happen," she said. "It's not so preposterous."

"You misunderstand," he said. "I already have."

The yellow-brown eyes flared.

"Here I'm never alone," he said. "The osprey speaks to me by day, the owl by night. The dolphins chase my canoe. And this one"—he pointed to a great blue heron who stood by the water's edge—"he's missing a leg. So he follows me everywhere, especially when I throw my net, and squawks for a handout." Iqi lowered his head. "I don't know how to thank you. You lifted a burden from me that I didn't even know I was carrying."

"Don't thank me. Love me."

He enveloped her in his arms and held her. In the brush behind them, morning birds sang, "Need you need you need you."

"When must you leave?" he asked finally.

"Tomorrow. But let's not speak of it, not now."

"Come with me again, then." Iqi took her hand. "I will show you something wonderful." He led her to his bayside canoe. They poled across the wide flat to a small channel that led into the heart of the island under a canopy of walking trees alive with crawling fiddler crabs. "You can navigate this channel only when the tide is about half," he told her. "Too low and the canoe won't float, too high and the branches will lop our heads off."

Under filtered rays that spackled their skin with patches of sunlight, they meandered through the narrow canal until it widened into a lagoon. "The lake was formed by a storm since last we were here. The entrance from the sea has silted in, though, so you can reach the lagoon only from the bay. That warms the water considerably. Look." There in the calm water basked a dozen or more manatees, huge and blubbery, snuffing air on the surface, then slowly descending to munch the sea grass or simply loll in utter relaxation. Aesha counted. A single breath could outlast fifty of hers. What gentle souls, she wondered, had come to reside in these peaceful creatures? She closed her eyes, trying to slow her breathing even further.

Thud. She was jolted awake by a hard thump that rocked the canoe. She looked over the side. One of the animals had drifted over and bumped its nose on the dugout. It did so again, twice, three times. She looked to Iqi in puzzlement.

"Go ahead," he said. "Pet it. That's what it wants."

Aesha leaned over to stroke the creature's thick neck. The skin wasn't the least bit slimy, rather tough, leathery, and covered with tiny hairs. As soon as she touched it, the manatee rolled over, exposing its enormous, lighter shaded belly. She rubbed the belly, textured like rough shagreen. The manatee lay perfectly still for the longest time before sinking from sight.

Aesha turned to Iqi with a rapturous smile.

Then up came the manatee another time, nose-first to the canoe. She rubbed its back again, and again it turned instantly stomach-up. She stroked its belly. It floated motionless, then sank leisurely to the bottom.

When once more it surfaced, she tested, gently touching its hand-like flipper with the four fingernails, but the manatee abruptly pulled back.

Neither did it like its nose stroked. But the back to belly combination, you could almost hear it murmur, "Ahhhh." Aesha giggled.

"That," said Iqi, "is the one sound I was lonely for."

She didn't even stop at the palace. Aesha climbed the ramp to the temple mound, the basket atop her head heavy and full.

Ishkara met her at the temple steps. "Ah, gifts for me." He began separating the mass of vines, roots and soil—with difficulty, for his bony hands were shaking.

"Let me help you," Aesha said, and she laid out the bay hop, sandbur, and disk vine plants she'd dug for him.

"I grow more useless each day," Ishkara sighed.

"Hardly. I collected these for you, but you must teach me how to use them."

"Little Bird, you humor me." His lips spread in a grin both sad and sweet. "But fortunately, that suffices for a feeble old man. So here is your lesson that you don't need. Tea from the leaves and roots of the bay hop—did you notice that they bloom only in the morning?—can bathe wounds or reduce swelling in the legs. I also boil the stems as a salve for jellyfish stings. A fussing child can suck upon the steeped leaves of the disk vine. And the sandbur is one of my favorites. A tea of its leaves reduces fever, relieves vomiting, and can aid a mother's milk in flowing. I hope you didn't step on it while collecting. The spikes of this marvelous plant can infect quite seriously."

"No, I'm well. More than well, actually."

"Yes, I see that. You love that place, don't you?"

She nodded.

"And the one there." It came out not as an accusation, just a declaration. "I know now that I cannot change your heart," Ishkara said softly. "Nor is it my place. But neither can I change your responsibility to Carlos and to your people."

At the sound of her husband's name, Aesha felt the glow within her smolder. "I accept it," she said simply. "I've returned."

"I worry for him," Ishkara confided. "His failures infuriate him, his successes only make him more ambitious. Now that young Tocobaga has succeeded his father, Carlos plans to issue an ultimatum: pay with tribute or with lives."

"Did Stepana put him to it? It could be another of his ruses."

Ishkara shook his head. "No. Carlos believes he can take advantage of Tocobaga's youth."

Aesha threw her arms in the air. "As if Carlos isn't young himself? A youthful cacique is all the more likely to fight."

"I agree. In fact, I said something . . . unimaginable. I told Carlos I sided with Stepana. I told him the idea was foolhardy and reckless. Now Carlos has turned his anger on me."

That night, the flames returned. When Aesha wakened in a sweat, she reached for a shell she'd brought from the Thumb. A crown conch, quite common, but this specimen was irregular, misshapen. Early in its life, the shell had been injured, leaving a blemish, rough and irregular. Eventually, though, the conch recovered, healed over, grew stronger, until now three rows of spikes, instead of the usual two, spiraled around it.

Aesha squeezed the lopsided shell between her hands and tried to calm herself.

☙ Ten ❧

In the moon of numbing waters, biting winds could heave the sea and make a choppy mess of the bay, rendering any journey a wet and miserable one. Iqi didn't relish traveling to Caalus. Perhaps he'd even be forced to take refuge at a settlement along the way. When the occasional traveler washed onto the shore of the Thumb, Iqi always warmed a pot of stew, invited the newcomer to share his lodge . . . and looked at him with a skeptical eye. Didn't the man know the weather? Were his canoeing skills deficient? Iqi didn't care to find himself in that position.

In truth, Iqi didn't relish traveling to Caalus at any time. It only dredged up the past. There, surrounded by an ever increasing population, he'd nevertheless felt isolated—not quite a noble, resented by the commoners and reduced to forcing a fake smile, always from a distance, for the woman he loved.

She loved him back. He knew that in a way that you can know something without having any understanding of it whatsoever. Here on the Thumb, Aesha's presence, though not physical, was far stronger than in Caalus, where she was wife of the cacique, more symbol than human. Her inexhaustible curiosity and deep reverence for the island were at his side as he made his frequent all-day journeys down the beach, around the base of the Thumb and back up the bayside mudflats. It was for her as well as for himself that he loved to linger on the final leg, observing the myriad of creatures that hopped, slithered, crawled, or simply lurked in the oozy muck.

Lately he'd been watching worms that lived in tubes. There were many: some artfully hidden, decorating themselves with bits of shell and seaweed, others as long as his arm, still others that revealed themselves with an eerie creaking sound. The flats, the walking trees, the channels, the beaches—all were alive with wondrous creatures. Aesha had worried about his solitude, but who could ask for better companions? Besides, the one-legged heron still trailed him everywhere, as if Iqi's shadow soul had taken the shape of the great blue bird.

More than two suns had passed since he'd come to the Thumb, flashing by in a wink of green, yet stretching, too, in a kind of timeless, unending arc that ringed back on itself to enclose him in a circle of contentment.

So why, then, on a bone-chilling morning when he could have been sipping bark tea was he instead packing his canoe and pointing it toward Caalus? The answer was simple: the shark. The bull shark's meat, though not the finest, would fill many bellies in this season that often brought hunger to the mass of commoners cramped onto Caalus. The fins would be boiled down for glue. The skin made excellent shagreen of a medium coarseness. Both were much sought after by Caalus's woodcarvers.

Even more prized were the shark's teeth. Iqi had carefully extracted and cleaned the jaw, leaving it whole. He'd present it to Carlos, who knew well how rare and valuable was a set of jaws from a healthy bull shark. The cacique would dispense some of the teeth to the craftsmen for cutting, drilling, and engraving tools. Most likely, too, he'd distribute some of the heavily serrated triangular upper teeth to the trading canoes to barter for spatterdock roots to make winter bread.

Undoubtedly, Carlos would turn the canines over to Stepana for weapons, maybe even a new war club for the great captain himself. An involuntary shiver ran up Iqi's back. There was a thought to make a cold day colder.

Iqi placed the heavy bundles of shark slabs slightly right of center in the canoe so that he could lean hard into his favored left-side paddling position. Then he set the jaws and skin carefully on top. Iqi knew that his catch would cause quite a stir. He would, of course, refrain from boasting. It wasn't difficult to get a shark to bite. Simply throw a line into moving current at night, with a fresh fish head attached, the bloodier the better. The challenge was in weaving a line that was strong, yet supple and of small diameter. Iqi preferred a four-ply agave-fiber twine that he attached to a buttonwood hook sharp enough to pierce the shark's tough mouth, but strong enough not to crack. He had led the fish in slowly, hand-over-hand, giving back line when necessary while avoiding slack that would allow the shark to succeed in its head-shaking attempts to escape.

No line, however strong, could pull a bull shark twice Iqi's weight onto the beach, though. To land it, he'd waded in shallow water, grabbed it by the tail, and hauled it onto the beach. Once you knew a shark's habits, it was not as difficult as it sounded. In shallow water, they invariably swam in rhythmic, back-and-forth motions. It was all a matter of patience and timing.

Patience and timing. Vital in more than one facet of life.

Iqi tucked another smaller wood bowl into the bundle, this one containing the shark's liver. The oil made an excellent base for paint and had the further advantage of repelling mosquitoes, so it was widely prized. Iqi remembered how welt-covered Ishkara's skin had become. He seemed to pay no attention to the biting bugs, yet scratched himself raw and bloody in his sleep. Iqi would present the shark's liver to the tirupo. He doubted Ishkara would keep it for himself, though. He'd save it to treat wounds and burns.

Taking a last walk to his shelter, Iqi secured the door against the wind, then returned to the shore. Though he was traveling south, he decided to paddle the short distance up the bay north to Open Mouth Pass and move to the open sea. He pushed the dugout forward with long, powerful strokes until the current of a strong outgoing tide took over, sweeping him into the pass. The choppy water rattled the craft like a child's noise-maker, but Iqi's high-bowed sea canoe rode the currents well, keeping his load secure and dry.

The sun, though low in the sky, had teased some of the bite from the air. It was a fine day, and Iqi paddled far out to sea. He loved the feeling of being a dot bobbing on the ocean. For all its vastness, though, the sea was seldom empty, and today was no exception. A split-tail soarer circled high overhead in search of bait, its crimson throat standing out against the cloudless sky. Flights of pelicans flew by low, riding the air currents effortlessly, swooping to touch a wing to water, then rising again. In the distance, a manta ray leapt far out of water and slapped down with a frothy splash. A dolphin surfaced close by, and Iqi drew his paddle through the water harder, trying to keep up. The dolphin swam with its head cocked sideways, smiling at him through the clear green water. Iqi's paddle dipped and pulled furiously. The dolphin glided alongside, then, with a flip of its tail, shot forward and disappeared.

With a following breeze, Iqi made excellent time surfing the swells. By mid-afternoon, he reached Tega Island and waved his paddle at the lookout high above in the sentry post. The man gestured and yelled something, but the wind took his words away. Iqi considered putting in to talk to the lookout. No. His grumbling belly reminded him that he had eaten no more than a handful of palmetto berries since morning.

The high hump of the temple mound came into view, then the broad plateau of the palace mound topped by the massive domed roof of the council hall and royal quarters. Closer in, Iqi began to see the mounds where the councilors and other nobility lived, lower in elevation but still towering above the commoners. These were the families that had perched their homes on generations of scrapings from their ancestors' plates, almost as if they'd eaten their way to the top. Iqi pinched his belly. Far too lean. Another reminder that he'd forever be a ground dweller.

Approaching the seawall with its row upon row of conch shells driven point-first into the sandy banks, Iqi heard a blast from the shell horn, too faint to distinguish what it signaled. He allowed himself a grin. Perhaps it announced his arrival. Adjusting his topknot, he tapped the shark bundles and sat up erect, feeling uncharacteristically keyed up. Iqi forced himself to slow his paddle, which wanted to race through the water. Stroke, feather, glide. There. Head up. Relax.

At either side of the mouth of the central canal, in the thatched shade-shelters that were favored gathering places, a cluster of people pointed and waved. Iqi held his paddle aloft and saluted. As he passed, though, the crowd ignored him. Instead, they kept talking in excited voices and pointing out to sea. Curious. Iqi kept paddling, discerning now numerous groups moving along the canal walkways. Unnoticed still, Iqi had to remind himself that the arrival of a stray paddler was an everyday occurrence in Caalus. He passed several side-channels and then another lined with partially constructed shelters that he was sure hadn't existed when he left the city. He imagined waking to the constant sound of post driving and found his head beginning to pound.

The farther into the interior Iqi paddled, the thicker grew the crowd. A solid line five or six wide filed around the edges of the wide water court at the central canal's terminus, filled the plaza, and continued up the ramp of the palace mound, straight for the council hall. So that was the meaning of the shell horn.

Iqi gulped, the knot of hunger in his belly turning instantly to fear. For what purpose were the citizens being called? Certainly not a celebration—the mood of the crowd before him was far too somber. He hurriedly moored his canoe to a pair of hitching posts and scrambled up the embankment onto the plaza, grabbing the arm of the first person he came to. "Who called the meeting?" he inquired. "What's happened?"

The man spoke only two words. "Wind ships."

Wind ships. For the second time today, Iqi's spine shook with an involuntary shiver.

Oddly, the thought of the Spaniards who steered them no longer summoned fear. There were Escalante, Barbu, and others. Each year, still, Spaniards were sacrificed. But wind ships? Iqi, like most others, had never witnessed more than the battered remains of shipwrecks that Stepana paraded before the people. Only Ishkara and a few of the elders had seen them on the water. But everyone young and old knew all too well of the colossal canoes that needed only the breezes to push them through the water, the floating cities that carried strange animals, thundering weapons, and ill spirits.

And now the wind ships were coming.

The council hall was jammed, abuzz with nervous whispering. Carlos sat on the ruler's bench centered on the platform that sprawled across the building's interior. Behind him, the nine councilors, each wearing the distinctive cloak of his clan, dabbed at their brows with bits of skirt moss. Stepana stood to the cacique's warrior arm side, heavy ear buttons pulling at his lobes. From the great captain's belt of polished tortoise shell hung a long bone knife. In his hand rested a massive atlatl nearly half again as tall as he, crowned by the carved woodpecker image of Aurr, oiled until it shone.

At Carlos's left crouched Ishkara, the fur of Otter draped over his shoulders and the mask of that animal, with its long, exaggerated whiskers, upon his face. Beyond the tirupo sat the women of the royal family, including two new wives that Iqi failed to recognize. Between Escuru, her belly swelled with child, and Piyaya, stocky and solid, sat Aesha, looking so slender she might have been mistaken for a child. From his place near the outside wall where he hoped the air might not be so suffocating, Iqi squinted to see that what hung between Aesha's breasts was the large crown conch shell she'd found on the Thumb. He touched that place on his own chest.

Carlos rose and rapped the ruler's staff three times, the wood-on-wood clatter resounding through the hall over the thrum of murmuring voices. He waited, then tapped three times more. The buzz lowered. He spoke slowly, deliberately. "My people, what you've heard is true. The wind ships have been spotted. You have nothing to fear. Listen now to your great captain."

Stepana rose, holding his atlatl high. "Here is what our lookouts tell us." He paused, his scowl quieting the last of the whispers. "Two wind ships have been spotted moving up the coast from the south. Our signal fires tell us they've passed Muspa and are skirting the great walking-tree maze. These are no merchant ships blown off course. The men on board carry weapons. They are warriors."

The great captain paused again, letting the rumble roll through the crowd. "There is, however, no danger. The ships are small, the warriors number less than a hundred. They're still a few days' travel away. We can capture them easily, take them prisoners or kill them. Or," Stepana wet his lips and blew loudly on his forearm, "perhaps we'll simply fart on them and blow them over, then collect their bounty of gold."

As Stepana returned to his place, the crowd erupted in cheers. Carlos stamped his staff sharply. "The people will use their ears, not their tongues. What say the gods? Let us hear from Otter Spirit."

At Carlos's prompt, Ishkara dropped to the ground and began to creep forward on his belly, using only his elbows to propel him. As he moved through the councilors, he raised his masked head and wiggled his huge whiskers. A few people tittered nervously. Passing the councilors, he tilted his head from side to side, attracted by some unseen object. Cautiously then, he wriggled ahead. Ishkara removed the otter skin from his shoulder and reached forward with the clawed hand, then retracted it. Again the mask wagged back and forth. Moving as if to turn a latch, he opened the invisible door and helped himself to the reward. Otter shifted to a sitting position and began to feed himself, making exaggerated munching sounds.

The spectators cheered as Ishkara returned to his spot beside Carlos.

Carlos tapped the staff once again. "Otter is a most clever animal, curious yet wary. He does not rush into danger, rather uses his wits. Is there anyone among us whose traps he has not raided? And so, Otter grows fat and lives an easy life.

"My people. We must prepare to do battle . . . with our wits. We will watch these wind ships carefully. We will not attack. If they approach, we will meet. We will talk, and we will listen. Let us remember, though, that the otter possesses sharp claws and teeth. Stepana's forces will be at the ready. If our wits fail us, our courage will not. The otter will defend its nest. Councilors, what say you?"

The councilors kept their silence. In the privacy of morning meetings, even in public council, they might speak their minds. Not today. They nodded their heads in unison.

Pedro Menéndez de Avilés, Adelantado and Governor of La Florida, stood at the bow of his ship, his sailor's legs anchoring his compact body more firmly at sea than ever they could on land. The brigantine was small, but its shallow draft was ideally suited for these treacherous waters. He was glad that he and Captain Diego de Maya, who steered a second brigantine, had outdistanced the five larger ships of his fleet. Progress would be much faster, and the ships could move in closer to land, the danger of running aground minimized.

The wind lifted a salt mist that teased the nostrils of Menéndez's elongated nose and stiffened the bristles of his curly beard. At forty-seven, he might be graying, but he always felt young when at sea. What a wondrous world the Lord had created, and how fortunate Menéndez was to be chosen as one of its discoverers. Why, then, did He test His children by populating this far corner of His world with such obstinate and ungodly beings? The influence of these Indians of Carlos with whom he sought contact reportedly extended clear across La Florida. Other tribes, proud and fierce in their own right, bowed low to them. And Carlos's Indians were known to enslave any Spaniards unfortunate enough to have landed accidentally among them. And to make human sacrifices.

Menéndez shuddered. His only son, Juan, had disappeared in the waters off La Florida two years ago and hadn't been heard from since.

If Menéndez wouldn't underestimate the Indians of Carlos, neither would he avoid them. King Felipe II himself had charged the Adelantado with a threefold purpose: to sow the seeds of colonization, to establish a military base for Spain, and to spread the Word of God. The Indians of Carlos lived in a highly strategic location near the mouth of the river said to bisect the peninsula of La Florida. Menéndez was determined, with an explorer's insatiable itch, to find it. And, if luck be with him, to find his son and other Spaniards lost at sea.

Thus far, God had surely smiled on his mission. He had established the fort of St. Augustine on the eastern coast of La Florida, defeated Jean Ribault and the French at Fort Caroline, and placed a third garrison among the Ais Indians farther south. It hadn't been easy. The march across the interior to surprise the Huguenots had been laborious, the battle bloody. There was simply not enough food to feed prisoners, and he'd been obliged to slaughter the Frenchmen to a man. Now conditions in the new settlements were so arduous that some of the colonizers were deserting, spreading the word of frontier adversity. Menéndez would execute them too, if need be. He would prevail. As he always prevailed.

After returning to Havana for provisions, Menéndez had sailed north, finding exactly what he'd been searching for: a deep-water passage between Las Tortugas and Los Mártires, the long string of islands running southwesterly from the tip of La Florida. Today he'd gone round a labyrinth of mangrove islands to the north. By tomorrow or the next day, he should reach the territory of Carlos.

Menéndez harbored no illusions. His men would surely be outnumbered. The impending meeting with Carlos would be another of the Lord's tests. So be it. The Adelantado thrived on them. Exactly such challenges had elevated the unremarkable one of twenty children of an ancient but modest Asturian family to command ships, men, and, above all, respect, not only from his underlings but from no less an authority than his King. Menéndez didn't intend to let Felipe down.

Iqi filed out of the council hall into a night that had already chilled the ground so it stung his feet as he made his way back to his canoe. Seeing the high silhouette of his cargo-laden dugout, he stopped in midstep. The shark. He'd completely forgotten. Well, it was cold enough that the slabs would keep until morning. But how to deliver the jaws and skin? He couldn't just knock on the cacique's bedroom door. He'd have to request an audience in the morning.

And the liver. The thought of approaching the temple alone and uninvited was only slightly less terrifying, especially given the tension of the evening. Yet Iqi felt a strong compulsion to deliver it. Before he could change his mind, he grabbed the package and set off, following the rows of torches that lit the path up the temple mound. Iqi was glad to see the glow of a coco plum seed candle in the sacred building. Good. That would be Ishkara.

When he peered into the outer chamber, though, it was not the tirupo's face the small flame illuminated, but that of Aesha. Her smile of recognition could have outshone the very sun.

"Were you at the council hall?" she asked. "I didn't see you."

"But I saw you." He pointed to her chest. "And the crown conch you wear."

"It reminds me of the island. It retains its strength and beauty, even when conditions are adverse."

He stepped closer to give her a quick embrace. "As do you." He whispered it.

She ushered him into the temple, closed the door, spoke in a low voice, too. "Come in, please. Ishkara is in the sanctuary. He spends much time there these days."

"It serves him well. His counsel was as engaging as it was wise."

"It's becoming such an effort. He grows older each day."

"But he moved about the hall so nimbly."

"An act. Even with the poultice of elderberries and firebush leaves I gave him, he'll hobble around for half a moon. I fear"—she dropped her voice farther yet, until it was barely audible—"I fear that when the wind ships arrive, his souls may depart."

"Is it true, then, that the wind ships are to land?"

"This new leader of theirs has done so on the mainland to the east. He leaves warriors to build settlements and guard them."

"But Stepana spoke of only a small force of men."

"They're only the first. There will be more." Aesha's hands went to her scalp, stroked her long black hair, causing a thick lock to fall over her left shoulder. Absently, but in a totally practiced manner, the hands separated the lock into three strands and began braiding them together. "There will always be more." She dropped the hair, pushed it back behind her ears. "But tell me—why have you come to Caalus?"

"I caught a bull shark. I brought the jaws for Carlos, and this"—he showed her the bowl, removed the lid—"is for Ishkara."

"Was it a large one? How did you catch it?"

Before Iqi could answer, though, Ishkara stepped out of the inner chamber. So sagging were his jowls, so wispy his faded hair that for a moment Iqi thought he had donned the mask of the pelican spirit. Even the tirupo's eyes looked like those of an aged pelican, milky and glazed.

"The gold, it whirls ever faster, and their gods speak so noisily they drown out the voices of our own. I cannot hear them."

Aesha dashed to his side. "My father, we have a visitor."

Ishkara blinked several times and squinted at Iqi. Finally, he smiled. "Forgive me. You hear the rantings of an old man."

Iqi pressed the bowl with the shark's liver into Ishkara's hands. "I've brought this for you. It's of a bull shark. And I have the meat, jaws, and skin as well."

"Your gift is much appreciated, Iqi. I fear there will be many wounds to treat in the coming days."

Aesha took Ishkara's hands in hers. "You speak often of fear these days."

"It's not the strangers' weapons I fear, nor even these dreaded wind ships of theirs. It is their gold and their gods. I've failed. I couldn't keep them away."

Aesha patted the wrinkled hands. "You've done all you can. Your counsel was wise tonight. Carlos accepted it."

"Bah. You know as well as I that tonight's performance was rehearsed. The decision was made earlier. For now, Carlos is proceeding cautiously. There's much pressure on him to attack, though. And he's becoming so erratic. He could change his mind in a bird's heartbeat."

"What can I do?" Iqi asked.

Ishkara looked away. "Something I'd never ask of you."

Iqi bowed his head low. "There is nothing I wouldn't do for you or Aesha."

"If that's true, then stay in Caalus. Stay as close to Carlos as you can. And to Stepana. Report to me what you hear. Calm heads must prevail."

"Then you've come to believe we can negotiate with the strangers, make friends of them?" Aesha asked.

"I believe nothing of the sort. But the gods seem to be saying we have to face these invaders. Beyond that, nothing is clear."

Aesha led Iqi outside. "I'd hoped you'd never have to return here. But I'm glad you have. The gods led you here. They have a purpose. As do you."

The sentry in the crow's nest shouted again. "There. To the east." Menéndez raced to the bow of the boat. Yes, it was definitely an Indian canoe approaching Captain de Maya's brigantine half a league ahead.

Menéndez quickly scanned the horizon. For the moment, he saw no others. Still, he sprang into action. "To your stations. Man the eighteen-pounders. Arquebuses at the ready. Oarsmen, double time. We must catch de Maya. And trim that sail." At times like these, no ship was fast enough.

Interminable minutes later, the single warrior stood before him. He was short, no taller than Menéndez. Strange, since these Indians were reputed to be of gigantic proportion. His long black hair was twisted around his head and bunched at the top, his face and chest painted red, indigo, and black. But for a belt and breechclout around his waist, the Indian was naked. For a moment, the two appraised each other, each perhaps recognizing the momentousness of the occasion. Then the Indian spoke . . . in Spanish! "Spaniards, brothers, Christians, you are quite welcome. God and Saint Mary told us you were coming. Thanks be to the Lord."

When Menéndez could unfreeze his lips, he managed to stammer, "I am Pedro Menéndez, Adelantado and Governor of La Florida. Who . . . who are you?"

"I am Hernando d'Escalante Fontaneda, son of García d'Escalante, loyal subject of the King of Spain."

"A Spaniard." Menéndez stared at the man again, unable to say more.

"Shipwrecked here in my youth, by my count seventeen long years ago, though I could not swear to it. Tell me, please, what year is it?"

"The Year of Our Lord 1566. Today is 13 February."

"1566. Thirteen February. Thirteen February." The man tossed the words on his tongue like exotic new tastes.

"And you have lived amongst these Indians ever since?"

The Indian who was not an Indian nodded.

Menéndez could not contain himself. "Tell me, are there others?"

Again, Escalante nodded. "Once, as many as two hundred. Now, regrettably few. I bring from them this letter." He withdrew from his belt a cross to which the letter was attached and handed both to the Adelantado. "We entreat you not to pass by without entering the harbor. Rescue us, Governor. Take us to the land of the Christians. We beg of you."

"I must ask. Do you have word of my son, Don Juan Menéndez?"

Escalante shook his head. "No word at all. I am sorry. But neither is he amongst those I know to have died."

Menéndez got upon his knees and held the cross aloft. "Let us pray together, then."

As they both knelt, the Adelantado stole a glance. The man prayed like a Christian and spoke like one. And his face, if one looked through the bizarre paint, had not the broad-nosed, rounded Indian look. Yet the whole of his appearance was so primitive, so alien, that Menéndez cringed. Could this have been the fate of his son? The Adelantado rose. "Let us find our Christian brothers. Can you show me how to safely navigate this channel?"

"With pleasure. You see before you Tega Island. It is the entrance to the Bay of Escampaba and the City of Caalus where lives the cacique Carlos. Your ship will easily pass through."

"Then join me at the bow, good Christian, and tell me all that you know of this Carlos and his Indians." To his men he shouted, "Bring this Spaniard some biscuits and honey and a nip of wine." Menéndez put his arm around the naked Spaniard.

And vowed not to trust him. Not yet. He would tell the Spaniard only that he carried gifts for the Indians, not the rest. Seventeen years with the savages. What would that do to a man?

"You see?" said Stepana to Carlos. "Escalante has followed my instructions exactly. He met with the Spaniards and led them to Hermit Crab Island. They can't possibly attack us by surprise in the night. It's too far away." Stepana watched the progress of Escalante's canoe back toward the harbor. "And now he returns. He did not, as you feared, run off into the arms of the strangers."

Carlos could not help but be impressed. "How were you so sure?"

"He is Calusa now. Besides, I promised him that to leave us would be to have the blood of every Spaniard in Escampaba upon his hands."

"Admirably done, Stepana. Rest well tonight, and tomorrow be at the ready. In the morning we will meet the strangers."

Stepana's hand caressed his bone dagger.

"I said at the ready. There will be no blood shed unless I order it."

✂ Eleven ✂

13 February 1566

Rescued.

Oh glorious day. Not even the Savior Himself would be more welcome. To have stood upon a Spanish ship, tasted Spanish biscuits, sipped Spanish wine, learned news of the King. Just to hear so many voices speak our lovely tongue. I wept openly.

And oh glorious night. The stars are out, the ones that will lead me home. Such a word, home. Would that I could leave tonight for Salamanca, the home I've never known. At least sleep with my brother Christians. But the Adelantado begged me to remain with the Indians, to open my ears, to relay any mischief they may have planned. This, as is my duty, I will do, but what cruel punishment to have to lie even one more night with my captors when my soul cries out, "Away."

I dare not tell Carlos my intentions. Let him think I'm loyal. I followed Stepana's instructions to the word, reported accurately the size of the Spanish force, the number of their guns. That gave nothing away—the Indian sentries had already counted them. Besides, they'll see for themselves soon enough. The Adelantado wishes to meet Carlos, to give him certain gifts. I will relay the words between them.

Then, I will leave. God willing, she'll come with me. She does not love Carlos. She is different from the rest. If I can take her away, I can save her. I've not told her yet. I pray I'll know when the time is right.

This will be the final page of my saga. Let me end it with the most joyful word to cross my lips in nearly twenty years.

Freedom.

Iqi and the three hundred archers in Carlos's guard followed the royal barge, beaching their crafts on the shore of Hermit Crab Island. How small the war canoes suddenly seemed, now as they stood a mere arrow's flight from the wind ships. The two Spanish vessels, moored one behind the other with the bow of the closest tethered to shore, were massive. Iqi had been prepared for that. What astounded him, though, was that a boat so large floated in so little water, even with a full load of men and equipment. Suddenly his breath caught as he saw the weapons, black and evil looking, long as a man, mounted on wooden carriages. Their gaping openings pointed straight at the clearing where the meeting was to take place.

Filing into the open field, bow held at the ready, Iqi felt the pulse pounding in his ears. He wished he were back on the flats. And yet, he'd promised Ishkara and Aesha. It was a stroke of good fortune to have presented the shark to Carlos the day before and to have been invited to stand with the guard on this momentous occasion.

The strangers had erected a platform in the still-deserted clearing. A single bench sat at the center. Iqi saw Carlos take his place upon it, with Stepana off one shoulder and Escalante the other. The nine councilors stood behind. Iqi and the guard backed them up.

At that moment, men began to file from the nearest wind ship, jumping to the ground without getting their foot coverings wet. There were perhaps thirty, and they moved in unison, like warriors, dressed alike in hard garments that encased them like seedpods. From their waists hung long metal knives, and in their arms they carried the heavy fire spitters known to kill from a great distance. Thin cords attached to the weapons burned with small, controlled flames that could mean only one thing: the weapons were at the ready. Iqi clutched his bow with sweaty palms. It felt at once like a child's toy, yet heavy, too heavy to lift.

The Spanish warriors marched to the opposite side of the platform and stood stiffly in a straight line facing the Calusa, their expressions grim behind hair-covered cheeks. Iqi stared back unblinking, since to drop his gaze would be a sign of weakness, until his attention, along with everyone else's, was wrested away as there emerged from the wind ship a final man. Like the other strangers, he was small in stature with a face so full of hair it made his head look tiny. He had a long, thin nose and dark, intense eyes set far apart that darted between his warriors and the Calusa, appraising the situation. He too wore the stiff garments, beneath which were fancy, ruffled cloths. Though he carried no fire spitter, his polished long knife glittered in the morning sun. He walked past his warriors with short, assured strides, mounted the platform, and sat beside Carlos. This must be the man called Adelantado.

For a long moment there was silence. Iqi grasped his bow more tightly, and he could see the Spanish warriors do the same with their weapons. Then, Carlos rose from the bench, knelt in front of the Spanish leader, and extended his hands, palm up.

Iqi gasped. The cacique was showing subservience to the Spaniard. And the Spaniard had apparently been tutored, for he extended his hands, palm down, to meet Carlos's. The cacique gave an order, and Stepana and the councilors, too, knelt before the Adelantado.

Carlos waited patiently for all to finish before he spoke. "Welcome. For many suns my people have awaited this meeting."

Escalante repeated the words in the Spaniards' tongue. The Adelantado rose and gestured to several men behind him, who approached the platform and deposited an array of gifts. First were garments. The Spanish leader showed them to Carlos one by one, beckoning the cacique to put them on: first, a covering of ruffled cloth similar to the Adelantado's for his chest, then a long breechclout of fine material that descended past his knees. Over both of these went another garment, puffy and colorful, covering his trunk and thighs. Last, the Adelantado placed a stiff-edged hat upon the cacique's head.

When Carlos turned full around, his motions wooden and awkward as he showed off the bulky garments, Iqi, along with many of the others, couldn't help but laugh, though what came out were nervous bird titters.

The Adelantado said something to Escalante, who in turn spoke to Carlos. "Captain General Menéndez wishes me to tell you how handsome you look. He has clothing, too, for your great captain, your councilors and wives. He has also brought from Spain"—Escalante pointed to a tray held by one of the Spanish warriors—"a modest offering of our biscuits and honey."

Carlos sampled the food and smacked his lips loudly, showing that he was well satisfied. Stepana and the councilors quickly emptied the tray. Carlos then tapped the ruler's staff, and a bar of silver was brought out. He presented the bar to the Adelantado, who felt its heaviness and nodded.

"More," Carlos said through Escalante. "Now I will eat more."

"I have not food enough for so many people as are gathered here," the Spanish leader replied. "It would be my very great honor to invite you to my brigantine. If you and your principal men will come aboard, I will feed them and give them many things for themselves and their wives." Thereupon, the Spanish leader strode toward his ship. His warriors followed.

The cacique would show no hesitation. He followed the Spaniards at a near-run. Iqi and the others scrambled behind.

As Carlos climbed aboard the Spaniard's vessel, he turned to wave to his counselors and warriors. The cacique was elated. Not even Caalus himself had set foot upon a wind ship. It was . . . solid, more like a house of wood than a canoe. He strode the length of it, his bare feet thumping on the hard wood planks. While much of what was on board was unfamiliar, Carlos took note of how orderly it all was, down to the neat coils of unimaginably thick lines. Organization meant discipline. It was clear that the Spanish leader held tight control over his warriors.

After Stepana, the councilors and perhaps another ten nobles had boarded, the Adelantado gave a command, and the lines tethering the wind ship to shore were cast off. Carlos's eyes narrowed.

"Do not be alarmed," Escalante translated. "This is the smallest of the Adelantado's ships. It can carry but few men, and we must put out to sea lest we sink under the weight of all your warriors. With your permission, the Adelantado will set sail."

Carlos waved off the rest of his archers who were crowding toward the wind ship. "I go on the wind," he told them, "as has no Calusa before me." The cacique watched as two rows of men seated upon benches pulled in unison on long paddles set in swiveling holders and poked through holes in the ship's sides. Carlos had to chuckle. They sat backwards. He turned to Stepana and the others. "These strangers must know much about where they have been and little about where they're going." Then, to Escalante, "Tell the Adelantado I am greatly enjoying his demonstration."

The wind ship was well off from shore now. At the Spanish leader's command, two cloths were raised on the long poles that reached high toward the sky. The cloths billowed and flapped until the breeze caught them, then filled with air. The ship's rate of speed increased greatly, even as it moved crosswise to the wind. Extraordinary.

As the ship cut through the bay's waters, the Spaniards served the Calusa more of the sweet treats, as well as a drink that tasted a bit like the juice of the sea grape. Carlos's head felt light. When the food and drink had been exhausted, Carlos turned to Escalante. "Tell the Adelantado that I am much impressed. Now, I will leave."

At that instant, two Spanish warriors rose to take hold of the cacique as another pointed a weapon at his heart. Simultaneously, Spanish warriors took hold of each of Carlos's party. As Carlos began to struggle, the men held him tighter. The Adelantado quickly interceded, bowing deeply to Carlos and instructing his men to let the cacique go. "I regret having to treat you so, for I desire to be your friend and brother," the Spanish leader said through Escalante. "However, the King of Spain, my Master, has sent me for the Christian men and women whom you now hold prisoners. I request that you release them. In return, I wish to bestow upon you many gifts."

"And if I refuse?"

"Then I shall have you killed."

Stepana broke free from his captor and reached for his bone knife. Carlos quickly called to him. "Do not struggle."

"You would give up the captives without even a fight? You show your weakness."

Carlos looked upon Escalante, standing next to the Spanish leader. "They're of no consequence to me. Let them go."

Escalante struggled mightily not to show the potent mixture of emotions coursing through him. Of no consequence? After all these years?

Carlos waited in silence while a party went to shore to fetch the Spaniards who now resided in Caalus. He kept his face impassive as inside he smoldered, his belly burning slowly, like the cords on the Spaniards' fire spitters. It would be so easy to spring up, to overcome the Spanish warrior closest to him. Or three or four or them. Not all, though. For the moment Carlos was too greatly outnumbered. He stayed put, glaring at the back of the Adelantado, who had moved away to confer with his warriors and was deliberately ignoring the cacique. With a sidelong glance, Carlos took in Stepana's smug expression. The great captain was enjoying this.

It was a short time and an eternity later that the party returned with five women and three men. The Adelantado, once again standing before

Carlos, thanked the cacique profusely and gave him many gifts, acting as if there had never been anything but the greatest friendship between them. Then Menéndez told the cacique that he was welcome to leave.

"Tomorrow you will come to my village," Carlos said evenly. You will meet my wives. They will thank you."

The Spanish leader immediately agreed.

Carlos departed to a waiting canoe, head held high even as his insides churned with a vile and seething anger.

Escalante followed the councilors and others into the Calusa canoes. Taking the last step from the ship's ladder was torture. But Aesha was not here, the time was not yet. Soon, he prayed. Very soon.

The Adelantado sniffed the damp air heavy with the scent of clam and fish as he watched the sun rise colorless behind a shadowy curtain of fog. He heard the cadenced chanting, accompanied by the rhythmic plop and splash of paddles, well before he saw the canoes, a dozen or more. His men heard, too, and scrambled for their weapons, but Menéndez warned them not to fire. A singing war party? Not likely.

As the canoes came close, Menéndez' hunch was confirmed. The Indians carried no weapons, only the fronds of palm trees. The chief himself sat at the bow of the lead canoe with the Christian Indian Escalante behind him. "The cacique Carlos has sent his canoes for you, Adelantado." Escalante said. "You and your men are to be carried upon the backs of his subjects. Carlos wants you to know that this is a great honor he bestows upon you." Escalante smiled and pointed toward the bay. Speaking in an exaggerated, singsong voice, he added, "He plans to ambush you, for hidden in the mangroves are many warriors."

So the interpreter was perhaps still a loyal Spaniard? Menéndez bowed and doffed his hat at Carlos. "Tell the chief that I thank him for his courtesy. However, I cannot accept his offer, for to carry us upon their backs is to treat us as gods, and that would make false Christians out of us. And I thank you, good sir, for informing me of this treachery."

To soften what he knew must be an insult to the chief, Menéndez ordered his brigantine anchored closer to the Indian town. Sounding two bugles and displaying flags, he signaled for the Indians to come board his ship.

But not a single Indian showed.

"The cat and mouse game continues?" asked Captain Diego de Maya.

"Cat and cat," Menéndez responded. "This Carlos is no mouse."

Having seen an Indian force of around three hundred, undoubtedly a small fraction of its total number, Menéndez decided that reinforcements would be prudent. The breeze had pushed away the fog now, and he sailed back to sea in search of his ships. Not finding any, he decided to make for a good deepwater harbor fifty leagues distant, where the rescued Christians had informed him lived three more Spanish captives.

The captives had either been killed or moved. Three days later, when Menéndez returned to the harbor of Carlos, he found that his five vessels had arrived. The men on board were jubilant. Captain Estéban de las Alas had led a hundred soldiers to the shores of the Indians' village. Seeing all the ships and soldiers, the Indians had sent canoes, dozens of them, to meet the Spaniards. There was no bloodshed, though. The soldiers dangled baubles and trinkets. The Indians understood their intention and returned with gold and silver.

Estéban was ebullient. "These Indians have no concept of the value of our gold. For a mere playing card, an ace of gold, I obtained a nugget worth at least seventy ducats. And for a pair of scissors, half a bar of silver, one hundred ducats at minimum."

Carlos knew not the value of gold? Fools. Menéndez knew a trap when he saw one. The Indian chief was dangling treasure in front of them, turning their heads, ruining their discipline. And it had worked. Menéndez quickly forbade his soldiers from returning to the village. But douse their celebration? You may as well milk a billy goat into a bottomless bucket. Late into the night they reveled, eyes glazed with drink, gambling away their newfound wealth with their latest form of entertainment: lice races. Imagine that—grown men crowding around a circle into which each has flicked his personal louse, wagering on whose would reach the edge first.

Menéndez himself kept watch through the night.

The next day Carlos came to sea once again, accompanied only by Escalante and a mere half dozen Indians. "Seize him," whispered Estéban.

"He's already freed the Christians in his hold," a terse Menéndez answered.

Estéban's voice was urgent. "This time we'll have his riches. To be set free, the chief will surely forfeit his entire chest of gold."

"And we ourselves will forfeit forever, for this act of knavery, the chance to earn the confidence of his people. Or ever to make them Christians."

"Adelantado," Estéban pleaded, "you are much in debt in both Spain and Havana. Have you such a short memory? And have you forgotten this Indian's intended treachery?"

"Forgotten? No. But I'll not succeed in conquering these Indians by force. There are too many, and they're of a sophistication I've not seen elsewhere. Now be still. This man is brave. He knows the danger, and yet he approaches. I have no advantage here." Menéndez bowed and extended his ladder. "Please, good Christian Escalante, welcome the chief again to my ship."

"Carlos wishes to invite you to his village," Escalante interpreted. "Five days hence, there is to be a great ceremony, a wedding."

"Another trap?"

"I do not think so."

Menéndez turned to Carlos. "I desire only friendship. I gratefully accept."

Carlos smiled broadly. "The bride is to be Piyaya, my older sister, whom I love very much. For many suns I've not allowed her to marry, not until I found a man of stature worthy of her. Now that such a man has appeared, I will pledge Piyaya to him and so take him as my elder brother."

"And who is the man so fortunate as to marry the sister of the paramount chief?"

"You, Adelantado. You will marry Piyaya."

No one could manage the preparations better than Carlos. Messengers were sent summoning all of influence to Caalus for the grand event. Fishermen threw their nets night and day; divers braved the cold waters to descend for the stone crabs that hid in the depths; women, children, and even elders dispersed far into the bay to hunt for oysters and clams. The girls' choruses practiced incessantly.

And all of Caalus, all of Escampaba, was chattering. Carlos's own sister married to the leader of the Spaniards? Would it work? Didn't the strangers know that marriages were arranged for Carlos's advantage? Could he really put the Spanish under his grip the way he had so many others? Would they reveal the secrets of their marvelous inventions? Would the Calusa learn to build the wind ships?

Many feared a trap. The five new wind ships were so monstrous they made the original two look like toy canoes. What terrible weapons and horrific beasts were hidden inside? Every Calusa chief and headman would be present. The Spaniards would seize the opportunity and turn loose their fire spitters, their gaping thunder mouths, and their killer dogs.

No, others said, it is Stepana who will attack. How many Spanish warriors could there be, five hundred? We will send five times that number at them.

All of you are wrong, claimed still others. We will use our wits, as our cacique has advised. At the banquet, we'll serve the strangers the meat of the sand tortoise that has eaten the poison mushroom. Then we will watch them die the gruesome, retching death.

But from the cacique came the directive: the Adelantado was to be his brother. He was to be welcomed.

She'd bathed and washed her hair. As Aesha opened the door to her quarters, the smell of her, steamy and fresh, nearly sent Escalante reeling. She blinked, raised those thin, expressive eyebrows. "Come in. What brings you here?"

"I . . ." he cleared his throat, "I wanted to inform you of what to expect from the Spaniards tonight."

"I'll be but a bystander, though. This is to be Piyaya's night."

"The Adelantado has gifts for both his bride and for the chief's wife. He instructed me to write words in your tongue for both of you. I've given them to him."

Aesha ran her fingers along the necklace of gold beads that Carlos had given her for the occasion. She shivered. It felt as cold as the disk Stepana had pressed upon her so many suns ago—the one, she remembered, she'd given to Escalante.

"I have it still," he said.

"You knew what I was thinking."

"Does that surprise you? We've grown from childhood to adulthood together." He paused, looked at her, then blurted it out. "Tomorrow I leave Caalus forever. Come with me. With us. We sail for Havana. There are priests there, holy men who can teach you the Gospels, make you a Christian."

"Tomorrow?" she stammered. "Forever?"

"I'm a Spaniard who has never seen Spain. I must. And you must see it, too. Have you not admired us these many years, our possessions, our knowledge? Imagine great buildings of stone no wind can ever touch. Imagine soft beds, a wardrobe filled with gowns. And our churches—

you'll stand dazzled in their light, blessed at last to be in the presence of the true God. I can take you there. All you have to do is be on board tomorrow."

Now the yellow-brown eyes were looking past him, flames of fancy and fervor trying to burn through a film of doubt and worry. Escalante saw the struggle in her, kept pouring the words out, fueling the fire.

"What greater good can you do for your people than to learn our ways? You can return whenever you want. I promise it. Surely you understand this: the Adelantado is here to stay. He becomes your brother tonight." Lightly, with thumb and two fingers, Escalante touched her chin. "Listen well to the words he reads. They bespeak your beauty."

Aesha blinked, forced herself to focus. She took his calloused hand in both of hers. "I—I must go now to help Piyaya prepare. I thank you for your visit." She led him to the door. "I shall see you tonight."

Escalante stopped at the threshold. "Remember," he said, "the words that come from the Adelantado's lips won't be his. They'll be mine."

As the backwards paddlers moved through the central canal, strange music filled the air. Iqi, stationed amongst a group of archers at the foot of the water court, made out three distinct sounds. The first was the familiar beat of drums, good deer hides stretched tight and struck with wooden mallets. The second resembled the conch horn, except that the notes rang with a brash clarity. The third reminded of the bone flute, high-pitched and airy. Put the three together, though, and the combination of them was utterly foreign. The strangers' music came not from the sea or rain or birdsong. It came from somewhere else. Iqi listened intently. The notes weren't sinister. Just different.

Save for the sound of the Spaniards' music, it was eerily quiet. The hordes of onlookers lining the canal hardly dared to breathe, creating the kind of hushed silence that only a massive crowd can make. Men clutched their women, and mothers gripped their children tight, lest they try to break loose and run. As the Spaniards arrived at the water court and filed out of their wide canoes, Iqi quickly counted heads. More than two hundred. Most carried weapons, the small attached cords once again lit.

They marched in step up the ramp to the council hall, led by the Adelantado and a man who carried a pole topped with a square of cloth, red and white with the likeness of a great panther-like beast, the same one that flew high above the wind ships. When the Spaniards reached the plateau, they stopped. The Adelantado shouted an order, and his warriors dispersed to circle the building, positioning themselves in small groups opposite the windows. Then the leader and about twenty others went inside.

Menéndez had seen the great round building from afar. Up close, he couldn't help but be impressed. Notwithstanding their crude tools and methods, the Indians had produced a palace of grand proportions, with a high domed roof he estimated at seventy feet tall. Entering, Menéndez's eyes grew large. There must be a thousand Indians inside this room alone and easily that number outside, all within earshot of their chief and warrior captain. Despite their superior weapons, the soldiers he had posted were hopelessly outnumbered. The Adelantado made his usual quick decision. This was no time for timidity.

Menéndez strode confidently toward Carlos and his wife, who were seated on the platform in the middle of the packed room. Carlos's face and chest were, as before, covered in black paint, and many necklaces and bracelets adorned his body. Menéndez was surprised to see that the chief's wife looked far older and that she was a plain-looking woman shaped like a sack of flour.

As the Spanish leader came near, Carlos rose from his bench and beckoned him to sit. Then Carlos repeated the palm-up greeting ceremony. The Adelantado tried to look into the eyes of the chief who knelt before him, but the man held them low. His wife performed the same ritual, as did the other Indians on the central platform. Menéndez recognized many of the men from the encounter on his brigantine. The women must be the chief's other wives. Multiple wives. Such ignorance and shame.

The chief tapped a wooden baton then, and there appeared in the windows, ducking under the line of Menéndez' soldiers, row upon row of brown-skinned girlish faces. At a signal from Carlos, they began to sing in high-pitched voices, the sounds somehow both sweet and guttural. As they did so, the Indians on the platform commenced to dance, not with each other but in a single mass, hopping first on one leg then the other, arms flying, heads snapping to and fro. Menéndez was astounded at the age of some of the dancers. Craggy faces displaying toothless grins, they must have been ninety or a hundred years old.

Turning his attention to the music, for he was a great lover of that medium, Menéndez found that the girls sang with great zeal and orderliness. From their budding figures—these girls, like the rest of the heathens, were naked from the waist up—he estimated their ages ranged from ten to fifteen years. In just one of the five groups, he counted exactly one hundred heads. Half sang at a time, then the other half, the voices filling the huge room.

Carlos addressed Menéndez through Escalante. "My people have prepared what the sea gives us. Now, we will eat."

"If it pleases the paramount chief, allow me first to speak some words in your own tongue."

Carlos looked most satisfied.

Menéndez pulled Escalante's paper from his pocket. "Cacique," he read, "It is my privilege and pleasure to sit beside he who commands the mightiest of all the tribes of La Florida. From the cacique of my own people, whom we hold in great reverence, I bring also greetings and salutations. Yours is a reputation of courage and wisdom, and I have traveled many long days to meet such a great and storied leader. I am humbled to be invited into your home and honored to be your guest."

Menéndez paused, taking in the startled expressions of both audience and those on the platform, many of whom were pointing excitedly at the lines from which he was reading, as if they thought the paper itself were speaking. He turned now to the chief's homely wife. This was the hard part. Yet Escalante had assured him the words were perfect. Menéndez supposed he shouldn't be surprised that the Indians' estimation of beauty was as flawed as their religion. He took a deep breath and continued. "And you are the loveliest light in this exotic land. Your beauty beams like the anchor star itself, shining in splendor, winking in mystery, standing firm as all else turns 'round you. Yours is the smile that guides the way. Yours is a beauty for now and forever. I am doubly honored to meet not only the cacique but his wife as well."

Once again, the Adelantado paused, and once again he saw astonished faces, though this time mixed with a different emotion. Confusion? Dismay? Why? He looked to Escalante suspiciously as Carlos mumbled something to the interpreter.

"Adelantado, forgive me. The cacique wishes to say that he is pleased you are so taken with the beauty of our women. This is, however, not his wife to whom you speak. Rather, it is his sister Piyaya, your betrothed."

Menéndez shot a dart of accusation at Escalante for not having stopped him. But the Adelantado would have to deal with him later, for his irritation at the interpreter was already giving way to a far more dire thought: this near-naked, oversized, dark-skinned woman his wife? Menéndez crossed himself and said a quick prayer. *Lord and San Antón, who have guided me on my mission, please help your humble servant. I will never sin against the church by taking a second wife. I must, however, win over these Indians peaceably. Please know I take these actions in the name of Jesus.*

He rose and took the woman by the hand. If the interpreter were tricking him again, Menéndez would personally break each finger of his writing hand one by one. And slowly. He read from Escalante's other paper and prayed that the words were as he intended, more subdued and formal, though complimentary nonetheless. The cacique's sister looked on silently, her broad face frozen, expressionless, revealing nothing.

At least the crowd didn't react this time. Menéndez hoped he was back on course. Turning to Escalante, he ordered, "Ask the chief to bring forth his principal wife, whom you yourself have told me is very beautiful."

When Aesha stepped from the back of the platform, Menéndez knew Escalante hadn't lied. She was as tall as the chief's sister, but slender and fine-featured, with thin nose and lips and quick yellow-brown eyes that appraised him even as he was assessing her. She wore at her throat a collar of large pearls and stones. A necklace of gold beads hung over her shapely bare breasts. Menéndez forced himself to ignore her nakedness, looking instead into her eyes. She stared unflinchingly back, not in defiance, but with a composure that belied her apparent youthfulness.

Menéndez took her long fingers into his hands and seated her between Chief Carlos and his sister. He then spoke again the words written on the first paper, and saw her beauty amplified a dozen times as her lips turned up in a modest smile.

Carlos was perturbed. This occasion was to be Piyaya's, not Aesha's. "Return to the back of the platform," he hissed at her.

Menéndez recognized the chief's tone, if not his words. Through the interpreter, he said, "Please, allow your wife to stay. I have brought gifts for her as well as for your sister." The Adelantado then took from Captain Diego a large box and pulled from it two green chemises. He gave the larger to the chief's sister, who had to struggle to pull it down over her wide hips. Slipping into hers, Carlos's wife looked stunning, the shift clinging loosely to her subtle curves. Then Menéndez gave the women beads, scissors, knives, bells, and mirrors. When the two took stock of themselves in the mirrors, the crowd of Indians surrounding the platform, who had heretofore been quite silent, cheered and laughed.

Then Menéndez gave Carlos another doublet, two hatchets, and two machetes, these last aimed at showing the chief he could be entrusted with what might be considered weapons. Menéndez let his eyes take in the entire scene: his men stationed behind the girl's chorus, the vast number of Indians. If trouble broke out, the few hatchets and machetes would make precious little difference. Continuing, he passed trinkets to the others on the platform. As he did so, Menéndez instructed Escalante to explain that all of these were simply gifts, that he expected nothing in return.

Carlos called for the food to be brought in. He had spared no effort. The oysters came raw, steamed, and roasted. The fishermen's catch, both roasted and stewed, included whiting, redfish, sheepshead, snapper, and three different varieties of groupers, including two giants that weighed as much as three men. Baskets followed of shrimp, blue crab, scallops, and clams, and there were stone crab claws, too, some as big as a man's hand. It was a feast no occasion had ever surpassed, made all the more spectacular because Carlos had pulled it off in the season of cold and hunger.

Menéndez was determined not to be outdone. His men produced a table and four chairs, complete with tablecloth, napkins and four place settings of china. He sat at the table with Carlos and his wife and sister, augmenting the Indians' food with offerings of his own: biscuits and molasses, wine, sweetmeats, and quince preserves. Menéndez ordered the balance of the hundredweight of biscuit distributed to Carlos's principal men and women.

The audience had disbursed now, congregating around half-log tables laden with more food. They ate noisily, sucking and smacking, tossing their shells on the ground. They drank just as loudly, slurping from shell cups a hot liquid ladled from a communal bowl. Outside, the girls' voices continued. Menéndez closed his eyes and heard the sound of revelry that could have come from a Christmas or Easter banquet, not from this alien scene.

"With your permission, Cacique, I'll offer up some of our music," he said through Escalante, whereupon Carlos waved toward the windows, immediately silencing the chorus. The chief stamped his heavy rod on the wood platform, beckoning the crowd to a semblance of quiet. Then Menéndez ordered the drummers, fifers, and buglers to commence, along with a harp, a guitar, and a psaltery. Menéndez saw the Indians take note of the stringed instruments. Good. It was crucial to impress at every turn. Now, for the icing. Five of his men, fine singers all, sang along.

The Adelantado had one more surprise. Up to the platform hopped Dwizel. The tiny dwarf he had brought all the way from Spain purely for the purpose of entertainment was in his element. Dressed in bright blue, yellow and orange, he flung his diminutive body in time with the music, leaping and pirouetting, landing softly on his stockinged feet. The room exploded with laughter and cheering. Soon the Indians were dancing, too.

Menéndez helped himself to another oyster and sipped a cup of the Indians' liquid that had been put in front of him. Some kind of tea. A touch bitter but not unpleasant.

Beside him, Carlos ate like a starving peasant, huddled over his plate, popping his lips, taking long slurping sips of wine with a loud "heh-emm." Menéndez made sure both plate and glass were constantly refilled. Dwizel danced on.

Menéndez surveyed the room. The event was going rather well, the Indians obviously enjoying themselves. Then his eyes stopped as he saw one of the heathens emptying his stomach out one of the open windows. Others around the poor retching wretch roared in laughter and patted his back. Strange custom. A vivid reminder of the Indians' lack of civilization.

When Carlos finally pushed back from the table, he rubbed his jelly-smeared lips with the back of his hand, then licked them clean. Menéndez called up Escalante. "Tell the chief that I have eaten enough for three days, and that now I must go and rest."

"I've prepared a room for you," replied Carlos, "Piyaya awaits her new husband."

Menéndez was surprised to find the sister's chair empty. How had she managed to slip away unnoticed? "Thank you. However, being a sailor, I must take my sleep on my ship."

Carlos's eyes narrowed, and he spoke in a serious tone to the interpreter. "My beloved sister I give you as wife. Do you hold her in so little regard? You embarrass and insult her . . . and me."

Menéndez spoke just as firmly. "Christian men cannot sleep with women who are not Christians."

There was a tense silence, the two men locking eyes. Then Carlos's expression brightened. "You need not worry. She is already Christian."

Menéndez asked Escalante to translate again.

"I have taken you, a Christian, for my elder brother. Therefore, I am Christian, and so too is Piyaya."

Menéndez crossed himself again. *Lord and San Antón, grant me patience. These Indians are as children.* "In order to become a Christian, you must learn many things. You must know of the wisdom and the power and the goodness of the Lord our God. You must worship Him alone, and do all that He commands. You must pray and give thanks and bless Him all the rest of your days. Do so, and you will be rewarded by going to heaven, where you will remain always, never dying."

One of the old men on the platform leaned over to whisper to Carlos. "This is the cacique's father," explained Escalante. "He wants you to describe your heaven."

"Gladly." Then, nodding to the old Indian: "Heaven is the land where we live forever in the loving arms of our Lord. Our families are there, our wives, children, brothers and friends, and we are always joyful, singing and laughing. But"—Menéndez paused—how would he explain this to a child? "But if you do not worship the one true God, you serve only the Evil One, the Devil, who is like a very warlike and deceitful chief;

and when you die you will go to him, and be forever weeping and cold. Or hot. Sometimes burning hot. But never will you be happy in that other place."

Carlos rose then, holding his still spotless napkin in his hands. "This cloth is very fine. So, too, your table, your food, your music and your dancing man-child. I wish to learn much from you. You will begin by bringing my sister with you. You will teach her your ways. Stepana will take you to her. That is all. I have spoken."

Before Menéndez could respond, Carlos marched from the room. Menéndez allowed himself to be led by the enormous painted Indian outside and around the building to a room on its far side, where the chief's sister waited, a small band of Indians clustered around her. The green chemise had come off. Menéndez gestured for the entire entourage to come with him, hoping beyond hope for safety in numbers.

She hadn't glanced at him when Menéndez read the words. Following Carlos's and the Adelantado's departure, Aesha had stayed at the table, removed from the chaotic clamor of the tribal feast, stroking the table-cloth, turning the plate round and round in her hands. Escalante understood. She was weighing his offer. He did not disturb her. But that didn't stop him from watching.

Menéndez had had to excuse himself, the sudden onset of nausea sending him racing from her room. He'd reached the bushes just in time, then fled from the shouting and cheering, this time directed at him, to his brigantine. On deck, the Adelantado's head always cleared. Tonight was different, though. A windless evening, yet it felt as if he were being battered by twenty-foot swells.

"You must go through with it," advised Captain Estéban. "Only then will the Indians trust us."

"I cannot. It is an abomination before the Lord."

"The Lord knows this marriage is not sincere. He knows your true purpose, to spread His faith to the heathen."

"If you want to make believers of them," suggested Captain Diego, "let them hear our guns."

"No. I'll not attack. But there must be another solution. Leave me now."

When his captains had departed, Menéndez gazed at the night sky, that vast space ever a source of both wonder and comfort, so predictable and yet so mysterious. He thought of Ana María waiting at home. His distant cousin turned mate, once a charmer herself, had long since accepted Pedro's lifelong love affair with the sea. But he'd remained faithful to her always. The visits to whores in ports of call were nothing, mere releases that no man of the oceans could avoid. The Lord hadn't struck him down for those. Would this be so different? Let the Indians term this union whatever they wanted. There'd been no ceremony before an altar. He'd spoken no vow. Estéban was right. There was no other way out.

He called back his captains. "I will take part in the masquerade. The Lord will understand. Look at the woman. Would I actually choose her over my Ana María?"

Both captains held serious expressions. This was no time for manly joking.

"First, though," the Adelantado continued, "this woman will be properly baptized . . . and clothed."

Thank the Lord for the Christian women he'd rescued. They bathed and dressed the Indian woman, and she was baptized that very night, given the name Doña Antonia. Menéndez ordered erected on the plaza several tents and returned there with his new "wife." The music and merriment lasted long into the night. At Menéndez's request, many of his soldiers danced with Antonia and complimented her on her beauty. To her credit, she accepted the flattery, translated by Escalante, with quiet dignity.

In the wee morning hours, Menéndez took Antonia to his bed and did what he had to.

"My sister is pleased this morning," said Carlos as he boarded the ship. "So I am pleased, too."

It was just the opportunity Menéndez had hoped for. "We must give thanks to the Lord," he said, "for it is to Him and Him alone that all thanks are due." With that, Menéndez knelt before the large cross he had ordered constructed and kissed it. Doña Antonia, as he had instructed, did likewise, her attendants following.

Menéndez addressed Carlos: "You wish to learn our ways? The praise of our Lord Jesus Christ must come first."

Carlos conferred back and forth with Escalante for several minutes. "I do not understand. This is an idol you worship, my brother."

"No." As simply as he could, Menéndez explained the story of Jesus. "And this cross represents the one upon which he died and thence rose. So, you see, it is not an idol at all."

Carlos spoke rapidly to Escalante, his utterances punctuated with the rising tones of questions. Escalante translated. "Another god, this one named Jesus? He asks why you profess to worship a single god when in fact you bow to two, not one."

Menéndez sighed. There was much work to be done here. "No, one God, now and forever, but two representations. Three, actually. The Holy Trinity: the Father, the Son, and the Holy Ghost." He crossed himself.

"I've seen Escalante make that motion," Carlos said. "Three gods. Yes. Three is a sacred number. Three souls and three gods: Sipi, Nao, and Aurr."

Menéndez knew there was no point in further discussion. He held the cross before Carlos. Carlos knelt and, ever so briefly, let his lips brush against it.

"I must depart now for Havana," Menéndez said. "I cannot stay longer, for my supplies have dwindled to naught. I'll take Antonia with me, as well as any attendants she desires. I leave you this cross, which you must erect on your island and go to every morning and worship before. It must be guarded as if it is your most valuable treasure, for in truth it is."

The chief promised he would do so. Menéndez did not believe it for a minute, but he pushed on. "And you must destroy your other idols, for they are false ones and are an insult to the Lord."

This time Carlos shook his head. "I cannot do so," he said, "until Piyaya and the others return. If, after learning from your wise ones, they tell me to do it, then and only then will it be done."

28 February 1566

I did not believe that ever again I'd set pen to paper in this foreign land, and yet here I write anew, as if my rescuers had never come. Pitiless fate has ensnared me in her trap, left me to suffer her unending cruel joke. Or have I a higher purpose here? I pray for an answer as the cards fall in an endless game of chance whose wager is my very life.

I went to the Captain General's ship to converse with the seven Christians still on board and to wait for her, for I'd convinced myself to have faith in her affirmative decision. We couldn't fathom that we were actually leaving any more than we could grasp that two of our kind—women both—had chosen to stay behind with their Indian husbands and children. Piyaya arrived, and with her three of the councilors and four noble women. The Captain General spoke to us all, telling us that we were to depart for Havana, where the Indians would be delivered to Juan de Ynistrosa, the Adelantado's deputy for the affairs of La Florida, there to be treated as royalty and indoctrinated into the Christian religion. Captain General Menéndez said that he would return in three or four months to take the Indians back to Caalus.

When Piyaya, whom the Captain General now desires us to call Doña Antonia, understood through my translation that her husband was not accompanying us, she let forth a wail of pure grief, as the Indians are wont to do here. The Captain General explained to her, in the most soothing and patient tones, that it was his duty to explore the Mártires, which the Indians call the Gator Tail Islands, there to discover some good port in the Bahama Channel and make friends with the Indians in those places. And he told Antonia that she must devote all her efforts to becoming not just a Christian but a proper Catholic one, which was a thing that would be explained to her in Havana, and that she should not lament, for when she returned she would spread the Word of God to all her people, and this was a very good thing. And she accepted it then.

Before he took leave of San Antón, for he had decided to name the harbor of the Calusas after that blessed saint as well, the Captain General called me aside. Escalante, he said, you have proven a very valuable asset to me with the Indians of Carlos. I do not know what I should have done without you.

I agreed with the Adelantado and told him so, for what he said was true, and told him also that long had I waited for my rescue, and that it was all worthwhile, for this was the day I'd anticipated for seventeen long years. And then the Adelantado cleared his throat and said to me, I must, good Christian, ask of you one thing more, and I said, of course, my leader, what is it?

And he said I want you to stay here with the Indians.

I could not speak. My mouth opened but no words came out, and I shut it, fearing that I'd cry out in the Indian way. The Captain General addressed me then in the same gentle tone he'd earlier used with Antonia: Only for a short while, until I return. You will, of course, be paid handsomely, for you will be in the King's service. And the reason, in addition to all I've enumerated before, is that someone must watch over the cross. We have gained much in our sacred mission here. If the cross is removed, all will be lost. I have observed that you command the Indians' trust. I leave its safekeeping to you.

I knelt before the cross myself and prayed that the Captain General would return safely. And as I prayed I had two insights. The first I shared with the Adelantado, advising him to deliver the cross not to Carlos but to Stepana, who is feared more by the Indians than even the cacique. The Captain General agreed and called for Stepana, who carried the cross on his shoulder with great reverence to the land.

Then, I watched all seven ships sail away. And repeated the second revelation to myself. She wasn't on board, and neither was I. We were still together.

But now several days have passed, and I've not seen her. Things seem exactly as before, with no change save the cross erected on the temple mound. I pray it works its wonders.

❧ Twelve ❧

Ask anyone, child or elder, ground dweller or noble, which moon marked the change from dry season to wet and they would answer the same: it was the moon of the purple hands. With the warming of the sea came moist air borne on gentle breezes, blown by the sun from the east in the morning and from the west in the afternoon. And rain, blessed rain that filled Caalus's cisterns and brought Escampaba into bloom. Bay bean, sabal palm, sea grape, and a host of others bloomed in a profusion of white, yellow, red, and orange. Bracken and leather ferns sent up their curly shoots. Everywhere, bright green growth tipped branches as consistent warmth and moisture returned to the bay.

It was a moon of change for the birds and fishes, too. Schools of pilchards, menhaden, threadfins, and sardines moved through like billowing underwater clouds. With them arrived their pursuers. The snook returned from their cold-season hideaways far up the mainland rivers. Fat speckled weakfish laid their eggs in the shallows of beaches and bay. A few silvery tarpon could be seen rolling at the surface. The manatee returned too, no thinner for having wintered to the north in temperate freshwater springs. The young of ospreys, high atop nests in dead trees, screeched constantly for food. As they grew, they began to peek from the nests, to perch and flap their wings, and finally to fly. Other birds seen only in winter, like the bright red cardinal, feasted on the ripening early berries before beginning their seasonal journeys to other lands.

The people feasted too, and no indulgence was more popular than the sweet, juicy fruit of the mulberry. Turning from white to red to a purple so deep it challenged black, the berries grew as long and thick as a thumb. The people congregated beneath the mulberry trees, sucking the sugary berries from their stems, gorging until they could eat no more. Children climbed the branches, tossing them down to their mothers, who filled basket after basket to be taken home as a treat for the men, or else dried for later use.

And everyone's hands were purple. The dark fruit stained so thoroughly that not even sand scrubs completely cleaned the fingers. But who wanted to scour away the tantalizing smell of mulberry anyway? Hence, in the moon of the purple hands, so too were stained the people's lips and tongues. Some called it the moon of the purple noses, for the prolific blooming of flowers and trees brought forth watery eyes, runny noses, and incessant sneezing. Still others labeled the moon that of the purple rump, for the fruit was known to bring on desire; many couples could not seem to keep their purple hands off each other.

But not this year. The waters and weather warmed, but the rains did not come. Flower buds dried up and fell off. Fern shoots turned brown. The mulberries were shriveled and sour. So were the people's faces.

Ishkara sat beneath the Spaniards' cross that had been erected just outside the temple. Each day he'd come here, waiting for the sacred symbol of the Christians to reveal its secrets, and each day he'd returned to the sanctuary unenlightened. No more. Now, he would sit. Sit for as long as it took to understand this idol that was not an idol, which was said to be the doorway to everlasting life in the land beyond death. Could it be that they who harnessed the wind to explore the edges of the ocean had also probed that secret passage? Or was this a mere show of power? Ishkara would not leave until he found the answer.

All day he sat as the cross's edgy shadow shrank and then grew again until it cast a shroud of darkness upon the temple itself. All night he sat as clouds blew past, obliterating the stars but releasing not a drop of rain. Black. All Ishkara saw was black. The doorway remained hidden. If one existed at all.

Under that dark, alien silhouette placed so high on the Calusas' homeland, the people suffered. Sipi was angry, and it was all too obvious to Ishkara why. What was as murky as the clouds that brought no rain, only false hope, was how the cross's magic worked, and what could be done to control it. There was nothing for Ishkara to do but strike out into the darkness, into the shadow itself. Whether there would be light or whether he'd be lost forever in the shapeless night, there was no telling. Ishkara knew only that he must go, and that in order to do so he had to let go of all that was precious to him, his loved ones, his plants, his very self.

Sitting, waiting in the darkness, he let the layers of his memories peel off like skin from the babe left too long in the sun, until he was no longer tirupo, no longer leader or father or brother, until he could no longer be defined by others or even by himself, until he merged into the formless night. Only then, when at last the thoughts no longer came, did it happen. He felt suddenly weightless, exhilarated, flying through the air. Free of both body and mind, Ishkara flew through the darkness in looping circles, soaring round and round in timeless arcs that reached ever farther outward. He saw blurs of light—yes, yes, they must be the stars— and his will interjected itself then, telling him to slow down, to move toward them. But there was no steering. The sensation began to change. No longer was it merely thrilling. Now he was wobbling out of control, dizzy, shaky, faint. A hand stretched out for him, and he praised Sipi, but when it reached him it was instead a crab claw that clamped down on his head, mashing it as easily as a ripe mulberry, producing crushing pain, sending deep purple juices squirting into the void. And then there was nothing.

The councilors wrapped their furs around their shoulders as Stepana's words bit into the chill of the pre-dawn meeting. "You showed only weakness. You bowed palms up to the fur-face." Stepana's scorn rained down at Carlos.

"I did what I had to. It means nothing."

"You kissed their wooden idol."

"And it is you who erected it at the temple, you to whom Escalante has entrusted its safekeeping."

"I will destroy it today. Just give the order."

Carlos shook his head. "No. We play along. We use the strangers to suit our purposes."

"Ha. And what purpose is that? To become their slaves? They've already made a slave of Piyaya. Your own sister. Ah, perhaps that's your plan. Since you've brought forth no heir yourself, you've left it to Piyaya to bear the new cacique. Hail to the fur-faced cacique."

Stifled sniggers broke out amongst the councilors.

Carlos stamped his staff so hard that, had it been made of any wood but the rock wood, it would certainly have split. So they were laughing at him. Stepana and the councilors both. And—Carlos had no doubt—surely the Spaniards, too. Let them. What did it matter if he kissed their idol, if he bowed palms up, as long as he achieved his aim? An alliance with the Spaniards would make his power impregnable. Let Stepana have his fun. Carlos had to ignore the taunts.

He gripped the staff hard, forced calm into his voice. "My plan is sound. We must use our wits. Let the strangers believe in our friendship. Let them believe they control us. In the meantime, we gather their gifts, their gold, their power. Soon, we'll be invincible."

"Cacique." The voice came from a guard at the door. "Aesha needs you. It's urgent."

Carlos glared for a long moment at Stepana, then at each of the councilors, bringing quiet to the room as he strode out. Good. He'd silenced them . . . for now.

Aesha's face was ashen, her hand cold as a dead eel as she gripped his elbow. "It's Ishkara. Something's happened."

Hurrying to the temple, Carlos found Ishkara sitting beneath the cross. He wasn't sleeping, for his eyes were open; but he gave no sign of recognition, even when Carlos shook his arm.

"He's been here three days now without food and water. He no longer responds at all."

"Suffering brings vision."

"But look at how frail he's grown. The wooden idol—it's like their gold. It sucks his strength as it sucks all of Escampaba dry."

"What am I to do? I dare not destroy it. Stepana challenged me to do exactly that, just now at the council hall. Called me weak. He ridicules my every move."

"But it was Stepana who formulated the plan to capture their leader, a plan that failed miserably."

"And I that take the blame. More slippery than catfish slime, Stepana is. No matter what happens, he twists the results to suit him." Carlos lowered his voice. "Someone advised the strangers in advance that our warriors lay in wait."

"Escalante?"

"I chanced not to confide in him. He can no longer be trusted. It couldn't be . . . unless he was warned by someone else."

"Stepana," she said.

"Why sabotage his own plan, when its success would have brought him such glory?"

"It's all so confusing." Aesha stroked Ishkara's arm. "For him, too. That's why he's gone away."

Carlos leaned close, spoke into Ishkara's ear. "Father, I need your strength and wisdom. I fear I've lost a sister. I must not lose you, too."

Ishkara floated deep in the void.

For nearly four moons Piyaya had languished in this strange city called Havana. Languished in the foul air of a room that didn't breathe. Languished in garments that bound her like a bundle of thatch, making her sweat and stink. Languished amongst those who pointed and stared, lips flapping in their babbling chatter. María, a Spaniard who had accompanied her from Caalus, translated the lessons that introduced her to the Christian gods, but that made them no more understandable. These weren't stories of the earth and the animals and the sea, but rather of a man-god who died but somehow still lived. And he was both the child of their only god yet still a part of that god in some way that didn't survive the journey from the Spanish tongue to her own. What did survive, though, was that Sipi was a false god, and so everything Piyaya believed and knew was false, too. Or so she was to accept.

And all the time, no husband. She did not even know if the Spaniard Menéndez still lived.

The others who'd accompanied her from Caalus had fared even worse. The strange food that at first seemed so exotic poisoned their bellies and pushed through their bowels undigested. It happened so fast. Fever flared in their eyes, shook their wasting bodies. Disconsolate and melancholy, they suffered, then succumbed. Five of the seven had died already in this unhappy, unholy place. Their souls would never find the land beyond.

Four moons: the moon of whelk egg cases, the moon of purple hands, the moon of mosquito hatching, and now the moon of the reflection soul fish. How she loved this magical moon when the mighty tarpon, at the height of their numbers, were constantly seen rising to the surface, flashing their silvery sides, somersaulting in the air and slapping back down into the water. It was more than a spectacle, it was a sacred phenomenon; each time a shimmering fish surfaced, beams of dazzling light burst forth, as if the reflection soul of the sea itself rose with it. The sight made the elders pause and drove the boy-men wild. They'd give chase in their canoes, try to tempt the silver giants with a small fish or crab; but their gorges would break, their fishhooks wouldn't penetrate the hard jaws, their lines would part, or the fish would wear the young pursuer out until the end of the line slipped from his raw, bleeding fingers. To bring a tarpon home for the fires was a rarity, and though Piyaya found the taste unsavory, it was an occasion to be celebrated by festive gathering and rapt listening to a story that inevitably grew with the telling.

Celebrated by others far away, growing more distant each day, as was the hope that she'd ever return home. Soon would come the moon of turtle laying. Piyaya stared out the small window of the home of the Spaniard Alonso de Rojas, a friend of her missing husband. The man's wife came every day to sit with her, play with her hair, fuss with her garments, having long since given up trying to get Piyaya to leave her room. The city of the strangers held no interest to her. Only one subject did, and for that, there was never an answer. *Cuándo va a volver mi marido?* She had learned to ask the question in the strangers' tongue. When will my husband return? The wife could only shrug. Piyaya's tears would come then, and no one could comfort her.

Piyaya didn't delude herself. The man she called husband was a stranger. He'd given her gifts, yes, but there'd been no love in his eyes, even in the wedding bed. Carlos, though, had entrusted her with this vital mission to wed the Spanish to the Calusa. The survival of her people might depend upon it, upon her. And so she clung to this driving purpose. She would be the Adelantado's wife. She would carry his child. If she could find him.

Then, maybe he would carry her home.

Mutinies, desertions, insubordination, lack of food and supplies, Indians who attacked in the dead of night. Menéndez had faced these hardships and more in the past four months. Though he had lost many soldiers, and though St. Augustine itself had burned to the ground, the casualty of flaming Timucua arrows, Menéndez's forces had survived and ultimately triumphed. He had rebuilt St. Augustine, this time on the more easily defended Anastasia Island, and reinforced it with artillery.

And in the midst of all these trials, Menéndez had himself seen the Hand of God. While exploring north along the east coast of La Florida, the Captain General had encountered an old chief named Guale. Guale was at war with a more northerly chief named Orista, whose lands Menéndez wished to explore. Through diplomacy and the persuasive power of biscuits and honey, Menéndez managed to persuade the two chiefs to make peace with each other and even to attempt to embrace Christianity.

The Lord, however, was not satisfied with the surface level of the Indians' faith. And so, He wrought a miracle. It had not rained in that country for nearly nine months. On the very day that Menéndez scolded Guale for not truly embracing the Lord, the day on which Guale finally broke down and kissed the cross in earnest, saying that he accepted the will of God, the Lord interceded. The skies opened up and the rains poured down. When lightning struck a tree near the village, the Indians scurried to take the blessed broken branches to their homes. Then they threw themselves at the Adelantado's feet. They believed.

Menéndez knew then beyond all doubt the righteousness of his mission. And he felt the tide turning.

He arrived in Havana in late May to reprovision the forts at St. Augustine and San Mateo and to root out some of the deserters who had taken refuge in that island city. Menéndez spent two frustrating days on the hunt for money and men. Neither task went well. So busy was he that he could not help putting off another duty that waited: he had to see his "wife."

He dreaded the reunion. The baptizing of Antonia, while a necessity, had been a sham. She had no more understanding of the Lord than a rock. He hoped that the catechisms provided under the guidance of Alonso had helped, but he had no delusions that she'd act like a Christian woman. That night in Carlos, all Antonia had wanted was his malehood. She'd reached for it the moment he entered the room and never let go. It was awkward . . . odd . . . embarrassing. Worst of all, pleasurable. For the sake of his immortal soul, Menéndez must not lie with her again.

So, he brought along friends, musicians, and gifts to the house of Alonso. Her face, thinner now, dark and moody, came alive briefly upon first seeing him, but she soon turned melancholy, even as he handed her three newly sewn blouses. "Why are you so cheerless?" he asked through Antonia's attendant.

"Two days you've been back in Havana. The wife told me. And yet you did not come. I am wife. A wife eats and sleeps with her husband. If I cannot do so, I want only to die. This all-powerful god of yours, let him kill me now."

Menéndez had to think quickly. Pointing to the medallion on his doublet, the cross of the Order of Santiago, he said, "A soldier who wears this cross, upon returning from battle, may not sleep with his wife for eight days. Would that the eight days were gone, for you know how much I love you."

Doña Antonia listened misty-eyed to María's translation. "If only I find you are telling the truth, I will then be happy."

Counting on his fingers, Menéndez showed that two days had passed and only six more remained. Then he rose and whirled her to the music. Slowly, as her body moved, her face too began to come alive. He decided now to ask the question that could only multiply her joy.

"Would you care to return with me to Caalus?"

Her eyes turned to his, questioning.

"Tomorrow," he said.

Doña Antonia danced with such delight that she almost possessed a touch of beauty.

In bed at midnight, Menéndez slept the dreamless slumber of the exhausted. Only his training as a soldier enabled him to awaken, for the intruder had been noiseless. He jumped from his bed, found his saber, and in the next instant spun to face his attacker. Perish at the hands of God he might, but not at those of a cowardly deserter turned night stalker.

But the assailant held only a candle. It was a woman. Doña Antonia.

"What is the meaning of this?" Menéndez demanded.

A much-flustered María, standing near the door, managed to stammer, "She told me you sent for her. I . . ."

Menéndez' head shook in wags of relief and incredulity. So the wiles of Indian women were not so different from those of our own. He smoothed his nightshirt, addressed Antonia as tenderly as possible. "I know how you feel. How I wish, too, that the eight days were over. However, I must obey our solemn law."

"Now that I've seen that you sleep with no other woman, let me lie in just a corner of your bed," the Indian woman begged. "My brother must know that we slept together. I must not lie to him." Her face furrowed. "And you mustn't make him angry, or he will never be your friend, nor will he ever become a Christian."

Menéndez pressed his face close to hers. "The Lord will strike me down, but if you wish it, if you wish for me to die here and now, then disrobe yourself and get into bed with me."

This Lord of his vengeful for husband lying with wife? She did not, could not understand. She threw her arms around him in a quick embrace, then left the room.

Propelled by a favorable wind, they reached Caalus in three days. With only thirty men aboard, Menéndez didn't risk coming ashore. He anchored in deep water.

Antonia tugged his arm. "Come with me now to the town."

"I cannot. I must go to look for Christians that can instruct your brother."

"I've taken the lessons. I'll instruct him myself. Come. I'll show you."

Menéndez stroked his chin. "I will confide this to you because of how much I love you. I fear that the families of those who died in Havana will think I killed them and will want to do evil to me. Then a war will break out between your brother and me. I would regret that deeply, for I love him as I love you."

"But the eight days have yet to pass. Will you not stay here with me?"

Menéndez did not have to answer, though, because at that moment Doña Antonia erupted in tears of joy and grief. Several Indian canoes had appeared. The torrent of Indian words poured down like the rainstorm in Guale.

Shortly, when Carlos, his warrior chief, and six nobles arrived, Antonia's hysterics erupted all over again. Menéndez ordered the instruments to be played and corn and manioc served. He brought out more knives and scissors, mirrors and bells. Carlos and his Indians looked well pleased.

Now was as good a time as any for the question. "Cacique," Menéndez asked through Escalante, who'd arrived with the chief, "are you ready to become a Christian, to cut your hair, to come with me to Havana and to return with my priest, who will teach your people?"

The Indian chief was silent a long minute, then responded, "I must speak with my great captain and councilors privately, and then I will give you an answer."

As the Indians moved to the ship's stern to confer in low voices, Menéndez noted how their bodies talked. The warrior chief Stepana stood solid, slicing the air with his hands, while Carlos shifted his weight constantly from one foot to the other. Interestingly, even as Stepana addressed his chief, he seemed always to keep one eye on the remaining Indians, as an actor might on his audience. Finally, the chief returned. "This my people will not allow, not yet. They have certain . . . expectations of me. Nine moons we must wait, then I believe they will be prepared and will not rise up against me and kill me. You must go now and return then."

Though his goals were not yet accomplished, Menéndez was only too glad to hand Doña Antonia back to Carlos and return to Havana.

The moon of turtle laying. The moon of deadly winds. The moon of turtle hatching. And still no rain. The fruits had long since dried up and fallen, mixing with mats of brown leaves that crackled underfoot. Hot, scorching winds rattled palm fronds dry as thatch. For the people, even the sea brought no relief. Soup-bone waters, they were called. They left you hot to the core and coated with a layer of scum and salt.

The waters oppressed the fish, too, which moved from the shallows to potholes and channels but soon found even those deeper places too hot. So the fish followed the tides out to sea and did not return. With them went the seabirds. The Bay of Plenty and its lush green islands lay brown and half dead.

Half dead, half alive. Such was Ishkara's state, too. He had come back from his journey, so close to finding the light and yet never reaching it. The hand—the claw—had unclamped itself, and he'd returned to the world of the breathing. But not completely. His left arm hung at his side like an anchor stone, and his left leg refused to bear even his birdlike weight. The right side of his face drooped, and, in a merciless irony during that terrible time of drought, drool flowed from that side of his mouth in a continuous waterfall. The clouds in front of his eyes had darkened, too, storm clouds that teased of rain, yet delivered only a dusky gloom. Ishkara lived between worlds, the spirits of the land beyond still near and solid, the loved ones nearby distant and shrouded.

They surrounded him now on his mat in the inner temple. He recognized the voices: Carlos, Aesha, Piyaya. He heard their words clearly, and yet his own speech refused to form on his tongue. When he managed to push out a sound, his voice sounded foreign, the babble of an infant blended with the wail of a dying animal.

"There've been more fires," Carlos said. "Tomo has been destroyed."

"The home of my mother burned?" Aesha wailed. Was this the vision she saw? A shudder ran up her back.

"From a lightning strike. Lightning, but no rain." Carlos laughed bitterly. "Another of Sipi's cruel jokes."

Look at me, Ishkara wished to say. I am yet another.

"We must pray," Aesha said.

"Pray to whom?" The words exploded from Carlos's mouth. "If Sipi won't bring rain, perhaps the Christian god will."

"It's true. My husband made it rain," Piyaya said. "First at Guale, then Otina."

"And why not Caalus?" Carlos demanded. "Why not Escampaba?"

Piyaya shrugged. "I don't know. Perhaps he knows your heart isn't true, that you seek his friendship only to use it for your own purposes."

"Our purposes," Carlos said. "Calusa purposes. My policies, my power ensure our survival. If we couldn't trade for roots from the interior, the people would be starving."

Only Sipi has power, Ishkara tried to say. And he is using it to punish us.

Carlos stamped his staff. "You must be wife. That is the problem. You do not sleep with him, and so you mean nothing to him."

"I try," Piyaya cried. "But he has rules. Christian laws."

"And we have drought and famine." Carlos made to stamp his staff again, but before he could, Aesha kicked at it, sending it skittering across the room. The two glared at each other.

Carlos broke eye contact first, turning to Piyaya. "You must go to him. At the first opportunity."

From that close distant land, Ishkara heard music and laughter. "I hear you," he said. "I'm coming." But what escaped his lips was an animal grunt.

"Look at what the Spaniards' god has done to him," Aesha said softly. "To all of us. We fight each other. Soon we'll all be dead . . . at their hands, or at our own. Now leave me with him."

When they'd left, she stroked the limp hand and sang:

Tireless, they lift their load and carry it with pride.
Mama's gonna sing you a song of the tides.
Moving moving moving, resting. Moving once again.
Moving moving moving, resting. Moving once again.

The rains came at Falko. The festival of the burning stars was washed out, turned into a starless, soggy event, at once joyous and puzzling. The people wondered. Had the Adelantado prevailed upon his god to send the rains from whatever distant shore he sailed? Or had Carlos's prayers to Sipi finally been answered? And what of the timing? Certainly the rain was a miracle, the replenishment of the cisterns a blessing, especially coming during what should be the beginning of the dry season. Yet, the same clouds that finally loosed their water obscured the stars night upon night. Not a single burning star was seen. The passions that Falko ignited were doused by the downpours that lasted for days.

For Aesha, desperation closed in with the rain clouds. The heavens were out of Carlos's control. The people saw that, and Carlos saw that they saw. When the cacique busied himself in overseeing the construction of new and larger cisterns, Aesha heard the ever growing resentment in his terse instructions and continual criticism. Ishkara, poor Ishkara was not only unable to help, he needed constant attention. Dear Iqi came to his rescue, moving his sleeping mat to the temple floor, and Iqi was a great comfort to her, too. Still, Aesha's all too familiar feeling of foreboding intensified. The showery skies invaded her dreams, but instead of dousing the flames of her vision, they produced only steam, fog, and more confusion while the flames danced 'round, unabated.

Once again, a wind ship arrived. This time, the Spanish leader was not aboard. Instead, he'd sent one of his lesser chiefs named Francisco de Reynoso, along with fifty warriors. This Spaniard had a long purple scar on his right cheek, and the top half of his right ear was missing. Squat of leg and thick at the waist, he walked with short, purposeful steps to greet Carlos, his long knife and armor clanging like one of the Spaniards' bells. Speaking in a voice as gruff as a growl, he produced a letter from the Adelantado to Carlos. Escalante translated. It ordered Captain Reynoso to build quarters for his soldiers on Caalus and entrusted their safety to Carlos, "my good friend and brother."

Carlos made a show of welcoming Captain Reynoso and ordered a lodge built on the palace mound, not an arrow's distance from the palace itself. "I ask only one favor of you," he addressed the burly Spaniard. "Return my sister to her husband when your wind ship departs." To this, the captain willingly, and Piyaya tearfully, agreed.

"The marriage is key. It will bind the Spanish to us," Carlos told Aesha afterward. "And here in Caalus, all will see how I look down upon the Spaniards and keep them under observation."

What the people soon saw, though, was a fence-surrounded Spanish lodge sharing the palace mound, looking down upon them.

A second cross was erected at the Spanish compound. The Christian warriors and not a few Calusa came morning and night to kiss it. Along with this development came an even more disturbing one: the Spanish soldiers and the gifts they offered were becoming very popular with Calusa women. It was as if the ardors of the rained-out Falko had not been extinguished after all, but rather redirected. When the men became jealous, Carlos issued a stern warning. Anyone who touched a Spaniard would himself be touched—three times on the flesh with a hot stick.

At council, Stepana continued his mockery of Carlos. "Soon, all our children will have curly hair and beards. I tell you, Cacique, we should massacre the Spaniards. There are only fifty. I will gladly do it myself."

Yet Stepana knew full well that Carlos would not. Piyaya's presence in Havana, though it might perhaps fortify the Spaniards' friendship, had an unintended consequence: it ensured the Christians' safety in Caalus.

Spaniards sharing the palace mound. The chattergulls dispersed on the winds, spreading juicy tidbits to the provinces and beyond. Carlos's allies turned apathetic; his enemies smelled opportunity. Trade envoys were attacked, captives taken. His grip was loosening daily.

The difficulties escalated even further. Aesha traveled to Tomo to see the ruins of her mother's home and to help rebuild. Carlos feared for his wife's safety, for Tomo was far to the north, close to Tocobaga waters. Over Aesha's vehement objection, he insisted that Stepana escort her. It would take the great captain away from Caalus, remove his incendiary words at least temporarily from the councilors' ears. Besides, not even a scheming Stepana would risk allowing harm to come to Aesha. What happened was just as disastrous. Tocobaga intercepted their canoe. Stepana escaped with Aesha, but Escuru, who had accompanied them, was taken hostage.

Carlos's own sister prisoner of Tocobaga. Could there be a greater insult? And once again, Stepana squirmed out from under the blame. Though he mourned the capture of his dear wife, he enthralled the people with the tale of his heroic rescue of Aesha.

Carlos frothed and bubbled like a pot of all-in-one stew.

Finally, there came an occasion for the cacique to reclaim a morsel of dignity and influence. One day Captain Reynoso requested an audience before him. "The Adelantado is due to return shortly." Reynoso leaned closer. "He would be angry if I told you this, for Captain Menéndez is a great explorer. But one feat eludes him. He has been unable to discover the water passage through the interior of La Florida, though long has he heard that one exists. If you could but describe the route, he would be most grateful."

Carlos immediately seized upon the opportunity. "I will do better than that. I will lead him to it."

"It is close?"

"No. Far from Calusa waters. The interior waterway begins near the home of Tocobaga."

The Spanish captain looked confused. "But we thought, that is, your trade route runs up the great river that empties into the bay not far from where we now sit."

"Yes, but we must cross much high ground. Tocobaga guards the far easier river route."

"I have heard of him. He's your enemy."

Carlos spat. "He's a salt mosquito, no more. If he lands on you . . ." Smack! Carlos slapped his arm, then flicked a finger, flipping the squashed Tocobaga to the floor. Then the cacique licked his finger thoughtfully, savoring the taste of blood.

Each morning, Aesha arrived early to see how Ishkara had fared during the night and to give Iqi a respite. She walked the same course with Ishkara each day, from the temple to the nearby Christian cross. The going was slow, for Ishkara's left leg still dragged behind him, all but useless. He insisted, though, and he greeted the Christian idol each day with a twisted half-smile.

Aesha had long since learned that, though the tirupo could barely see or speak, he still heard and understood everything. She described the capture of Escuru by Tocobaga. "They waited for us in ambush. They knew we were coming."

Ishkara grunted. "Stp."

"Yes. Stepana. He's wangled it so Carlos must seek revenge. He can only be intending to have Carlos killed. Then, in the void, Stepana will take over."

Ishkara nodded his agreement.

"Carlos has a plan. He's enlisted the Spaniards to attack Tocobaga."

Ishkara raised his good eyebrow.

"It's so. He told Captain Reynoso that a water path exists through the interior and that he will guide Menéndez to it. Carlos said the river begins at Tocobaga. He aims to rescue Escuru and kill Tocobaga. Such a bold act will revive his authority, and it will demonstrate to all that the Spaniards are the Calusas' allies."

Ishkara's grunt indicated a question.

"I do not know if the plan will work. That is what I am asking you."

Ishkara turned his milky eyes skyward. Sipi would provide an answer. In his own time.

⤠ Thirteen ⤟

12 March 1567

Despite his promise, I did not believe the Adelantado would ever return. As great a leader as he was—is—still the man does not know these Indians as I, only I, do. I pleaded with him not to leave so small a contingent, only fifty men, in Caalus; but now I am a soldier and must obey orders. Calm yourself, Escalante, he told me, for though we may be outnumbered, our Lord and our artillery will protect us. And then he left.

I moved my meager belongings to the miserable fort on the palace mound and set about the impossible task of keeping the soldiers safe. They made it all the more difficult, ridiculing the very Indians who brought them food and water, bedding the Indian women at every opportunity. I reported diligently every threat, every plot I got wind of to Captain Reynoso, but the man has the disposition of a street brawler and was always spoiling for a fight. Wildfires and tempers flared all that dry and wretched summer. I struggled to keep a full-fledged battle from breaking out, a battle that could have only one victor. I, in the employ of the Adelantado and wearing a soldier's uniform now, would have perished with the rest.

How oddly Aesha looked at me in my doublet and armor, broad-sword glinting at my side. I see that those coverings hurt your feet, she told me, and I couldn't deny it, for the boots had rubbed raw blisters on my unaccustomed heels. Why do you not throw them off, she asked? What purpose do they serve? I tried to explain that a soldier's uniform demonstrated his respect and loyalty, even as I secretly ached to do just that, to fling the strangling leathers into the sea.

You look different altogether, she told me.

As do you in your Spanish robes, I said. At my urging, she had dressed in the watered silk gown the Adelantado had given her, the long one that covered breasts, legs, and even feet. Smiling, putting on my most confident face—for these Indians can smell assurance as readily as they can weakness—I told her then that her beauty and modesty would turn every head in Salamanca. Soon, I told her, though I didn't believe it myself. We'll be leaving very soon. And I explained that when Captain General Menéndez sailed for Spain, he'd promised to take me with him, and she, of course, would accompany me.

She was silent then. I do not think she knows what to make of my newfound boldness any more than she does my uniform.

Through the rains that came so late and then a dreary, sunless winter, I carried on my peacekeeping mission, slogging between the two groups, not really belonging to either. The soldiers looked at me with suspicion as I moved so freely about the island; the Indians saw only my uniform. Such was destined to be my fate until the Adelantado returned. If ever he did.

Three days ago he arrived, and for the second time, I wept. This time his flotilla included six brigantines and one hundred fifty men, still a paltry number, though an improvement nonetheless. He carried with him from Havana Piyaya—Doña Antonia—as well as two missionaries who had helped educate her. There were six Indians aboard whom I recognized as nobles of Tequesta, one being, in fact, that chief's brother. The Adelantado told me that he wished to make peace between Tequesta and Carlos. That is certainly needed, for Carlos has made war upon Tequesta ever since that chief refused to deliver some Christian prisoners to Carlos.

It is good you've come, I told Captain General Menéndez, and with reinforcements, for your soldiers here are in grave danger. I told him of the many times Carlos had threatened to overrun the fort. Captain Reynoso, who was at my side, confirmed the accuracy of my account, adding that his men had been hearing the same warnings from the Indian women they'd befriended. I had to bite my lip to keep from blurting out that these very liaisons were the root of much of the Indians' resentment.

The Adelantado told me how fortunate he was to have me in his employ and assured me that he would keep his men safe from harm, that no purpose was dearer to his heart. Then he asked me to arrange an audience with Carlos, for the purpose of presenting the nobles of Tequesta.

Before the Adelantado could even bring them into the room, though, Carlos started in about Tocobaga. The hatred between those two caciques is of such grand proportions that you might almost suppose them two opposing civilizations instead of bickering heathens, as truly they are.

Help me make war upon the dirt-eating worm, Carlos ordered me to translate, and I will show you the water passage you seek.

I cannot wage war upon Tocobaga, Captain General Menéndez said, for the King of Spain is my master, and he has sent me rather to make friends and would cut off my head if I disobey him. I will meet with Tocobaga as I have done with you and will ask him to become a Christian, too, for if you will all do this as I say, then when you die you will meet in heaven as friends and brothers.

I alone among civilized men know Carlos intimately. A breath of air that escaped his lips alerted me to his deep perturbation, but he ordered me to translate as thus: While I deeply regret your decision, still I will accompany you to show you the way. Take me and twenty of my nobles with you to Tocobaga, and there we shall see whether we can negotiate a peace.

I added, for the Adelantado's benefit, that he should not trust Carlos, and he nodded, telling me he had already well learned that lesson. Then the Captain General called forth Tequesta's brother and his Indians and made them and Carlos pledge friendship each to the other.

We leave tomorrow for Tocobaga, the Adelantado concluded. I will need an interpreter.

My stomach took to the sea with the apprehension of what might come to pass between those two great enemies, yet my heart leapt at the prospect of leaving Caalus not as a slave but as a soldier of my King aboard a Spanish brigantine. High adventure waited, and I was to be in its center.

Then the Adelantado asked if there were another Christian who speaks the tongue of Tocobaga, enough to get by, and he said to me, you of course must stay in Carlos. You are far too valuable to me here.

And I was too shocked to answer immediately, so I corrected him. The city is Caalus, not Carlos, named for the former cacique, not the current one. And he said that it was much easier to get the name Carlos off his tongue and did it really matter, anyway, and I agreed. For if I am never to leave this place, nothing matters. Then I answered, for it was my duty to do so. Yes, Captain General. Arturo González can translate for you.

Three days at Carlos was long enough. Menéndez had already done what he could for the moment: directed that a home be built for Doña

Antonia and ordered a chapel constructed for Father Juan Rogel, whom he intended to install permanently at the Indian capital. A Jesuit missionary who had come to Havana in October on a Flemish galleon, the priest had already been severely tested. First, his ship had passed by the entrance to the harbor at St. Augustine and wandered along the east coast of La Florida for a month. Rogel had witnessed a fellow priest, Father Pedro Martínez, die at the hands of Indians in that land merely for the offense of asking directions. Then, returning to Havana, Father Rogel had contracted a nasty case of malaria. Menéndez hoped the priest's hardy constitution would bear up. In Carlos, he'd surely be tested again.

Promising to return soon, Menéndez charged the other Jesuit, the lay brother Francisco Villarreal, to look after the six Tequesta nobles. Despite the poor security at the haphazard compound, the Adelantado wasn't overly concerned about attack in his absence. Carlos would be aboard his ship. Menéndez left only a small supplementary force behind.

Traveling northward with Carlos, headed for the lands of that chief's bitter enemy, Menéndez knew he should be feeling apprehension. But on the sea a fair March breeze filled his lungs and the sails of his brigantines. The discovery of a waterway through the interior of La Florida awaited him. Though Menéndez himself had sailed safely now many times through Los Mártires and the Bahama Channel, still the waters there could be most treacherous. A route through the interior would save much time and avert the danger for the colonizers who would soon be coming. The Adelantado felt reinvigorated.

They'd sailed past sunset into a cloudy, moonless night when one of Carlos's Indians pointed to starboard, directing him into the entrance of a large harbor. In pitch dark the guide led him with certitude the last twenty leagues up a wide tidal river to where Tocobaga was said to reside. They arrived in silence an hour before dawn.

"We've not been noticed," Carlos whispered through Arturo to Menéndez. "This is a sign from both my gods and yours. We can kill the tailless lizard and burn his city before he awakens."

"Tocobaga has done me no harm," Menéndez replied. "Such an act would be contrary to Christian law."

"Then my warriors and I will do it ourselves."

"I cannot allow that."

Carlos was so frustrated that he wept. "The belly-crawler holds my sister."

"So I have heard," Menéndez acknowledged. "But I am here to make an honorable peace between you and Tocobaga."

Carlos's fist clenched and unclenched. But he did not dare to raise it against the Spanish leader.

The Adelantado put his hand on Carlos's shoulder. "I will force him to give up his Calusa captives. This I promise you." Then Menéndez went in a small shallop with only Arturo and eight soldiers to Tocobaga's village. In a loud voice, Arturo announced in that cacique's tongue not to fear, that the Spaniards had come as friends.

So frightened were the villagers upon awakening and seeing the six wind ships that they fled en masse to the woods. Not so Tocobaga himself, who remained in his palace. He sent a Christian of his own to speak to Menéndez.

"Tocobaga wishes me to thank you for not killing him or burning his village. His people are much alarmed and have abandoned him. Tocobaga, though, remains in the temple of his gods. He would sooner die than forsake them. He invites you, Adelantado, to land and to give him life or death, as is your choice."

"Who are you, man? Indian, by the look of you, but Portuguese, by the sound."

"I am Joam Amrrique, of Tavila, which is in the Algarve. I have been prisoner here six years, cast ashore in a storm while bound from Campeche to New Spain. Ever since, I have served the cacique Tocobaga, cooking and carrying wood and water for him. But I knew you were coming. For the last eight nights, I have dreamt it."

"Praise God. Tell me, the passage to the interior, where is it?"

The man shook his head. "I do not know. Tocobaga keeps me here. I haven't traveled ten leagues from his village."

Menéndez told Amrrique to inform Tocobaga that he had come in friendship and that Tocobaga could tell his people to return, for they would not be harmed. The Adelantado chose not to mention the name of Carlos. He wanted to meet Tocobaga first himself.

The ceremony was becoming familiar. Menéndez was given the seat of honor on a high bench looking down upon the Indians. Tocobaga and then his wife and principal men bowed before the Adelantado. The chief himself looked much like his enemy Carlos, with long black hair tied atop his head, sun-bronzed skin intricately painted, bone and shell jewelry dangling. He carried himself like the Calusa chief, too, erect and proud, assessing Menéndez's every move with intense, intelligent eyes. There was one difference, however. Where Carlos had made a show of power, even at the first meeting, with his three hundred braves, Tocobaga met Menéndez with but six men and his wife. He was, Menéndez hoped, a humbler leader.

Tocobaga spoke eloquently through the Portuguese interpreter. "For many moons there have been Christians in our land. They called themselves our friends and asked us to give them corn, but when we said we could not, that our bellies were empty, too, they killed many of us. Afterwards, more Christians came who killed these first ones, and we loved these new Christians greatly." He looked at the Adelantado with steady, even eyes. "Which kind of Christian are you?"

Menéndez returned Tocobaga's calculating gaze. "The first were false Christians, and being so, it was I who ordered them killed. I've come not to enslave you, but rather to show you the way of the one true God."

Tocobaga bowed again before Menéndez and kissed his hand.

When the Adelantado then announced that Carlos was at that very moment aboard his brigantine, a wave a shock rippled across Tocobaga's face. "He comes to make peace with you," Menéndez reassured. "You ought do the same with him, and you must start by releasing Carlos's sister and the others you hold as prisoners. If you do so, and if you and your people agree to become Christians, I will leave my soldiers here to defend you, as I have done with Carlos."

Tocobaga sat inscrutably still, his face quickly refrozen into its mask of measured composure. "This decision I cannot make myself," he answered finally. "I will assemble my chiefs. You must wait."

"How long?"

"Three or four days."

Menéndez didn't like this turn of event. Nor, he realized, could he do much about it. "I invite you to my ship, where you and Carlos will meet and begin your friendship," he said.

"I will come in the morning."

Daybreak. From the mangrove-lined shores, birds were beginning to squawk, honk, and cackle their morning greetings. Menéndez stood on deck, glad for the light that allowed him to rise from a restless night, when through the thin mist that hung over the wide salt river, he spied an Indian canoe approaching. Tocobaga himself was in the bow. Menéndez bid him to board.

"I've come to meet Carlos. Where is he? Does he hide from me?"

"Not from you nor from any man." Carlos materialized behind the Adelantado. He stood tall, arms across his chest.

For several minutes, the two men eyed each other, neither flinching. Menéndez, though tensed and ready, knew not to interrupt. Then Tocobaga spoke. "I wish to invite you to my lowly village."

Carlos quickly accepted.

"I promise you safety."

"I do not fear you."

"Nor I you." Tocobaga nodded toward Menéndez. "I merely aim to show our Christian brother that we can live in friendship."

"Friendship? Is that your term for capturing Escuru?"

"Or yours, for taking our fishermen as slaves?"

"If they stray into our waters, our nets capture them. They are no different than fish."

Tocobaga swallowed hard. "I am releasing your sister and the others."

"I will come get them."

Tocobaga signaled to his men, who readied the canoe.

"A moment, please," Menéndez said, his mind racing. The two brown-skinned chiefs before him were enemies perhaps, but both were clever and powerful. The one—Carlos—he knew he could not trust. The other was at best a question mark. Leave them alone together and one might kill the other, or perhaps they'd unite against him. Either way, it was a formula for disaster. Yet, the Adelantado desired not to anger Carlos. He thought quickly. "I would ask that my interpreter and your own Christian Joam Amrrique accompany you."

Hurriedly, he urged Arturo to stay at Carlos's side and be sure that the chief did not speak ill of the Spaniards. Menéndez watched the Indian canoe disappear. He spent the rest of the day pacing the deck.

When Carlos returned with his sister and the other Calusas, Menéndez breathed a deep sigh. But the sigh turned to a startled gasp two days later, when Menéndez found more than fifteen hundred Indians, arrows at the ready, at the landing. Where had they come from? How could his men have had not even an inkling of their arrival? But Menéndez had no time for speculation now. He strode boldly forward and gestured to the huge mass.

"My soldiers are most joyful," Menéndez had the Portuguese interpreter tell Tocobaga. "They have come all the way from Spain and have not yet engaged in battle. You've provided a pleasant amusement for them. They are eager to employ their weapons."

"You misunderstand," answered Tocobaga. "These are my close advisors. They simply wish to hear the Adelantado speak."

Menéndez now had his answer as to trusting Tocobaga. "I am most grateful for the reception. However, it will be much easier for me to address a smaller delegation."

Tocobaga turned away, his point made.

The next day Menéndez met with twenty-nine chiefs and about a hundred of Tocobaga's braves, plus Carlos and his small band of Calusas. Tocobaga and Carlos were cordial, each promising peace, each agreeing that, should one make war on the other, the Spaniards would come to the aid of the aggrieved side. Tocobaga formally requested that Menéndez leave a delegation of Spaniards behind to enforce the truce and to begin instruction on how to become Christians.

Menéndez ordered a contingent of thirty soldiers to remain, under the command of Captain García Martínez de Cos. The Adelantado allowed himself a small chuckle. The captain had stolen three casks of wine. He deserved this dangerous assignment.

"And what of the watercourse through the interior?" Menéndez asked Tocobaga when the ceremonies were completed.

"You have not nearly enough warriors with you," the chief answered, "for the route passes through the territory of Macoya, who has many warriors and will attack you."

Menéndez departed Tocobaga without finding the route through La Florida. Disappointed, yes, but all considered, a most important mission had been accomplished. The Adelantado had now made peace with Carlos, Tequesta, and Tocobaga, the three most powerful chiefs in La Florida. Increasingly, Menéndez understood that the colonization of this new part of the world depended less on the taming of the land than of the devious, warlike race of heathens who inhabited it.

On the return voyage, Carlos acted considerably less than tamed. When a sailor accidentally dropped the end of a rope on the chief's head, Carlos savagely attacked him, smashing the rope back in the man's face and then hefting the startled Spaniard on the chief's husky shoulders. Carlos nearly had the sailor overboard by the time Menéndez interceded. Explosive, this Indian. The Adelantado ought to hang him as he would one of his own soldiers for such insubordination. This powerful chief was so like a petulant child. But Carlos's influence over the tribes of La Florida made him too valuable to harm. Menéndez would have to put up with his tantrums. So long as they didn't turn deadly.

⇜ Fourteen ⇝

Finally, a flock of his own, a purpose. The endless string of misfortunes, of suffering, anguish, and loss, that had so long accompanied Father Juan Rogel only strengthened his conviction that at last he'd found his sacred calling. On this island of savages, he was utterly without support, for the soldiers the Adelantado had left behind seemed near as much in need of spiritual counsel as the Indians. Nevertheless, the priest had all the loving companionship he could want. The Lord was near. And though it might have appeared so time and again, the Lord had never abandoned him. Now the time had come to do His work.

Father Rogel's path to his ultimate purpose had been a long, circuitous one. The youngest by four years of seven sons and four daughters of a prosperous if not moneyed Pamplona wool and cloth merchant, Juan hadn't grown up deprived or unloved, simply apart. His sisters bent themselves to the loom; his brothers helped his father cart the materials to market. Juan was superfluous. At home, he was lumped in with his nieces and nephews, babied. When he tagged along with his father and brothers, they warned him in no uncertain terms that his single duty was to stay out of the way. Young Juan wanted desperately to be noticed. The one time he took the reins, though, so to speak, ended in disaster.

Determined to show his mettle, he rose before dawn, hitched horse to cart, and drove the load of linen smocks, chemises, and coifs through the dark streets of Pamplona, promoting his wares in his high, boyish voice, arousing the sleeping bargain hunters. He succeeded. The thieves stole not only the goods but the horse and cart as well. Juan almost relished the beating from his father—it was attention, at least. He took no pleasure whatsoever in his long-term sentence, though. His father relegated him permanently to the loom.

Juan was a sickly child, too, with a chronic perturbation of the bowels that forced him to carry his chamber pot everywhere. Teased without mercy by his schoolmates as the boy with the brown lunch bucket, spurned by his father and burly brothers, he turned sullen and morose. Even when his brothers began to fall, one smothered by an overturned cart of capes and tunics, another rendered mindless by a horse's kick in the head, his overprotective mother refused to let him from her sight. Juan felt useless. He retreated to his room, spending endless hours alone. Bored and brooding, he taught himself to juggle. He'd become a jester, renown for his skills, doing command performances in the highest places. Maybe even in the King's court. That would show them.

But Juan's juggling skills were woeful. Try as he may, he could master no more than three turnips at a time. Nonetheless, the thought stuck. His only solution was to get out. So his application to the university at Alcalá wasn't so much a calling as an escape. He failed the entrance exam twice, leaving him more despondent than ever. On the third try, he cheated, bribing an older brother to take the exam for him. When finally Juan was accepted, he announced with finality to his family that he was never coming back.

Wrong again. A year later, his father and oldest brother were killed during the Festival of San Fermín, trampled by bulls and neighbors. Finally, Juan was needed in Pamplona. Now, though, he found that the tasks that had seemed so appealing during his childhood were back-breaking, boring, and repetitive. His life was pleasureless and devoid of meaning.

Until he met Marguerite. Daughter of a competing merchant, she stole glances at his wares and then, quickly, his heart. Finally, good fortune came his way. They married, had a son and daughter. But the brief period of bliss soon came to a crashing end. Marguerite died birthing their third baby. Not long after, the other two succumbed to the little leprosy, the spotted disease.

Dazed and overcome with grief, Juan continued working the wool, but heavy taxes drained the profits. One by one, his remaining brothers left for more lucrative pursuits, until only Juan and his idiot brother remained. Finally, Juan's lack of motivation doomed the business. He sold the remaining goods and equipment to his father-in-law for a pittance. Juan was left to care for both brother and mother, whose mind had fled so that she no longer recognized him. At the age of twenty-six, Juan was alone, insolvent, and, with his bowel malady worse than ever, incontinent, too.

Wandering the streets of Pamplona, Juan found himself at the foot of the citadel that, forty years earlier, Ignatius of Loyola had attempted to defend. The founder of the now burgeoning Society of Jesus had been a miserable failure. The fortress fell to the French, and a cannonball nearly tore off Ignatius's leg. While recuperating, he was extremely bored and asked for romance novels to pass the time, but all that was available were copies of *Life of Christ* and *Lives of the Saints*. The calamity ended up turning his life around. He went on to study at Alcalá (as Juan himself had begun to, at least), Salamanca, and Paris, eventually coming to the priesthood, founding the Society, and serving as its first Superior General. Great things could happen to unlikely candidates. Juan, like Ignatius, was the youngest of a large family. Why not he, too?

Empty of pocket and nearly so of faith, he finally found the Lord.

Juan began to study a copy of Ignatius's *Spiritual Exercises*. The set of meditations, prayers, and mental exercises taught to find God in every moment and aspect of one's life. The concept was as all-embracing as it was comforting; it meant that his failures and suffering had a purpose, that God had been preparing him. He used the last of his savings to hire a housekeeper for his brother and mother and, like Ignatius, re-entered university at his advanced age of twenty-seven. Immersed in the loving-kindness of God and buoyed by the harmonious companionship of colleagues, his emotional scars began to heal. He was ordained. When the King called for recruits to spread the word to the New World, Father Rogel volunteered. He was terrified of leaving Alcalá, but he had much to prove to himself. And he owed it to the Lord.

Certain that he'd made the right decision, Father Rogel believed the rest would be easy. It wasn't. He had no stomach for the sea, and the voyage across the ocean left him weak and pallid. Then he witnessed the slaying of Father Martínez. And finally, malaria. Only the bleeding and purging saved him.

And prayer. Weak as he might be physically, for in trying times his bowel disorder always flared up, his spirituality was robust and resilient. This savage wilderness might be his first pulpit, but with the Lord at his side, how could he not succeed? And so, he plunged into his new assignment with passion. Neither the Adelantado's absence nor that of Chief Carlos were cause to delay his mission. Through the interpreter Escalante Fontaneda, he set about learning the Calusa language and spreading the Word of God to the Indians.

Opening the crude brushwood gate and handing out a bit of maize as an enticement, the priest managed to attract a few dozen Indians to the fort. At first, Father Rogel was hopeful, for when he preached to them about the oneness of God and His being the creator of every good, the natives readily agreed. They willingly kissed the cross and repeated the interpreter's translations of the priest's readings.

The day the maize ran out, the Indians disappeared.

No one came to the fort the next day either, save for an old Indian accompanied by a young and quite comely woman. The old man's behavior was bizarre. He limped around the compound, sniffing the lines hung with drying clothes, then shaking some kind of rattle and chanting in a kind of moan that sent shivers up the priest's spine. Odd as the Indian's behavior was, though, Father Rogel found his gaze locked on the young escort. She was thin, with delicate features and shining long black hair, and she dressed in the typical native style, with only a moss skirt to hide her modesty. The priest felt his face color. He must get used to the nakedness, try to understand it as innocence, not shame.

Escalante introduced her. "This is Aesha, principal wife of Carlos and daughter of the great leader who gave this city its name. She has come with Carlos's father, Ishkara, who is tirupo to the tribe, a kind of priest and doctor both, though he has grown old and infirm, as you can plainly see." The interpreter conversed quietly with the Indian woman for some time then, quite ignoring the priest.

Father Rogel loudly cleared his throat. "Please welcome her—both of them—to my humble place of worship."

The Indian woman—Aesha—studied him with intense yellow-brown eyes that never left his. "The prayers that you ask my people to recite," she asked finally. "What is their purpose?"

"The Our Father and Hail Mary? They serve for speaking with God and for asking Him everything we might have need of."

"And these things your god grants to you?"

"He grants that of which we are deserving."

"Why do you not ask him for more food? Your own men go half hungry. They depend upon my people to supply them with fish."

Father Rogel explained that God, in His wisdom, had a plan for the whole world, and that while men could pray and study and seek to understand His ways, they would never fully understand them, for only God was divine. "But those who follow faithfully the righteous path will be rewarded in the next life." He saw Aesha's brow crease in confusion. Simple, he reminded himself, he must make this simple. "If you do good deeds during your life, you will go to heaven in your next. And heaven is the land of plenty. No one goes hungry there."

"This heaven, where is it?"

The priest pointed to the sky.

"How does one travel there?"

"When you die, your body stays behind, but your soul is freed and can journey anywhere."

"Which soul goes to heaven?"

Now it was the priest's turn to furrow his brow.

Then Aesha described her people's fantastical beliefs of not one but three souls: one the *niñeta,* the little pupil of the eye; another the shadow that each one casts; and the last the image of oneself that each one sees in a calm pool of water or in the clever reflecting mirrors that the Spaniards used. She explained, too, that when a man dies, two of the souls leave the body and the third one, the little pupil, remains with the body always. "And so we go to the burial place to speak with the departed ones," she concluded.

"And they speak back to you as if they are alive?"

Aesha shook her head. "They speak back to us as if they are departed."

Father Rogel's lips formed a solicitous smile. "And what of the other two souls?"

"The stories say this: those souls enter an animal, perhaps a bird or a fish. And when that animal dies, the souls move to yet a smaller being, and so on until eventually they are reduced to nothing."

The priest chuckled. "No, child. I assure you that the souls of all men and women as have ever been in the world are alive, either in heaven or in hell. Either way, they cannot die."

"Ah, but they can," the chief's wife interrupted. "Ishkara could tell you; he rescued the shadow soul of my own father, protected it with the fire ritual. But it left again, as did his reflection soul. Not long after, he departed for the land beyond."

Father Rogel took stock of the skinny old man. Some kind of witch?

Well, he looked harmless enough now. The old Indian's glazed eyes stared off into space. He must be mostly blind. And deducing from his non-responsiveness, probably deaf, too.

Aesha continued: "I believe that my father's souls yearned to explore the place of the setting sun, a place that no man can reach. It is true, as you have said: his body was left behind. As for his eye soul, Ishkara says it lives in the temple with his bones. But I know that sometimes it wanders. I have seen and heard him in another place, a very special place far from here. Perhaps you could answer. Could he be in both locations?"

The priest frowned. So many misconceptions. Where to begin? There was little doubt where her father, an unbaptized heathen, had gone. Father Rogel wanted to answer honestly, yet there was no reason to alienate this important Indian female. "No. One place only."

The old man came close to Aesha then and grunted something, after which the chief's wife asked, "Heaven. It is at the end of a dark tunnel?"

"Yes. It is full of light and more beautiful than any place on earth."

Aesha put her arms on the old Indian's shoulders. "You will help Ishkara find it? He tried to go there, but he could not reach it."

"I will help him, yes. And so will God, when the time comes."

"I think the time will be soon. You will come to the temple to help him prepare?"

Father Rogel didn't doubt that the old Indian's death was fast approaching. But lead a man to heaven who protects souls with a fire ritual? Well, the priest would try. It was his sacred duty.

Returning to the temple, Aesha prepared a pot of tea from the leaves of the rock tree, for Ishkara was sure to be stiff and sore from overexertion. "Have you learned what you set out to?"

Ishkara pointed to Aesha.

"What have *I* learned? The Spaniard's beliefs are not so different from our own, though he says that they are."

Now Ishkara pointed to the sky.

"His heaven? I do not believe the Spaniard knows the route there, though of course he says that he does."

With a wistful look, Ishkara shrugged his shoulders and turned away. Aesha knew the meaning. Despite the Spanish tirupo's claims, the land beyond death was still the great mystery.

Father Rogel started. So intent had he been upon his prayers—for the strength to surmount his doubts and fears in this strange and foreign land, for the patience and wisdom to guide these poor, lost, brown-skinned souls toward the light, and, most urgently, for the Adelantado's safe return from his dangerous mission to Tocobaga—that he hadn't noticed the approach of the giant, naked Indian. Now, as the priest knelt at the cross, the man stood over him, a scowl etched on his broad, black-painted face. Or was it a smirk?

Father Rogel rose. Even standing, he barely reached this man's wide shoulders. Black lines painted around biceps and thighs accented the Indian's massive muscles, and around his thick neck hung enough jewelry and trinkets to fill the small trunk that held the priest's every earthly belonging. Yet, neither the copious jewelry nor the fearsome body paint could wrench Rogel's attention from the Indian's most prominent feature: an enormous belly. How anomalous it was, in this land where the lonely soldiers of San Antón joked that starvation was their one sure companion.

Courage, now. Father Rogel forced himself to raise his gaze to study the man's face. He couldn't venture a guess whether the Indian's age was greater or less than his own thirty-one years. All that was clear was that the painted native exuded an unmistakable air of authority. Then the Indian startled Father Rogel again. He knelt, trinkets tinkling, and kissed the cross.

"Bless you," said Father Rogel. "You come here often to pray?"

The Indian did not reply.

"Do you love God?" the priest rephrased.

By the rood, the language barrier. Father Rogel had quite forgotten he was speaking to the Indian in Spanish. "Escalante," he fairly screamed. "Come quick."

Fortunately, the interpreter was close at hand. "He is Stepana, warrior chief of the Calusa." Then, after conversing with the Indian, "He wishes you to know that it is he who has protected the cross at the temple, and that he is in your service."

"Thank you, my son," The priest said through Escalante. "You serve God well.

"I wish to become a Christian."

His first convert a highly placed Indian. Father Rogel couldn't believe his good fortune. "Christ is ready to receive all His willing children," he told the Calusa.

Stepana gestured, and two Indians came then and laid presents at the priest's feet, feathers and woven mats and a bowl of ripe, purple-black berries. Pointing at the former two items, the Indian said, "These were collected from those who pay tribute to us, valuable not only in themselves, but also as symbols of Calusa authority. The berries"—he patted his huge belly—"are precious too."

"I have heard much about the tribe of Carlos. It is the most powerful in all of La Florida. That is why I've come here, for the spreading of God's word must begin with the mighty."

Stepana's scowl hardened. He whispered something to Escalante, who spoke back to the Indian. Then Escalante addressed Father Rogel. "Stepana asks whether he may speak to you in confidence."

"Of course," the priest promised. "When my children speak to me, it is always in confidence."

"Stepana begs your pardon. However, he wishes me to correct you. His are not the people of Carlos; they are the people of Caalus."

The warrior chief spoke again, pointing both bulbous thumbs at his own chest as Escalante translated: "Carlos, who now is absent with Captain General Menéndez on the mission to Tocobaga, is neither the rightful ruler of Caalus nor of the people of Escampaba. Carlos has no right to rule. That right has been stolen from me. I will tell you how if you wish to hear it."

Father Rogel said the silent prayer that was dominating his ever more frequent pleas. *Captain General, please return.*

The Indian was grunting again, rapidly and at length. "The ruler of my people was Caalus, the uncle of Carlos and my uncle, too. But he was more than that to me: by his own decree, he became my adoptive father, for Caalus had no sons. Wishing me to rule Escampaba, he gave to me the royal insignia. When I was but a young child, those indicia were wrested from me by Caalus's brother, the tirupo Ishkara, and given wrongfully to his son Carlos, who wears them now on his forehead and around his legs. And Ishkara stole from me, too, my dear wife Aesha, the daughter of Caalus, and thrust her upon his son. Carlos rules only by Ishkara's trickery. It is I the people love, I who am the rightful cacique."

Father Rogel's astonished look needed no translation.

Stepana continued, his meaty hands chopping the air. "Out of devotion to her and to my people, I serve Carlos. I do not rebel; I remain silent. Now, though, I must speak." Again, Stepana addressed Escalante in a whisper.

"He asks again that you pledge confidence."

Father Rogel crossed himself. "As a man of God."

"Do not trust Carlos. He smiles at the Spaniards, but he does not love them. He plots to kill you all."

"Why? How?"

"When he returns, watch him well, if you value your head." Stepana turned to leave. "It is very dangerous for me to be revealing these secrets to you. I will try to warn you . . . if I can."

"Please," Father Rogel implored. "I must know why you tell me these things."

"I must speak with candor before the Spanish god. Let him reveal my words to be true or false. If the Spaniards desire a friend in the lands of the Calusa, they must look to Stepana, not Carlos."

"Can I trust this Stepana?" Father Rogel asked Escalante after the Indian had departed.

"He killed my brother and threatened my life. Yet for many years now, he's confided in me. But trust him? Wiser not to trust any of these Indians, Father."

"It's true that Aesha, the chief's wife, was once the wife of Stepana?"

Escalante nodded. "When she was but a young girl. She harbors no love for him. Nor does she for Carlos."

"I am confused."

Escalante shrugged. "I have lived amongst these Indians for more than seventeen years now, and I know not their hearts. Be wary, Father, and be brave."

"I will pray on it."

"You will need to."

At long last—for strong south headwinds had forced the brigantine to tack far out to sea—Captain General Menéndez reached the Indians' homeland without, thank the Lord, further incident from the brooding Carlos. The Adelantado's first order of business was to fortify the compound, if that's what it could be called. There wasn't much to it, a cluster of rectangular huts with woven mat walls and thatched roofs, surrounded by a fence of brushwood faggots that a strong child could push over. He shored up the fence as best he could and along each wall stationed two eighteen-pound culverins, their black muzzles exposed for all to see. Menéndez decided to increase the complement of soldiers to a total of seventy-five, even though he knew full well that neither the cannons with their serpent-shaped handles nor the added manpower would stop an all-out assault from an enemy with overwhelming numbers. The weaponry and soldiers were a show. So far, they were all he'd needed. He was hopeful that his luck would hold.

The reinforcements were completed in a few days. Menéndez was eager to depart for Tequesta to inform that chief of the peace between Carlos and Tocobaga. That such an accord, however tenuous, had been reached would no doubt impress every Indian in La Florida.

He had, however, one more duty to carry out. Though he'd managed so far to steer clear of her, the visit to Doña Antonia in the crude hut he'd built for her was obligatory.

She didn't mince words. "You are neither husband nor friend."

When he placed before her a blue taffeta gown his tailor had just finished, she threw it back at him. "A friend of Tocobaga is no friend of the Calusa."

"I am friend to both. I have two hearts."

"Two hearts, yes. One for Tocobaga and one for yourself. For me and for my brother, you have none."

Menéndez's fingers double-timed his whiskers. "My dear Doña Antonia, I will try to explain, though I cannot expect you to comprehend. I come with a higher purpose, to bring all the children of this world into the fold of the one Supreme Being. I am brother to Calusa and brother to Tocobaga both; we are all God's children. I leave behind Father Rogel. Continue with his lessons. You will begin to understand."

Antonia raised herself to her full height so she looked down upon her husband. "I have already begun to understand."

Antonia's malignant demeanor, Carlos's sulking, and Father Rogel's account of his conversation with the Calusas' warrior chief compelled the Adelantado to reconsider. It was too dangerous to leave the garrison on Carlos's island. At least temporarily, he would have to move his forces. He chose the smaller nearby island where they had first landed, reasoning that separation by water would constitute a greater safety factor. In a short while, as with children, the Indians would cool down. In the meantime, he would appoint a work detail to build a more fortified garrison in the Indians' settlement. Menéndez ordered Escalante to speak to Stepana. "Tell him the work party is not to be harassed. We will see how far his boasted authority reaches."

Menéndez sent Escalante with a second task. "Ask Chief Carlos to supply us with a dozen canoes and paddlers to aid us in moving our supplies." Then, anticipating the interpreter's response, "Yes, I'm well aware of the danger."

And it was that very evening that Father Rogel came breathless to Menéndez's quarters with the news that he had just been visited by Stepana. Carlos planned to attack the canoes full of Spaniards. Menéndez sighed. The chief was becoming far too predictable. Perhaps the Adelantado had overestimated him.

"The warrior chief told you this in confidence?"

"Yes, but God will never allow foul play. It is my moral imperative to inform you."

"You explained that to Stepana?"

The priest shook his head. "I thought that unwise. He's beginning to trust me. I don't want to place that in jeopardy."

"Ah. Apparently he was shrewd enough to deduce that himself."

Stepana's undermining of Carlos now was obvious. What was not so clear, as Menéndez reflected on it, was whether the planned attack was real or contrived. To risk his soldiers, though, would be foolish. The Adelantado made the move using his own small shallops. There were only two, and the process took all of a long day and half of the next. The Adelantado was growing weary of this game of cat and cat, and he was itching to return to the high seas. As the last load was delivered, he bid his men goodbye and made for his brigantine.

Father Rogel sat in the clearing beneath a sky so pregnant with moonlight that the priest had no need of a candle to read his verses. The move from the Calusa city hadn't deterred his work. During the day, he said Mass to the soldiers. At night, beneath the Indian sky, before the Indian waters, he preached for the benefit of that brown-skinned race. And he prayed that the Lord made them hear.

His eyes skimming the familiar Latin words, Father Rogel began, as always, at the beginning. "In the beginning God created the heaven and the earth. And the earth was without form, and void; and darkness was upon the face of the deep. And the Spirit of God moved upon the face of the waters." He read on to Verse 20: "And God said, 'Let the waters bring forth abundantly the moving creatures that hath life, and fowl that may fly above the earth in the open firmament of heaven.' And God created great whales, and every living creature that moveth, which the waters brought forth abundantly, after their kind, and every winged fowl after his kind: and God saw that it was good."

Good, yes. The priest fingered the hem of his fraying cassock, stroked the stubble of beard between his goatee and long sideburns. The conveniences in this alien land were few, yet how much more appreciation he had now for the Lord's work. This very evening, he had beheld a truly wondrous sight, right in the clearing. He'd been watching the slow crawl of a hermit crab onto a small piece of beach, marveling at the tiny creature dragging the heavy shell. As he watched, more and more of the little fellows appeared, until there seemed to be a whole congregation of them. Then, at the sounding of some unheard signal—surely the bell of the Lord—the crabs all crawled out of their shells, and, as in a child's game, scrambled for another. Father Rogel had chuckled at the scrawny creatures, little more than a single, hand-like claw and a pair of eyes, as they tried on shells and, either satisfied, made for the water, or displeased, crawled out to seek another.

"'Tis the hand of God," he'd said aloud, and laughed so hard at his own joke that he had to wipe away the tears.

Ah, it felt good to laugh. There had been little merriment at this island. The men were always on edge. Whenever Indian canoes approached, they rushed to their weapons, lighting the matchlock fuses on their arquebuses. Chief Carlos himself was a frequent visitor, bringing fish and other provisions. It seemed that his anger had passed. Yet he could not be trusted. Neither his behavior at Tocobaga nor Stepana's warning would soon be forgotten.

Besides, another common visitor was Stepana. Always he sounded the alarm. Chief Carlos was obsessed with revenge for what he considered the Adelantado's treachery in forming a pact with Tocobaga. He wanted only to dance with the Spaniards' heads.

The soldiers, of course, followed the Captain General's lead and trusted neither. Yet, Father Rogel had seen Stepana kiss the cross. The Indian war chief continued to pledge his love for Christ. Stepana's credibility further increased when one of his predictions came true. Carlos, he cautioned, had sent word to his vassal villages: kill the Spaniards, and you shall be rewarded. Indeed, one morning a group of unfamiliar Indian canoes—the men now recognized those of Carlos—approached before dawn. When the sentinels called out the alarm, the Indians dispersed. It was too dark to see clearly, but the soldiers judged that they saw weapons, not trade goods.

How was Father Rogel to make any progress in this atmosphere? All too familiar feelings of isolation began to grip him. He was preaching only to the moon.

In a fortnight's time, the garrison near the Indian palace was completed, triangular now with reinforced ramparts and a heavy wooden gate. A continuous moat surrounded the compound, more of a shallow ditch really, but at least it would slow an enemy down. Inside, a fort had been built of beams and wood, brushwood faggots and earth. Father Rogel persuaded Captain Reynoso to accept Carlos's proffered aid of three canoes to help the soldiers on their return. No warning had come from Stepana. And there were only three canoes. Surely the Indians, outnumbered, would not try the now familiar tactic of attacking the soldiers in the water.

Yet that is exactly what they did. The Indian paddlers rose up and overturned the canoes, then set upon the soldiers in the water. Other soldiers, at the ready, came to their aid, and soon the water was red with Calusa blood. Captain Reynoso crowed. Father Rogel felt only pain.

Aesha put her hands on Carlos's neck and shoulders. Every muscle was as taut as the strings on the Spanish music makers.

"I'll kill Stepana," he said. "I'll kill the Spaniards too, kill them all."

Nothing seemed to stop Carlos's rant. Such a sad state he had been reduced to. Yet Aesha had no time for pity. "You yourself have argued repeatedly that you mustn't, that to do so is to assure the return of even more Spaniards and an alliance between them and Tocobaga."

"My people consider me a coward. That is worse."

"It's Stepana who has manipulated the people. You must find a way of exposing him. He's your real enemy."

"Expose him? Never. He's too devious. It wasn't I who ordered the attack. Stepana commanded it, though he well knew it was doomed to failure. He cares not that his own warriors die, as long as it subjects me to ridicule. There's only one way. I must do what I should have done long ago. Eliminate him."

"Be very careful. His warriors are loyal to him."

"I trust no one. I'll do it myself."

"How?"

Carlos's teeth clamped down on his lower lip: "I will find a way." Then he let his shoulders slump under the pressure of Aesha's fingers. Such a wonderful touch she had, firm yet light. He must give her the attention she was due. When this was all over.

His head snapped back up. "The people sting from this last humiliation. They seek revenge. But never will I have it while Stepana is alive.

He hides behind his warriors, or else the skirts of the Spanish tirupo. It won't be easy to get close to him."

"Expose him in the Council. Isolate him."

"They'd applaud his valor in attacking."

Aesha knew there was no reasoning with Carlos. He was like the fish stunned by fish poison, flopping in helpless circles while the nets tighten around him.

Was it only Carlos that lay within the snare of the net, or was it all of Caalus, all of Escampaba? What could be done?

Aesha took her questions to the temple. "Carlos cannot take action. He behaves as if he is paralyzed."

Ishkara raised his left arm with his right.

"No, it's different. You may have lost motion, but not your power to act."

Ishkara pointed a finger at Aesha.

"Me? I would act, if only I knew what to do. That's why I seek your counsel."

Now Ishkara touched her eye.

"Yes, I still see the vision. Still the flames braided to my own hair."

Ishkara shuffled off then, disappearing into the inner temple. When he returned, he clutched a whelk shell dipper. He held it out to her, his bony hand—the good one—pale and shaky.

Before Aesha realized it, a flood of tears came. This was no ordinary cup; it was that of the right-handed whelk, the ceremonial casine dipper. Only the tirupo could possess it.

He placed the cup in her hand, wiped her eyes tenderly with the back of his arm.

"But what does this mean?" she stammered.

He stamped his good foot then; his look of impatience stung her.

Aesha forced herself to think clearly. He'd thrust upon her his spiritual authority and responsibility. There was only one problem; such was not his right. Only the cacique could choose a tirupo. So what was

Ishkara saying? She kissed his lopsided lips. He'd said all he could. She would do her best.

Ishkara sighed and looked to the sky.

Father Rogel felt like a prisoner. He dared not step outside the fort. Since the Spaniards' return to the island city, the situation had gone from bad to worse. Accompanied by Escalante, he had visited Aesha and Ishkara at the temple. The old Indian witch doctor had invited the Jesuit into his inner chamber—a rare privilege, according to Escalante—and shown the priest his idols and masks, treating the devil-inspired man-beasts with the greatest reverence. When Father Rogel attempted, in the gentlest fashion possible, to correct Ishkara's misconceptions, the Indian became agitated, donning one of the hideous carved and painted masks and dancing, in his limping style, about the temple.

The priest was sympathetic but firm. Speaking through Escalante, he asked Ishkara, "Do you wish still to go to heaven?"

The old Indian nodded his grotesquely covered head affirmatively.

"Then you must give up your worship of these false idols. There is only one God. You must worship Him alone."

Ishkara held up three fingers and pointed to his repulsive statues.

Father Rogel crossed himself, then shook his head. "No. The Lord is One."

"That motion you make—does it not pay homage to three gods?" Aesha asked.

"The Holy Trinity recognizes three elements, yes: the Father, the Son, and the Holy Ghost. But they are all embodiments of the one Lord."

"As are our three gods, for Nao and Aurr cannot act but by the permission of Sipi, who rules all. You see, it is the same."

Father Rogel felt his ears begin to purple. "No. Not the same. These idols are false. They must be destroyed, or Ishkara will surely burn in eternal hell." He quickly left the temple; he would listen to no more.

Soon thereafter, there was an incident. It occurred at the single time Father Rogel ventured out from the fort each day to do a thing that could not be avoided. Three Indians jumped upon him, covered his mouth and tried to carry him off. Fortunately, sentries guarded the Father even in his most private of moments. The Indians were driven off.

So there the priest remained, half a world removed from Pamplona, dropped in the midst of soulless Indians who desperately needed his guidance and yet walled off from them. Though he continued to invite the natives inside the fort, baiting them with more maize, none came now, no doubt on the order of Carlos.

Furthermore, Doña Antonia had abandoned her hut inside the garrison and returned to her brother. Father Rogel shuddered when he thought of the likely purpose: incest. Aesha, Escalante explained, had failed to produce an heir. The people were impatient. Doña Antonia would be an acceptable if less desirable alternative. Father Rogel could only shake his head sadly. Long had the devil roamed free in these uncivilized quarters. The matter was all the more troubling because Antonia professed to be a Christian. It reminded the priest of how much work he had to do. What could he accomplish, stuck in the fort? He was frustrated beyond words, yet he saw the situation for what he knew it must be: the Lord's trial of his faith. Father Rogel would be patient. He would prevail. The Lord would ensure it.

The priest was not so sure of the patience of Captain Reynoso. Carlos's constant threats were wearing on the Captain. Following Father Rogel's near kidnapping, Captain Reynoso had exploded. "I'll take his head with my own sword. Just say the word, Father."

"No, you mustn't. 'All they that take the sword shall perish with the sword.'"

"I am a soldier. If perish I must, I am ready."

"I beg you, be patient. Our work is only beginning. The Indians will settle down. You will see."

"No, it is you who will see. They will settle when their leader has fallen."

Dawn's cheeks were blushing as Aesha, padding lightly on bare feet, found Iqi outside the temple watching the shadows lift from the bay. Though he stood as straight as ever, lines of age and worry had begun to etch small tidal streams into his face. They emptied into eyes that were pools of longing. Aesha's breath caught momentarily at the unguarded moment. A small "Oh" escaped.

Iqi turned and brightened briefly, but then his face went somber. "He's been awake all night," Iqi said, tilting his head toward the temple. "Preparing."

"Preparing for what?"

"I didn't disturb him. He's inside the sanctuary. I heard him limping back and forth, heard scraping and rubbing sounds. That's all."

Aesha looked at the temple wall, then back to Iqi. "I owe so much to you. Soon this will be over and you can return to the island. What I've done to you, it's not fair."

Iqi took her shoulders in his hands, squeezed them briefly and then turned her around. "You've done nothing to me, only what you had to for me and for others. Him especially. Go see him."

She reached back to place her hands on his hips and leaned into him. For a moment they held the pose. Then he pushed her, gently, toward the temple.

Masks lay all over the sanctuary floor. There were the warrior masks, bearing likenesses of the woodpeckers—pileated, redheaded, red-bellied, red-cockaded, and ivory-billed—carved from dark, gnarled blocks of wood and painted to display those birds' blood-red heads; the disease masks, depicting the spider with its eight exaggerated legs; the supremacy masks, mimicking the crocodile's jaws; the grieving masks, portraying the black, featherless face of the vulture; and the single mask of death foreseen, that of the white pelican. Ishkara sat in their midst, dipping a whelk ladle into a pot of boiled manatee fat, dripping a bit on each mask, then rubbing it in with the heel of his good hand, all the while chanting garbled prayers only he could understand. Aesha could see he'd been at it quite a while. The masks shone with the glint of malevolence.

Aesha reached down to rub the old tirupo's bony neck. Beneath the loose skin was no muscle, only bone, as if she grasped the frame of a skeleton. He turned to blink at her with milky eyes and struggled to his feet.

"Please," she said. "Sit down. It is too much effort."

Ishkara shook his head violently. He jabbed a thumb at his own chest, then raised his arms, forcing the bad left one to lift so that it made a full circle with his right.

Aesha guessed at the gesture's meaning. "You have something to say to all of Caalus."

He nodded, then pointed to the masks, then outside.

"Yes, I understand. The masks are to be brought out. When?"

He took her hand, limped from the temple. Indicating the sun, he made a wide arc with his right arm across the sky to the west.

"At sunset."

Nod.

"And for what purpose?"

Ishkara's mouth twisted into its left-sided grin.

Aesha had known what she needed to do. Dusk was just yielding to night as she finished preparations. She and the group of councilors and elders clustered together on high as the people gathered below. When the long lines had finished filing into the plaza, she helped the great white pelican to his feet. Following his lead, the long procession of masked visages began their march down from the temple. Slowly and solemnly, they descended, each holding a coco plum seed candle, until they reached the wide plaza at the foot of the water court. The throng of onlookers parted for them, and the procession wound, in single file, to the plaza's center. At a signal from Pelican, nine drummers began to pound their deer hide drums, three beats and a rest, then three beats again. Next, the shell horns joined in, sounding their upturning melodies in time to the drumbeat. Finally came the chanting of the hundred-girl chorus, delivering its three-word prayer in intentional dissonance to the notes of the shell horns: "Hear us now." The crowd sang along and stamped its feet in time.

The production raised such a commotion that the gods could not help but hear.

Pelican lowered his candle and lit the central fire that had been laid on the plaza floor. Other masked figures moved to the perimeter, igniting the nine smaller fires. As light leapt from the fires, the sound of crackling and popping wood mixed with the voices and instruments. Pelican began to dance then, hopping on one foot, shaking the crab claw rattle that flashed orange in the fire's glow. Around him, the other animal beings began to dance, too. They spread out on the plaza, skipping faster and harder as the drumbeat quickened. The horns blew louder, and the girls sang at the tops of their lungs. The dancers whirled and shook, then began leaping over the fires, their shadow souls appearing, then vanishing into the night air. Grabbing the onlookers, the masked dancers pulled them into the melee, until soon the plaza resembled a nest of disturbed ants.

Pelican stood still now, watching the frenzied dance, his rib cage heaving as he struggled to catch his breath. A single calm figure in a sea of fury, he placed something into the central fire and sat down next to it. The dancers wound themselves in a circle, spinning and twirling around the now-serene figure of Pelican. Round and round they revolved, stabbing the air and pounding the ground, sweat and tears mixing as they danced for their tirupo.

At length, Pelican reached into the fire, pulled out a flaming piece of wood and held it high above his head. Smoke rose from it to the sky.

A buzz went through the crowd as they recognized the shaft of burning wood: Caalus's staff, inherited by Ishkara, plucked from Stepana's hands. The hot embers of the dense wood burned beneath his hand, turning the hand transparent, like that of a departed soul. If Pelican felt pain, he didn't show it. With the dancers still whirling around him, Pelican began to move slowly from the plaza. But not back to the temple. He aimed for the ramp to the palace mound and the Spanish fort.

Father Rogel peered through the space between the gate to San Antón and the heavy timbers to which it was latched. Flames flickered from the plaza below, and the sound of animal-like chanting rose wild and riotous, raising the hairs on the back of his neck. There could be no doubt. The devil was about. He stood transfixed, dumbly watching the satanic chaos.

Then, there was pattern to the movement down there, as the dark clot of Indians funneled from the fires and away from the plaza. Father Rogel's bowel nearly let loose as the realization hit him. The mob of angry Indians was moving toward the fort.

Clutching the crucifix at his neck, the priest gathered all his strength and faith. "Turn back," he shouted. "Turn back. I command thee." But his words were lost in the tumult of heathen drumbeats.

Up the ramp came the mob, the mass twirling and hopping, circling in frenzied Indian fashion around a slowly plodding central figure. He was wearing some kind of disguise, one of his masks probably, but he walked with a pronounced limp that the priest could not mistake. It was the old witch doctor, Ishkara.

Closer and closer came the devilish horde, until Father Rogel could see now the tortured likenesses of beasts, birds, and fishes that had hung on the inner temple wall. The old man himself hid behind the long-beaked mask of a pelican, painted a ghastly, ghostly white. In his hand, he held a burning torch. No, not a torch. A stick burning from end to end. Smoke swirled from beneath the old man's fingers, yet he flinched not a bit.

Now Father Rogel knew beyond doubt that he was facing the devil in-carnate. "Turn back," he yelled again. But the mob inched ever forward, bringing the evil one to the very foot of the fort's outer gate.

"Stand aside," spoke a voice behind the priest. It was Captain Reynoso. And before Father Rogel could react, the captain thrust open the gate and plunged into the mass of Indians. Brandishing his half lance, the Captain rushed straight to the center and struck at the visage of the pelican. As he did so, the masked Indian flinched and bowed his head. The blunt end of the heavy instrument landed full on the Indian's un-protected skull.

The pelican figure crumpled. The circle of masked dancers froze as Captain Reynoso swiftly slipped back into the fort. From the stunned silence sounded an anguished wail, and up rushed the woman Father Rogel recognized as the chief's wife. She threw herself upon the stricken body, curled now in fetal position. Blood had spilled out onto the ground, pooling in a dark, dust-shored lake. The old man did not move.

ᗡ Fifteen ᗡ

Aesha cradled the breathless body, light as a child's. "What were you trying to do?" she whispered. "Burn the fort? Did you take my vision as your own? Is that its meaning?"

Ishkara didn't answer.

"Or did you mean to force the Christians to recognize the power of our gods?" She sat numbly, her eyes following the smoke from the still smoldering staff. It wafted toward the now-closed gate of the fort, found the cracks and spaces, and entered the Spaniards' compound.

Two of the masked councilors bent to help her up, but Aesha curled in a ball over Ishkara. He'd known. That's why he'd worn the mask of white pelican. But why hadn't he given her a sign so she'd recognize him in the land beyond? Now what was she to do? His death clarified nothing.

Aesha pulled the mask from the tirupo's blood-soaked head. His features were tranquil, lips pulled into a serene and full smile. From his eyes, no longer clouded, shone the polished pearls of a pure, unblemished soul.

"Kill them. Burn the fort." Anger boiled around her, yet no one dared act. They were waiting to be led. Aesha closed her eyes. *Help me, Ishkara,* she said silently. *Let me see clearly, as you do now.* She fought to maintain her calm, to ignore the voices that assailed her ears. Still huddled over Ishkara's limp body, she felt its heat seep through her, spreading upwards until it lit the dark space behind her closed eyelids with the familiar flames of her dreams. So be it. Her own vision must lead her. She concentrated, peering through the smoke, following the tendrils of flame that radiated from her hair. But they reached not toward the gate to the Spanish fort. They went elsewhere. And something more. Elsewhen. Not now.

She opened her eyes and faced the fort. Through the brushwood fence, she saw the eager flickering of the burning cords that would unleash the Spaniards' weapons. No. Not here. Not tonight.

She rose, Ishkara's body folded in her arms. "Let us not dishonor Ishkara by dying needlessly. That wasn't his purpose; that isn't our fate." She turned from the fort, carrying him silently down the slope of the ramp.

The people followed.

In the stillness of the soft and hazy morning, Captain Reynoso swung open the fort's gate. He thought there'd been a sound. Not the usual singing and chatter as the Indians went about their morning routines, rather something both far-off and familiar. In fact, what he observed in the village below was . . . nothing. No gathering of nets from the drying racks, no fetching of water, no laying of kindling on cooking fires. No teasing smells from their pots. It was as if the city below him had died.

Though this might have given the captain cause for concern about attack, Reynoso wasn't worried. Once the old man had fallen, the others had lost their nerve. They hadn't laid a finger on the captain; they'd skulked back down the ramp like whipped dogs, just as he thought they would. This morning they weren't preparing for battle. As a military man, he'd sense it, smell it, even if he didn't hear or see it. No. For now, the fort was safer than ever.

Reynoso was satisfied. Bold action had been called for, and he'd taken it. The Adelantado would approve. Did, in fact; that was why he'd appointed Reynoso not just captain but governor of San Antón. Reynoso was so proud of the order that represented the pinnacle of his thirty-year career, he could recite it word for word: "I name you as captain of the aforementioned fort and people, and governor of that destination, and as such, I order all the people, sailors, and soldiers of merchant ships and military fleets that might go there and reach port, and all the people of whatever quality and condition they may be, to obey and observe and respect you as such, and to fulfill your commands."

All the people to obey. That meant the Indians, too.

He felt the ragged edge of his mangled right ear. It had been torturing him ever since he'd arrived at the fort, the mosquitoes and sand flies chewing on it incessantly, leaving it thick, crusted with blood, and constantly throbbing. Not so this morning. No itching.

The sound came again. There was no doubt now. It was the voice of a ship's boy calling out the time to the pilot. Supplies were coming. Reynoso ran about the compound, rousing his soldiers. "Stir yourselves. The *Espíritu Santo* has come from Campeche. Don't dally now. She'll carry maize. Hardtack, too, and wheat flour. Can't you smell the cassava? And wine by the barrel. Lively, men. Let's unload her before these Indians put their breechclouts on."

As he led the soldiers down the ramp, flanked by arquebuses just in case, Reynoso sang. After all, he'd been a ship's boy himself.

Blessed be the light so good
And blessed be the Holy Rood
And blest the Lord of Verity
And the Holy Trinity.
Blessed be our souls—God save them.
And blessed be the God Who gave them.
Blessed be the light of day
And God Who with it lights the way.

As the shallow-drafting brigantine moved into the Indians' canal, Reynoso saw that their luck was even better than he'd hoped for. There was livestock aboard, cattle and pigs. Fresh meat.

Soon, while the rest of the attachment hauled supplies, his cooks were slaughtering the fattest steer and feeding a huge cooking fire. Spurred by the tantalizing smell of roasting meat, the unloading went quickly. Some of the Indians peeked out from their huts, but most just cowered inside. There were no incidents. That task completed, Reynoso raced his men to the fire. Drawing his broadsword, he began hacking off slabs of the barely seared beef, dispensing the still bloody hunks into the clutching hands of the meat-starved soldiers.

Off to the side, Father Rogel ate his fill to the accompaniment of a growling belly. Let the others celebrate; he could not. He could be of no benefit to the Indians now. Their sullen silence would eventually turn to anger, no doubt directed at him as much as at the captain. The priest had already made his decision. San Antón would be better off in his absence. When the boat, reboarded by men drunk on wine and gorged to groaning on good beef, prepared to sail for Havana, Father Rogel took his leave in it. He would return when the situation calmed down. Or if.

By the afternoon after his father's death, Carlos had formulated his plan. He dispatched messengers to spread the news of Ishkara's passing. The nine-day mourning period would begin immediately with fasting and running. Upon the last day, a great festival of singing and dancing would be held, capped with the sacrifice of Ishkara's servant, Iqi. As the canoes prepared to depart, Carlos bade Stepana personally to deliver private messages to Tanpa and to Muspa: Escampaba was in crisis. They must come personally and bring their stores of silver and gold to trade with the Spaniards. And their warriors as well.

There. The nets were set.

Carlos could even now hear the hushed exchange between Stepana and the Spanish captain. "It's a trap," Stepana would say, relaying the intercepted message. "Carlos does not trust that the citizens of Caalus, his own people, will follow his orders, so he orders distant villages to do his bidding. He knows well that the Spaniards love their silver and gold. While they are occupied in trading, Tanpa and Muspa will attack."

"The solution is simple," the arrogant Spaniard with the chopped-off ear would reply. "We'll refuse to engage in barter."

"Then they'll simply break open the gate to the fort. There are too many; you'll never stop them. Carlos has nothing to lose. He must do this. The people demand it."

"Then you will have to help me."

Stepana would try to disguise the panic in his voice, but Carlos could hear it, taste it. "Don't you see? Carlos aims to trap both of us. I'll be left with the impossible decision of sending my forces against their own cousins, or of watching the slaughter of my Spanish friends."

But the exchange between Stepana and Reynoso couldn't take place until Stepana's return. That was the beauty of Carlos's plan—part of it, anyway. Making Stepana personally deliver the message to both Muspa in the south and Tanpa in the north ensured both that Carlos would have plenty of reinforcements and that the Spanish captain would have no time to get word to his superior. What would Reynoso do? Put up a stand inside the fort? Carlos thought not. The captain was a man of deeds. He'd shown that in his slaying of Ishkara. More likely, he'd mount an assault. Then Carlos would have him. Outside the fort, he'd be a shark on land, wriggling helplessly, full of teeth that snapped at air.

The victory would be Carlos's alone.

The cacique had spread out still another net, one he should have set long ago. He'd been too soft. No more. The third net was for Aesha. Live up to her breeding or down to that of her lover. The choice was hers.

Carlos was treating her fairly. When she'd shown him the casine cup Ishkara had given her, Carlos had taken it from her. The decision as to who'd be the next tirupo was his alone, and he had other ideas. He did, however, allow his wife to perform the rituals with Ishkara's body. Odd.

Instead of grief for the passing of his father, he felt only gratitude. In the wake of Ishkara's sacrifice, the ulcerous festering of troubles facing the cacique had all risen to the surface. Carlos had only to lance them like boils, cut out the abscesses. Blood would have to be shed, but afterwards the blemishes upon his authority would heal, and the cacique would have his seat back. And his revenges.

Carlos was not oblivious to the fact that the people of Caalus were stunned and outraged. He could hardly expect otherwise. Grieving over Ishkara's slaying, restless for Spanish blood, they were calling him a coward and a traitor. When they learned that Carlos intended to trade with the Christians, they'd boil over. Trade with the Spaniards when they should be dancing with their heads? They'd demand Carlos's instead.

His opening for success would be brief. He intended to make good use of it.

"He's given us no choice. We must leave for the island before it's too late."

Iqi recognized the look on Aesha's pallid face. It was that of the snared rabbit. "We must be calm," he answered.

"Calm? How can you be calm?"

"It's a great honor to be sent to serve Ishkara in the land beyond."

She stared at him in horror.

"I'm calm only on the surface," he admitted. "Inside, the voice I've always trusted, the one that has given me patience and fortitude, is asking why I must depart with our love still unfulfilled. I'm not prepared for the life beyond life, not prepared to leave you. But I'm a ground dweller. I accept."

"I'll not let him take you. Carlos ordered it only to spite us. There's no requirement for a sacrifice. Only when the cacique dies. Ishkara was tirupo, and before that only regent, never truly ruler."

"The people loved him as one. I loved him as one."

Behind their veil of wetness, Aesha's eyes burned fierce now. Rabbit no more. "Do not speak to me of love. No one loves Ishkara better than I. But this act of Carlos comes not from love. He scorns my barrenness, resents my independence. I think that's his true intention. He knows I'll aid your escape. Then, he'll banish me. Not even I can violate his command without punishment."

"That is not your fate. You've seen it otherwise too often in your vision."

"Then I'll burn with you. Maybe that's my destiny."

Iqi bowed his head low. "I leave knowledge of our destinies to you."

Aesha's arms flew out to envelop him. "I know only this. Ours are tied together." She squeezed his head tight to her breast.

Iqi breathed in hard, then mumbled something too muffled to make out, and Aesha was forced to release him. "It still smells faintly of the mud flat," he said.

"My breast?" And the two of them were suddenly awash in a spasm of laughter, a convulsive release of tension and tears. As it began to die down, Iqi wrinkled his nose and sniffed loudly, bringing forth a new eruption.

"No," he said finally, "the crown conch. You still wear it."

She fingered it, feeling its shape, malformed but smoothed. "Will our lives ever begin to heal over?" she asked.

"I can't say," Iqi answered.

"I can't, either." She hugged him again, the shell pressed between them, exuding its faint smell, singing its faint song. "But I can believe," she said.

Tanpa and Muspa arrived as ordered with their gold and silver displayed and warriors painted for feasting, not fighting, bows and atlatls stowed beneath skins in their canoes. Before long, a messenger came to tell Carlos that Captain Reynoso had called for him. Good. Stepana was acting as expected. It was interesting that the captain was seeking to negotiate. Perhaps as a warrior he understood the impossible odds against him. Or perhaps Escalante had convinced Reynoso to show some consideration for Carlos's power. The cacique pressed his fingers together thoughtfully. This might be even better. He would simply deny his intention to attack, expose Stepana's trickery once and for all. Incident by incident, in front of Tanpa and Muspa, Carlos would reveal how all the overturned canoes, all the threats and schemes from the very beginning had been hatched by Stepana, not Carlos. Then he'd begin dangling gold, piece by piece. Carlos didn't care if it took all of Tanpa's and Muspa's stores and half of his own. Of one thing, the cacique was sure: the Spanish captain's allegiance could be bought.

The cacique would call for Stepana's execution then. Oh, sweet revenge to let the Spaniards take care of him. But if in the Adelantado's absence Captain Reynoso proved reluctant to order Stepana's killing, Carlos had a fallback plan. Stepana claimed he wished to become a Christian. Let the Spaniards take him to Havana. Better yet, to Spain. Carlos knew that Menéndez himself planned to return there with some of his newfound pets. Let Stepana be one of them. Either way, removing Stepana eliminated the single obstacle to a genuine Spanish-Calusa alliance.

Yes, this turn of events boded far better. He was surer than ever that Ishkara had foreseen it all.

He summoned Tanpa and Muspa to share casine. "I have arranged for you to meet the Spanish captain," he told them. "You will see him bow before me."

"Due in large part to my warriors, who stand ready," said Tanpa.

"Your loyalty will be rewarded."

"How?" The chief from the north was blunt.

Carlos took a sip of the black drink. He'd been gulping it nonstop since the night of Ishkara's death, and it had given him clarity of mind such as he'd never before experienced. "You are to become my great captain upon Stepana's dismissal. And you, Muspa, will be tirupo."

The two looked at each other, then back to their cacique. Then Tanpa spoke: "Stepana will never step down voluntarily."

"That is why you've brought your treasures. Stepana is a traitor. Support my position and you'll be rewarded. Oppose me and all three of us may die. Now, to the fort, and heft your treasures. The captain awaits us."

The two chiefs exchanged looks again as Carlos made for the door.

"Now," growled Carlos, and this time they followed as the cacique led them the short distance from the council hall to the Spanish fort. The crowd lining the path, called out by Carlos for the occasion, scowled at him and spat on the ground. But Carlos was no longer angry. The people's vision was clouded with grief and fury. Only the cacique saw clearly.

Carlos paused in front of the Spanish fort. The gate was about to open to him. Scorned by his wife, his councilors, his people, only Nao had stood by him, helping him to get the gate to yield not by the force of might but by that of cunning. As his subordinate chiefs struggled with their heavy bags of gold and silver, Carlos felt profound satisfaction. The promises of high office had not been too high a price to pay. Ishkara had been right all along about one thing: the glittery metals were crucial. In the absence of their supreme leader Menéndez, the Spanish soldiers would be unable to restrain their appetites. The wealth that had been brought to Caalus would send them into a frenzy of greed. And no one was easier to control than the glutton.

"My brothers," he said to Tanpa and Muspa, "prepare to meet your pale-skinned servants."

As the gate closed behind them, the three faced a dozen pairs of glinting metal pupils. The last thing Carlos saw was a flash of light.

⊱ Sixteen ⊰

12 July 1567

Poor Father Rogel. How he suffers in the sun, the heat building up inside his black cassock, beads of sweat running down his sideburns and staining his collar. The soldiers joke that the reason he holds his head so high in the air is to spare his nose from the stench of his body. We all smell, victims of either too little water inside our prison of a fort, or else too much. Of late, it is the latter. We put up with rotting feet, heat rash, and insects that swarm inside our porous quarters. Sometimes I find myself longing to shed my ruan tunic and breeches, smear my body with shark liver oil. Then I pray: I must not turn heathen, not now after being rescued. A small price this misery, to save my Christian soul.

Despite the Father's agonies, he tries to convert souls. Upon his return from Havana, he erected a new cross and attracted many of the leading families to his morning lessons. Even Felipe came for a time. Such a spectacle, hearing the Indians recite the Our Father and chant their Hail Mary's in their mimicked, uncomprehending Spanish. The Father quite forgets his discomfort as he preaches in all earnestness about the oneness of God and how He created the world, then the first man and woman. Father Rogel smiles most sincerely as I repeat his words in the Indians' tongue.

He fails to see that the Indians have always one eye on the maize.

I'm grateful the Jesuit didn't return from Havana until after the rituals. He could never have stomached the slaying of Carlos's servants, could never have accepted that to the Indians it is an honor to be so chosen. The families of the sacrificed were placed on seats of honor, so close they were sprayed by the scarlet fountains spurting from the gashed and gurgling throats of their loved ones. The Father would have wept.

As did I. I saw not the servants up there, but my brother, and I wept. Something has changed in me since the return of my brethren. I've awoken as if from a nightmare of mutilation and mayhem, where all manner of ghastly practices are conducted and I am not mere bystander but willing participant. I'd sworn never to forget my brother's slaying, and I forgot. So shamed am I now. I pledge once more ne'er to slumber.

What made the servants' sacrifices even more revolting was that Aesha presided over them, as she did over the other rituals, the fasting, the running, the feast that ended the grieving period, and the interment of Carlos's body, which now lies in the temple next to that of his father and of Aesha's own father, Caalus. She is tirupo now, just as Felipe is cacique, crowned with the huge pearl for his forehead and the fringed leggings in a kind of pagan coronation that Aesha officiated over, too.

Felipe. It was the Father's idea to rename Stepana for Our Lord and Majesty, though of course Aesha, as tirupo, had to proclaim it. Stepana protects his new name as a hungry raccoon guards a fish carcass. Already he has severed the tongues of several Indians who slipped up. With these tactics, they learn fast.

I was astounded at first that the enmity between Stepana and

Aesha did not explode, even as I was astonished that the Indians didn't storm the fort after the deaths of both Carlos and Ishkara. But in all my long years with these Indians, the only thing I know for certain is that I'll never understand them fully. I suppose they were stunned by the two slayings so near in time. And Felipe—I'd best get used to calling him that, lest I too lose my tongue—must have found the path of truce and negotiation preferable to that of battle; for he has succeeded in securing the support of both the Spanish and of the daughter of Caalus, endorsements that have bought him time and legitimacy.

I'd have sacrificed a year of freshwater baths to have been hidden inside the temple within earshot of the negotiations between Felipe and Aesha. Now I wonder if perhaps they'll marry. Remarry. A sickening thought, yet no more so than seeing her order the slitting of throats. Maybe she only cooperated with Felipe in order to save the head of her lover. I will never know her innermost heart. Such folly to have thought I could save her. She's lost to me forever.

Danger lurks everywhere on this island. So I told Pedro Menéndez Márquez when he delivered the Father back here last month. When Felipe declared himself a vassal of Spain, pledging tribute to the Adelantado's nephew with feathers and mats and other miserable things the Indians value, I warned Pedro of the Indian's insincerity. He thanked me and told me how indispensable I am to the soldiers and to the Jesuit. He is right, of course.

So now it is left to Father Rogel to convert the Indians. Or rather, left to me, for the Father still trips over the simplest of their words. No matter the evidence to the contrary, the priest still believes he can win Felipe over to Christianity. Ever the innocent, just as Captain Reynoso is ever the bloodthirsty. I've come to realize that the Adelantado knew all this, knew the fort would fail without my presence. That's why he left for Spain without me. If ever he returns and I have my due reward, my homecoming to that dear and distant land

will reveal my significance, declare my celebrity. Perhaps an audi-
ence with His Majesty himself, the true Felipe, is not too far-fetched a
dream.

If I survive. If the fort survives. Would that the Adelantado return
soon.

The task of saving souls was arduous, one that required patience, perseverance, and purity of spirit. Though Father Rogel struggled mightily
with all three, he had to allow himself a tiny pinch of pride. Certain successes were beginning to manifest themselves.

Regularity. That was the first of them. Routine and repetition were
the treads of the Lord's staircase. Twice each day, once for the men and
once for a group of leading women, Father Rogel went to the cross to
catechize the Indians. Afterwards, exhausted by the heat, he repaired to
the chapel to read the Bible. Frequently, many of the Indians followed,
even though they'd already consumed the bits of food he'd brought to
the cross. The natives were coming on their own.

It was clear that they were fascinated by the Good Book. They pressed
close to see and touch the images and to run their fingers across the
words, as if by stroking them they might absorb their wisdom. Father
Rogel didn't discourage the strange action. It was a sign of the power of
God's Word.

He also took the Indians' visits as an opportunity, through the interpreter, to discuss the teachings of holy faith in clear language, though,
of course, only in the simplest of terms. Now there was a lesson oft repeated. Just today, the priest had tried to explain the creation of the angels and the fall of the bad ones. Even after Escalante translated, the Indians' faces bore looks of pure confusion.

"Angels are persons who God created in heaven. They do not have a
body," the Father explained.

"They are souls, then," one of the Indians commented.

"Yes, like them, as they cannot die." Better to communicate imperfectly than not at all. He'd gone on to inquire of the group why they prayed.

"Because you ask us to."

"But I have witnessed you pray of your own volition to your idols. What do you pray for?"

"For victory over our enemies," answered one.

"For an abundance of fish for our pots," answered another.

"For health and long life."

"And you know, as I have been telling you, that all thanks for these things are due to the one God?"

Heads nodded, if slowly.

"To ask for these things from your idols is to do God great injury. It's the work of the devil."

Now the confusion shifted toward consternation.

Father Rogel cupped his chin. "Let me pose a like situation. Suppose one of your own people, a very citizen of Caalus, were to pledge allegiance to Tocobaga. Cacique Felipe would be greatly angered, would he not?"

The chatters and nods confirmed that this, at least, was universally acknowledged.

The priest stabbed the air with an accusing finger. "The one who appears to you in the images of your idols is the devil, the enemy of God. It is he you have worshipped these long years. That is why it is so urgent for me to bring you into the fold."

But the faces turned opaque.

Father Rogel knew he needed the aid of the cacique. That's why this latest development was so worrisome: Don Felipe had been conspicuously absent the past three days. Father Rogel was determined to meet the situation head on. He could no longer afford to be fearful of the new chief. He sent a messenger, requesting that the ruler come to the chapel inside the fort.

Don Felipe appeared within minutes. To the priest's question, he replied, "The duties of my new office weigh heavily upon me. Regretfully, I am quite busy. I do not ignore my Spanish brother, though. When you call, I come."

Father Rogel was firm. "If you wish to become a Christian, you must commit to it with your heart, your soul, and your time."

"I promise you. I shall become a Christian as soon as the Adelantado returns."

"But he may be gone many months, if not years."

"This is the same pledge my predecessor made. I am an honorable man. I will abide by it." Felipe rubbed the huge pearl he now wore on his forehead. "You must realize, however, that since the deaths of Ishkara and Carlos, my people fear the Spaniards greatly. They believe that you wish to ravage them and carry them all off as captives. They wish either to rise up against you or else to flee. It is I who persuaded them to remain peaceful. And to learn about your one god. Are you not grateful for my actions?"

"Of course, of course," said Father Rogel. "But why must you await the Adelantado's return?"

"The customs of my people are ancient. They cannot change like the tides. If I do not follow my people's wishes, they will no longer allow me to lead them. As cacique, I must command, but I must also obey."

"But the people—your followers—say they cannot become Christians until you do."

"Patience. You must learn it as I have."

Yes, patience, persistence, and purity. And prayer for the Adelantado's return.

Cacique Felipe. Nearly forty suns he had awaited the day, and now that it was upon him, he was more than ready to rule. His first task—the task of any new leader—was to consolidate his authority. He ordered that extensive amounts of gold and silver be heated and hammered into amulets bearing his personal dolphin motif, then distributed the pendants to those pledging loyalty. Like the dolphin, he spread his seed freely amongst an ocean of new wives. When the first challenge inevitably came—the defection of two northern villages to Tocobaga—he dealt with it promptly. The heads of four of the leaders now hung on poles at the entrance to the temple. It would only be a matter of time before he tracked down the rest.

Relations with Aesha had even achieved a level of—how to say?—stability. She'd made no move to block the mounting of the bloody heads. The discussions with her were almost friendly. They both knew that the Spaniards were sniffing for weakness in the aftermath of Carlos's death and that a unified front was essential. He'd suggested that they give the world further evidence of their harmony. "Your own father commanded it. Let us once again wed."

"Never," she answered, her eyes narrowing to cold notches.

"You still love the ground dweller?"

"I warn you: leave Iqi alone. He serves me at the temple. You will not touch him."

"Your charms haven't dimmed a bit," he'd said. "In return for my benevolence, you will bestow upon me a new name, taken from the cacique of all the Spaniards, lord of even Menéndez."

She agreed. They both needed each other. For now.

Only the Spanish priest continued to harass him. It was a constant annoyance, having to feign devotion to the Christian god, promising wild concessions like cutting his hair or banishing his wives once the Spanish leader returned. Once, it had nearly led to disaster when Felipe's daughter Esquete, only four suns, had fallen seriously ill. Convinced that she was dying, Father Rogel pestered Felipe day and night to have her baptized as a Christian. "Please," the priest pleaded, "by virtue of the holy baptism, the child may well be cured. And should it be God's will to take her, her soul, having been baptized, will go to heaven. Otherwise she'll be left in limbo."

Distraught, Felipe ordered Aesha to assemble three children to be sacrificed upon Esquete's death. Instead, Aesha brought her to the temple and gave her smoke and herbs. The next day, Esquete's fever broke, and she returned to the living.

Felipe cursed at how close he'd come to consenting to the priest's demands. Yet, what had the Spaniard done? Claimed credit for the healing. Felipe was proud of himself. He didn't lose his temper, didn't lash out at the Spaniard's arrogance and ignorance. Instead, the cacique kissed the cross. At times like these, a leader had to trade the war club for diplomacy. Felipe needed the Spaniards as he needed Aesha. For now. Until their leader's return.

The hand touched her, stroking her long hair, parting it to rub the back of her neck. It was a strong hand, yet not rough and calloused like Iqi's. Aesha lay motionless in that place between dreaming and wakefulness, not caring which world he was coming to her from. It was enough that Carlos was here, massaging her gently, showing her tenderness, unencumbered now by the demands and pressures that had turned him harsh and arrogant, led him to his seemingly senseless death.

"I'm leaving," he said.

Don't, she cried out in her mind. Your hands are so warm. Stay with me just a bit longer.

"I'm leaving," he said again, and this time it jolted her awake, for the voice did not belong to Carlos any more than it belonged to the world of dreams. It was Piyaya's; she knelt beside Aesha's sleeping mat. Aesha sat upright, rubbing her eyes.

"To the fort," Piyaya said before Aesha had a chance to ask. "To become a Christian. To await the return of my husband."

"To live with Carlos's murderers?" Aesha was fully awake now. Too awake in this nightmarish reality.

"In the house my husband built for me."

"It makes no sense," Aesha said.

"It makes perfect sense. With Stepana—excuse me, Felipe—in the palace, what use am I here? My brother was right. If I'm to be of any value, it must be as the Adelantado's wife."

"You'll be alone. He may never return."

"They open the gate to those who pray with them," Piyaya said. "Besides, I've been alone before."

"How do you know they won't slay you as well?"

"Murder the wife of their leader? Why? They want me to be their Christian. Carlos wanted it, too. It's necessary. And it may help us."

"But the people love you."

Piyaya patted Aesha's hand. "It's you the people love and always have. It's your duty to stay with them, keep them from Felipe's grip. But it's I the Adelantado married. You must follow your fate; I must follow mine." She glanced out Aesha's window. "It's getting light out. I must leave."

Aesha rose with her, hugged her tight.

"Don't grieve," Piyaya said. "I'm not going to the land beyond the living, just to the one beyond the fence."

"But, Piyaya . . ."

"Call me Antonia. I'm a Christian."

No matter how many times Don Felipe proved himself insincere, Father Rogel would continue to work at saving his soul. It was clear that the Indian chief was struggling with his faith. He pondered carefully the priest's teachings, admitting freely concepts like the oneness of God and the Lord's ability to raise the dead. Yet his indoctrination into his heathen and unholy beliefs continued to blind him, and Felipe continued to fornicate openly with multiple wives. Father Rogel would not be duped; so depraved were these actions, the new chief might prove incapable of being saved. But the priest would never give up.

One day, he called Don Felipe to his chapel. "I have heard a rumor," he explained through the ever present Escalante, "and I must ask if it is true. Do you plan to take your own sister as wife?"

"It is tradition. My people demand it."

"It is an abomination before the Lord. You must not go through with it."

"I'll leave her when I become Christian, when the Adelantado returns."

Father Rogel pounded a fist onto the half-log table that served as his writing desk. "No, it is not so simple. You sin knowingly. You'll not be easily forgiven."

"I kiss the cross daily with all sincerity."

"And what will you do with all your other wives?"

"They simply bind me to my people. They're merely a convenience. What harm do they cause?"

"Harm?" Father Rogel struggled mightily to control his rising fury. "You are violating the law of God. When God created the first man in the world, He put him in the company of one woman only. All Christians are descended from this single man and woman. To become a believer of the one true faith, you must share your life with one legitimate wife alone."

Felipe paused, lost in thought for several moments before responding. "I will tell you a story. One day, Egret was wading in the water. He waded as deep as he dared, but still the small fishes he stalked were out of reach. Tarpon and Redfish, who were near, saw this and taunted him. 'Simply plunge in. What are you so afraid of?' But Egret dared not, for that is not how egrets hunt. He returned to his nest without food for his young.

"In the nest were three chicks, two that were white and a third, all black, who complained the loudest. That is when Egret had an idea. 'You are different,' he said to the dark-colored chick. 'Being so, you will be able to swim.' Believing his father as all children do, the chick took to the water, returning with a belly full of fry. Soon that hatchling left the nest, no longer Egret but Cormorant, the finest diver of all the birds." Felipe stopped, hooking both thumbs under his painted biceps.

"You prove my point exactly," said Father Rogel. "To change, one needs merely to believe."

Felipe smiled solicitously. "That is not the point at all. It is a very troublesome and difficult thing for men to change who have been accustomed to one way of living since infancy. I am afraid that your attempt to strip old men of all their customs and to make them perfect Christians is not achievable. Perhaps you should work, instead, with the children and youth. Teach them how to swim."

The priest felt heat searing at the back of his neck. Patience, he reminded himself for the thousandth time. The stakes were exceedingly high. If Felipe were to embrace Christianity, the faith of our Lord Jesus Christ and his holy Gospel might spread peaceably to all of La Florida. If not . . . this cacique had been the Indians' war chief. Father Rogel preferred not to think of the consequences.

"Two," Felipe said at long last. "When I become a Christian, I will keep no more than two wives."

Father Rogel would have to interpret this as progress.

The inner temple. The sacred sanctuary of all that was holy. So familiar were its contents: the masks, the likenesses of Sipi, Nao, and Aurr, the carved buttonwood box that held the remains of her father. So familiar, and yet everything was altered now that the refuge was no longer Ishkara's private domain but Aesha's retreat, now that the great bowl of casine before her was not to share as a guest but rather hers to brew and consume. The air inside the sanctuary had grown heavier, more somber. Another change: the two temporary plain pine boxes that lay at her feet, so similar that Aesha feared she might mistake the remains of the two.

She grieved for both of them. For Ishkara, of course, but for Carlos, too. He'd been demanding, trying, petulant with her and with the people as well. But he'd loved them and, she supposed, her too. That she couldn't love him back was regrettable. She could at least do honor with his remains now, not simply out of duty but with sincerity.

Aesha sipped the casine thoughtfully, the bowl nearly empty now, her head full of revelation if a bit woozy.

"I'm here."

She jumped back, nearly knocking the crane mask off the wall, her face a mask, too—of puzzlement.

"You've forgotten me already?"

Of course not. She recognized the voice instantly, though it wasn't the jumbled, grunted intonation of his final days but rather the rich tones of his prime, the ones that could chime with humor one moment and slice with irony the next. Like a pot of all-in-one stew, Ishkara's voice.

"Will you just sit there, or will you pour me a cup of the black drink before you guzzle it all?" The voice emanated from the right-hand box.

"No. Of course. I . . ."

"Just set it on the box."

She heard a slurping sound and a loud "heh-emm," but the contents of the cup remained untouched.

"Sadly, the delights of the previous world are denied us here," Ishkara sighed. "I'm still getting used to it."

"But where is 'here?' You are in the box, no?"

"No. I mean yes. But elsewhere, too. Do you understand?"

Aesha considered. "Yes. I think so. It is like the feeling I had in front of the fort, that the flames of my vision rose not only in another place but at another time, even as I saw them before me. Elsewhen as well as elsewhere." She stopped. "You must know. Tell me where and when my vision will be fulfilled."

"You ask the wrong question. It is quite irrelevant, for the answer is everywhen and nowhen, too," said the box.

"You must help me," she pleaded. "Felipe—Stepana—is cacique now."

"It was you that gave him the new name."

"I sanctioned it, yes. What choice do I have but to accept his rule? If the Spaniards see dissension, they'll annihilate us."

"I don't doubt the prudence of your action. You're now tirupo. An extraordinary appointment for a woman, even the daughter of Caalus."

"But now what?" She pressed her fingertips to her forehead, which pounded like a deaf man's drum. "I beg of you. Now what?"

"What makes you think I can help?"

"You live in the next world. To see its nature is to see as the gods see, to know as they know."

"That's a rather high standard you set for a pile of bones inside a box."

"Why do you joke with me? I—the fate of my people depends on me. That's too heavy a burden."

"Then carry it lightly. Heh-emm. A delicious brew, I'm sure. Enjoy it."

With that—she was not sure how she knew—his presence was gone. Aesha took the still-full cup and sipped it slowly down. Ishkara's passage to the land beyond had changed nothing. Her burden was her burden. Yet, he had given her an insight. Everywhere and everywhen. The very limitlessness of that concept demonstrated something of supreme importance.

Escalante met her at the gate, escorted her through the compound. He walked rigidly, didn't look at her, didn't speak. Didn't need to—his manner shouted of resentment. Aesha regretted it, but it irritated her, too. There was little she could do at this moment.

He led her into a small, haphazardly built building, its brushwood walls blocking much of the breeze but few of the insects, the choked air inside stale from the odor of men who bathed too seldom. No masks graced the walls; no mats adorned the dirt floor. Yet Aesha recognized it as a temple nonetheless, not only from the cross and the altar but also from the quiet it captured inside the soldiers' compound.

Quite oblivious of her entry, the Spanish holy man was seated at a small table, a finger zigzagging across the pages of his book, lips moving silently. Dark half-moons of sleeplessness hung below his sunken eyes.

The man was not well. Still, his face, though gaunt, looked relaxed and peaceful at this moment.

She touched Escalante's arm lightly, felt him stiffen even more. "Thank you for bringing me here, and thank him for receiving me."

The priest glanced up and closed his book with a loud thump. Rising, he stared at her from a corner of his eye. Then, wary as a starving animal scenting a baited trap, he approached. "Welcome to my humble chapel. To what do I owe this honor?"

"I've come to speak to you about our gods."

Father Rogel clutched the crucifix that hung from his neck. "I know of your gods. There is nothing to say. They are false idols. They must be destroyed."

She replied calmly. "You misunderstand. I wish to speak of your god and the Calusa god. I have had an insight. Your teachings are correct. The one true god rules over all peoples."

Father Rogel wanted to be relieved. He wanted to embrace the Indian woman. Not so fast, though. This was the Calusas' so-called holy priestess, responsible for perpetuating their heathen beliefs, and—Captain Reynoso had informed him almost gleefully—slitting the throats of several servants in the aftermath of Carlos's death. Was it not like the devil to take the shape of a beautiful woman? "You wish to become a Christian, then?"

"No. I do not."

Hah. He wasn't so gullible after all. "Then you will burn in eternal hell. But you know that already, for that is from whence you come."

Aesha shut her eyes momentarily. Burn, yes, perhaps. Still, she must try to explain. "This is what I wish to say. I believe that the true god, the one you call the Lord and the one we Calusa call Sipi, are one and the same. He simply reveals himself in a way each of our tribes can understand. He speaks to you in your tongue and to me in ours. Tells you to worship him as a Christian and wishes me to honor him in my people's fashion. The book you held when I entered—your holy book—my people tell me it's full of beauty and truth. So, too, are Calusa practices. I am convinced that's what Ishkara meant to show you the night he departed this world."

In all this time, Father Rogel still hadn't mastered the Indians' language, hadn't even learned enough to converse without the translator. Still, the sincerity in the woman's voice was unmistakable. It made Father Rogel long to accept her argument. But no, that's not what had happened that unfortunate night. If Captain Reynoso hadn't acted so quickly, the Indians would have burned the entire fort. The elder who expired in her arms died a heathen. He'd be waiting for her in hell. How dare she suggest that Calusa abominations—fornication with multiple wives and human sacrifice—were acceptable to God. No. The devil was ever persuasive.

He began to formulate a scathing reply, to muster all the righteous indignation he felt in his heart, but then he stopped himself. If he were ever to progress with the Indians, he had to deal with their priestess. There was only one sure way to banish the devil: with the light of faith. And the truth.

"I am pleased that you have respect for the Bible. Will you come to catechism? Will you pray with me? Will you learn further of our God?"

"I will. And will you learn further of ours?"

The priest reluctantly nodded. "I will try." How could he say otherwise?

"The time of Falko, a great festival of our people, is nearing. I wish to invite you to the celebration."

Go out amongst the Indians during their pagan ritual? Father Rogel felt a flush of heat and a sudden dizziness, as if he were teetering on the edge of a precipice, looking down on the very fires of hell. Steady. That was what he needed: the steady stability of faith. And the latrine. "I will come. Now, please excuse me."

"He's not well," Aesha stated to Escalante after the priest raced from the room.

He scowled at her.

"You won't speak to me?"

Escalante's lips parted reluctantly. "Only because it's my duty. He sleeps little. The heat afflicts him."

"Why does he fear me?" Aesha asked. "He wouldn't even look at me."

"Your nakedness still gives him discomfort."

"This hiding, covering up, I don't understand it." She glanced at him. "I've known you since our childhoods, and yet I barely recognize you in your Spaniards' robes. Are they not uncomfortable?"

"They make me miserable."

"Then why do you wear them?"

"They represent who I am." He paused. "Who I've always been."

She paused, too, before responding. "Yes—I understand your meaning. You and I—we've always yearned to see each other as someone else. You envisioned me a Spaniard, and I pictured you a Calusa. But only in our minds. Our real natures never changed."

Escalante glowered at her again. "You've shown yours by allowing the slaying of servants. Ordering it. But I noticed you convinced Felipe to spare Iqi. *Hipócrita.*" He used the Spanish word. "There is no Calusa equivalent. It means you are two-faced and duplicitous."

She was stunned. "The sacrifices were required in the one instance and not in the other. I followed the law of my people. And tell me, was your captain following Spanish law when he bludgeoned Ishkara to death? Luring Carlos to the fort to slaughter him was not deceitful?" She touched the fabric covering his arm. "So this is who you are. Such fools we've been. The differences are too great."

"I loved you," he said, speaking the words to the ground. "I tried to show you the way, just as the priest did. I know now you're not worth saving." The bitterness oozed from his voice like pitch from a slashed pine.

"And I loved you, loved your marvelous inventions, your writing, even your god who speaks to all Christians through those strange symbols. I've pledged to your holy man that I'll learn more of your beliefs. But"—her words came out like a wail now—"think of all that *you* could accomplish. You alone have lived in both our worlds, speak both our tongues. Help bring us together, find a way to live with each other. It's ever clearer: my people's survival depends upon it."

"And what of my survival? But that's never been your concern. It's not me you loved, only what I represent. Deception. There's nothing more to you than that."

His words crashed into her like waves, threatening to knock her over, wash over her in a relentless, sour flood. Dance between them? She wasn't sure she could anymore.

Escalante took something from his pocket then and put it in her hand. The gold and silver disk she'd given him so long ago. To earn his trust.

It burned her hand with cold, and she wanted to drop it or fling it at him. But she maintained her composure. "I'll keep this for both of us," she said softly. "But there's a purpose far larger than you or me. It's up to you to see it or not."

Father Rogel steeled himself when, the next day, Aesha joined the "queens," as he called them, the group of noble women who came for daily instruction. He was hopeful that the others would help him to point out to the Indian priestess the errors of her beliefs. Key amongst the queens was Doña Antonia. An enigma, that one. After Carlos's death, instead of spurning the Spaniards who'd slain her brother, she'd moved back to the fort. Father Rogel was unsure why. She seemed genuinely to want to live as a Christian and as the captain general's wife (though that would cause problems of its own when the Adelantado returned). Perhaps there'd been danger for her in what was now Felipe's palace. On the other hand, who knew with these Indians? Maybe she was spying on the soldiers, searching for weakness, reporting back to Don Felipe.

At any rate, she now lived in the hut the Adelantado had ordered constructed for her, a happenstance that Captain Reynoso was delighted about. He called her his volunteer hostage. Father Rogel didn't know what to think. Doña Antonia was a most able learner, willingly singing and reciting. Yet otherwise she was cold and taciturn. She managed to live inside the compound while quite ignoring the soldiers.

No matter their disposition, the priest was grateful for the mere presence of Doña Antonia and the other queens for one simple reason: he wouldn't have to face the Indian priestess alone. Why then did a nagging voice keep telling him that that was exactly the challenge the Lord would someday place before him?

Aesha proved an attentive and inquisitive student, probing the Bible, asking the priest to explain apparent inconsistencies. Not surprisingly, the most difficult area of all was the Holy Trinity. Father Rogel knew, of course, the complexity of the subject. He had even struggled with it himself as a child. How could a single person have three representations? Like children, the Indians lacked the capacity for higher reasoning. He had tried to get beyond the issue by describing it as a mystery—weren't the Indians' lives, because of their lack of education, already filled with mysterious occurrences? But Aesha pressed him. "Then you are saying that we cannot know the real character of your god."

"No, not true at all. A mystery by its nature is something that we know is valid but cannot fully comprehend. God's wisdom is infinite. We can know that, although we cannot fathom its entirety. So it is with the Holy Trinity: we know of its existence, for God has revealed it to us. We accept it, even if its inner depths are impenetrable. That is the character of faith."

"So God is three persons in one body."

"Three persons in one *nature*. Let me give you an example. Does it ever happen in your society that there are multiple births of children identical in every way?"

"Yes, it is uncommon, but twins do occur."

"What of triplets?"

"Exceedingly rare, though not unheard of. I understand your point. It would be like having one person with three bodies."

"Not my point at all. Identical triplets would be so close they could communicate to each other without even speaking. This would be a case of three persons sharing one nature. So it is with God: three representations share one divine nature."

"And your book, your Bible, explains all this? Perhaps if you can speak its words to me, I'll better comprehend."

The priest drew a long breath. "No, the Trinity is not mentioned in the Bible. But God the Father is, as is Jesus Christ his Son. The Holy Ghost is described as well. Yet, as I've oft repeated, our Scripture tells us that there is only one God. Now, if you have followed my teachings, you well know by now that God cannot contradict himself. The Holy Trinity explains that seeming contradiction."

Aesha and the other queens conferred in low voices for several minutes. Then she said, "We understand. One god, three depictions."

"Yes."

"And the father god is the mightiest of all."

"They're all divine, but in a sense, yes, for he was here in the beginning."

"Three is a most sacred number, then. That's what you mean by the Holy Trinity."

He nodded in agreement. A breakthrough at last?

"Exactly as in our teachings," Aesha said enthusiastically. "Only Sipi created the world, yet he is represented also by Nao and Aurr. One god, three depictions. And three souls, too. Three is indeed the most holy of numbers."

Father Rogel felt the breakthrough flutter away.

As the days passed, the oppressive weather began to cool on occasion. But Father Rogel could take no solace from the beauty of the star-filled nights. His mission was failing miserably. He was converting no souls. Don Felipe, living in the most disgusting of sins with his very sister, continued to promise to change only when the Adelantado returned. Aesha persisted either in challenging the Bible's teachings or else in attempting to appropriate the very tenets of Christianity as those of her own pagan beliefs. The leaders would not be changed. Nor would the people change until their cacique and priestess told them to.

That sinking sensation of uselessness fell over the Jesuit. There was nothing more he could accomplish until the captain general's return from Spain. Once again, Father Rogel ached to leave Caalus. Hearing that the Indians of Los Mártires were more tractable, that they had already thrown some of their idols to the sea, he attempted to convince Captain Reynoso to lend him a brigantine. The captain couldn't spare the men. In desperation, the priest asked Don Felipe to lend him a pair of canoes and Indians to man them. But Captain Reynoso convinced the cacique to deny the request. What if the priest were killed? The Adelantado would blame Felipe.

Word came too that the soldiers at the fort at Tocobaga were suffering greatly. With recent prolific rains, all their food was rotting. Again, Captain Reynoso refused a trip of mercy. To reduce his force by even one soldier might give the Indians of Carlos an excuse to attack.

Patience, purity, and perseverance were the priest's mantra. The closer the time came to the Indians' festival, though, the more agitated he became. He dreaded a repeat of the same behavior that had led to the death of the former holy man, feared that Aesha would whip her people into a heathen frenzy and attack the fort. But there was something more that yanked at him with invisible, unseverable strings, something dark and truly terrifying. He feared for more than his life. He feared for his soul.

For a moment, Aesha awoke young again, tingling with anticipation as she had before her very first Falko. It didn't last long. Before she even opened her eyes, a thick fog of dread descended upon her. So far she'd utterly failed to persuade the Spanish priest of anything. At best, he treated her like a child; at other times, he didn't even attempt to conceal his disdain for Calusa ways. Try as she may, Aesha couldn't understand his attitude. The more she learned of Christian ideas, the more she saw parallels to her own beliefs, if not in all the details, then surely in the general precepts. Why did Father Rogel fail to see them, too?

Aesha rose from her sleeping mat and added wood to the still-hot coals of last night's fire. Above, a huge pot of casine brewed. She inhaled a steamy nose full, then added a few more leaves. Perhaps the events of Falko would accomplish what her words had been unable to. The Spanish priest couldn't help but be impressed at the array of wares on the plaza, works of love painstakingly produced by the finest craftsmen in all of Escampaba. Love: didn't he keep preaching of his god's love? Love of life was at the very core of the Falko celebration.

Sacrifice, too. The priest spoke constantly of the sacrifice of Christ. Aesha would be sure to remind Father Rogel of the purpose of the festival: to honor Sipi's sacrificial burning of the stars in the sky. No—she corrected herself. God's sacrificial burning of the stars. She would try not to use Sipi's name. It too agitated the Christian.

She placed a shawl of skirt moss around her shoulders. Bare shoulders were something else that agitated him.

Aesha was thankful, at least, that Father Rogel had received permission from Captain Reynoso to leave the fort unescorted. It wouldn't be wise for Spanish soldiers to be present at Falko. The pots of stew could too easily boil over.

She went to the garden. Iqi was awake, sipping wild sage tea and chewing on hackberry seeds. Following Carlos's death, she'd tried to send him away, back to the island life he loved. He refused, insisting on staying at the small hut he'd built in Ishkara's garden. "Our fates, as you told me, are intertwined," he'd said. "I'll leave when you do. Besides, I can't stop eating these." He crunched down on another mouthful of the crimson seeds.

Aesha didn't overrule him. She needed him here, needed his strength, his comfort.

"Stick close to the Spanish priest," she instructed him now. "I want him to experience the joy of Falko, but I want him to feel safe." Aesha felt the effects of the casine cutting through the blanket of gloom. Ultimately, she told herself, the priest was well intentioned. The day held promise. It had to.

Father Rogel, too, arose beneath a dark cloud of his own making. He dressed in his fresh cassock, went to kiss the cross and pray, adding a small plea to God for his bowels to quiet and his resolve to return. The Jesuit ate his small breakfast of cassava bread, repeating over and over to himself that the Lord was with him, that as long as he believed, he'd be protected.

When the sun rose above the compound's fence, Father Rogel willed its rays to chase away the shadows of doubt. He reminded himself that today he'd be released from the prison of the fort to walk freely amongst the Indians, to observe them at close quarters in their own environs. True, with Felipe as cacique, he had marginally more leeway to visit the Indians' village to minister to the sick and dying, but only under guard, only for limited times and purposes. Simply venturing outside the compound was reason for cheer. The experience would prove invaluable in his mission. If he were ever to turn the Indians from their pagan beliefs, he must observe them firsthand.

Patience, perseverance, purity, and prayer.

Aesha awaited him at the gate, dressed modestly, thankfully, with a grass shawl covering her breasts, as well as a skirt that hid her privates. Accompanying her was a large man, nearly as massive as Don Felipe himself, but with a flat, muscled stomach. The man was unpainted and wore only a breechclout and a simple shell necklace. His face was weathered from years in the hot sun, yet there was a glowing vitality evident in both face and body. He walked behind Aesha—a bodyguard? Why was one needed? The priest felt his stomach flutter.

The village was a tumult of activity. Strolling the crowded plaza, Father Rogel had to admit that the native artisans, though primitive, demonstrated a good bit of skill. A wood likeness of a deer was eerily lifelike, with muzzle, nostrils and jaw delicately formed and ears whose tips curved just as in nature, their interior painted with a creamy pinkwhite pigment over which black tufts of hair were brushed on with thin, delicate strokes. The priest found himself transfixed by the eyes, which seemed to stare back at him with doe-like wetness. Aesha spoke in her tongue and, with the help of her miming, Father Rogel understood that the eyes were made from the shell of a turtle and the whites from some gum-like substance.

The sights, sounds, and smells were quite overpowering. Everywhere, women stirred huge black pots of simmering stews whose aromas teased pangs of hunger from Father Rogel's shrunken stomach. The girls' choruses sang and danced; young boys raced back and forth, unable to contain their excitement.

At the sound of a shell horn, the Indians' attention turned to the water court. Aesha's bodyguard led the priest to a vantage point at the water's edge, where dozens of canoes, each paddled by a single young man, sat at the ready. At a signal from Don Felipe, who looked regal in an enormous feathered headdress and a hundredweight of dangling bracelets and necklaces, the paddlers raced off, pushing their canoes into the central canal. Their skill in forging ahead while avoiding each other was remarkable. The crowd cheered, and the paddlers whooped, too, their roars fading as they disappeared from view.

Father Rogel studied the onlookers as they chattered, pointed, and poked each other, promoting their favorite contestant's skills in a way that needed no translation. It seemed but a few minutes before the paddlers reappeared, having completed their circuit around the island. Glistening with sweat, the winner of the race was surrounded by well-wishers, who lifted him from his canoe and tossed him into the water.

The priest began to relax. If you could ignore their near nakedness (some were even fully nude, the Father could not help but notice, though he struggled to avert his eyes) and their harsh, coarse-sounding language, the event almost could have been a San Fermín festival of his youth. And far from shunning him, the Indians treated him as a celebrity, offering him bowlfuls of stew from their communal pots. He gratefully accepted the dishes heaped with meat, fish, and oysters and found them quite delicious. With full belly and light heart, Father Rogel joined the merriment by juggling three coco plums. The large crowd that had formed around him roared approval as he performed his grand finale, quickly transferring the fruits from hand to mouth and back again, even as he kept them in the air, devouring them until only the seeds were left. He spit them on the ground and bowed low to raucous cheers.

As the sun set beneath the sea, Aesha led Father Rogel to a seat of honor in front of a large fire in the central plaza. As hundreds gathered around, she murmured a prayer in Calusa language, that, with Father Rogel's rudimentary language skills, he could not quite make out. She then passed around cups of tea to Don Felipe, the principal men and women seated in the front, and one to Father Rogel as well. The assemblage watched their cacique drink his tea first, then they followed suit. Father Rogel drank his down. Delicious. His cup was instantly refilled.

As the twilight quickly vanished, a group of younger women began to dance around the central fire. Lithe and limber, they leapt and whirled, then jumped sideways this way and that, each imitating the dancer in front of her. The leader fell into a prone position, supporting herself on one arm and leg, the other leg kicking to the side; and the others followed suit, their bronzed faces beaming. Then the opposite arm and leg. So spellbound was Father Rogel that it took him several minutes to realize that the dancers were completely naked. His head abuzz—was it the day's excitement or the tea?—Father Rogel couldn't keep his eyes off their bare, bouncing breasts and gyrating privates. They rose again, snaking around and around until suddenly the undulating line broke apart, each dancer choosing a man from the spectators to rub up against in the most vulgar of ways. To his horror, the priest felt his manhood rising beneath his cassock.

From a distant place, his brain told him he must resist. But a louder voice shouted why, what could be the harm? He was simply observing the Indians. It would help him in his work. A girl barely more than a child approached him, giggling, and thrust her crotch inches from his face. Father Rogel grabbed for her, but she slipped away, wiggling her bare buttocks at him and throwing him a seductive, backwards glance. Another came then, brushing up against him, and he inhaled the heady smell of her womanhood, so foreign, so exotic, and yet, in the deep recesses of his consciousness, so familiar. The priest nearly swooned.

Then he felt a thin, watery taste in his mouth, and almost instantaneously his insides began to rise. The priest did not even have time to turn from the fire. All the bowls of stew came back up, gushing onto the fire and, amidst loud hissing and popping, quickly turning black.

The crowd applauded and thumped Father Rogel on the back, as if he had just done something wonderful. But, yes, it had been. Even as he continued retching, the priest wept for joy. The act had broken the spell. His inflamed privates relaxed. Praise the Lord. He had intervened, saving the priest from further embarrassment. Nay, saving him from eternal damnation.

Gathering his cassock, Father Rogel leapt to his feet and raced for the safety of the fort.

Aesha hurried to follow, calling after him. But the priest would not turn around. He would not be tempted again.

"Where were you?" Aesha was furious. "You were supposed to protect the Spaniard."

SONG OF THE TIDES 255

"I assure you, no harm came to him. I followed him to the fort. He arrived quite safely." Iqi was baffled. What could have happened?

Aesha shook her head. "The Christian priest is sworn to a vow of chastity."

"Yes, so? There was no coupling."

"The dancers frightened him."

Iqi tried to absorb Aesha's statement. He didn't doubt her wisdom, but perhaps in this case, not being a man, she failed to comprehend. "I saw for myself," he countered. "They didn't frighten him, they aroused him. He even tried to pull Sacaspada toward him."

Aesha let out an exasperated sigh. In truth, she didn't understand either. The dancers terrified and attracted the priest at the same time. His purging made him weep and run. It was no different than with Escalante. She'd been deluding herself all this time. The differences with the Spaniards were too great.

They both saw it at the same time, she and Iqi. A flaming arc of light curving across the sky, its billowing smoke trail etched into the night for an instant. And in the next, all traces of its existence gone.

⤜ Seventeen ⤛

Never again would he put himself in that position. Father Rogel was devastated by the weakness he had shown, but angry, too. Exploiting vulnerabilities was the devil's signature. Aesha the temptress had lured him into a trap; in his arrogance, he'd strolled right into it. The Lord had rescued him from the precipice of the sins of vanity and lust once. He might not do so again. There was no choice now. The priest had to leave San Antón.

Praying constantly for forgiveness, the Father secluded himself in his chambers, going out only to say Mass, once a day for the soldiers and once for the Indians. For the latter task in particular, he could muster little enthusiasm. He even avoided Don Felipe's visits, feigning illness. Nothing had changed. Father Rogel could do no good here until the arrival of the Adelantado.

Finally, in early December a frigate came bringing both supplies and an excuse for his escape. The *San Felipe*, which was to have provisioned both San Antón and the fort at Tocobaga, had come scantily supplied. Employing all his powers of persuasion, as well as a pitiful whine that he abhorred but could not control, Father Rogel convinced Captain

Reynoso to let him go to Havana to plead for more rations. The Jesuit knew that the soldiers would think he was running from the hardships at San Antón. He didn't care. He was terrified of another encounter with the Calusa she-devil.

In Havana, Father Rogel sought out Pedro Menéndez Márquez and urged the nephew of the Adelantado to reprovision the two forts. The effort took no less than a month to accomplish. In the meantime, Father Rogel made amends by throwing himself into his work, hearing confessions, catechizing the children of the Church of San Juan, and spreading the word of God amongst the native people as well as more than a hundred black-skinned slaves. The sessions with the slaves were especially rewarding, for though they were as ignorant as the Indians, they asked no troublesome questions.

As he did the Lord's work, Father Rogel began to feel the shame retreat. The incident at the Calusa feast hadn't been his fault. He'd survived another of the Lord's tests and had been sent here to Havana where he could do so much more good. He took up the cause of Estame, an Indian woman—Calusa, no less, brought earlier by Captain General Menéndez—who wished to be baptized. When he probed her motives for becoming a Christian, she replied, "I believe as you have told me, that after this life there is another, and in that life God will punish those who did not do His bidding on earth and will reward those who have." And then she said, "I believe this more than the lies of my people. Please. I fear I will die before you bring me to God."

How sweet were those words. Father Rogel invited every Christian in Havana to the baptism and begged García Osorio, the governor, and Doña Flores, a leading lady of the town, to serve as godparents. The ceremony was held on the Feast of Epiphany with the entire village present. Upon its completion, Father Rogel glowed. After so many months— it was now January 1568—he had finally saved a Calusa soul.

A few days later, the ship was ready to leave for Tocobaga and San Antón. Father Rogel was loath to leave this place in which, he told himself, he was so effective. He was comfortable in Havana with other priests and civilized people. His scourges of prickly, itching skin had dissipated; his gripping, griping bowels had relaxed. There were receptive souls here, both Indian and Negro, to be added to the Lord's ranks. The Lord had called him here.

But the Church had assigned him to San Antón. Temptress or not, he must return. He spent most of his last day in the latrine.

In Tocobaga, to his horror, he found both the fort and village abandoned. Two soldiers were discovered dead on the beach from arrow wounds, their blind eyes staring heavenward. Despite several days' search, no more could be located. Before leaving, the Spanish soldiers set fire to the entire village. Watching the temple of idols burn, Father Rogel felt grim satisfaction.

Guebu, Enenpa and Comachicaquiseyobe knelt before Felipe, extending their palms upward. "Rise," said the cacique, but the three continued to cower.

"If I wanted your heads," said Felipe, "I would be holding them already."

"We returned voluntarily," said Guebu, the oldest of the three cousins. "We throw ourselves upon your mercy. We wish only to go home to Tomo."

"What happened at Tocobaga?"

"The Spaniards were mean-spirited," answered Guebu. "They mistreated everyone except Tocobaga himself and Mocoso, his great captain. When their food rotted on them, they blamed us. They poked us with their weapons, forced us to feed them. We were suffering, too, and yet we had to let our bellies go empty so that we could fill those of the Spaniards."

The traitors' sunken eyes and protruding ribs confirmed their story. So did their smell. They stank so foully of rot and runny bowels that Felipe dared breathe only through his mouth. "Go on," he ordered.

"One day two soldiers stole food from an elder," Guebu said. "The people had had enough. They rushed the fort and broke down the gate, then carried off the two offenders. When the Spanish soldiers tried to come to their brothers' aid, a fight broke out. The fire spitters slew many, but the Spaniards were soon overwhelmed. Tocobaga's warriors slit their throats and disemboweled all but three who were kept alive as servants."

"When we heard the Spanish ship coming, we disposed of those last ones," put in Enenpa, a ghoulish and foolish grin on his emaciated face.

"Mocoso ordered it," added Comachicaquiseyobe. "Tocobaga was gone from the village."

Felipe cuffed the youngest cousin on the side of the head. "Are you sure you're remembering correctly?"

Before Comachicaquiseyobe or Enenpa could answer, Guebu cupped his hands over their mouths. "No, I remember clearly now. Tocobaga was present. He ordered the slaughter."

"Yes, Tocobaga ordered it," Felipe nodded. "So you would swear if questioned by the Spaniards?"

"Of course," said Guebu. He poked his cousins. "Of course," they said in unison.

"We have an understanding, then."

Three enthusiastic nods.

"I accept you back among us," Felipe said. "You won't return to Tomo, however. I may need you here. Now, go."

As the three bolted from the palace, Felipe called after them. "And don't disappoint me again."

Father Rogel went about his work at San Antón with stalwart resolve. He had rescued one soul. He *would* save others. With the help of a quantity of maize, he attracted even more of the principals to the chapel each day, thirty or forty men in the morning and a like number of queens in the afternoon. When Aesha, too, appeared, the soldiers turned her back at the gate, giving the priest's apology. Out of respect for Calusa religion, Father Rogel would not attempt to catechize their priestess.

The Indians came willingly to the smell of the lure and listened to every word with great attention. Father Rogel further encouraged them to study in their lodges at night by awarding prizes each fifteen days to the ones who could best recite the prayers and answer his questions. The fishhooks, knives, sickles, hatchets, adzes, and nails worked even better than the maize. Those who confessed that they'd been living a lie were awarded the greatest prizes. Father Rogel saw the Indians awakening, as if from a dream, from the blindness in which they had lived. The teachings of the Lord were beginning to sink in.

The priest's strategy was working. Once the principals had been won over, the commoners would convert. As for Felipe, he could choose to lead or follow. Either way, when Captain General Menéndez returned, the cacique's hand would be forced. Best of all, Father Rogel could accomplish all this without venturing from the fort, a contemplation that filled him so full of trepidations it haunted his dreams as much as his bowels.

In late February it happened that one of the cacique's councilors, Coyobea, took ill with a pain in the side. Father Rogel watched the man deteriorate to the point where he was convinced Coyobea was going to die. Yet the good councilor, even in his weakened state, continued to come to catechism. Here was surely a soul crying out to be saved.

To scrutinize the councilor's sincerity, the priest questioned Coyobea strenuously. The Calusa was not only earnest but almost eloquent. He believed in God and Jesus Christ his Son, who became human in order to make men the friends of God. He believed that Jesus died on the cross for the sake of all men, and that on the third day He rose from the dead. And Coyobea promised that, if God should spare his life, he'd give up his idols and never adore them again.

Hallelujah!

When the illness tightened its grip to a stranglehold, Father Rogel baptized the councilor. And, praise the Lord, from that point on, Coyobea began to recover. Father Rogel took the councilor in his charge, feeding him from the Jesuit's own provisions. The Father borrowed clothes from one of the soldiers and dressed the Indian as a Christian. And Coyobea responded, returning every day to avoid a relapse into his heathen religion. Soon he was so well he was eating most of the priest's rations.

Here was an example of the Lord's miracles before the Indians' very eyes.

Then Father Rogel learned that the priestess Aesha was to perform a certain ceremony involving masks and other pagan idols, at which all the councilors would be present. Screwing up his courage, he dared to leave the fort to plead with Felipe to relieve Coyobea of his duty to attend. The cacique—didn't this prove his heart was turning Christian?—agreed. Bless him.

But that very night, the man threw off his Christian garb, wore a heathen mask, and danced before the pagan idols.

The devil had won another skirmish.

Felipe breezed into the inner temple like a man entering his own sleeping chamber, as if it were his right. Which, since he'd become cacique, it was. Aesha could only grumble.

He got directly to his purpose. "Why did you let Coyobea take part in the moon-tide ceremony? Just to irk me?"

"He came of his own free will. He wanted to."

Felipe glared at Aesha. "I ordered him not to."

"Take it up with him."

"I will take it. His head, that is."

"Do you really think it wise to slay the only man the Christians believe they've won over?"

"This isn't a child's game we're playing," Felipe admonished. "The

Spaniards must believe we are—how do they say?—folding in their robes. If they suppose us a lost cause, they'll burn our city, just as they did at Tocobaga."

Burn. Despite her vexing anger, Aesha shuddered.

"The Spaniards are eating from my bowl," Felipe continued. "They're frightened to death of those fools Guebu, Enenpa, and Comachicaquiseyobe. They're convinced the three are spies for Tocobaga and plan to kill me and then steal back to Tocobaga with instructions on how to overrun the fort. I've assured the priest and captain that I'm aware of the planned treachery and have the suspects under observation. I even extracted confessions from them that it was Tocobaga himself who ordered the attack on the Spaniards."

"Your deceptions amaze me."

Felipe grinned. "I appreciate the flattery." Then he turned serious. "Don't doubt my intentions, though. I've succeeded. The Spaniards are my allies; they've focused their wrath on Tocobaga."

Aesha let her eyes wander slowly around the sacred room. "And what will be the end result? If they give us their handouts long enough, some day we'll all be Christians."

"That's your concern, not mine. What difference does it make what we call ourselves, as long as we prosper? The Spanish tools, weapons, and ships are what we need. Their Christ does no harm."

"How dare you speak such words in this holy place. Have you learned nothing as cacique? If you anger the gods, they'll destroy us all."

"You've inverted the truth. If the Spaniards destroy us, *that* will anger the gods. But by then it will be too late."

Silence. Aesha glanced at the plain pine box on the mat. Ishkara, help me. But there was no response.

"Enough of this. I didn't come to quarrel, but rather to give you a gift." Felipe handed her a box-shaped object the size of a large anchor stone. "The priest presented it to me, but I think you'll have much more use for it here."

She took it, felt its leather cover, knew it to be the Spaniards' holy book, though not the one she'd seen the priest reading from. Fanning its hundreds of thin pages with her thumb, she felt its weightiness. "The words of the Christian god. Recorded and memorialized forever," she mused aloud. "Yet, in the end, does this object hold more power than our stories? I've tried to reason with the priest. We don't insist that he change his beliefs. Why must he demand that of us?"

"And the result of your discussions?"

"He won't even see me anymore. I must find a way."

"Save your good will. It's the nature of all men, dark-skinned or light, to be so convinced of their moral superiority that they'll fight to the death to assert it. Be happy the Spaniards still believe they can win us over. Once that conviction dissolves, they'll be left with only one other option. It's you who has learned nothing. If we fall, it will be to the thunder of the Spaniards' weapons. Tocobaga made a fatal mistake. Do you think the Adelantado will allow the slaughter of his soldiers to go unavenged?" Felipe paused, that ever ready grin spreading again across his wide face. "I mean to make sure the Spaniards finish the extermination. The burning of the village was only the beginning."

Aesha shook her head in wonderment. Was ever a man born more skilled at turning another's misery to his advantage? "You'll become a Christian, then?" she asked.

Felipe hesitated. "So far I've successfully avoided it."

"Why, then, if it makes no difference?"

"The people won't allow it."

Aesha shook her head. "You may make that claim to the Christians, but you and I know otherwise. If you lead, the people will follow. Even over my opposition."

Felipe folded his arms across his chest. "I hold out my conversion the same way the priest holds out his handfuls of maize. With myself as bait, I aim to attract no less than the Adelantado. You, my beloved child bride, aren't the only one with heroic blood. When he returns, I'll do as my father did before me: rid the Calusa of the Spanish leader. Then, and only then will they flee." He blustered from the temple.

So sure was he. How could she oppose him, with her doubts, her confusion? She longed for comfort, for confidence, for confirmation from the gods or the departed. As hard as she strained, though, Aesha could make out only the faint crashing of waves. The winds were up, the song played on the seawall surrounding Caalus chaotic and uncadenced.

And the Christians' holy book now resided alongside the Calusas' most sacred objects.

In March, the maize ran out. Father Rogel had been forced to give half to the soldiers, who had promised him they would eat no meat during Lent. The prizes ran out, too. And so, once again, did the Indians.

All except the cacique. Don Felipe came often to dine with the priest. Always, he asked when the Adelantado was returning, for he was most anxious to become a Christian, though his people would not allow him to until he was so ordered by the Spaniards' supreme commander.

Father Rogel explained how great the distance was, how difficult the transmission of messages. And the Adelantado had other urgent matters to attend to in Spain. Don Felipe must not use Menéndez's absence as an excuse. If the cacique wished to convert, there was nothing holding him back. "In fact," the priest worked up his nerve, "failing to do so, you are a sinner. Your soul will be condemned."

Felipe's eyes filled with tears. "The things that you tell me all make sense. Our gods are false and evil. But our fathers' fathers have lived under these laws from the time of quiet. I do not wish to listen further. You must let me be."

Father Rogel didn't hide his disappointment. "In everything you do, Don Felipe, you show yourself to be a great friend of the Spanish. You have alerted us to many potential dangers, and you always discuss matters truthfully with us. But," he shook his head sadly, "you are far from becoming a Christian."

Don Felipe didn't answer. He drank down the wine Father Rogel had poured him and held out his glass for more.

12 July 1568

A full year since my last writing. A year of hope receding, drifting away on an ebb tide that flowed to Spain, never to return. In my most disconsolate moments, I follow that tide in the canoe I built long ago, paddle to the lookout island and beyond, searching for the tall mast of hope renewed. I throw off my clothes and go naked into the sea, the home that Salamanca will never be. I dive to the limestone ledges to swim amongst the grouper, grunts, and snapper. So peaceful it is six fathoms down. I hold fast to the rock and will myself to stay forever.

But always a force within pulls me back to the surface, to my soldier's duties, to my existence no matter how miserable. I paddle back, battling the tide, always ebbing, always flowing away.

Father Rogel has left again, gone to Havana to await the Adelantado's supposed return. I shall probably never see the good priest again. I hope he finds the peace there that eluded him here. The Indians laughed at him, called him the Man of the Rising Gown; and when the soldiers learned the name, they snickered, too. A mean and disheartened lot they are, depending on the sporadic supply ships or bartering with the natives for fish. They treat the Indians badly and so are spurned in return. When the Father was here, bless his naive, magnanimous spirit, he preached constantly of kindness. And even though I saw him struggle mightily with the trickery of Felipe, he never conceded defeat in the battle for the cacique's soul; for he confided to me one day that to give up on Felipe would be to give up on himself and on God.

Nevertheless, the Father is gone, and the Jesuits have sent another, Brother Francisco Villareal, in his stead. When I first saw him, I could think only of how much I myself have aged. His appearance is markedly boyish, his face still round and smooth-skinned despite

the deprivations so universally shared amongst the pilgrims. He ar-
rived from the fort in Tequesta, at the mouth of the Mayaimi River
where he was stationed for ten months, having come within a blade's
edge of leaving his mortal remains there after one of the soldiers in a
pique of temper slew the former chief for but a trifle. I plead with the
soldiers here to heed the lesson. The Indians of Tequesta, being of no
Christian morals, flew into a rage. They murdered three soldiers, in-
cluding the offending one, taking his head and dismembering him.
The fort was under siege, the soldiers' munitions and food dwindling,
and the rest would surely have perished had it not been for the fortu-
itous arrival of Pedro Menéndez Márquez, who drove the Indians to
the woods.

Brother Francisco arrived here in early April, along with sev-
eral soldiers from that ill-fated fort. Like Father Rogel before him, he
preaches most sincerely to the Indians, and as before, they come only
as long as he brings food. As for Felipe, when he found out Francisco is
but a lay brother, he shunned him. Besides, Felipe is otherwise occu-
pied. Upon the slightest rumor of disloyalty, he hunts down the sup-
posed offenders and slaughters them brutally and publicly, then in-
vites his vassals to dance around their heads. Yet, he is ever careful to
remain on friendly terms with us. No Calusa would dare attack us
when we go amongst them to barter or to unload the supply ships.
They ignore the soldiers' affronts, knowing that if they disobey Felipe,
the next heads hung on display will be theirs.

Thus my pitiful life continues. No longer have I even the meaning-
less pleasure of playing third man in the drama between leaders. No
longer do I even encounter the one I could have loved. Father Rogel
warned the Brother in the most colorful terms of her. The She-Devil,
he called her, the Temptress. Of course he's right. She played me all
those years like a psaltery, plucking my strings, extracting the music
from my soul, leaving me silent and songless, like the tide, in eter-
nal ebb.

➥ Eighteen ➦

Aesha sat in the sanctuary's candlelight, casine cup at her side, the heavy Christian text resting upon her moss skirt. She bent to put her nose on the tawny outer covering, inhaling its ancient, leathery aroma. Opening the cover, she began to turn pages, not even looking at what was on them, just marveling at their perfect uniformity in size and thickness. Several pages in, something drew her attention. A painting. She pulled a candle closer to inspect it. Before her was a drawing of great intricacy, its detail sharper than even the finest of Muspa's wood etchings. The drawing contained several rectangular panels. In the center stood an old man, the hair on his head and face pure white. Undoubtedly the Christian god. He held a long ruler's staff—another similarity to her own people's customs that the Christians would undoubtedly dispute. The two long panels on either side depicted beings that blew long horn-like instruments like the ones the Adelantado's musicians had played. She wondered if they were the angels Father Rogel had described, but then remembered that angels were said to be bodiless. Puzzling, these figures. Aesha couldn't even tell if they were men or women because they were dressed in long robes. Similar with the two babes—children of the horn blowers?—holding hands in the panel below. They had no genitals. Perhaps the figures were like the girl-men of her own people, women in men's bodies much revered for their sensitivity and vision. Yet another parallel?

If the drawings were confusing, still Aesha found them wondrous works of art. The top panel contained no humans, only stylized curling designs that looked as if they'd been carved in wood by a master craftsman with the finest shark's-tooth blade. In all these suns, her admiration of the Spaniards' accomplishments hadn't dimmed. How much effort went into this single page of this single copy of the Christians' holy text.

The candles in the room began to flicker, as if the wind had found its way inside the sanctuary. Strange. She examined the page opposite the drawing. It consisted entirely of two columns of letters. Aesha traced their coiling paths with her fingers. Escalante had explained that they were written in a tongue altogether different from the one the Spaniards usually spoke, an ancient language used now mainly by the holy men. Perhaps that explained the inconsistencies in the Christians' beliefs. Maybe the words didn't survive conversion into their tongue any better than they did out of it. Yet hadn't Escalante impressed upon her that the precise benefit of written stories was their constancy? She remembered a long-ago argument with Ishkara during which she'd put that idea to him, then called him old and pinched when he disagreed. She'd been so confident of her position; now, she wasn't so sure.

"Aha. You admit I was right."

So that's why the candles had sputtered. Ishkara. She should have known. "You've been listening in on my thoughts?"

"Quite a puzzle, this idol of the Christians. Tell me, what do you make of it?"

She hefted the book up and down in her hands, as if its very weight should provide the answer. "I'm convinced that it holds the key to our survival. The priest is ever using it against our people. But it's not even written in the Spaniards' tongue. Such a beautiful object, and yet it seems to bring only death and destruction. Long have I tried, yet still it eludes me. I can't avoid the conclusion that it's full of discrepancies."

"The priest, too," Ishkara said, "is full of discrepancies."

Aesha closed the book, set it down. "He's departed again, gone to Havana to meet with his superiors. He says the Adelantado has left Spain and will soon arrive."

"What then?"

"Felipe plans to kill the Spaniards' leader."

"Felipe? Forgive me, my Little Bird, but I still cannot get used to that name. As if it gives him some power over the Spaniards."

"But you yourself gave the name of the Spanish king to Carlos."

"So you think I'm infallible, child?" Ishkara's booming laugh filled the room.

Aesha's teeth clenched tight. Ishkara's departure to the land beyond hadn't diminished his ability to exasperate her.

"So now you want help with this idol of theirs, is that it?"

"Do you really think it an idol, no more?"

"No, Little Bird. I think it an idol, no less. That makes all the difference."

"What do you mean?"

But with that, the flames flickered again, and Aesha knew he was gone.

What *did* he mean, "an idol, no less?" She had only to look around the sanctuary to the solemn images of Sipi, Nao, and Aurr to remind herself of their significance, to her people at least. Of course. The reason the Spanish priest kept insisting that the Calusa burn their idols had to be that he recognized their power. Maybe even feared them. Suddenly, she knew what to do. Ishkara himself had revealed the way long ago, when she showed him her first writings. Taking hold of the Spanish text, she placed it above the candle next to her, held it open over the flame until fire licked the edge of a page, and then another. Flames, yes. She froze, mesmerized by them; then, with a yelp, dropped the Spanish idol to the floor. The book closed shut, and the flames snuffed, leaving a haze of acrid smoke and a few smoldering pages hanging, suspended in the air, the charred letters still visible.

How could she have been so innocent as to think her burning of the Christian book would make a difference? The flames of her vision were taunting her. But they were still somewhere beyond reach. Still elsewhere. Still elsewhen.

The small patache rolled and pitched on a slate-colored, mocking sea that mimicked the stormy sky. Father Rogel leaned over the rail of the reputedly swift and sturdy craft one more time, his stomach convulsing to empty its already empty contents. Nineteen days they'd been at sea, nineteen days for a voyage that, in fair weather, could be accomplished in two. And the irony, the utter irony of it, was that the priest had prayed for just such an occurrence: to be blown anywhere but back to San Antón. But the vessel was under the command of Pedro Menéndez Márquez, and the nephew of the Adelantado had inherited his uncle's famed determination. "I will deliver you there," he'd assured the priest, "or we shall both drown in the attempt." Neither Father Rogel's misery nor his pleading made a difference. The ship was not returning to Havana.

Havana. He'd been useful there. Contented, too, in the company of others of the cloth, Fathers Álamo and Sedeño, the priest's peers; Father Juan Bautista de Segura, the vice-provincial; Brothers Carrera, Juan de Salcedo, and Pedro Ruiz as well. There the wilds of the New World were tempered by an almost collegiate atmosphere that harkened to Father Rogel's days in seminary. Their daily duties and ministering were followed by lively theological discussions. There, under God's winking heaven, Father Rogel felt his spiritual strength and security return, and the healing spread through him clear to his intestines.

The priest was especially thankful for the presence of Father Segura. The leader of the Jesuits in La Florida bore a spirit of unflagging optimism, no matter the circumstances. And Father Segura had certainly been through some of the worst, arriving from St. Augustine empty of stomach, having given away all his supplies, even those needed for the return voyage, to the unhappy settlers there. The vice-provincial threw himself and his small cadre of priests into his latest plan: to start a school in Havana for the children of both Indians and settlers. Let us start with the children, he reasoned, in a location where the hardships are not so overwhelming as inevitably to diffuse our efforts.

Father Rogel was delighted to be a follower. If occasionally his mind drifted to his unfinished business with the Indians at San Antón or to the well-being of Brother Francisco, the priest turned the thoughts aside. The settlements simply could not yet support missionaries. And Father Segura was praising his important work here in Havana.

For six months, from April through the brutal humidity of the tropical summer and into September, Father Rogel had toiled in Havana. Yet the heat had proved more tolerable, the maize more digestible, and the Indians, thank the Lord, more malleable.

Why, oh why had he been sent back to Carlos? Yes, of course he understood that Brother Francisco couldn't hear confessions. He appreciated— and imagined all too vividly—the soldiers' need of the confessional. But why him? He'd pleaded with Father Segura to send one of the others. But Father Álamo was ailing and Father Sedeño slated to sail to Tequesta to try to reestablish that mission. Besides, the vice-provincial concluded, Father Rogel was intimately acquainted with both the soldiers at San Antón and the Indians of Carlos as well. Hadn't he touted his influence with the new cacique?

Father Rogel dared not argue further, dared not reveal that he'd promised Don Felipe he would return with the Adelantado. Where was the captain general anyway? The rumors of his imminent return had swirled through the islands for months. But they proved to be as fickle as the winds that battered the ship and ruined the priest's constitution; then, after making him endure such wretchedness, delivered him to the dreaded destination anyway.

Aesha sat in the shade of a mastic tree while Iqi dug a depression in the earth with a clamshell hoe near a grouping of wild petunias, giant and scarlet milkweeds, blazing stars, and purple coneflowers. The plants, and the sweet bay tree which provided partial shade for them, drew an abundance of butterflies that flitted and fluttered in carefree delicacy. Iqi too looked free of cares, totally absorbed in his digging, not even taking notice of the vivid winged beauties that lit on his back and shoulders, attracted to the salt of his sweat, or maybe just to him.

She really shouldn't disturb him, but their moments together were too few and her time too precious. "What are you doing?" she asked.

His head snapped up. "Starting a pond for water hyssop. It attracts a butterfly that is white with black spots and orange borders around its wings. There were some at the edge of the lagoon on the Thumb where we saw the manatees. Do you remember?"

"But it's nearing the dry season."

"I know. Perhaps it will take. Perhaps we'll have to wait another season."

"Perhaps we won't have another season." Her voice was more strained and cross than she intended.

But Iqi let the comment flutter by him.

"Why do you do this? What's the point?" Aesha just couldn't help herself. He looked so content. Yet she had to provoke him.

"It doesn't please you?"

"Of course it pleases me. But it's so . . . unimportant."

He leaned on his hoe, wiped his brow with a forearm. "Tell me what you'll have me do, and I will do it. I thought you wished me to take care of Ishkara's gardens."

"I did," she said. "I do. For the fruits. For my herbs and teas."

"And why not for beauty?"

She started to retort, but then the impact of his words hit her. Her existence had been whittled down to one with no time for beauty. She looked at Iqi, at a brilliant orange and black butterfly perched on his right shoulder, and began to cry.

He put down his hoe and came to her. She clung to him, buried her head in his chest, the frustration and sorrow pouring out, her tears mixing with his sweat.

He waited a long time before speaking. "We should move to the pond I was just building. We could fill it now. The hyssop loves saltwater."

She drew her head back, looked up at his kindly smile. "I couldn't go on but for you." She hugged him harder.

Her embrace squeezed hard on his ribs, forcing the air from his lungs. "Nor I without you." He sucked in a long breath. "But what you say is true. We won't have another season of quiet. For far too long, the smell has been in the air. The clouds have gathered; the storm must follow. I cannot say if we'll survive it. And yet, what am I to do? Digging the pond that may never be filled, attracting the butterfly that may never arrive, I can't help but feel that Ishkara is watching . . . and approving."

"He spoke to me. But in riddles. And he laughed."

"Laughter is not such a bad thing."

"But why doesn't he help me more? Why do Carlos and even my father ignore my pleas? And why do the gods not intervene?"

"Perhaps it's because you're doing all you can. Perhaps their silence indicates agreement, not the contrary."

"Only one thing is certain," she said. "You are my one true friend."

"You have another."

Her eyes asked the question.

"He's perched on your head."

* * *

Coyobea shuffled into the cacique's chambers, careful to keep his head bowed. It wouldn't bode well for Felipe to see resentment in the eyes of the former councilor whose role had been relegated to that of messenger boy. "The Spanish ship approaches."

Felipe studied the man briefly. With his shorn hair and Christian clothes, he looked as ridiculous as he did uncomfortable. Good. And he cowered, too. Let him ever remember the consequences of defying a cacique's order. "A single ship only?"

"That is what the lookouts say."

"How many aboard?"

"Not more than thirty. It is not a large vessel."

"And the leader, Menéndez, he's among them?"

"The scouts cannot tell. The ship hasn't come close enough yet."

"Leave, then, and don't return until you can give me an answer."

Coyobea limped out, grimacing from the open blisters on his feet.

Felipe chuckled. Fitting punishment, was it not, making a runner out of Coyobea, a runner in white man's boots? The meting out of justice was at the core of a cacique's responsibility. It was a task at which Felipe excelled. He pressed his fingertips together, feeling them tingle with anticipation. Nearly six moons now he had awaited the Spanish holy man's return with his great leader. Felipe had long since grown tired of toying with the new priest. He was but a baitfish. Felipe's net was woven for the big catch. And the net was ready.

When the ship unloaded its men and cargo that night, Felipe allowed them to pass unmolested, wanting to make sure the Spanish leader Menéndez hadn't remained on board. He sent Coyobea to the fort, requesting an audience. The messenger returned a short time later. The cacique would be welcomed the next morning.

"You've done well. I wish to reward you."

The former councilor flinched.

"Meet me at the palace in the morning," said the cacique, "and lead me to their Adelantado. He'll be most impressed to see my Christian councilor."

Felipe paused at the gate. This was a risk. Carlos had perished in exactly this way. But it was an opportunity, too, to sit with the headman of all the Spaniards, an opportunity that Felipe couldn't afford to pass up. His hold over his own people depended on his continued favor with the Christians. But, he reminded himself, the opposite was also true. The Spaniards needed his friendship equally. Carlos's failure was one of confidence. Felipe would not repeat it. He'd come without knife or war club, without guard save for the worthless Coyobea; but he'd brought his self-assurance. It would carry him through; it had to. The gate swung open. Adorned in only his breechclout, his egret-feather headdress, and the cacique's fringed leggings, and carrying only his ruler's staff, Felipe entered the Spaniards' lair.

The captain Reynoso and several soldiers who led them through the compound were dressed in clean, identical half-sleeved coats that hung to knee-length. Good. The Spaniards, too, recognized the importance of the occasion. When they reached the Christian temple, the holy man Rogel threw his arms around Coyobea, then greeted Felipe with downcast eyes. The priest looked pale as a ghost crab and just as skittish.

The cacique surveyed the room once, then again, hardly believing what he saw, or rather what he didn't. There were only the priest, the captain, Escalante, and the soldiers. No Adelantado.

No Adelantado. Felipe struggled to control the rage rising inside. There was a tangible feel to it, a taste and odor, too, like that of sea grapes fallen from the tree and fermenting on the ground. "Your leader," he hissed through clenched teeth. "Where is he?"

The priest squeaked something to Escalante. "Detained," said the translator, "but I promise you—"

Felipe cut him off. "You dare to return without him?" Before he even realized it, Felipe's ruler's staff waved and waggled over his head, the thick, heavy, rock wood baton light in the same surprising way of a large bird held in the hand.

The priest cowered, placing a forearm in front of his face. The soldiers rushed to his side, the Spanish captain quickest of all. His long knife drawn, he charged Felipe, who turned to face him, ruler's staff still dancing. But before either could act, the priest dove for the ground between them, a single piercing "No!" uttering from his throat. Both men froze for an instant.

The prone priest took hold of one leg of each and held on for dear life. The desperate action had the desired effect: both men glowered at the other, but neither lunged. With a supreme act of will, Felipe made himself lower the staff. The captain's knife followed suit.

"Soon," the priest pleaded, picking himself up and brushing dust from his robe. "I promise you. The Adelantado will return soon. I'm going to Havana to meet him."

Felipe glared from the priest to the captain and back again. "Bring him two messages," he growled.

"Yes, of course."

"The first: I demand that Menéndez declare war on Tocobaga. The worm is a murderer of Calusa and Spaniards alike. He ordered the killing of your soldiers. The captain"—Felipe locked eyes once again with Captain Reynoso—"if he has a shred of honor, will vouch for that. He heard the confessions of Guebu, Enenpa, and Comachicaquiseyobe."

The priest looked to Reynoso for confirmation. The captain was breathing heavily through his nose, snorting almost. The scar on his cheek was a white knife blade against his scarlet face. Just barely, his head nodded. Father Rogel whispered something to him, and the captain moved his hand from his weapon . . . though not very far. "I will tell the Adelantado," said Father Rogel to Felipe. "And the other? You said you have two messages?"

In a flash, Felipe's staff rose up, then came crashing down. But not on the priest. Instead, it landed square on the head of Coyobea. There was a splintering sound, and the councilor collapsed to his knees, then fell forward, blood pouring from his skull.

Father Rogel knelt beside Coyobea. Captain Reynoso drew his blade.

Felipe's staff stayed down. "This man—as you well know—was a false Christian." His voice was calm now, in command. "Tonight we will dance around his head. I will set it out to remind my people that I won't tolerate falseness. I do this as a service to you, as the friend to the Spanish that I've always been. Remind the Adelantado of how well I treat my friends." He stooped and threw the limp Coyobea easily over his shoulder. "I'm sure he wishes to remain one." Felipe strolled casually for the door.

When Captain Reynoso made to block the exit, Father Rogel threw his arms around the soldier's waist. "No. Touch him and we'll all die."

Grudgingly, the captain allowed the cacique to pass. He turned to Father Rogel, disdain splattered across his flushed face. "You have it wrong, Father. Backwards, in fact."

"They'll be back. You don't doubt it, do you?" Aesha stood at the steps of Felipe's palace, watching the backwards paddlers convey the priest from the harbor.

The cacique dismissed them with a wave. "Next time I think they'll remember to bring their leader."

"With an entire army, no doubt. You've ensured that."

"Let them come. I'm already gathering a force of my own. Every able man in Escampaba."

"You mean to destroy them in battle, then?"

Felipe broke out his toothy smile. "Destroy the Spaniards? Of course not. My warriors are merely preparing to vanquish Tocobaga. I'll assure my Spanish friends of this. With such an impressive force, I'm sure they'll want to help."

Aesha watched as, in the distance, the smaller boat reached the larger one. Sail cloths raised, it pointed away from Caalus. "And if they won't?" she asked, knowing full well that Felipe would have an answer. "What if the Spaniards attack us instead?"

As the wind carried away perhaps the last chance of reconciliation, Felipe replied. "The people of Escampaba will be ready."

Moving, moving, moving. They're moving once again. The tides were gathering.

ᴖ Nineteen ᴖ

He hadn't intended to stay so long in Spain, just long enough to secure the King's support and financing. But when Pedro Menéndez arrived in Madrid, back in July the year past, he'd had to refute the slanders of Governor Osorio of Havana and of the handful of deserters from La Florida who'd returned safely to Spain. Osorio's motives, Menéndez told King Felipe, were a transparent attempt to cling to his governorship, and the deserters were weak-willed cowards. What really convinced the King, though, was the parade of Indians Menéndez had brought with him. The six chiefs strutted their naked, painted bodies in front of Felipe, whooping and grunting in their native tongues. Then they bowed before Menéndez.

Felipe declared Menéndez Captain General of the West and Governor of Cuba, charged him with defending the Indies against all enemies, and gave him the means to do so: 200,000 ducats, 2,000 soldiers, and 12 galleons.

The Adelantado's biggest problem was that the King trusted him too well. Felipe asked him to ready a fleet to take the King to Flanders. Menéndez wasted months doing so, only to have Felipe change his mind. It was December 1568 by the time he finally returned to Havana.

Too long had he been absent from La Florida. A year and a half, and in that time, his forts had been overrun, his soldiers murdered. Only San Antón at Carlos remained. Menéndez called Father Rogel, who had lived with those Indians, to the governor's quarters.

At the mention of Carlos, the priest took on the look of a sailor in his first high seas. "You mustn't return there. It's far too dangerous."

"Let me be the judge of that," the captain general said as softly as he could. "Just tell me what has occurred there since I've been gone. I am aware only that the chief, Carlos, is dead."

The priest poured out his story. "Carlos was killed by Captain Reynoso at the fort. The new chief is friendly. He took the name Felipe to show his devotion. I've spent many long hours with him and know his heart. He sincerely wishes to become a Christian and awaits only your return."

"Yet, you just told me that would be too dangerous."

The priest's eyes jumped in quick, jerky movements. "There's another factor." He looked at the floor. "The priestess Aesha. I'm convinced she's ruled by the devil. She has much power, that one, as much perhaps as the chief. She's poisoning her people and Felipe as well."

Menéndez' eyebrows arched. "Aesha. She was the wife of Carlos, as I recall."

"With the death of Carlos's father, she's become the defender of their heathen ways."

A dash of bemusement brightened the Adelantado's face. "Ah, yes. I remember the first time I met her. I thought her the sister of the chief. Not one of my finest moments. Quite beautiful she was. Charming, too. I remember her smile."

"Please," Father Rogel bleated. "Don't underestimate her. She is the daughter of those Indians' greatest chief. Some say the chiefdom should rightly be hers."

Menéndez considered the enemies he'd faced over the years: privateers and savages, slaughterers and backstabbers. Then he pictured the slender, bare-breasted beauty . . . and feared he would laugh aloud. He bit his index finger hard, composed himself. "And the situation now in Carlos?"

"Felipe's hold on his chiefdom is tenuous. Upon my last departure, he was dancing around the heads of four of his own tribesmen: three who had betrayed him and a fourth whom he called a false Christian. But I know"—the priest dropped dramatically to one knee—"as God is my witness, that Coyobea was sincere. It was Aesha who turned him from the light. I pray, don't blame Felipe."

Menéndez cradled his bearded chin, stroked it with a thumb and two fingers. "You've gained the confidence of the new chief, then?"

"He dined at my table countless times," Father Rogel replied. "Through the interpreter, we delved into the deepest spiritual subjects. I cannot overemphasize Don Felipe's importance. He's the most powerful chief in all of La Florida. If we can turn him to the Lord, all the rest in those vast lands will follow." The priest cast his eyes skyward. "How I've prayed for your return. It's the Lord's work you're doing. Your success will be His."

"And how, pray tell, do we accomplish this feat if it's too dangerous to visit that place? Can that really be so? The fort is still operating. Why don't you go there with me? We'll talk to him together."

The priest's hands clutched at his stomach. "No. I can never return there. It would be my death sentence and yours."

"Then what is your plan?"

"Bring him here, Adelantado. Bring him to Havana. Away from that she-devil, he will show you his true heart."

Menéndez' fingers played with a curly white hair that had come off his beard. A painful and all too frequent reminder that he was no longer a young man, that time had become an ever narrowing funnel. Who knew when the king might call him back to Spain? But the priest's plan should not cause undue delay. "I suppose your idea has merit," he said.

"I know not whether I can entice him to come, but I'll dispatch a galleon forthwith."

Felipe's plans proceeded swiftly. Caalus was frothy with activity. Shell hammers pounded, saw teeth bit, and shagreen scraped as the people turned out atlatls and darts, arrows and bows, bone knives and saber clubs. Canoes scurried here and there with tools and materials. To free the men for their labors, the populace made do with stews of pinfish, whelk, and conch. Felipe made it a point to consume the rubbery meals himself, exhorting anyone within earshot to "savor the taste, for it is that of victory."

It was not advisable to complain.

Aesha fretted as Felipe whipped the people into a fury. By day, they honed weapons. By night, they danced around the never ending display of bloody heads, too frenzied to consider that the executed had been their friends and neighbors. War with Tocobaga or war with the Spaniards, it was all the same to warriors whose blood lusts had been roused. Aesha felt powerless, her voice a silent, unheard cry. And matters would only worsen. The cold season upon them, the people were beginning to suffer. Aesha found herself watching almost hopefully for the approach of a Spanish vessel.

The fortress at San Antón sat in the midst of the commotion. Captain Reynoso did not dare send anyone outside the gate except for Escalante, who still seemed to enjoy a favored status with the Indians. Expecting an attack at any minute, Reynoso doubled and redoubled the night watches, until the men grew bleary-eyed and irritable from lack of sleep. Soon the Indians would starve them out. The captain resolved never to let that happen. He'd die fighting first.

Then the ship arrived, anchoring well outside Tega Pass. The Calusa lookouts reported that it was the largest yet, with square, rectangular and triangular sail cloths, six in all, set on towering poles rising from a deck already high above the water. Below the wooden floor were two rows of windows, one above the other, as if three dwellings had been stacked on top of each other. Only a few dozen Spaniards were visible. It was impossible to tell how many hid below.

Felipe's forces gathered, preparing for the Spaniards' attack. Rows of archers lined the harbor entrance. Warriors slipped away to nearby islands to hide in the thickets of walking trees, ready to attack the Spaniards from behind. Instead of an assault, though, a lone Spanish canoe appeared, manned only by two backwards paddlers and a single messenger, not the Adelantado, not even a noble. Felipe ordered his warriors not to molest the Spaniards. Calling Escalante from the fort to translate, the cacique waited at the foot of the plaza.

Felipe stood dumbstruck. He'd envisioned a dozen possibilities, but this one had escaped him. The Adelantado was calling him to Havana. The cacique's mind raced, considering the alternatives. Go, and he'd be utterly exposed. Without his warriors by his side, what leverage did he have? But if he refused Menéndez's invitation, he was missing the opportunity to engage, finally, the Spanish leader. He doubted he'd get another chance.

The cacique wasn't one to hesitate on even the most difficult of decisions. Clearly, the Adelantado feared facing Felipe on his home grounds; otherwise he would have appeared in person. Yet that would have to be Felipe's exact mission: to lure Menéndez to Caalus. The cacique was unsure how he'd accomplish the feat; that detail would have to come later. For now, he addressed the crowd of onlookers gathered on the plaza. "My people: I will go now to Havana to meet the Spanish leader. I will stand at the bow of his ship; I will be his honored guest. I will tell him of our readiness to fight"—he turned to face Escalante—"to vanquish Tocobaga, alongside our Spanish friends. I will bring their Adelantado back to Caalus."

The warriors hoisted their bows and stamped their atlatls. The people cheered. Putting on his most self-assured face, Felipe stepped into the Spanish canoe.

As the wind ship entered the Spaniards' harbor, Felipe's belly went sour. Before him, spreading across the waterfront stood a massive stone structure, unfinished still, yet already unmistakable: the Adelantado's stronghold. It was high, high as Felipe's own palace and council hall, and broad, with two vast wings extending from a central body, as if the building were a great gray stone bird. Men were working on the fort even as he passed, their metal tools glinting as they chipped and shaped and set the blocks, each one straddling two others. Other workers were digging a deep ditch to surround the building, as if to make an island of it. Felipe struggled to keep his face impassive, even as the sourness threatened to eat through his belly. The structure would never burn; it would be near impossible to attack. An all-stone fort surrounded by water would stand forever.

Disembarking, he followed his Spanish escorts through the narrow, dusty paths of the city called Havana. Here, Felipe counted no more than sixty buildings, a few of stone and wood with two living levels, latticed windows, and enclosed squares of open space, though most were built of palm strips, small and unimpressive. And easily burned. Attack, his warrior's instinct demanded. Now, while the numbers are still small, before the stone fort is completed.

Everything about this island was strange. It smelled of smoke and dung. The latter could be traced to the pens that held the huge, docile grass-chewer and the grunting mud-wallower that the Spaniards favored for food. That explained the former smell, too: they smoked the meat to preserve it. There was a different kind of smoke in the air too, akin to a fire of wet grass, that baffled Felipe until he saw that some of the men were inhaling the smoke of tightly wrapped, smoldering leaves. It was a practice he'd heard of, though never seen. Did it create visions? Were all these strangers tirupos?

Felipe studied the men walking the paths. Some must be Spaniards, for they closely resembled the soldiers at Caalus. Others, who he judged to be speaking the Spanish tongue but had darker complexions and broader faces, must bear mixed lineage with the Tainos native to the island. Where were the Tainos themselves, though? They seemed to have disappeared. Instead, here and there black faces gazed out. Negroes, Escalante had called them when occasionally one was brought to Caalus amongst shipwreck survivors. They were slaves and looked it. One man's back was a snarl of interlacing purple welts. Three others' right ears were missing. They stared not at Felipe but at their homeland, unfathomably far away. Or perhaps at the land beyond, for they looked dead already, though their bodies didn't yet know it.

Then Felipe heard a most surprising sound. From inside one of the buildings, several women were laughing loudly. He veered toward them. They were dressed only in the garments the Spanish women wore underneath their hot, voluminous long robes. The men inside were smiling too, the first happy Spaniards he'd ever seen.

Abruptly, Felipe was taken by the arm and led away from the happy house, taken instead to the home of the frowning priests. The Man of the Rising Gown was there and two others, as well as an interpreter, another Spaniard—Felipe couldn't remember his name—whom Carlos had released three suns before on the Adelantado's first visit. The priests hovered over the cacique like sand flies, pestering him with the same annoying questions he'd been asked a thousand times. Yes, he was prepared to become a Christian. Yes, he would send away his wives, renounce his gods, burn his idols. Of course he was genuine. He knelt and kissed the cross with all sincerity.

A group of Spaniards filed in. He recognized several from the happy house. They were fully clothed now. They marked themselves and prayed and listened to the priests babble on. They didn't smile. Then they left.

Finally, the Adelantado arrived. He was shorter than Felipe remembered, and when the cacique stood before the Spanish leader, he noticed that the circle of curly hair atop the man's head had thinned considerably. Lose your hair, lose your power, Felipe thought, and he held his pose over the Adelantado an extra-long moment before bowing. Menéndez took Felipe's hands and signaled him to rise. There were gifts of clothing and of glittering beads. The Spanish leader insisted that Felipe dine with him at a table heaped with meats and starchy roots. Even better, there was a variety of cane grown in fields behind the houses with a skin full of needle-like hairs that could be peeled and split open. Felipe sucked on its sweet juice as the Adelantado entertained him with singers, musicians, and dancers. The cacique ate until his belly was as hard and round as a woman overdue for birth. He drank cup after cup of wine.

But he kept his wits about him.

His chance came late in the evening. The platters had been cleared, the exhausted singers and dancers excused. Felipe sat alone at the table with the Adelantado and the interpreter. "You've regaled me in most impressive fashion. Now, I must pay you back. You will come to my home, and I will put on for you a festival such as you've never seen. There, before my people, I will pledge my faith to the Christian God."

The Spanish leader stared at Felipe with a piercing, steady gaze. His hand went to his hairy chin to pat his curly hairs, shape them to a point, pinch the ends, but his eyes never left the cacique. Then he nodded his head, spoke to the interpreter. "The Adelantado accepts your invitation," the translator said. "He is dispatching a ship to take you home tomorrow. He will follow in a few short days. He asks only that you postpone the celebration until after your conversion to Christianity, which is a most solemn event."

"I will do so, my friend and brother," said Felipe, taking the Spaniard's hand. "And then together we will destroy Tocobaga."

The chilling moons fell upon Caalus with the touch of a dead man's hand. Trees shivered, some even dropping all their leaves. Fish grew sluggish and refused to swim to the nets. Birds plumped their feathers and stood facing south, their backs to the bitter winds blown from the frozen mouth of the anchor star.

The people, too, looked south to Havana, awaiting their cacique's return. Unlike their plant and animal kin, they stubbornly refused to accept the abnormal cold. Around bonfires built to drive back the chill, they danced the war dances, stomped their feet and pounded their fists, compelling their blood to stay warm. Felipe's lieutenants stoked the fires and urged them on.

Aesha attempted to break through the madness. Wearing the mask of sea turtle, she descended from the temple. She would urge the people to rest, to slow down, to conserve their energy. When she reached the fires, though, two men were skirmishing, not mock fighting as they would in training, but lunging and thrusting at each other with their bone knives. Both were bleeding badly. Around them, the crowd rooted for their favorites. Her arrival went totally unnoticed.

She moved to the center of the circle, finally catching the attention of one of the combatants. As the man looked her way, the other plunged his knife deep into his opponent's throat. Gasping and gurgling, the first man fell.

The mob cheered louder. The victor, rewarded with a silver amulet bearing Felipe's dolphin design, danced in triumph.

Despondent, Aesha retreated to the temple. It was impossible to pray, for her ears were filled with the shrill cries of voices bellowing for war. She didn't even try to go to her sleeping mat, knowing it would be useless. Instead she stepped outside. A cold wind blew her hair behind her, wet her eyes and penetrated her body, carrying with it the unrelenting war cries that screamed now through her bones. She wandered aimlessly through her cold, shivering gardens.

As dawn's finger dabbed the sky above the mainland, still the warriors continued. But with the light, too, came the voice of the first morning bird: "Tee deedle tee deedle tee deedle tee. Tee deedle tee deedle tee." Over and again it called, incessant and cheerful, insistent and assured. She found herself drawn to the bird, pulled to the call so contrasting to those that haunted her. "Tee deedle tee deedle tee deedle." She followed the song to the edge of Ishkara's grove. There, perched in the brush, stood a hand-sized brown wren with a long white eye patch and white throat. Exhausted as she was despairing, Aesha submitted, let its voice become the only sound in the world, a peaceful moment such as she hadn't had for a very long time.

"It sings to live. It lives to sing." Iqi, behind her, hands on her waist.

She slumped into him. "Existence can be so simple . . . for others."

"And why not for you?"

"I have the weight of the people on me."

"Perhaps that's the problem. Part of it, anyway."

She felt herself stiffen. What she needed from Iqi was support, not criticism.

He rubbed a thumb gently along the tendons of her neck. "Who can improve the fortune of others without attending to their own? The wren sings the song it was born to. What is yours? Surely not self-pity. Sing it, my love. The people will hear."

Now, though, yet another sound intruded. The call of the conch horn. A wind ship approached.

11 April 1569

A most unsettled, unsettling time. First, the news that the Adelantado had returned. Oh, how I rejoiced, wept like a child, only to have my tears turn bitter yet again when I learned he had called Felipe to Havana and was not coming to San Antón. I understood the strategy. The captain general would have been in grave danger here. Yet to have come so close to my rescue, after twenty years—twenty!—then to have been abandoned again was more than I could bear. I wandered amongst the Indians, fully expecting to be slain, for Felipe had left them in a fever for blood. I did not care. I was ready to join my brother in heaven. I had nothing to live for.

A severe winter it was this year, rare in these tropical lands. Some of the natives wore animal skins, but most still walked naked and barefooted, suffering, as I know they do, stoically, uncomplaining. I stood in my soldier's uniform as I listened to the Indians howl for the blood of their enemies. They didn't beat me, didn't touch me. Whether from familiarity or from fear of reprisals from Felipe, I cannot say. I walked amongst them like a ghost, a specter floating in a cloud of fog.

It was the soldiers instead who might have slain me, so piqued were they at my unreliability. They'd entrusted to me their dwindling supply of trinkets to trade for food. Instead, I gave them away and returned empty-handed. Captain Reynoso protected me. In all this time I haven't lost a single man, he said. You'll not be the first. I need you.

I was there when Felipe returned. Dressed in Spanish finery, he boasted of his triumph, of the banquets, the gifts, the promises. The Adelantado was coming with wind ships, soldiers, and weapons, all meant for Tocobaga. A new mound would be built on that enemy's lands, a Calusa mound, with Tocobaga's worthless body at the base.

Such fervor there was, such a frenzy of stomping and stamping that the very ground beneath me shook.

Two months have passed since Felipe's return. Despite the ripening of the purple berries, no celebrations called forth the warm season, no giddy play. He sustains the people on a diet of promises, guaranteeing them new fishing grounds and oyster beds, pearls and gold. He keeps his warriors stirred up with blood games, sacrificing the weak and skeptical. And through it all, where is Aesha? His night fires seem to ward her away. She no longer ventures from the temple. She is as dead.

And I am, too. I believed none of Felipe's assurances. The Adelan-

tado wasn't coming to aid the Indians. He wasn't coming to rescue me. He wasn't coming at all. Then, this morning it happened. The conch horn blew once again.

Finally, the Adelantado had come to him. A wind ship was anchored in deep water beyond Tega Pass; this time, the Spanish leader was on it. He had sent a message that he wanted to meet Felipe, but he was being cautious. He declined Felipe's invitation to dine at the palace, turned down the offer to meet on neutral ground at Hermit Crab Island. The Adelantado preferred to meet Felipe on the sea. And alone, save for the interpreter.

A trap? Felipe thought not. Menéndez could have disposed of him in Havana. The Adelantado was just being wary, as well he should. He was in Felipe's domain now, and the cacique was set for all contingencies. He'd worked hard to convince his own people of the Spanish leader's allegiance, but Felipe wasn't counting on it. He was counting only on his own preparations.

Launching a solo canoe from the water court, Felipe paddled past the crowds lining the canals. They weren't cheering. Felipe understood. They'd grown weary of waiting. Well, so had he. Now, finally the decisive moment had come.

Felipe left the harbor with Escalante paddling a respectful distance behind. A spark of recollection struck of a long-ago Falko, of Escalante besting him, of threats hurled in both directions. Maybe the interpreter was the one up to mischief. Let him try. Felipe's paddle, long and heavy, was all the weapon he needed. Oh, yes. And the bone knife hidden in his fringed leggings.

The sun was high, the air crisp and springtime dry. Felipe's canoe moved easily across the bay. In the pass, where tide met wind, small waves slapped at the dugout's sides. The cacique powered through them, aiming now for the small Spanish canoe in the distance.

The figure approached, his back to Felipe, short arms pulling the twin paddles with authoritative if choppy strokes. No mistaking the build; it was the Adelantado.

As they drew near, the two crafts slowed and stopped. Bobbing on the small swells, the two men appraised each other. Felipe detected no weapons. Not counting on that either.

"I am delighted to see my Spanish friend again," Felipe said when Escalante had caught up. "It saddens me, though, that I cannot greet you in the style befitting a man of your stature."

"Ah, but for a man of the sea, there can be no greater pleasure." Pushing with one paddle and pulling with the other, Menéndez positioned his craft closer to Felipe's—though still with a canoe's length between them. "I trust your journey back to your home was a pleasant one."

"I have much admiration for your vessels. Even the smaller one you are in now. Its maneuverability is remarkable."

"Though yours undoubtedly is the faster."

A flight of pelicans passed in a perfect line, each gliding and dipping, then flapping its wings lazily to rise once again. The two men watched them disappear into the distance.

"You know the purpose I am here for," Menéndez said.

"To help me defeat our mutual enemy. My warriors are ready. We will leave in the morning and reach Tocobaga's lands under cover of night."

"Tocobaga has wronged my people. He must be punished," Menéndez said. "This I've promised. But"—the Adelantado's head shook from side to side—"I have come for a greater purpose than that. Are you ready, as you've pledged, to swear your allegiance to the one true God?"

"As soon as I return with Tocobaga's head."

Menéndez's head shook again, even as his warrior's gaze remained locked on Felipe. "You are a great leader, Felipe, and of course the choice is yours. I've brought my priests with me and will send them ashore in the morning. They are here to guide you to the light of Christianity. I pray that you will follow. Tomorrow will either be a blessed day or something else entirely. There is nothing more to say." With that, the Adelantado reached for his paddles. Still eyeing Felipe, he began to back away.

The knife pleaded to be thrown. The paddle begged to be waved, a signal to the warriors hidden on Tega Island to intercept Menéndez and attack the Spanish ship. But Felipe sat motionless. The Adelantado had proved his friendship by coming to Caalus. To defeat Tocobaga once and for all, Felipe needed the Spaniards. First Tocobaga. Then Menéndez. If it meant one more tiresome ceremony, Felipe could endure it.

The three priests were dressed in identical black robes and three-cornered hats. Felipe had to study their solemn faces for several moments before realizing that they were all ones he'd met only recently in Havana: Álamo, Sedeño, and the older one that was their leader, Segura. The Man of the Rising Gown wasn't among them. Amusing, though hardly surprising.

The lead priest's words echoed in the near-deserted council hall. "Cacique Felipe, are you ready to become a child of God, to shun forever your graven images, to worship instead the one true God and his living Son?"

"I am." Ready to be done with this tedious ritual, that is.

"And will you repudiate the sister you have taken as wife and the other wives as well, and repent for those sins, and throw yourself on the mercy of the Almighty?"

"I will. Yes, of course. As I've promised." At least until Tocobaga is dead and my authority firm throughout the region.

"Then bow your head."

The lead priest recited words that Escalante didn't translate and sprinkled water on Felipe's head. An odd custom, though harmless enough. When the black robe finished, he reached up to place a hand on Felipe's bare shoulder. "You have been received by sacred baptism into the loving arms of God and the world of civilized men. Now, in the name of the Father, and of the Son, and of the Holy Ghost, you must give proof of your sincerity not only by your words but also by your deeds. Lead us now to your temple."

Felipe's shoulder stiffened beneath the cold hand. "Our temple is the domain of the tirupo. Just as is yours."

"We serve, though, only under the good graces of our Lord and Majesty in Spain," the lead priest countered. "His servant, our Adelantado, humbly requests this action by you. He says that if you are the supreme leader of your people, surely you can accomplish this simple deed. Destroy your idols. They are evil, as is anyone who protects them."

So close. This was the final leap. The gods would have to understand.

All morning she'd prayed, begged for help, wept. As she caressed the treasures of her people, her mind hunted desperately for a solution. Hide the masks and sacred images of the gods? No. The answer could never lie in such shameful action. Fight both Felipe and the Spaniards? Her people would fracture, and against a confused and splintered enemy, the Christians would be ruthless. Aesha's head pounded in searing pain. The flames were coming. She could not stop them.

They marched up the ramp toward her, Felipe in the lead, the three priests and Escalante trailing behind. She let Felipe walk past her and into the temple. But the priests were a different matter. She addressed Escalante. "Tell them they may not enter the temple."

Escalante conferred with the lead priest. "He says that is quite unnecessary."

Aesha's breaths came in short, shallow puffs. Would the gods allow the temple to be violated? Would Ishkara intervene? Her father? She looked around expectantly, saw only pallid faces staring from black robes. A strange feeling came over her as she watched the events unfold, as if she were watching from afar. Felipe stepped back outside. He carried the masks of otter, sea wolf, and dolphin, placed them on the ground at the priests' feet, then ducked back inside, this time reappearing with the mask of the crane.

A thing of beauty with its long, slender neck and bright feathers, a marvel of fabrication with its hinged, working jaw. As it crashed to the ground, the lower beak broke off.

Time after time Felipe returned, adding to the growing mound the tirupo's skins and feathers, her claws and rattles, her casine bowl and gourd. Sea and land turtle, cormorant, vulture, spider, alligator, and raccoon lay skewed and cracked at the top of the heap, the vacant souls of their empty eyes staring in all directions. Aesha tried to shut her own eyes to the horror. She could not. She stared on just as vacantly.

Felipe reappeared once more, this time with a lighted candle, Ishkara's wooden bowl of shark's liver oil, and Carlos's ruler's staff. He dipped the staff in the healing oil, then emptied the rest of the bowl onto the mound of masks. Felipe held the candle beneath the staff. It was the tassel holding the lock of Aesha's hair that caught first. The small flame traveled up the tassel until the staff itself was burning.

All eyes focused on the flames. Without so much as glancing sideways, Felipe tossed the staff onto the pile. For a long moment, there was silence. Not even breathing. Then there was a loud "whump," and instantly flames were everywhere. Sparks popped and crackled. Tongues of fire licked the masks, thrust through the empty eye slots, and danced luridly skyward.

Aesha could not mistake the flames she'd seen so many times.

When next Felipe appeared, he carried a figurine. He threw the perfect carved woodpecker onto the fire. Aurr. So this was to be the fulfillment of her vision, more horrible than she'd ever imagined it. As in her dreams, Aesha tried to cry out, but her tongue was frozen, her words voiceless.

The feline figure of Nao crashed onto the fire, sending a shower of sparks whirling into the air, rising toward the heavens. And still, Felipe wasn't finished. He entered the temple once more.

The heat was scorching her face, smoke stinging her eyes. Aesha stared on, unblinking. Felipe was gone for a very long time. When at last he reappeared, he walked very slowly, holding the object in front of him ceremoniously, with both hands. Aesha gasped. It must be Sipi. But when the smoke cleared momentarily, she realized it wasn't the Old One, wasn't the ancient white deer hide that Felipe clutched. Yet was this act any less depraved? Felipe threw the object on the fire. Flames engulfed the buttonwood box with the osprey's likeness. The box that held the bones of her father.

Expressionless, Felipe walked slowly from the fire and down the ramp to the plaza. The Spanish priests followed, nodding to each other in satisfaction. Escalante lingered behind, staring at the blazing container. He bowed his head then, tapped his forehead, chest, and then shoulders in the way of the Christians. When his eyes rose, they sought out Aesha. "My God will help you through this," he said.

You pray to a god who allows this? She tried to reply, but the words would not come out, and she swallowed them back down, vile and sour, and turned her back on him until he, too, departed.

The fire burned on. Aesha knew what would happen next. The flames would reach out for her, take her in their grip, pull her to them, engulf and consume her. She tried to brace herself to resist, but her legs were weak. It was all she could do to remain standing.

Paralyzed and helpless, she looked on as the sacred objects of her people blackened beyond recognition. But the flames came no closer. Could this conceivably *not* be her end?

It was in that instant of numb confusion that, at the edge of the fire, Aesha noticed a single mask that had escaped the blaze.

Felipe reached a plaza as silent as it was filled. He addressed the gathered multitudes, ordered the warriors among them to take up their weapons and prepare the war canoes. The Adelantado was waiting. The moment of triumph was before them. Tocobaga, at last, was theirs.

The crowd didn't move. The people remained on the plaza, their stunned eyes locked on the temple mound.

He'd anticipated this. What the people needed now was leadership, firm and decisive. "Go. Now." he roared. He pushed at the people, guided and steered them, swinging at those who refused to move, viciously clubbing several to the ground. The crowd cowered, shrank from his saber club. But they didn't leave the plaza.

Two priests were back-paddling out of the central canal; the third accompanied Escalante toward the fort. "Stop them," Felipe called to the frozen crowd. He was in a rage now, running to and fro, club waving, herding the people from the plaza as a fisherman drives mullet to a fish pen.

Mindless, bewildered, they began to stumble off, not toward anything, just away from the crazed cacique.

Then, there was a voice. A song, melodious and clear. Once again, the movement stopped as the people turned back toward the temple. A figure was descending from that mound, wearing a mask, charred but distinct, of a small brown wren.

Aesha sang. Sang the song of the morning. Sang of loss and of hope. Sang of change as inevitable as the shifting tide. Arms flapping, she ran onto the plaza. She flitted about, lighting here and there, singing, always singing the songs of the wren, and of her mother and father, husband and uncle, until all finally blended into a new song, a song that was her own.

Straight into the crowd she flew. The people shrank from her, too. They were too shocked, too confused.

Felipe bellowed. Aesha sang. Felipe's club swung. Aesha's arms waved. The people veered this way and that, away from the cacique, away from the tirupo. Finally, the cacique took notice of Aesha, turned to face her. Between them, the crowd parted.

He had no words for her now. Instead, in a smooth, fleet movement that belied his bulk, Felipe erased the distance between them, his war club already in motion. The club came down. It bit into flesh.

But not Aesha's. It was Iqi, who had followed her from the temple, who had kept close to her, and who now darted between the two, his hand outstretched to block Felipe's thrust. He managed to deflect the blow away from Aesha, but it caught him on the shoulder, the bull shark's teeth tearing a deep, jagged gash. In the next moment, Felipe was on him, his momentum so great that the two toppled to the ground. The full weight of the cacique fell on his opponent.

The breath rushed from Iqi's chest and he couldn't capture another. Felipe used the moment to search for the club, which had flown from his hand on impact. Too far to reach. He grasped for his bone knife. That instant, though, was enough for Iqi to recover. He knocked Felipe's hand aside before it could touch the weapon, then squeezed his muscled arms around the cacique's broad biceps.

Arms pinned, Felipe buried his forehead in Iqi's shoulder, butting it, ripping and mangling the wound, soaking the cacique's face in bright red blood. Grimacing through the fiery pain, Iqi held on and heaved, straining to push the heavy body from his. The men began to roll over and over one another. They reached the plaza embankment and tumbled over the edge.

As they plunged into the shallows of the water court, Iqi lost his grip on the cacique. Felipe scrambled to his feet, already drawing his knife. "Ground dweller." He spat out a mouthful of Iqi's blood. "I'll drink the rest for breakfast."

Aesha stood above the two, at the front of the huge crowd. Stood still, but was frozen no longer, just calm. There must be a victor. For the people's sake. She would not stop the fight.

Felipe took his time now, feigning and slashing with the pointed blade. Iqi dodged the thrusts, backing into water that was knee, then waist, then chest deep. Timing his move perfectly on Felipe's next lunge, instead of drawing back Iqi dove beneath the surface, tackling the cacique's legs. Felipe fell backwards, and for a long moment the two scuffled underwater.

Iqi came up first, clutching Felipe's legs, the pain in his shoulder inspiring him now, giving him strength. The cacique flailed wildly, kicking his legs and thrashing his arms, trying to find flesh with his knife. Felipe's giant belly, though, got in the way. Hard as he struggled, he couldn't bend close enough to strike another blow. And he began to tire. Iqi lifted the cacique's legs higher, forcing Felipe's face underwater.

Now it was Felipe's turn to strain for air. He lay back in the water, sculling his hands to keep his head up. Iqi glanced toward shore, looking to Aesha for guidance. It was just the opportunity Felipe needed. His legs lashed out violently, breaking Iqi's grip.

Free, the cacique charged, his knife slashing downward. But in the deep water, and spent as he was, the thrust was too slow. Iqi danced away from the knife and, grabbing Felipe's left arm, spun behind him. Iqi's hands ringed the huge belly and locked on the knife hand, forcing it down and outward until Felipe's wrist threatened to crack.

The knife popped loose and fell to the bottom.

Iqi heaved the cacique from the water. Coughing and sputtering, Felipe doubled over his quivering belly. Aesha ordered him bound with heavy rope. The cacique did not resist.

The circle of spectators stood as stiff as fish in the sun. "My people." Aesha, the mask now shed, strode to the platform at the center of the plaza, her yellow-brown eyes blazing like miniature suns. "Even in our darkest moment, the gods have spoken. Felipe went too far. His time is over." She held the wren mask high over her head for all to see. "It is time now for song, not war. For creation, not destruction. We will carve our masks again, carve images of the gods even more beautiful than before. I've failed you once. I won't fail you again. Return to your homes. Pray with your families. And sing."

Ever so slowly, still dazed and reeling, the people complied.

⪼ Twenty ⪻

Iqi sat on a low stool in the temple's healing area as Aesha boiled firebush leaves, then poured the hot brew on a moss poultice and pressed it hard to his shoulder. "There's no need to thank me," he said. "Leave me now. The people need you. Your people."

"I made them promises I have no idea how to fulfill."

"You led them away from war. Now lead them toward something better."

"And what is that? The Adelantado may have departed, but what will he do when he learns that Felipe is my captive? The priests see only evil in me. They'll convince him to attack . . . if he even needs any convincing. Of what use will my songs be against his thunder mouths?"

"I cannot answer," Iqi said, "but I believe in you. You must believe in yourself. Now go, please. I'll watch him." Iqi's head jerked toward a far corner of the room, where Felipe, swaddled in ropes, sulked.

"If he speaks, turn your ears elsewhere," Aesha cautioned. "Any moment now, he'll regain use of that slimy tongue of his and talk his way back to the palace. He still has supporters. They were simply too stunned to act."

"Will you go to the palace yourself, then?"

"I cannot. Not while the flames still burn. If I am to lead my people, I must know how. The answer will come, if it comes at all, from the fire. Now sit still." She removed the blood-soaked bandage and applied a new one, binding it tight with braids of cypress bark. "Don't move your shoulder, or the bleeding will begin anew."

She returned to the fire of a vision yet unfulfilled. She couldn't, wouldn't let it die. So she began to tend it, raking the dwindling heap ever closer together, sifting through the blackened pieces. She found the charred remnant of Carlos's ruler's staff and used it to poke through the coals and ashes, searching for the contents of the box Felipe had thrust last on the fire. Locating the pearl eyes that had adorned the container, she wiped them clean of soot, rubbed them until they shone again. But Caalus's bones were nowhere to be found.

Believe. In the smoldering aftermath of desecration, she must yet believe. The flames would burn again. They would lead her to her rightful destiny. She had to persevere.

Filled with dread, she lit a candle and went inside the temple. Bracing herself as if leaning into a fearsome gale, she entered the sanctuary. Even then, the emptiness nearly blew her over. The walls were stripped, the altar that had held Caalus's remains barren. In Felipe's frenzy, he'd flung the thatch floor mats to the side of the room. Aesha lay prostrate on the dank, grief-saturated dirt floor before the lone and lonely image of Sipi. "You are still here, Old One," she whispered. "I ask you today not for guidance, only for strength. The weight upon me is great."

Though Sipi was silent, Aesha felt a presence in the room. There was no sound, no movement. Yet still a presence. "Ishkara?" she said aloud. "Father?"

No answer.

She rose, rubbing her arms to smooth the shiver bumps that had erupted. "You can speak or not," she said. "I know you're there."

She waited.

As she peered about the dim room, something teased at her memory.

Felipe had emptied the inner temple, save only for Sipi. Or had he? Then she knew. The pine boxes. They'd never been placed on the fire. Whatever the bedlam of the day, she couldn't have missed that detail. In the shock of the aftermath, though, she'd overlooked it. Now she was drawn to the side of the room. She removed the pile of mats, and there they were, the boxes and something else. A final mat wrapped around a large mass. With shaking fingers, she unrolled it. Bones. And a lidded bowl. She broke the seal to open it. A pair of yellow-brown eyes stared at her, through her, beyond her.

Like storm waves over a seawall, the emotions crashed over her. Felipe had saved all the remains, even as he'd destroyed everything else. Those eyes, her father lived still. Ishkara, too, and even Carlos. She wasn't alone. And yet, would they help her?

Steadying her trembling hands, she resealed the lid, secured the bundle, and placed it on the altar with the pine boxes flanking it. Then she made for Felipe. "Why did you do it?" she demanded. "Why did you save the remains of our leaders but destroy all else? Did you think that somehow justified your actions?"

Felipe looked up with one eye. The other was swollen shut. "I did what I had to," he mumbled wearily. "I was so close to victory. With Tocobaga out of the way, no one could have opposed me."

She regarded him, incredulous. "Oppose *you*? It's the Spaniards no one could oppose. How can you not see that?"

"I needed them only to defeat my enemies."

"You became their dupe. You couldn't rule except with their assistance. You would have turned us all into Christians. The price is too great. It is like telling the fish to take to the sky. How will he swim? What will he eat?"

"A deceit," Felipe said bitterly. "It was all a deceit. I saved the white deer hide, saved the bones of your father. It's the remains that matter, not the vessel, however ornate. And my trickery with the priests worked. They believed the buttonwood box to be the image of Sipi. They know only that we worship three gods. They've never seen the Ancient One. Few have."

"It's a sacrilege that you're among those that have."

Felipe's jaw was set in an expression she hadn't seen before. There was neither smile nor sneer. "You may never agree, but I did what I had to. Destroying the objects doesn't destroy our beliefs. You said yourself that the masks and idols can all be replaced. Only the image of the Old One can't."

"You're right. I'll never agree," Aesha snapped back. "You're no hero. You bullied the people and defamed the gods."

"Do with me what you will, then. I'm ready to die."

"No. You still have a purpose to serve. I'm sure of it. I only wish I knew what it is."

One eye shone clear. The other fluttered and oozed. "You need me," Felipe said. "Admit it. The time has come for us to join together."

She willed her ears not to hear.

"It's as our fathers intended."

He was securely tied. All she had to do was turn her back on him and walk out. But she couldn't stop the dreadful thought from invading her: what he was saying made sense. "Why should I trust you?" she demanded. "How can I know you won't twist the situation to your advantage, bring the Spaniards back into your camp?"

"Because you defeated me and the people will never again take my side over yours. Because you've already recognized that you cannot defeat the Christians on your own. But there's another, more important reason. And that is because I love the people as much as you do. Set me free, Aesha. Let me help."

If she were wrong, she'd surely perish. But if she did nothing, all the people of Escampaba would. What she was about to do was foolhardy. Dangerous. Desperate. But there was no other way. Drawing a silver-handled knife, she sliced the cords that held his hands. "Here." She handed him the knife. "I do need you, and you need this."

Felipe severed the remainder of his ties with the sharp blade, rubbed his reddened wrists, then tossed the knife from hand to hand. "This will do quite well. It was Ishkara's, no?"

"May he watch over you."

Felipe's laugh thundered through his bruised ribs. "There's a jest befitting a cacique," he said, wincing in pain. "The old crow looking out for me, and I for you."

"What do you intend to do?"

"You'll see." Felipe rose, grimacing. His first two steps were stiff and tentative. By the time he reached the door, there was spring in his stride.

The freshly carved mask was crude in construction, and the eye slots had had to be oversized to fit Felipe's still-swollen orb; but it was a fair representation of its object, and that was what mattered. When Felipe appeared at the gate to the fort, chanting, nickerbean rattle in one hand, blazing torch in the other, he commanded immediate attention. Soldiers. Captain Reynoso. Escalante. And the priest who'd stayed behind, Father Álamo.

"What's the meaning of this . . . this sacrilege?" Father Álamo demanded from behind the closed gate.

Felipe slithered rhythmically back and forth, flicking, then retracting his tongue through the mask's mouth hole.

"Open the gate," Father Álamo said to the captain. "He's been possessed by demons. We must take him in, purify him."

"Just what he wants us to do," said Captain Reynoso. "I can't allow it."

Felipe danced with abandon, chanted with joy.

"I was taught long ago that the snake is sacred to the Indians," Escalante explained. "They say it was created by Aurr, the war god."

Father Álamo pounded his fists on the gate, trying in vain to get the cacique's attention. "But you destroyed your gods in the fire," he called. "You bathed in the holy water. You are a Christian, one of us."

Behind the mask, Felipe couldn't contain his grin. His life was on the line; his heart was light.

"His meaning is clear," Captain Reynoso said. "Your Christian has shed his skin and donned quite another. Did I not warn you?"

"His immortal soul is at stake," Father Álamo pleaded. "I must help him. Open the gate. Please."

While they argued, Felipe acted, leaping forward to place the torch beneath the gate. Flames began to shoot up. Quickly, a soldier brought a bucket of water to douse the fire. When the smoke dissipated, the cacique was gone.

His message was not. Captain Reynoso ordered the three culverins fired, a distress signal to the small patache the Adelantado had left behind. It was a risk, sending away the one ship that if need be could carry his men to safety. But the captain needed reinforcements. There could be no doubt concerning Felipe's actions. He had nothing to lose. His bold move was an attempt to regain support. If even some of his warriors rejoined him, he'd throw himself at the fort. Reynoso hoped the Adelantado would make haste. In the meantime, the captain took up the night watch himself. The Indians would attack in the dark. Captain Reynoso would be there to greet them.

Thin threads of smoke rose into the night sky, reaching toward a half-moon circled with a ring of mist. The small flame still burned. But not much longer. Aesha brought the last of the coals inside the sanctuary, where she nursed them and prayed for inspiration. And fumed. Felipe had stirred the Spaniards up again. There were sure to be reprisals. He must have known he couldn't succeed in burning the fort, not that way. He'd simply turned all the attention on himself. As usual.

"Which is exactly the opportunity you need." The words came from a pine box.

"Ishkara!"

"What are you waiting for? Felipe has shown you the way." Laughter erupted from the container. "Sipi is ever the master of irony."

"Shown me the way? Don't tease me yet again, Ishkara. Truly, there is no time left. The coals are almost spent."

"So add fuel. It lies before your nose. As does the solution."

"All that lies before me are the boxes holding your bones and Carlos's."

"Just so."

"But . . ."

"Burn them." A second voice. Her father! "Felipe was right. The containers don't matter."

"We don't need them." Carlos now.

"But you do," Caalus said. "Keep the sacred flame alive. Do what you must, First-born. Lead your people."

"Do what we could not," said Carlos. "You're the last hope."

"The flames," said Ishkara. "Take them to the people."

Before she could even get out the words "Stay with me," they were gone. In that same instant, though, she knew what to do. Of course. Felipe had shown her the way.

Before fear and doubt could seep back in, she acted. She opened the boxes, removed the bones and eye bowls, wrapping them hastily in floor mats. Then, using Carlos's staff, she broke apart the boxes and began feeding splinters onto the sacred fire.

The time the boxes bought her would have to be enough. She would take the flames to the people. It would be up to them to do the rest.

Quietly, behind closed doors, the people began to prepare as Aesha had ordered. The canals were empty. No fisherman ventured forth to set his nets. Instead, the fish pens, teeming with catches from the warming spring waters, were emptied and distributed. In the kitchens, blades chopped and cauldrons boiled. Chisels shaved and sharks' teeth cut in the workshops. Piles were sorted and resorted.

Despite the activity, though, the city was hushed, the paths empty save for the occasional errand runner sent to a neighbor's for twine or a spare basket. Parents sent their small children out to play, yet even they huddled silently together, understanding instinctively the significance, if not the substance, of what was happening.

Two full days and nights and into the next the people labored. Only the plaza bustled, though not with the voices of citizens gathered to argue, sing, or discuss. Rather, a group under Iqi's leadership collected downed trees and branches, dragged them to the plaza, sawed and chopped and split them, then piled them in twenty distinct piles.

It would be a feast to end all feasts, a fire to end all fires.

Warned by the escaped patache, Menéndez assessed the situation quickly. San Antón was in peril. Felipe had turned against him. He had to be made an example. Like Carlos, he had had his chance. He wouldn't get another.

The Adelantado would have liked nothing better than to carry out the execution himself, but he feared the king might call him back at any minute. The Indians of Carlos, whom he had hoped would help him spread the Word of God throughout La Florida, were now naught but another failure. The captain general could ill afford to waste more precious time on them. So instead he dispatched his nephew. Pedro was a worthy commander in his own right.

Menéndez Márquez wasted no time, either. He rounded up as many infantrymen as he could find, fifty or so, loaded his fastest galleon and set off. The winds were good, full and strong from the south. All sails were raised.

At midday of the third day, the citizenry began to gather at the plaza, their simmering pots releasing a medley of steaming aromas. A feast, yes, but the people's faces wore looks of solemn resolve. They spooned their stews in silence, keeping close to their families. It was purple hands moon, too, and heaping bowls of fat mulberries were passed from family to family, but with none of the frivolity that usually accompanied the occasion. This meal, each person knew, might be his last.

The sun fell. All eyes turned to the temple mound.

Aesha fed the last of the pine splinters to the fire. It had endured. Now, would she? Would her people? She felt the weight press down upon her, not just of the people of Caalus but of all the people of Escampaba, not just of today but of all those who had walked before. If tonight her people failed, with them would die the stories and deeds of the ancestors. The mounds would become tombs, soon to be covered over and forgotten. Once again the gods would be alone.

She pushed the thoughts from her mind. Night had fallen. The ceremony must begin. Aesha donned the round-eyed, pointy-eared mask that Iqi had fashioned for her, of she who sees and hears the dark. She lit a candle with the sacred flame, in turn used it to light those of the somber group before her, the councilors and headmen who wore the newly carved masks of their clans.

Felipe stood before her, too, wearing the mask of the snake. He accepted the candle she proffered, then bowed low, palms up. "Lead us," he said. "This night is yours."

Owl escorted the group down the temple ramp, the candles winking like a river of stars.

Reaching the broad, flat expanse of the plaza, the masked figures split up, threading their way through the mass of citizens. Aesha moved to the center, where the largest fire had been laid, and stood on a platform that placed her in view of the entire throng. Before her lay a large vat of shark's liver oil and two piles, one of palm fronds, the other of lengths of dead wood the thickness of her arm. She sprinkled a bit of oil on the palm fronds and placed her candle beneath them until they burst into flames. Moments later, nine other palm frond fires burned, too.

As the fires flared, the girls' chorus began, alone and unaccompanied, singing notes so sweet and sad that the people hugged each other, weeping openly. Aesha listened, moved to tears, too, uncertain whether she would ever hear the songs of the people again. She savored the sound, let it imprint in her memory, let it go on five verses longer. Then she beat on the platform, just once, with what was left of Carlos's staff. The chorus and crowd fell silent.

"My people." Her voice came out thin and choked. She cleared her throat, began again, this time strong and determined. "My people. You grieve tonight, and I grieve with you. We mourn because our great island city of Caalus has fallen ill. It's an illness we've long suffered, and yet, like the man plagued with toothache, we've deadened our senses to it, preferring the dull, constant pain to the sharp, stinging cure. And like the long-suffering infirm, there is but a single reason for our continuing misery." She paused, scanned the sea of faces, saw it, felt it too, thick and congealed like animal fat in cold stew. "Fear," she said. "We, the brave, fierce, and cunning, the Calusa, feel fear in our souls, fear for what we must do tonight, fear of moving toward an unknown future.

"And yet, is not change the way of the world? Do not the currents ever carry seeds to new beaches to sprout in the bare sand, to grow thick and tall, until they become mighty, invincible trees? And then, does not the even mightier storm inevitably come to strip the beach clean again?

"Change resides in the birth of every child, the cycles of sun and moon, the flow of the tides that move that greatest being of all, the ocean."

In the crowd, a smattering of heads began to nod. Aesha pressed on. "More than fifty suns ago, the sea brought strangers to us from a land beyond our imaginations, strangers whom we once thought were gods, then believed were devils, but now know as merely another race of men. We tried to cast them back into the ocean. Always, they returned. Now, they've taken root in our Bay of Plenty. Like those trees on a new beach, they grow thick, tall and strong."

Aesha gestured toward the palace mound. "We tried, too, to dwell in harmony with the strangers. We invited them to live with us. Instead, they have built a gated fortress that casts its shadow over our homes, our cooking fires, our lives. That darkness has become the shadow soul of our homeland. It hides behind us, follows us, weakens and sickens us.

"Now look here." She pulled from around her neck the gold disk given back to her by Escalante, the one she'd received from Felipe on their wedding day. "The strangers brought light, too. Their shiny metals sparkle and glitter and capture the sun. They capture our greed, too. We covet their riches, hoard their treasures. Their gold and silver flash from our necks and even from inside the closed chests where they are kept. Thus has the light of their riches become our collective reflection soul, dazzling us, luring us, blinding us."

Many in the crowd looked down in shame. A warrior near the front who wore the gold dolphin medallion of Felipe removed it, cast it into the fire. "My people," Aesha cried. "My purpose is not to scold, not to blame. But tonight I must speak naked truth. For as powerful as are the fort that shadows us, the metals that gleam, this new race carried with them something more potent yet. Just as our third soul, as contained in the pupil of the eye, is the single indestructible one, this third force of the strangers is unyielding, imperishable, eternal." Aesha stooped to pick up the object that Iqi had left on the platform for her: the Christians' holy book. "My people, the written word stands as the soul of the civilization of these men who call themselves Spaniards. Like an all-seeing eye, it captures their knowledge and beliefs in a way that is as permanent as the spark of life that stays with each of us even as we pass to the lands beyond death. It cannot be destroyed. This I know. I have tried and failed."

Aesha paused, drew a breath. Nothing but the naked truth. "I don't condemn the strangers' ways. Does not our own palace cast its shadow down upon the ground dwellers? Don't we Calusa delight in the luster of the rare, perfect pearl? And don't we too pass on knowledge to our children and grandchildren through our stories, just as does their holy text? I cannot even condemn the strangers' weapons, for do not we, too, manufacture exquisite instruments of torment? My people, I freely admit the Spaniards have fascinated me since I was a child. I've played with their trinkets, delighted in their inventions, studied their beliefs. What I understand now, though, understand in seeing the shadow that engulfs us, the glare that blinds, is that these beliefs that sustain the Spaniards do not nourish the Calusa. It is the one, single tragic failing of the strangers that they insist that their way is the only way. In so doing, whether motivated by conceit or benevolence, the result is the same: they seek to enslave us. This we can never accept. We are Calusa. We must be free."

Now, finally, the people began to stir. She felt the fear melting, the energy as tangible as the sun's rays. "My people, for fifty suns our leaders have tried words and reason, weapons and trickery, all to no avail. A great decision is upon us. We may bow, or we may take the final remaining option."

"We will never bow," a voice called from the crowd.

"We are Calusa."

"We must be free."

"Yes," said Aesha. "To be Calusa, we must be free. Now go to the fires. Spread the flames of our gods and of Caalus, Ishkara, Carlos, and Felipe, too. Use them as I've seen. Use them as you must."

With a bellowing cheer, the people rose to their feet as one. Forming circles around each fire, they pranced, stomped, and sang. The hide drums beat, the shell horns blew. Round and round the fires the people danced, drawing ever more strength from the music, chiming in with the girls' chorus: "We are Calusa. We must be free."

Aesha dipped Carlos's staff in the pool of shark's oil, then touched it to the fire. She held the blazing torch high above her head. "May these flames bring you freedom," she shouted. "Take them. They are yours."

The people followed suit, each in turn hoisting a stick of wood and anointing it with oil, then lighting and holding it high. A thousand, two thousand torches blazed.

Thus sprang to life the final flames of Aesha's vision.

Captain Reynoso saw the mass of fires below. So this was it. He had one more means of defense, and he aimed to use it. He fetched Antonia. Since the catechisms were no longer being conducted, the Indian woman had been all but forgotten in the hut the Adelantado had built for her, ignored by the Spaniards, cut off from her people by the locked gate. Now the captain opened that gate just long enough to lash her to the outside. He didn't really believe her presence would stop the crazed mob down there, but it might confuse them, allow him to kill a few Indians before the enemy's crushing numbers brought about the inevitable result.

As he went to close the gate with a stoic, silent Antonia securely tied to it, up rushed the onslaught. Reynoso readied and steadied his men. But before he could give the order to fire, he heard the voice of the onrushing leader call. In Spanish.

Pedro Menéndez Márquez and his men dashed into the compound. "We came as quickly as we could," said the commander. "None too soon, by the looks of it."

"But how did you get past them?" asked the dumbfounded captain.

"That matters little at the moment," replied Menéndez Márquez. "We landed on the far side of the island and made our way through the bushes. The Indians were otherwise occupied. But at what? That seems the crucial question now."

"It's a fire ceremony," said Reynoso. "They mean to burn us alive."

The two men peered down at the ten great circles of flames from which issued a chaotic sea of lights. One thing was sure: a great wave was leading toward them.

Menéndez Márquez's men hastily took up positions next to Reynoso's. The culverins pointed down the ramp. The fuses of the soldiers' arquebuses were lit. Captain Reynoso waited as the torch-bearing mob approached. It would have been easy to identify the leader even if he hadn't seen the snake mask before. That black and red painted body, the huge belly could only belong to Felipe. The cacique moved slowly, in no hurry. As if he were enjoying himself.

Aesha stood on the platform above the central fire, seeing before her eyes the scene that had haunted her dreams for so long, feeling her connection to her people and to their torches, as if they were pulling hard against her scalp, each attached to a strand of her hair. "Light the torches, every one," she called to them. "Go. You know what to do."

Then, from above, she heard the booming of manmade thunder. Felipe had engaged the Spaniards. She prayed that he'd held off long enough to draw into the fort the soldiers from the wind ship that had landed that day. It had been Felipe's decision to leave them unmolested, though it would make his task that much more dangerous. She didn't disagree. At least the Adelantado's men were off the water.

Aesha prayed for Felipe, prayed for the warriors who'd followed him. Then she turned her attention back to her people.

The captain's water crews were ready, snuffing the fires started by the Indians' hurled torches and spears. Smoke was everywhere, making it impossible to see the enemy. In the sooty chaos, it was only gradually that Reynoso realized that most of the smoke was emanating from his own weapons. And that no Indian had pierced the fort. Instead, they were surrounding it, staying just out of range. Either his tactic with Antonia was working, or the Indians were being cagey, forcing the Spaniards to expend their ammunition. The captain ran along the barricaded walls, shouting, "Stop firing."

By the time he returned to the gate, the haze was beginning to clear. He joined the Adelantado's nephew in peering out. There were Indians, yes. A hundred, maybe. But it was what he saw beyond that staggered him.

A great sea of lights that dwarfed the tiny contingent in front of him was spreading from the plaza, fanning out the entire length and breadth of the island. As the Spaniards watched open-mouthed, here and there the individual lights began to flash with intensity and grow, grow into columns of blazing flames shooting up into the air. The columns began to merge, filling the sky, until there was but a single gigantic flame. Only then did the awareness hit. The Indians were burning their own island.

Flame-tipped tendrils stretched in every direction, to the people's very homes and inside their doors, igniting the stacks of mats and bedding, children's toys and spare nets and other non-essentials piled inside. Aesha felt the flames pull at her hair, as if from all directions at once, as the sun shelters, the gathering benches, and the net-drying racks caught fire, as likewise did the walls and roofs of every home, until the entire city of Caalus blazed like a sky full of flaming stars. Like an end. Like a beginning.

Aesha turned to face the city's two high mounds. A brilliant tower of flames was eating the palace and council hall, exposing the colossal wood skeleton that had been Carlos's crowning achievement. Iqi had accomplished his work as well. The temple, too, was alight, a giant bonfire that reached toward the heavens.

Yes, Felipe had shown her the way. The temple had to burn, too.

From the fort, the thunder that had stopped momentarily began anew. Aesha shivered. Felipe and his warriors were doing their job, holding the Spaniards inside. But with no advantage in numbers, they would not prevail. Felipe would receive no funeral, no proper preparation of his bones; yet he would pass to the land beyond as a warrior. He deserved it.

In the end, there had been no other choice. Even a successful attack on the Spaniards would not go unpunished for long. The Christians would never settle for anything less than total dominance. And so, there was only one option left: to leave, to depart in such a way that the Spaniards would know the Calusa would never return. Let the strangers rule from their fort. Rule over no one.

And let the people be set free. She hadn't told them where to go. They'd have to find their own way. For now, Felipe would have no successor. Finally, Aesha understood a truth she hadn't dared to speak of even with her people: that they must be released not only from the Spanish invaders, but too from the grip of their own leaders, who had forgotten that they themselves were born of the people, not over them. How could she tell them that? So, she had to send them away to learn for themselves. Many, she feared, would die. But if the spirit that had made the Calusa mighty was to endure, it must be in freedom.

Let a new time of quiet begin. A time remembered by the old stories, not without struggle, not without conflict—both were inevitable—but without supremacy, without domination. This was her gift to her people. Should they reunite, let it be by choice.

Aesha laid the mask of the owl on the fire. She would not leave anything behind for the Spaniards to desecrate and could take little with her. Not even the remains of her loved ones. She'd placed them that morning on the Island of Bones, scattered them amongst the departed. They'd done much for her, those three. Now, she would leave them to rest anonymously.

A single group remained on the plaza. Women, the nobles who'd studied the Christian text, believers perhaps, or maybe simply supporters of Piyaya. They carried no weapons, only torches as they moved now up the ramp toward the fort. Aesha didn't try to stop them. This decision to leave their families, to die with Piyaya in Caalus or surely to be captured, was theirs to make. It hurt. Yet it had to be. That was the essence of freedom.

Beyond the plaza, the water court was filling as small knots of families scurried with their belongings toward their waiting canoes. With remarkable swiftness, the island began to empty, and the people made off down the central canal and out of the harbor, paddling hard to avoid the Spanish forces that were sure to give chase after finishing off Felipe.

Aesha watched the last of the canoes disappear, scattering into the Bay of Plenty, heading wherever the sea might take them. Then she, too, left the plaza.

Within moments the final canoe launched, carrying an ancient white deer skin, an injured lover, and the weight of a decision from which there was no return. She'd saved Sipi, yes, but the temple, the great city of her father, and its people—her people—all were gone. She didn't regret the decision; she could only mourn, already, their absence. The families would survive without her, without Felipe. Of that she had no doubt. But the people needed more than their freedom; they needed each other, too, needed their beliefs and their festivals and their voices joined in song. For only together were they more than women and men and children, more even than families. Only together were they a people. The great irony was that, in order to ensure their survival, Aesha's sole option had been to separate them. She could only pray that from weakness would come strength, from destruction rebirth, from division reunion.

Aesha turned for a final glance at the burning island, a smudge of orange blurred by a film of tears. From now on she would look only forward. She turned her focus to her paddle, dipping it into the bay's dark waters, pulling in time with Iqi's even strokes, lifting it through the confused night air, hot at her back, cool before her. Dip, pull, and lift. She threw herself into the work, leaning into each stroke, using shoulders, back, and stomach, faith and hope, too, until the heat upon her back cooled and the crackle of burning wood was drowned by the gentle slap of waves. The canoe reached the pull of an outgoing tide. Then, finally, the weight was gone, and the canoe moved not away, only toward.

He itched to rush the fort, to throw himself at the smirking face of the half-eared captain who hid behind the tied-up figure of Piyaya. But

Felipe didn't. He held himself back, held back his warriors. He couldn't get close enough for a kill, but this time, killing was not his purpose. And so, Felipe fought on for a new kind of victory, not for himself but for his people, a victory more important than winning, more important than his life.

The gate opened, and a swarm of Spanish soldiers rushed toward him, the captain and the nephew of the Adelantado in the lead. Felipe made aim at the nephew with his atlatl. He'd save his war club for Reynoso.

He didn't see the third figure, the one with a Spanish uniform and a Calusa throwing stick. Escalante flung the spear with twenty years of fury. It found its target, ripped into the giant, painted belly. Felipe froze, his arm still extended in throwing position.

Escalante let the soldiers charge on, their broadswords flashing and slashing at the retreating Indians. Only Felipe stood his ground, his fleeting look of surprise turning quickly to recognition. Then, as his legs crumpled and he fell to his knees, a knowing grin.

Escalante had learned well. The spear tip had been dipped in a slurry made from wild sage berries and the fruit of the fish poison tree. The death would be as agonizing as it was certain.

As the soldiers rushed on, slaughtering the dwindling contingent of warriors, a small band of Calusa women skirted the battle and made its way to the fort. Escalante didn't stop them when they freed Antonia from her bonds. Instead, he ushered them through the gate and closed it behind them.

The untrod sand beneath her feet squeaked its song of greeting. The palm fronds rustled their welcome. The sea and shore sang their booming duet. Aesha stooped at the tide line, sifting through the shells, examining each one large and small, not just the intact ones, the pen shells, bubbles, and baby's ears, but the pieces, too: the spine of a lightning whelk, the top to a shark's eye. Maybe especially them. For their tumbling journey from their offshore beds had laid bare their inner strength, their whorled beauty. She held them, traced her fingers around their spiraling curves, saw them now as more than chipped and broken. Saw them as promises.

It was to the shores of the Thumb that they'd paddled, reaching it the next afternoon. Aesha had helped Iqi to his sleeping mat, laid the image of Sipi in the corner of the hut that still stood. Now, on the beach she watched the yellow sun turn red as it plunged toward the sea, then flatten as the two mighty beings made contact with each other. The big red eye poured its lifeblood into the ocean, winked a final green farewell, and disappeared.

She went to check on Iqi, heard his heavy, rhythmic breathing keeping pace with that of the surf on the sand. Then she returned to sit on the tide line as night greeted twilight with a sky full of more promises. And made one to herself. The cat's claw bark, the herbs that brought her bleeding—she would collect them no more. She hugged her knees to her chest, awash in crests of joy and troughs of grief, each inevitably following the other, each impossible without the other's existence. The tide had receded down the sloping sand. Now it was beginning to rise again. She could hear its song.

∽ Twenty-One ∽

15 June 1569

The ship is loaded, its hold heavy with the Indians' gold. Even now the soldiers are boarding. A bedraggled lot they are, their scabbed, bony arms poking from torn uniforms, barely able to heft rusted weapons. The queens, Doña Antonia and the others, cluster together on deck, comforting each other. And searching seaward.

She's out there, Aesha is, watching, waiting. She knew. After we sifted through the smoldering wreckage and found their stores of silver and gold, what then? How long would we last in this foreign land? With the Indians fled, why would we stay? What else could we do but leave?

It was to no avail that the soldiers made chase. The Indians simply melted into the bay in numbers too small to be worth the effort. When, out of frustration, the Captain hacked his way through the jungle for hours, his only reward was an abandoned hut. We still see them, a canoe gliding in the distance, the smoke from a cooking fire. They wait patiently for the day they know will come. This day.

I try to turn my eyes to Salamanca, to the Spain I've yearned for so long. Instead, my gaze keeps turning back. Such a fool I am. Such fools we all are. The wealth we carry is as illusory as our victory. We leave behind the only riches that matter, the scorched land that has already begun to renew itself, the tide that will ever wash the shores afresh. I take with me naught but the memory of what could have been and wasn't.